She said, *How on earth did he get here?*

As if all you ever do is sprinkle shamus dust
and the police suspect of the year floats in.

SHAMUS DUST

HARD WINTER   COLD WAR   COOL MURDER

JANET ROGER

Matador, 9 Priory Business Park, Wistow Road, Kibworth Beauchamp,
Leicestershire, LE8 0RX
Tel: 0116 279 2299 Email: books@troubador.co.uk
Web: www.troubador.co.uk/matador Twitter: @matadorbooks

ISBN 978 1838590 437

British Library Cataloguing in Publication Data. A catalogue record for this book is available from the British Library.

Printed and bound in Great Britain by 4edge Limited

Typeset in 9.5pt Latin Modern Roman by Troubador Publishing Ltd, Leicester, UK

Matador is an imprint of Troubador Publishing Ltd

IN THE FALL OF WORDS

For as long as I remembered, I'd been sleeping like the dead.
Could slip at any hour, in any place, deep into that cool night
where the heartbeat crawls and dreams are stilled like small
animals in winter. Not on account of some inner serenity or
the easy conscience of an unspotted soul. It was a leftover, a
habit arrived in a war, when all that counts is to grab at sleep
and hold onto it whenever and wherever it offers. It becomes
a thing accustomed. So routine you take it as given, right
up until the hour it goes missing. Lately, I'd lost the gift.
As simple as that. Had reacquainted with nights when sleep
stands in shrouds and shifts its weight in corner shadows,
unreachable. You hear the rustle of its skirts, wait long hours
on the small, brittle rumors of first light, and know that
when finally they arrive they will be the sounds that fluting
angels make. It was five-thirty, the ragged end of a white
night, desolate as a platform before dawn when the milk train
clatters through and a guard tolls the names of places you
never were or ever hope to be. I was waiting on the fluting
angels when the telephone rang.

First light was hours away. It had been snowing for twenty. The telephone sat on a bureau between two sash windows looking down on the street. I slacked my shirt collar and shoelaces, let the ringing clear my head, rolled off the sofa and picked up on a cool, well-fed, commercial voice I didn't recognize. "We have not met, Mr. Newman. I am Councilor Drake." The delivery out of the box where they keep the City's anointed, but the name meant nothing to me. The commercial tone went on. "There has been an incident. A short while ago I received a telephone call from City Police requiring access to a property that belongs to me. My driver has the keys. You will convey them to the detective inspector who telephoned and determine what this incident amounts to. Whereafter you will report your findings to me. You are acquainted, I believe, with City Police."

The councilor believed right. We were acquainted. I waited for whatever else he wanted to tell me about my immediate future, and when he didn't, said, "You're mistaken about what I do, Mr. Drake. And you didn't mention where you got my name." Vehicle lights lit stripes along the wall and moved them clockwise round the room.

The councilor didn't miss a beat. "From your former employer, Mr. Lynagh. Why should I be mistaken?" Cold distilled off the window in waves. I watched a snow flurry beat against the glass. My last employer had been head of the City's insurance investigations; a shrewd, straight-talking Australian who moved in circles where you can say *whereafter* even in front of the servants. Also given to homilies. *Look, Newman, as far as the locals are concerned, we're both colonials. The difference is my lot play cricket with them and all is forgiven. Your lot are the tired and huddled masses that rhyme tomato with Plato, and every living Limey thinks baseball is a game for girls. Can't argue about the baseball, though.* The councilor filled the silence on the line, waiting his answer. "Mr. Lynagh commends your resourcefulness and discretion. Therefore, whatever prior engagements you may have, be good enough to do as I ask."

But it was early Christmas morning. I had no engagements. No argument with discreet and resourceful either, and still it didn't make sense. This was London. There were major league inquiry agencies on call around the clock, ready to jump. Instead, the councilor had taken a recommendation, called a number in the book, and was making it clear he was not somebody to disappoint. I put the mouthpiece under my chin and a double-hitch knot in my necktie. "Councilor, I'm one man. What I do mostly concerns people who go missing with other people's money. Hard to believe, I know, but in this mile-wide hub of empire and enterprise there are operators who rub up against other operators with fewer scruples than they own themselves. When that happens and they get taken to the cleaners, it's not a thing they advertise or mention to police. Not even to a high-class agency, on account of the embarrassment. So far, I don't see what your embarrassment is. Without it the job wouldn't be in my line."

Drake breathed a sigh in my ear. "You can have no idea yet, Mr. Newman, in what line this employment belongs. If, on the other hand, you are intending merely to bargain, there is not time. I propose that you double your customary fee and do not keep the detective inspector waiting. My driver should already be at your door."

The line sputtered and died. I put the telephone back in its cradle and cleared my breath off the window glass. Twenty feet below, Fleet Street was quiet as a prayer, newsrooms dark and presses shut down for the holiday. Parked as close to the curb as the snowfall allowed, a Daimler limousine waited with its sidelights burning, fanning exhaust across the sidewalk. I was curious. Curious that a City councilor with a problem would send his car to collect me first, and then telephone me second. Curious that he would double my rate and not ask what my rate was, or even how I voted. If all you want is a delivery made and some questions asked, it's a lot of trouble to go to. I got my jacket and coat off the floor and went down to the waiting car. Not out of curiosity. Not even for the siren call of an open checkbook. In the end, just to get some air on a night turned airless. That and because I thought I could be back before daylight, weary enough for sleep.

Ten minutes later the councilor's driver eased under a streetlight on West Smithfield on the hospital side of the square, climbed out and had the rear door open while the car still settled at the curb. He pushed an envelope at me, bleak-eyed in the falling snow, then got back in behind the wheel without a word and glided east along the deserted meat market.

The streetlamp hung off a half-timber gatehouse in the middle of a row of storefronts with offices over, there to light the gatehouse arch and a path running through it to a churchyard beyond. I ripped open the envelope while my fingers still worked, put two keys on a tag in my pocket and walked under the arch. The freeze was squeezing the ground so hard, the gravestones were starting to levitate.

The church had a square tower over a doorway framed in checkerboard stonework. An iron-studded door stood half open on a porch, a police officer hunched in its shadow. The pallid giant beat one glove against another in a slow handclap, then raised a salute as I walked up the churchyard path. I said I had a delivery to make to his detective inspector and asked was he around. The officer looked out at the night over the top of my head. "Detective Inspector McAlester, sir. He left. A motor vehicle connected with the incident is reported nearby." It was the third time I'd heard the word inside half an hour. "Incident?" The officer backed up inside the darkened porch, snapped on a flashlight that sent wild shadows shuttering across his shoes, then settled it on a bench that ran around the wall. The beam moved over a torso lying twisted under the bench, played along the lower body, and then moved up again to an arm outspread across the floor. It held there on a face in profile cradled on the arm. I squatted down. The *incident* was a white male in his early thirties, lean built, smooth shaved, hair thinning; good-looking once. A dotted rhythm of blood made an arc across the plaster wall. A flying jacket was zipped tight under his chin, sticky where his cheek nuzzled the sheepskin lining. He lay as if listening to the muffle of snowflakes falling, wrapped in a long-drawn night of his own. A faint, sweet violet hung on the air. "You found him?"

"No, sir. A nurse from Bart's stepped into the church before she went on duty this morning, it being Christmas Day. The deceased was a neighbor." He moved the beam along the sleeve of the flying jacket, fixed long enough on curled fingers to show their manicure, then snapped it off and went back to filling the doorway.

I got on my feet and looked him in the chin. "It being Christmas Day, officer, I'm thinking I ought to step inside myself." I took off my hat and held it over my heart, to let him weigh if he wanted a refusal on his conscience.

He nodded me at the door that led into the church. "Shouldn't see why not, sir. Compliments of the season."

St. Bartholomew the Great was so cavernous inside it was shrugging off ten degrees of frost. At right a halo of candlelight flickered, impossible to tell how far off. Up ahead, a blood-red sanctuary lamp burned and might have been a distant planet. The rest of the interior took its time to collect. A half circle of arches floated on squat, massive columns. Moonlight pale as butter slanted from high in the walls. I moved right, followed along a line of fat pillars, kept going and came level with the halo of light and stopped when it divided in two.

Inside the rail of a side chapel, on a wrought iron stand thick with wax, two tapers were burned almost through. At the foot of the stand, catching their glimmer, a nativity was bedded in a scatter of straw on the stone-flagged floor. It had a crib in a stable, an ox and an ass in a stall, shepherds on their knees beside the crib, and a pageboy a little way off, beckoning wide-eyed to three kings that they'd better come see. On a rise behind the stable, a somber angel who knew how it all would end was at the edge of tears. A warden with a salesman's eye had left an open packet of tapers next to a coin slot in the wall, where you could drop in a coin and hear the sound that pirate treasure makes. In the City it counts as therapy. I checked my wristwatch, emptied my pocket change in the slot and bought up the warden's inventory. The rest was two minutes' industry.

TWO

Cloth Fair was a narrow street running along the north side of the church, strung with vacant lots burned out on a blitz night six years before. Cloth Court was hardly more than a dogleg passage leading off the street, built around with black-brick row houses four stories high. At that hour only one house in the court was showing a light. I stood in a wind from Siberia watching snowfall cover my trail, reflecting on what I had.

It wasn't complicated. Not more than an early morning call from a City grandee, a nurse who came across her neighbor dead or dying before dawn on Christmas Day, and the dead neighbor's latchkeys in my hand. That and the voice that always whispers in my ear, soft as telling a rosary, that for every reason I might think I have for mixing in a murder, there are ten better reasons to walk away. I crossed the angle of the court, fitted one of the keys in its lock and gave it a quarter turn. As for the voice that whispers, I hear it every time I step uninvited into an unlit room. The trick is not to let it start a conversation.

A board floor cracked under my shoes. Somewhere a breeze snapped at a curtain. The hallway was thick with haze off an oil heater, and when you got underneath that, the hard, acrid smell of a bear cave. I walked my hand along a wall, scraped my knuckle on a line of coat hooks, struck cold tin and dipped a switch. A naked bulb hanging from a wire at the head of a stair, flared and rocked in a draft. I leaned back on the street door and let it latch, waited while my breathing steadied then grabbed the stair rail and climbed toward the light.

The second floor had a corridor with peeling yellow walls of geishas swaying under parasols and a small, rank kitchen at the far end where a curtain flapped at a wide-open sash. Beyond the open window, a fire escape dropped to the alley below and somebody who lately decided to use it had left a trail on the iron treads, hollows filling already with snow like footprints on the edge of a tide. I pulled my head back inside the window and let my eyelids unfreeze. It was cold enough for Lapland.

At the other end of the corridor there was a bedroom looking out over the court, and the only house in it that had been showing a light. The bedroom had a line of empty liquor bottles on a dresser that had likely come with the rental, and in front of the bottles, a portable gramophone in a chromium case that hadn't. At one side of the gramophone there were import-label records: McGhee, Hawkins, Hodges, Lester Young. On the other side there was a folded card frame with two photographs in ovals, one facing the other. The photographs were paired: one younger man and one older, both of them taken on the same lawn under the same trees on the same afternoon in high summer. The younger one was a college boy with a cool, even smile who wore a sports jacket and slacks, a shirt open at the neck and wrote *Henry* and added *Christmas Kisses* across the corner of his picture. The older man was in his middle thirties. He stood behind a garden chair wearing a brush moustache and a slim bow-tie, had a jacket hooked over his shoulder and soft, tawny hair that lifted in the breeze. The camera had caught him off guard, arching back from the knees, his head tossed in a broad, handsome laugh. I switched on a bedside lamp and took in the rest.

The Councilor's tenant was a collector of photographs. He had them pinned across the window drapes, slotted in the frame of his vanity mirror, taped to his bedroom walls and closet door. Not the kind of photographs that get taken at garden parties on summer lawns, and it was hard to tell if the boys in his collection were college types. But always they were boys. Boys who brooded alone, soft and wide-eyed and available. Boys who sat in each other's laps in twos and in threes. Boys coaching rouged and heavy-lidded older men whose otherwise sheltered lives left them short on companionable warmth and close affection. There was one exception, wedged in the top of the vanity mirror. Not a portrait of any of the regular ingénues, and younger looking in the photograph than when we'd first made acquaintance not half an hour before. The subject was stretched on a dark satin sheet, eyes hooded, hair ruffled, one arm hooked toward the camera and the other propping his head, framing a bored, glassy look that said *Remember me?* He couldn't have known it, but he might have been rehearsing for his final pose: spread in the beam of a police flashlight with a gunshot wound gaping where his hairline had been. I pulled the picture off the mirror and put it in a pocket. City Police would be making plenty of their own.

The rest of the floor was a tour of a very private and tax-free enterprise. A curtained passage at the side of the dresser had a darkroom leading off, strewn with brown glass bottles of chemicals and clear, still pools in trays. Pegged out to dry over the trays, more boys-only collector items, strung like flags waiting for a parade. Across the passage was the studio that went with the picture collection—a boudoir stage set from a Viennese operetta, walled around with gilt mirrors and choked in red plush. Center-stage was the oversize divan that featured in all the pictures, buried in pillows of rumpled red satin.

I left it at that, wound back into the corridor turning out lights as I went, and followed the reek of oil heater to a moldering bathroom. No surprises. The bathroom had a ragged square cut out of the wall over a washstand, and pointed through the square at the back of one of the boudoir mirrors was a Leica on a tripod; sleek, black and ready to go to work. All that was missing was the film. But then, not everything you open Christmas morning is a gift.

I knocked and waited at the only door showing a light, its two top stories boarded up, burned out in the same night raid as every other house in the court. The door cracked open on a nurse in uniform. Late twenties, medium height, standing in a cramped hall with a rag-rug on a red-tile floor and a photograph on the wall behind her, its frame plaited around with laurel twigs to mark the season. She was looking past me at the curtain of falling snow. I held up the councilor's keys where she could read the address tag. "It's about your neighbor, Miss ...?" Then made a rueful mouth at the heavens that asked if I could step inside.

The nurse edged the door wider and moved aside. "Greer. Miss Greer." She was buttoning a cape at her throat, touching a froth of dark hair at her forehead under the band of a starched white cap. The hall was an ice block, the tip of her nose red with cold.

I closed the door, took off my hat and stood dripping on her tile floor. "The report is you found your neighbor's body this morning, Miss Greer. Even for a trained nurse that must have been quite a shock. I'd appreciate hearing how it happened."

The question set deep lines in waves along her brow. She took a breath and said quietly, "There's little to tell. Since it was Christmas, I went into St. Bartholomew's on my way to work. When I came out, he was lying across the floor of the porch. It was unnerving. I had my pocket torch. If he'd been there when I walked in, I'm sure I would have seen him."

"I'm sure you would have. What time was this exactly?"

She bit behind her lip and put pale dimples in her cheeks. "Normally I leave here at around a quarter to five, a little earlier this morning so I could go into the church. I might have spent ten minutes inside. I'm afraid I don't know exactly." An idea was bothering her. It swung her gaze up off her shoes for the first time since I walked in her door. "I was told to wait until a policeman came. But aren't you American?"

In the photograph behind her a young flyer with a diffident smile looked surprised at finding himself in uniform. He was barely twenty, recently passed out of air school, still wearing the innocence he lost the first day he found out what the training was for. There is no way back to it, and every time she walked in the door it was the way she wanted to remember him. I opened the top of my coat, pulled a card from my wallet and put it in the fingertips peeking out from her cape. "I'm here for the owner of your neighbor's house, Miss Greer. Anything you want to tell me will help, but you don't have to say a thing. The only questions you absolutely have to answer are the ones a police detective will ask."

Nurse Greer blinked at the card, as if she recalled a promise she once made not to talk to strangers. "What else is there to say? When I first saw him lying there, I supposed it was someone sleeping off Christmas Eve. Then when I saw blood everywhere and realized who it was, I tried to find out where he was hurt, but there was nothing I could do. Nothing anyone could have done. So I ran to the nearest telephone box, in West Smithfield." She bit down hard on her lip again and waited for the story to grow on me.

"Did you know your neighbor, Miss Greer?"

"I wouldn't say I knew him. He was living opposite." Her chin jutted. "Most houses in the court are rented. People come and go. We spoke once or twice at most."

"You knew his name?"

"He said Jarrett. Raymond, I think. I told him mine. It was practically all the conversation we had."

"But you noticed his callers. I mean the good-looking boys and well-dressed older men."

Nurse Greer stiffened then took another breath. "No, Mr. Newman. I'm hardly here to notice. When I'm not at the hospital, I'm working behind a bar. Why don't you ask someone who has the time to pry? Now please..." She stepped across the hallway and reached for the latch, flattened against the wall not to get too close. You had to hand it to her. She hadn't any powder on her nose or color on her cheeks or lipstick on her mouth. The hospital would have its rules. But there in the hallway, close enough to feel the flutter of her breath, hospital rules were doing Nurse Greer no harm at all.

I put a shoulder against the door. "The call you ran to the square to make. Did you see anybody else out walking? Think about it, Miss Greer. When City Police arrive, they'll want to know."

For two seconds her eyes drew the light out of the room, then saw the whole idea was ridiculous and gave it all back. "Before five o'clock on Christmas morning, in this weather? Did you see anyone? Look, I've already told you everything I can think of. I want you to go."

"You didn't tell me you lit a candle at the crib."

Her knuckles whitened on the latch. She gave a small gasp of disbelief, put her head back against the wall and looked along the rose pattern on the wallpaper. "Because I didn't imagine it could possibly interest you. As a matter of fact, just lately I light two. If a real police detective should ask me, I'll be sure to tell him."

I pulled my shoulder off the door and stepped aside, to give her room enough to throw me out.

THREE

I was renting an office in the Thornburgh Building that year, a stucco-fronted block near the top of Snow Hill. It was about the one building on the rise that had a good war. Plenty of its neighbors hadn't come through so well. Barely a hundred feet downhill a police station had taken a direct hit. Beyond it on both sides, the street was level rubble. Where the curve of the hill dropped into Farringdon, buildings still billowed under tarpaulin as if they had plague inside. Uphill, on the crest of the rise, the blast of a near miss had taken out the stained glass of St. Sepulchre, and its mystery along with the glass. Next to it, all the Thornburgh had to show were the pickaxe scars of bomb splinters in a rash across its face. Its windows had been fixed, and the luck of it was, it never had any mystery to lose.

An office anyplace in the City was overpriced and hard to find. Harder still when the address had a ring to it and liked to guarantee a better class of customer. Maybe it did at that, if what you had for sale was fancy accounting or imported fashions or a quarter-mile of chalk stream running off the downs. But nobody had walked in my office yet in a better class of trouble, and all the Thornburgh was bringing me were better fed accents living past their means, wearing the high-hat manner in half sizes.

Sometimes they glided in, languid and exquisite, leading complicated lives they needed to make less expensive. Others came high-strung, hesitating before they stepped inside, looked downhill at a police station and uphill at a church and decided they were in their kind of neighborhood after all. But some were just plain scared, and looking up and down the hill was no help because police were a part of their problem and their problem was way beyond prayer. So they leaned on the buzzer, waited to be invited inside, and took the customer chair as if they'd found the last seat in a lifeboat. Lately, I'd been seeing my share of the scared variety.

Trouble was in the air. Right now there were Soviets in Berlin, Communists in Manchuria, Zionists in Palestine. And the Americans on Bikini Atoll weren't there for the beaches or the coconuts. But in the end, those were just headlines in the foreign pages. The City of London had troubles of its own. It had an empire waving goodbye, a currency stepping off a cliff, and some high-toned citizens with singular tastes and private arrangements they couldn't buy off anymore. Berlin and Bikini passed over their heads. What walked them through my door were the tastes and the private arrangements. A chrome-plated address on Snow Hill made no difference. They would have found me anywhere.

The fifth floor of the Thornburgh was one long corridor with offices either side, most of them with a name stenciled on a half-glass door, some of them with a string of letters after to impress anybody who wasn't in the business. Currently, their doors were advertising commercial agencies, bookkeeping or import-export, and for all I knew they were making an honest living in regular hours inside, doing just what it said on the glass. At daybreak Christmas morning the whole floor was hung with paper streamers and silent as craters on the moon. My office led off a waiting recess at the end of the corridor. I pushed open the door, switched on a light and picked up the telephone. It had been ringing since I left the elevator.

A woman's voice, clipped and wide awake, said, "I'm pleased to find you in your office, Mr. Newman." And in case I mistook it for a holiday greeting, introduced herself. "I'm Dr. Swinford, acting for the City forensic medical examiner, responsible for the postmortem on a body found earlier this morning. You were at the scene in some capacity. I have your card, together with a message you left for Detective Inspector McAlester, whose case this is. The inspector is currently unavailable. You might care to explain the circumstance to me."

I didn't know whether or not I cared to, but I explained anyway. "The circumstance, Doctor, was a gunshot murder, in the porch of St. Bartholomew's. I was there looking for the detective inspector but he wasn't available then either, so I stepped into the church. There were two candles lighted at a Christmas crib inside, left by the nurse who reported the body. I thought they could be important, and if they were then they wouldn't wait until McAlester arrived. So I snuffed them out and passed them to the officer on duty, along with the rest of the packet they came in. Burn a sample and it ought to tell you what time the nurse lit hers and confirm or deny whatever story she has, as well as the time your victim died, near enough. The message for McAlester was that I could explain what I just explained to you. In case he thought he had to beat a confession out of the candles."

The electrics in the elevator shaft whooped like a train in a cutting and shook the thin party wall. We had two seconds of silence while she thought around the situation. "I see. Well, you certainly were thinking on your feet, Mr. Newman. No doubt the detective inspector will be most grateful for your prompt action. To do as you suggest, of course, we should need to know exactly when you extinguished the candles."

"That's right, Doctor, you would. And when my notes get typed I promise to send a copy. Today, I don't have a secretary."

It was strictly the truth. Not Christmas Day, or any other day of the year. But then, I didn't have any notes to type either. We took another break while she absorbed it all. When the voice returned it had added an edge where the sparkle had been.

"No, of course not. But we might go through this sooner, mightn't we? Shall we say the Great Eastern at nine-fifteen, in the breakfast room?"

I said yes to that and the forensic examiner's stand-in hung up. I was still thinking about why the hurry when a chair scraped outside.

The lounge seats in the recess floated in a blue fog. In the middle of the fog, a heavy-set figure in a derby sat with his palms crossed on the silver top of an ebony cane. He wore a fox-collar coat open on a necktie with a City crest and might have been sixty, but it was hard to tell. His hand scooped at the cigar smoke as he levered out of the seat. I looked along the line of chairs and the magazines on a low table in front of him, at a dozen sprigs of paper holly pinned around the walls and thought, *Lucky man!* The floor linoleum wore a holiday shine. I had my window blind pulled down over the view and my name on the sugar glass in the door didn't have any letters after to confuse him. It would never look more enticing. I shooed the door wider and motioned him through. "Merry Christmas, Councilor. Won't you step inside?"

I took his derby, laid the hat next to his keys on the desk and let him get arranged in the customer seat, palms crossed over the ebony cane as before. His narrow eyes saddened. His hair shone in flat stripes across the dome of his head, where you could count them if conversation ran thin. "You cause me embarrassment, Newman, by not following my instructions. Our understanding was to deliver those keys, not to return them to me. I have received a further telephone call from Detective Inspector McAlester, requesting them urgently." His voice was level and deliberate, not as embarrassed as it made out.

I squared a pencil on the desk blotter and tilted back in my chair. "You had two instructions, Councilor. Making a delivery was one of them. The other was to find out why City Police called you in the first place. When I got to the address, it turned out the detective inspector was otherwise engaged and waiting there to talk to him wouldn't have worked. He's not the outgoing type. But I had your keys, so I took a look inside for myself. Now it's done and your driver can deliver them, along with an apology. As for the embarrassment, save it. Right now, McAlester wouldn't notice if you were rolling naked in the snow. He has other things on his mind." The councilor flicked ash off his cigar. "Indeed?" He had a way of tasting words before he uttered them. "And what might be on his mind?"

I flushed a cigarette from a hollow pack, tapped it on the chair arm and thought how McAlester would answer that. It didn't translate. "His immediate concern is a body discovered this morning. Male, early thirties, last name Jarrett, lately residing at the address you own. But his immediate concern will be as nothing compared to the ones he'll have when he uses those keys. Did you know your tenant, Councilor?"

Drake stiffened, lost some of his high color along with his air of irritation, and asked, *"Dead?* How?"

"Well I'm not the medical examiner, but my impression is that his wounds were not self-inflicted." I set my elbows on the desk edge, propped my chin on my knuckles and gave him the sad eyes back. "Councilor Drake, your tenant was paying for his expenses, his clothes, his records, his perfume and your rent by photographing good-looking young men on your premises. Pictures of the kind that circulate in plain covers to the jaded, who need a map to peek at before they can travel. As a going business, it was way outside the law, and that might be awkward for you. Just not as awkward as the photographs Jarrett was taking of the young men's admirers. Acts of gross indecency have been a felony in this country for sixty years. Which not only makes life difficult for citizens that way inclined, it invites other citizens to a land of wild opportunity. Your tenant was working a blackmail racket. Meaning that soon a City detective will be asking you the question I just did, and he'll notice when he doesn't get an answer. How well did you know Raymond Jarrett?"

Drake blinked and tasted words again, then squinted past the light on the desk. "As I recollect, not at all. You say he was a tenant. It is conceivable our paths may have crossed. Though I would hardly expect to have known him personally. I own many properties in the City, Mr. Newman. Residential and commercial, large and small. Naturally, records can be made available to any police inquiry that may follow. As for the rest, I had not the least idea."

I pushed back my chair and moved around the desk to bring him an ashtray for the cigar he was letting die between his fingers. "Well that's wonderful, Councilor. Tell it the same way to McAlester when he drops by. You'll have him spellbound."

FOUR

A cab dragged by on Liverpool Street hushed by snow, rolled past the entrance to the Great Eastern Hotel and used the empty rank at the rail station to turn around. Daybreak shied at the window of the hotel barbershop. I was its only customer. Louis had something on his mind.

"Did you know this was Bethlehem once, Mr. Newman? Right on this spot used to be the hospital of St. Mary Bethlehem. Bedlam. The madhouse. Only they don't put up a sign to say so." He coiled a hot towel around my face and kidded me with a high, keening laugh. Louis was compact and dapper, wore a wisp of goatee on his chin and a graying Cab Calloway over his lip.

I settled in his chair, drowsy on the fat smell of shaving soap, the hot towel chasing a murder out of my thoughts. "This whole town's a madhouse. Tell me about Christmas on the island."

Louis unwound the towel and considered. "To say the truth, Mr. Newman, I don't recall Christmas but as a child." I murmured nobody ever does and we agreed on that. He worked a brush in the soap and laid a stripe of lather from ear to ear. "The island starts Christmas on St. Lucy's day,

December thirteen. To a boy it seems holiday is come for good. So every morning I set off along the dirt road to Vieux Fort, to where it has a left turn to the ocean, a right turn to the sea, and a fig tree I could sit under and decide which way to take. Most days, the breeze in that fig tree would make up my mind. But the Atlantic in December is always too cool. No matter what breeze was blowing, Christmas Day I went swimming in the Caribbean." His fingertips eased out my jaw.

"Sounds hard to leave."

"Mr. Newman, when you get invited to a war you leave. Hard or not makes no difference, you know that. All I decided when it was over was to see the country I was fighting for. I had an officer tell me I would be made most welcome and I took him at his word. Now I think of it, I don't believe that lieutenant ever did reside in Limehouse." The high laugh again while the razor flopped on a leather strop. A thumb gouged soap off my mouth and stretched the beard along my jaw. Louis took one stroke from my ear to the point of my chin, wiped the blade on the heel of his hand and started back in a figure eight. We got to what was on his mind. "You hear about the shooting last night, Mr. Newman?" I said I'd heard. His wide eyes lidded. "It's unchristian to say ill of the dead, I know, but that man had a real bad reputation. They say a boy he was running on the street is skipped out."

He had my nose pressed flat against a stud on his jacket, working across my cheekbone. The blade scraped my top lip and snapped back in the bone handle. The rest of the lather wiped off with a towel. I could still see his fig tree swaying in the breeze. "You didn't learn this business barefoot on the beach."

His palms patted talcum into the razor burn. "I did not. Momma had a chandler store, and five growing boys to fetch and carry around the port. It made fine, free living. But I was a young fellow that relied on eating and I needed to take a trade. Choices you make, Mr. Newman, are not such a complicated thing." He stepped behind the chair, took away the cotton cloth and wound the seatback upright.

I peered at him in the mirror. "The boy who skipped last night. Does he have a name?"

Louis' head tilted. "All I hear is Reilly. Took his custom from the rail station, they say. He has a friend works as housekeeper right here in this hotel. I never saw the boy myself, but I don't doubt he's better off and gone. You want to know about him, most likely Miss Dillys will know. She'll be where she always is at this hour." We went back to small talk. Louis brushed off my jacket, handed me my coat, then went ahead to pull open the door. Not the door to Liverpool Street I'd walked in by, but his exit at rear of the barbershop that led into the hotel foyer. I checked the coat at a counter by a curving stair, called over a bellhop and sent out for cigarettes, then followed a sign pointing upward to the breakfast room.

Breakfast at the Great Eastern Hotel was a colonial affair, a hush of chintz and chiming silver where ancients in fly collars sat under a colored-glass dome and waded through kippers and kedgeree. There were barely a dozen people still eating, scattered through the room in ones and twos like an anarchists' convention. Along the south wall there were window bays looking out on Liverpool Street high above the sidewalk. In the farthest bay, remote from the other customers, Dr. Swinford sat at a table for two.

The doctor seemed entirely at ease with the broad expanses of the room, its faded patterns on Indian carpet, its bowed attentiveness; with the kind of Englishness that accommodates to privilege effortlessly, because it never noticed it had any. We hadn't met before, but the temporary medical examiner wasn't hard to spot. She had honeyed hair and a cream-colored coat draped across her shoulders, dressed for wisdom and experience when she looked hardly more than thirty-five. Which made us more or less contemporaries, the only customers the Great Eastern was entertaining that morning who obviously hadn't been at Mafeking. By the time I walked up, a waiter in a white mess jacket was unloading from a tray, the bellhop was leaving my cigarettes on a napkin and the doctor was fingering her wristwatch, motioning at the seat opposite. "The coffee is for you. We're rather late starting."

I slipped the pack of cigarettes out of the napkin and into my pocket, poured a half-cup of burned black coffee from a silver pot, added some scalded milk from another and watched the result churn and clot in the cup. The doctor had a slim document case zipped open in her lap. I lit one of my own cigarettes, waved out the match and asked, "So who was he?"

Dr. Swinford straightened a small cameo pinned at the throat of her blouse, hesitated, and then lifted out a file, opened it flat on the table in front of her and set the case by her ankle. She had a high, clear forehead, and a mouth that might have a spectacular smile. Just not here or for now. For now, the doctor would let me decide myself who Raymond Jarrett was, and for that she cut a furrow across her brow and began reading to me softly from the file.

Raymond Jarrett had been thirty years old, a sometime street hustler hauled in once on a gross indecency charge seven years before. After his brush with the law, he'd moved off the streets and worked a string of addresses in the City, noted in his file. That was all. There were other priorities in wartime. From his one and only bust, right up until his final crowded hours, the victim's police record amounted to postcards on a career grifter that Vice always knew where to find.

Evidently Jarrett had been working his Christmas holiday. Dr. Swinford hadn't completed her postmortem, but preliminaries showed he was hopped to the hairline and trade was brisk. The next thing certain put him in the driver's seat of a Singer Roadster, abandoned without its keys on a bombsite in Cloth Fair, with evidence indicating Jarrett had been shot there from the passenger side of the convertible. His assailant had pushed a .38 into his left side below the armpit, and fired once. The bullet had lodged in the angle of the car's bodywork behind the seat frame on the driver's side, removed part of the victim's shoulder traveling through, and left a sweep of blood and muscle that started at the roof lining and trailed slantwise across the windshield. Perhaps because the killer hurried the shot, it hadn't killed Jarrett where he sat. Or else the victim saw it coming and scrambled to get out of the seat. Either way, the gunshot and his weight on the door had pitched him outside the car.

From there, Jarrett had picked himself up and headed in the direction of St. Bartholomew's church. Blood in the snowfall traced his route along Cloth Fair. There were cuts on his palms and wrists where he'd fallen, his arms were bruised, but still he kept going. So did his killer. Jarrett had flopped on the bench inside of the porch when his assailant caught up, pressed the .38 in the back of his head and fired a second time, inward and downward, left side again. No more getting up and running. The second gunshot had sprayed Jarrett's brains in a shallow arc across the whitewashed walls and embedded itself in the bench's backrest. The body carried no identification or any keys, but that lost City Police no time at all. The nurse reporting the incident had also given the name and residence of the victim and since the investigating detective happened to know the owner of the building was a City councilman, all he did was call him to get access right away.

The doctor's gaze lifted, deep and distant as hills after rain. "Nurse Estelle Greer who found the body claims she was inside the church and heard nothing of the gunshot. You were there this morning. Do you really think she might not have?"

I pushed aside the clotted coffee. Wondered if the doctor had any idea of the noise the .38 would make inside a church, then decided it was the wrong question anyway. You didn't have to believe Nurse Greer's story, but it was hard to picture her shooting Jarrett twice over, and trailing him in the snow like a wounded animal to do it. Harder still to see her leaving him for dead and then coolly calling in the murder to City Police. Nurse Greer had been edgy and guarded when we talked, but fall across the bloodied corpse of a neighbor early Christmas morning and edgy is how you're supposed to be. "It's possible she didn't hear. On the other hand, if you really want the nurse for this, she didn't have to be inside the church at all. She could have been in the porch standing over a dead man, pointing a smoking .38. Though if she was, she would have been a mess. Two gunshots at less than arm's length would bloody her hands, her face, her clothes, her hair. When you run to a callbox to report a murder it's not how you want to be remembered by a chance passerby. Unless you think she had time enough to go back home and clean up."

"She might. I timed a taper you took from the Christmas crib inside the church to compare it with the two Nurse Greer left burning there. I'm not sure it's science, but it seems they were lit at least an hour and a half before the police officer says you arrived. That was around six o'clock this morning, meaning she might well have left the church before four-thirty. Yet it was after five o'clock when the duty officer logged her call to Bishopsgate police. Once we know exactly when you extinguished the candles at the crib, we can be more precise. Don't you agree?"

It wasn't an inquiry. She laced long fingers under her chin and stitched back a frown while I went on wondering about her. Dr. Swinford was straight-ahead and determined and a little intense, probably well-connected, and schooled where they don't burden you with diffidence in dealing with your fellow man. It had made her innocent of needing to fit a system, handed her a gift for making a room grow small around her, and a dress sense there is no other way to acquire. Taken altogether, it's a start in life. "If it isn't science, Doctor, it won't make any difference if I agree or not. Anyway, how temporary are you?"

The pale eyes rounded slow as moonrise, her mouth working at a basement obscenity. Then, unhurried as if she wouldn't want me to lose her meaning in translation, "I was physician here at the City Police Hospital for more than three years, trained under Dr. Templeton in legal medicine. Until he returns from Christmas leave, I'm standing in for him as forensic examiner. Hard as it may be for you to take in, Mr.

Newman, the police board did not appoint a novice. Not even temporarily. Try not to be disappointed."

I ground out the cigarette and watched a faint stripe flush at her throat above the cameo. Besides the chime of china cups, it was the loudest thing in the room. "Then why the rush to make an impression? Leave the nurse to City detectives, stay out of their hair and don't think of trying to ritz them the way you've been ritzing me. It's quaint of you, but those boys have no notion of gallantry. They'll poison their own grandmothers before they ask your advice." She stiffened and caught her breath, then relaxed extravagantly, squared Jarrett's file in her lap and slotted it in the case down by her shoes. "The roadster Jarrett got shot in, was it his?"

The doctor straightened up, put a festive mood in her voice and gave me the bright-eyed smile that said never mind that this had been strictly business, she would always look back on our half-hour together as the high spot of the holiday. "No, it wasn't his. The car belongs to Professor Michael Garfield. You may have heard of him. Principal Archaeologist to the City Corporation, discoverer of our Roman fort in the City. These last six months he's been all over the broadsheets and wireless talks. Highly regarded from Mr. Churchill on down."

"Does he say his car was stolen?"

"So far as I am aware, he's not answering his telephone this morning."

I shrugged. "Maybe he's still making friends at wherever Jarrett was partying last night. Do you know the professor, or is he just a pinup in the police canteen?"

She hoisted the slender case to her knee, kept the bright, tight smile posted and still resisted wasting the obscenity on me, however gratifying it might be. "We've never met. Now excuse me. I have Christmas presents to deliver."

I got to my feet and stayed there while she threaded the room, past an all-weather type in heavy tweeds and ginger moustaches, breakfasting alone. He had soft, dewy eyes that searched for pheasants croaking in stubble fields, waiting for the beaters. I'd been watching him feed bacon rinds off his plate to a liver-colored Springer that lay huffing under his chair, close enough to hook its tongue around the rinds without a strain. The doctor skirted his table and nodded wistfully at the tweeds, got back a shuffle of the ginger moustaches and went out through the double doors. Her waiter loitered under the room's Christmas tree, appreciating her exit. When he'd gotten the rubber out of his neck, I waved him over.

"Sir?"

"Breakfast." I pointed at the customer with the dog. "I'll take whatever the colonel had. No coffee."

The waiter fluttered his lashes at the dining room's longcase clock. "Breakfast is served until ten o'clock, sir. Luncheon service will commence at midday." And glided away, past tables laid with linen crisp enough to cut him off at the knees. The long hand of the clock moved to two minutes past the hour.

I pushed out through the foyer's revolving door and lit a cigarette at the top of the hotel steps. It was hardly mid-morning and I'd had four different conversations about the murder of a hustler whose loss nobody regretted, but still made them uneasy. It troubled Louis to speak ill of the dead, no more than that. Why the nurse and the councilor and the City's acting examiner were on edge was harder to tell.

While I stood there, a figure in an ex-army greatcoat made an abrupt about-face off the sidewalk and started an untidy diagonal up the hotel steps. He was steadying a briefcase tucked high under his arm, deep-breathing for the ascent, and when his progress slowed only five steps short of the summit you wanted to urge him on. I snapped the cigarette, went down to meet him and put a hand under his elbow. "Things being equal, pal, you're about to enter the Great Eastern Hotel. On the whole they prefer decorous and sober, but they absolutely insist on collar and tie. Want to change your mind while you're still ahead?"

He had to be older than he looked, wore a shadow across his lip for a moustache, a pallor the gray putty of overworked glands and an air of unraveling surprise. I didn't doubt he heard me, but in the way a deckhand hears breakers in a fog. It took time for the idea to percolate. When it did, he braced against the hold I had on his arm and with elaborate politeness announced, "I can absolutely promise to be decorous." He was high as a kite. I got him up the last steps and into a quadrant of the revolving door, where he could hold steady with the brass rail. Once in there, he squared up, filled his lungs and said cordially, "You're a pal, pal." Then leaned his forehead on the glass and let the revolve propel him inside the hotel foyer. I left him to it and dropped down to the street. I had a Christmas present of my own to deliver.

Eighty yards along Liverpool Street, past the empty cab ranks, was a high, narrow, soot-brick alley named Sun Street Passage for a joke. It ran between two City rail stations, each the size of a small country town. On its east side, Liverpool Street terminus was closed for the holiday. On its west side, Broad Street station was a stretch of abandoned platforms, walled-off and bombed to dereliction. The alley was so sheltered, the night's blizzard had stopped dead inside its maw, a scatter of powder stirring on the flagstones as if it had blown in under a door. Brick arches with deep recesses ran its whole length, and on a dead winter forenoon Sun Street Passage was passing for warm if you were desperate enough. Dillys Valentine was sitting hunched on a packing crate in one of the east-side recesses. The one she called her morning room.

She was gazing over a private horizon with an elbow rested on a knee. Wore a flyblown trench coat belted tight at her waist and a red beret with a raddle of mouse-blond hair pushed under. Her chin propped weightless on one gloved knuckle. A cigarette hooked under the knuckle was trying to set the fingers of the glove alight.

"Mind if I sit down?"

She rubbed a thumbnail under her nose and didn't look up. "Oh, for God's sake, Newman, it's not a private parlor.

Got a cigarette?" The voice was gravel. The face worn beyond a powder disguise. I took out the pack of Passing Clouds the bellhop had brought me and put it beside her on the crate. Her fingers dropped the lighted cigarette stub under a heel.

"Louis said I should talk to you about Reilly."

Miss Dillys's gaze flickered. I sat opposite her on the tread of an iron stair that climbed to the level of the station platforms. She coughed thickly and took a long minute to consider. "Terry's all right. He was here earlier. Left me a present." She patted the weight of a bottle inside the trench coat. "And now you're here. Must be Christmas."

"I heard he disappeared last night. I also heard Jarrett was his wicked fairy."

Miss Dillys made a mouth. "If it wasn't Jarrett it would have been some other sod. Terry needed somebody keeping an eye on him."

"Now he needs somebody else. You saw him last night?"

She picked up the Passing Clouds and turned them over and around. The pack was pink, of the kind that can get a petunia a reputation, and in the center a portrait of a cavalier, languid in lace cuffs and hat feathers, shimmering in silks. "My, my, are these for me? Not your color I suppose."

I shrugged a why not and she asked, "Why would I tell you about Terry?"

"Because when a cop asks, sooner or later you'll tell him. And I'm twice as polite."

She pushed open the flap and pried out the foil with a fingernail, waved the open pack under her nose and pouted, then slotted an oval cigarette in the pout. It stayed there while I found a match to light it. "Louis sent you?"

"That's right."

Miss Dillys turned back to her private horizon, flattened the silver foil across her knee and smoothed the creases while she thought about that, "I didn't see Terry last night. I saw Jarrett." She sniffed and tilted her chin at the stair behind me. "At the office." The iron stair climbed to a platform at the west edge of the station, freight-only since wartime, where a clerk left a stove burning in a waiting room after the last night train left. In a winter freeze and a coal shortage, Miss Dillys's office was her special draw, for a fading clientele and acquaintances alike. "Jarrett said Terry was working. He was expecting him. But come one in the morning there's no Terry and Jarrett ups and goes. It was the last I saw of him. Then an hour after, a City type walks in. Nice clothes, not bad looking. Never saw him before. I thought Christmas had come early. Then he asks me where he can find *Mister* Jarrett, as if he's lost his bleeding bridge partner. Well how would I know? Nice manners though. I said to try *Mister* Jarrett's social secretary next door along and he wished me goodnight." She pushed a rat-tail back under the slope of the beret with the lift of the chin that was her social secretary impression. "You know the rest."

"Some of it. Would you recognize the City type again?"

"We'd recognize each other, wouldn't we?" She dragged a heel across the powder of snow. Something in the conversation made her nose twitch and set her head on one side. "Are you kidding me, Newman?"

"Kidding about what?"

"About City coppers being interested in how Jarrett got himself killed. Do me a favor. They'd have to explain how come they left him alone all these years wouldn't they? It would embarrass the poor dears. Not to mention their employers." She wagged a gloved finger in front of her mouth, the lips painted the same front-door red as her beret. "You *are* kidding me."

"Miss Valentine, I am not."

She leered at that and dug in her pocket for Terry Reilly's Christmas gift, prized the stopper from the bottle and wiped a palm across the neck. "Come off it, Newman. They only ever call me *Miss* Valentine in court. Just for that, you can have lesson one on *Mister* Jarrett and City Police."

Her hand held out the bottle. I was halfway to taking it. And then I didn't have her attention any longer. She was looking straight past me slack jawed, eyes wide and fixed in wonder, her free hand brushing past her mouth so that the glove smeared red across her cheek. I rolled hard against the rail at the side of the stair and jumped an elbow high alongside my face. Just not high enough or fast enough to beat a black, pulping blow that bit deep behind my ear and pitched me across her knees. I felt thin arms around my shoulders. Smelled cheap perfume in her lap. Heard shattering glass. Then the high, distant wail of a small girl playing in the street who trips and grazes her shins. Nothing serious, just unexpected. Then the wail shut off like the closing of a vault.

My head felt as if somebody was trying to break in through the roof. Every lift of an eyelid made me clammy and sick. I was learning how to breathe and not move a hair when a sudden, sour smell of barroom filled the back of my throat and I gagged, rolled on my side and sat up. A bloodied mess trickled through my fingers. Glass splinters sparked like diamonds on the blue-brick floor. I found a handkerchief and ripped it in two strips, knotted them around my hand with my teeth and looked over at Dillys Valentine.

She was just out of touching distance, knees drawn under her chin and arms at her sides, slumped against the packing crate with the beret slanted across an eye. Her hair fell loose. The rat-tail dabbled in a stain that covered the shoulder of her coat, saturated her upper arm, welled in the crook of her elbow and spread in a pool at her hip. The jagged end of the whisky bottle had hit so hard it was still bedded in the angle of her jaw.

I was sitting alongside her up against the crate, my hand cupped at the pulp behind my ear, caught the next wave of sour liquor and started retching again. I got on my feet, stood long enough to steady my head, then left her to the snow zephyrs dancing in from the alley and climbed the stair out of there, one step at a time.

"They don't help just looking at them, Mr. Newman. You want to say what happened? Because I don't think it was a bus that hit you. Not today." Louis took his aspirin bottle and shook some in my hand, screwed back the cap and dropped the rest in my pocket. I swallowed six, said no to his hip flask and looked around the tiny storeroom where we sat, walls lined with slatted shelves empty from floor to ceiling. In the end a death announces not in words but in the fall of words.

"Miss Dillys is dead, Louis. Nobody I saw. I got in the way, just not enough in the way."

Louis' gaze marked a beat. He set the hip flask on a shelf at his elbow without taking his eyes off me. "That could be most difficult for you, Mr. Newman."

He was right. And the more he knew the more difficult it could be for both of us. "I didn't want you hearing it on the radio. Now help get me out of here." Louis' lip pursed and crinkled his moustache and we left it at that. He put a hand under my arm and the other around my wrist, the way you hoist an invalid aunt out of a bath chair, and by instalments got me from his storeroom to a service exit in the hotel basement. We didn't talk. Likely we both were entertaining unchristian thoughts. But his look said getting in the way is never the complicated thing. The complicated thing is when you decide to make something of it.

A wide, green-tile corridor dropped underground from the service door to the hotel's own rail siding. From there I followed along the tracks into the deserted station, crossed a dozen and more stilled platforms floating in winter light and found the waiting room with the stair behind it that dropped down to the arches on Sun Street Passage. Dillys Valentine grew cold there where she had fallen, with nothing in her pockets to tell me anything and enough whisky on the air to give her hopes for better things to come. I sat on the crate beside her one last time, long enough to make our short goodbye. Then left her there—where she always could be found at that hour—and walked back along the alley named for a joke, into a day still weeping snowflakes.

On Liverpool Street, a line of phone booths stood empty outside the entrance to the subway. I stepped inside one, dialed an emergency operator, left a message with the desk officer at Bishopsgate police station and hung up. It would be his second reported murder of the morning, in a square mile where the only thing you're meant to die of is surfeit, with your stock certificates gathered around the bedside.

FIVE

A directory in the callbox gave me an address for Professor Garfield in Cross Key Square. But it wasn't a square, it was an oblong with an access off Little Britain that opened on a courtyard planted with limes. It had been the yard of a coaching inn once. Snowed-in on a Christmas morning, it was a picture book collection of crowding mews houses, as deserted as the rest of the City. Over the entrance into the court a janitor's apartment had a light showing and smoke drifting from its chimney, and beside the janitor's mail slot was a board listing names against the house numbers. I walked the left side of the oblong as far as a blue painted front door and leaned on the doorbell, and kept leaning until a latch turned.

The door was opened by a slim-built college boy dressed in a corduroy three-piece and a knitted necktie, wearing no trace of the smile he used for photographs. He set his feet apart and pushed his hands deep in his pockets for the look that comes with family money.

"I'd like to talk to Professor Garfield. Mr...?" I held out a card and waited while he read it through. We waited a little longer while he took in the state of my coat and the makeshift bandage around my hand and then sighed and motioned me inside. We climbed to a drawing room at the top of a stair, where three squat windows looked out across the snow-white branches of the lime trees in the courtyard. The rest of the wall space was lined with display cases, like some forgotten wing of the British Museum. I glanced in at medals and dull coins, colored glass thin as eggshell, statuettes of gods and heroes inches tall, and small, bright patterns of mosaic. Every one of them labeled and dated.

The college boy said, "Michael's collection. I daresay it won't make much sense to someone in your line of business. I'm Henry Beaufort, his personal assistant. You'll gather he isn't here." He had near-set eyes, features a touch too fine, and hair tousled like the portraits on the coins in the professor's glass cases. I wondered which came first, the way you wonder about people and their dogs.

"In my line of business, the only thing that doesn't make sense is poetry. Everything else I get by on."

He gave me his resigned smile. "We write our poetry in Latin, anyway. Look, I'm tidying up. You may as well sit down while I make some tea."

The room had two armchairs; leather boxes that you sit in with your knees pinned and your elbows either side of your ears, like a swimmer waiting for the start gun. They were set in the center of Garfield's museum collection, either side of a low table. A large book lay open on the table with a magnifying glass on the page, next to a carousel of gilded angels that would turn and chime small bells when you set alight the candles. It wasn't Christmas decoration. The house didn't have any. Not crepe streamers or paper lanterns or presents under a tree. Not even a tree. As for the angels, they never would play the chimes because nobody would ever light the candles. The carousel was a collector's item, like everything else in the room. I jammed in one of the armchairs and picked up the lens.

The book was an exhibition catalogue, open at a double-spread reproduction of a very fine ink drawing, taken from an original that would have filled an entire wall. It showed a bird's-eye view of the bombed-out City, so detailed that even without the magnifying glass it took the breath away. Look through the glass and I could follow every step I'd taken that morning. Fleet Street, West Smithfield, the house on Cloth Court. The Great Eastern, Sun Street Passage, Cross Key Square. Even the windows of the room I was sitting in, with the catalogue open in my lap. Henry Beaufort walked back in the room with a black lacquer tray, set it down and aimed his conversation for tea at the vicarage. "Remarkable isn't it? The original was drawn during the war from a barrage balloon. You can see exactly where Michael discovered our Roman garrison fort. I was expecting he'd be here last evening when I got back to town. Why do you want to talk to him?" All delivered in the listless manner that signals rank and society for the benefit of strangers. He slid the lacquer tray along the table and folded in the second armchair, lifted the lid from a china teapot and trailed a spoon around inside it, the way he'd trail a finger in the water if I ever rowed him on the river.

I set the catalogue beside the tray. "A Singer convertible was found abandoned in the City overnight. He hasn't reported it missing yet, but the car is registered to Professor Garfield. Leave that aside for now. Do all his assistants get a house key, Henry? Or are you special?"

Henry swallowed hard and forgot about his tea ceremony. "I stay here sometimes. Since the snow put an end to our fieldwork, I've been spending some days in the country with my mother." The idea narrowed his mood and clouded his look. His mouth whitened around the edges. "Anyway, he spent those days with someone else. So, I can't be that special, can I?"

"Do you know that he did?"

Henry had been raised to let his disappointments show. "I know he did last night. When I got back, I went into the Raglan to see if he was there. It's our local bar. They told me he'd been in earlier and left with someone. You're an investigator, work it out for yourself."

"What then?"

"There are two flats above my father's offices in town. We keep one for the family. No one was using it so I stayed there overnight. When I telephoned Michael this morning and still got no answer I came back here to wait." Then, as if he ordinarily wouldn't see the need, added, "My father's an architect. Beaufort Partners."

I nodded and put a cigarette on my lip. "Tell me about Raymond Jarrett."

Henry fluttered his eyelashes. "I don't recall the name. Should I?"

"Maybe. He knew yours. As a matter of fact, he kept your photograph framed on the dresser in his bedroom. It ought to make him easier to remember. That is unless you autograph all your pictures." I put a light to the cigarette and described the photographs on Jarrett's dresser. Two people having fun on a shaded lawn one high-summer afternoon.

It got me all of Henry's attention. His society air evaporated. He gave me his lip-chewing repertory and then unbuttoned a hip pocket, took out his wallet and found two small square photographs the size of postage stamps from Samoa. He handed them across the lacquer tray with the look of Young Werther. "Both of us, taken last summer. I had two larger prints made from them and put in a frame for Michael's Christmas card. Who the hell is Raymond Jarrett?"

But I hardly knew the answer to that myself. I got Jarrett's study-in-satin out of my pocket and let Henry get the gist. The pounding in my head was starting a cold sweat. "He was a known male prostitute, getting a little worn at the edges for trade. Lately branching into camera work and blackmail."

"Was? What does he do now?"

"At around four-thirty this morning he was sitting in the professor's roadster and had his new career cut short. What he does now is take up space in the City morgue."

Henry groaned, and while his eyes crimped shut and his head lolled, we made a simple exchange. I put his two summer garden pictures in my pocket with Jarrett's and left my business card slotted in the sugar bowl on the tray. Against the hour when Henry got anxious about his boyfriend.

SIX

The Raglan's saloon bar stepped down from the sidewalk on St. Martin's le Grand. At Christmas Day noon it was a solid wall of noise and sweated faces at a line of tables that ran parallel with the bar, hot as a boiler room and swirling in a blue tobacco haze like river fog. I pushed inside and worked along the counter under loops of rocking paper chains. It was slow progress.

Half the room away, a coal fire licked in a wide brick hearth. At the bar, a customer was easing down off a high stool an inch at a time, as if one slip could start an avalanche. I was level with him, standing in his way, put a hand flat against his chest and let him slide to the floor on his feet. At ground level he began taking an interest in his surroundings, still trying to get a bearing when he checked himself and peered in my eyes as if we might have belonged to the same library once. The mountaineer climbing the hotel steps, with the glassy smile and the smudge moustache, asked, "Have we met before?" His trademark way with conversation, three inches from the knot in my necktie and still couldn't get me in range.

I nodded in the direction of our last talk. "At the Great Eastern. You were decorous and sober. I was young and innocent. And if you're thinking of leaving the building let me tell you there's oxygen out there." A recollection ghosted behind his eyes, but exploring it meant going back all of two hours and he swatted it away before it started nagging. By way of parting, he put his hands in front of his stomach, pulled in his chin and belched lightly, then patted my arm and stepped into the crush. I watched him leave, then climbed up in his place at the bar, took out a handkerchief and mopped under my lip. I was sweating like a stoker in a steam bath.

A figure in the crowd had been following the pantomime. We caught each other's eye in the mirror behind the bar. He wore a camel coat with a dark velvet collar, carried a briefcase under his arm as if nobody had mentioned it was Christmas, gave me a wry look and raised his glass. All I did was nod back in the mirror, but it was a mistake. The wry look in the camel coat floated off across the crowd. I made a giddy grab at the edge of the counter and missed. The room turned somersault, high laughter fluttered and broke in splinters, my knees went to milk. Then for the second time that morning, nothing.

When I came around, there was a scent in the room I didn't recognize and a wad of handkerchief taped behind my ear. I was trying to claw my shirt collar off the lump under the handkerchief, with a hand padded like a pitcher's glove, when another hand pulled it away and a voice said, "Let it alone, it ought to have stitches. I've bandaged your hand as well. When you're ready, your jacket's hanging behind the door. You'll find me along the hallway."

Floorboards creaked. A door clicked shut. The Raglan's inn sign careened in a snow squall right outside the window. I sat up on a chaise longue, leaned my head against the wall to stop my brains spilling on my shoes and looked around. The chaise was in a tiny parlor with a side table alongside it crowded with china figurines. A gas fire burbled in a corner. In among the curios, a painted china clock was chiming a quarter till four.

There were kitchen sounds along the hallway, and opposite the kitchen a door open on a dining room where another coal fire burned. It had a dozen places set at a table where the eating was finished, a sideboard littered with dishes, and three grown-ups with two livewire children seated in between them pulling Christmas crackers and fitting on paper hats. One of the grown-ups glanced over when I walked in the door, turned away from the children to pull aside a chair and asked, "Can you eat?"

My stomach crawled to the edge of a pit and looked in the abyss. I shook my head. Nurse Greer wore the two lines that stitched across her forehead frowning or not, and a high, dark wave of hair fixed behind her ear with a tortoiseshell comb. She smoothed the skirt of a fashion-house dress in polka dots, and in an undertone that said it might be better than I deserved, "You look as though you've been hit by a bus. What are you doing here?"

"It's a theory, but it's discredited. What are *you*?"

She glanced around a room otherwise engaged, got up and walked to the sideboard and came back with a glass and a bottle. "I told you. When I can, I work here."

I sank the brandy she poured, too brittle to carry a conversation, and while the liquor worked its medicine, took out the miniature of Henry Beaufort in a summer garden and laid it in front of her on the table. She poured me a smaller one and waited. "He says he called in here last night. You recognize him?"

She looked over the picture. "Last night? Yes, he was here. I worked the hours before closing. Who is he?"

"When last night?"

An eyebrow lifted and made her frown lines three. "I couldn't say exactly. We were crowded. What has this to do with?"

"Try, Miss Greer. About what time would you say you saw him?"

She pouted, annoyed, coloring a little. "You really don't care for anyone else asking questions, do you? He came in looking for someone late on. They come here together sometimes. It might have been around ten o'clock. I told him his friend had been in earlier and left."

I found Garfield's picture and laid the two side by side. "He's older, has lighter-colored hair, sports a brush moustache."

"His friend? Yes."

"Did you ever see either of them with Raymond Jarrett?"

Perhaps she hadn't seen it coming. Or perhaps she needed more time to think what the answer ought to be. Either way, it put an end to Christmas. Her napkin tossed at the photographs. Her chair scraped back. She chiseled an incendiary smile. "My *neighbor*? Is that what this is about? I told you already, I know nothing about him. Why won't you listen to me?" She got up, smoothing out the dress again, and between bared teeth in case she wasn't making it obvious, "You have no idea how hard you are to like when you're awake."

The grown-ups and the livewires had already drifted to the kitchen across the hall. A figure collecting dishes at the head of the table looked over in my direction, stopped what he was doing and came around to where I sat. He pulled eyeglasses from his shirt pocket and fitted them on his nose, leaned across me and took a closer look at the photographs on the table. The Raglan's landlord had chins to spare and yellowing hair brushed in tight waves off his forehead. He wore a lime-check vest that might have struck his patrons as a little flat for Christmas Day, but that was before he remembered where he put his carnation-pink dress shirt and the stickpin for his purple tartan cravat. His mouth hooked down at the corners. A finger tapped Garfield's photograph. "He was in here before nine o'clock, waiting for somebody who didn't turn up. Then a youngster went over and got bought a drink. They left not long after."

The way he told it, they both might have been late for Bible class. I asked, "The boy he bought a drink for, he's a regular?"

"He was here again today lunchtime. I never saw him before last night." I prodded Garfield's picture aside and left Henry Beaufort's. The Raglan's landlord peeled off the eyeglasses and folded them back in his shirt. "Like Miss Greer said, he came in later asking after his friend and got upset when she told him he'd left with somebody else. Look, Mr. Newman." He put a large hand on my shoulder and squeezed. "Young Estelle had a shock this morning. The matron sent her home. Lucky for you she didn't want to be on her own and came in here, because we don't have disorderly at the Raglan. I was for putting you on the street when you passed out. It was Estelle who said you were genuine." He went back to collecting dishes for the kitchen and we left it that today was my lucky day. I drained off Nurse Greer's painkiller and was last out of the room.

SEVEN

Superintendent Littomy kept his office on Snow Hill like a hothouse. At five o'clock on a late December afternoon it was sweating down the window glass. The superintendent lifted his gaze out of a file he was reading, jabbed a pencil at the seat opposite, winced from behind his desk lamp and launched the conversational opener of the day. "Good Christ, man, were you hit by a bus?"

I put down the travel grip I was carrying, pulled out the chair and waved his question away. "It's Christmas. There aren't any."

He twitched his jug ears and levelled the pencil between his fingertips, and didn't ask what I was doing there. A photograph on the wall behind him showed his children standing at attention in a line. They looked apprehensive. "Season of Goodwill though this may be, Newman, our newspapers tomorrow will be reporting not one but two murders on our doorstep. And while you may think that between these two high crimes my energies would be sufficiently occupied, you would be wrong. For as he dined today, Commissioner Stearns received a telephone call, a complaint that you called this morning at the home of a university professor and adviser to the Corporation, to question his junior assistant. In the name of all that's wonderful, the commissioner was taking Christmas lunch with his family. This is the City. What were you thinking?"

Littomy said the City. Not the city. In '47 London was a metropolis crowding three million people in a hundred square miles, sitting at the heart of an empire and playing a long, losing hand to keep it. A city like no other or just like any other, depending what you had in mind. Most of the possibilities were on offer, and part of its charm was that while you were deciding which to go after, it would give you benefit of the doubt. Stay clear of trouble and its police would salute, hold the traffic and walk you across the street. Step out of line and they'd lose the rulebook faster than you could answer your name. Yours to choose. The city was liberal that way.

The City of London was different. A single square mile, financial heart of the metropolis, where banks and insurance offices, trading houses and exchange floors mined the motherlode and squeezed out every other way of living. It had a resident population that could fit in the back of a limousine, and when its offices emptied and headed home at nights, they left behind a ghost town. Meaning that the possibilities for lawbreaking were rarefied, best appreciated by men who wore club ties and returned home late to wives with headaches and hearts of diamond. Meaning also that its police were left to concentrate on those things closest to the City's heart. It had twelve hundred officers paid to keep the traffic moving, eject undesirables not the City's own, and otherwise maintain an atmosphere congenial to the making of loud money. Ordinarily the setup worked like a Swiss timepiece. In the City a killing was strictly a figure of speech. Most days of the year you stood a better chance of getting shot at in a lighthouse. But the real beauty of the arrangement was this: all twelve hundred of its officers answered to nobody but the Corporation, and inside the one square mile they policed, no London metropolitan officer of any rank had any kind of jurisdiction whatever. The City's finest were the City's own.

Which was cozy. Because they had their streets nailed down and barely a handful of residents to protect and serve. As for the Corporation, it decided long ago that who got law and order inside that one square mile was nobody's business but its own. I unbuttoned my coat and jacket and waited to hear what came next.

"Professor Garfield's car was found abandoned earlier today; stolen, we may assume, in connection with the nearby murder of a known male prostitute. Meanwhile, your barefaced questioning of the professor's young assistant has affronted the boy's father. We have calmed the man, confirmed to him that Professor Garfield is subject to no police inquiry of any sort, and assured him we shall establish what in God's name you thought you were doing interviewing his son." He held up a hand to break his own flow. "There is more. It need not concern us."

Littomy was tall even sitting, better than six feet and a half, gaunt-thin in a uniform jacket. He ran one hand across a sparse, gray hairline and pinched the knot in his necktie with the other. His eyes hooded as he reflected. "Beauforts are society, Newman. This evening, Sir Hector and Lady Stearns will attend their Christmas ball. He will not have the Beaufort family troubled. We endeavor to locate the professor merely to seek his assistance regarding the presumed theft of his motorcar. However, since the matter also touches on a murder inquiry, it follows that your interest is at an end. Your questioning of the Beaufort boy was a grievous error of judgment. The commissioner has explained the same to his father." He leveled out in his chair. It was the only way his knees fit under the desk.

"And if it wasn't an error?"

Littomy didn't move a hair, just let go the club manner the way he would drop a shirt in the laundry, and talked at shadows on his ceiling. "These are two vice killings. As inconsequential as they are most certainly connected. Detective Inspector McAlester will investigate them as such. And though our newssheets will doubtless question police vigilance and the safety of our streets, it's eyewash and they know it. The victims were a common pimp and a whore, inhabiting the self-same gutter as their assailants. The perpetrators will be duly apprehended. Meanwhile, understand that Beaufort will not have his son even remotely connected. We have cooperated in the past, Newman. We shall again. Forget the professor. Forget his young assistant. Neither is your concern." Then, as an afterthought, "Your client is a City councilor."

Fine dust drifted past the light on his desk, rising on the dry sourness you breathe in all police stations everywhere. They refine it out of passing falsehoods, routine evasions, threats and mean deceits. I flicked a speck off the band around my hat and motioned at the file on his desk. "The victim lived at a property belonging to Councilor Drake. I got a call from him to deliver keys to McAlester. When we missed each other, I returned the keys to the councilor. Your file ought to say the same."

Littomy put his hands behind his head and stretched against the seatback. "Perhaps. Though why, I wonder, would Councilor Drake dispatch a private investigator on an errand any of his own employees might have performed?"

"He didn't say. Besides, looking up the professor was my idea not his. I was curious, Garfield wasn't home, so I talked to the boy. And still I'm curious. But then I don't have a medical examiner on hand when a question occurs."

The superintendent's gaze flickered across my face. "What question occurs?"

Craning up at Littomy was giving me a crick in the neck. I pushed back my chair and stood behind it. "The court the professor lives on has a janitor. I didn't see him when I went there this morning, but a visitor isn't a thing a janitor misses. So, this afternoon I dropped by again to introduce myself. He doesn't get a lot of company. We got along. I told him Professor Garfield couldn't be located and how people were getting anxious, left a card and asked him to call when the professor got back. He promised he would do that, but evidently something was bothering him. When I asked him what it was, he said an odd thing happened after I left this morning. The professor's young friend walked out of the house with a gift-wrapped box, emptied a garbage can in a corner of the yard and dropped the box inside. Then he put the garbage back on top." Snowflakes drifted past the window. The room went on sweating. "It made the janitor wonder if the refined thing nowadays is to Christmas-wrap the trash. So when the boy left, he went over to find out. What he found in the garbage was a stylish leather travel grip, loose-wrapped in gift paper, with a classy winter coat inside. He thought they both might be worth money cleaned up and so set them apart. Then I arrived and the idea lost its appeal." I reached down beside the chair and lifted the grip onto Littomy's desk. "Because what needed cleaning off were blood stains. Maybe the janitor thought the professor's Christmas turkey had put up a fight, but when he heard Garfield was missing, he could add things together as well as you or I can. Difference is, you can ask your medical examiner who the blood might belong to."

When I closed the door, Littomy was still strung out in his chair, fingers laced behind his neck like Huckleberry Finn in a hammock.

EIGHT

My taxi crawled west on Holborn, followed a snake of tire ridges past the City boundary and made south toward the river. On Kingsway the going got easier, the cab circled Aldwych and Bush House, then drifted left across the traffic to a marquee with a red pitched roof connecting the Waldorf to the curb. A doorman stepped up in livery and a tall hat, shook open an umbrella, pulled on the cab door and let me out. He looked me over, let a greeting die on his lips and moved directly to a dove-gray Armstrong limousine waiting next in line. I was at the hotel entrance before I glanced back to where the doorman had the umbrella lofted over a woman getting out of the back seat. She was stretching an ankle for the curb and wore a flawless, high-shouldered fur that might have been matched for the pearl-white tuxedo following her out of the car. But I didn't think so. Related, very probably, but one look said neither the fur nor the tuxedo would notice if the other was walking barefoot on glass. I moved into the lobby, checked my coat and followed the crush. I had on my dark navy suit, a sober tie, a mirror shine on my shoes, and blended so well with the money I could have been wearing my rainbow silk pajamas.

This was Christmas night with the Beauforts, not Monday Night at Minton's. The party was gathered in a ballroom lined with fluted columns and side aisles hung with streamers and cut-out Santa Clauses, its tables crowding three sides around a dance floor and a low dais where a band was playing. The band's brass section sparkled under a glitter ball. A dozen couples walked through a version of *Body & Soul* with the lift taken out of it under anesthetic. The rest was a hubbub of loud talk and high spirits at a hundred tables, stylish women dressed to dazzle, exotic as birds of paradise, and men seated in between them dressed as a milking herd of Friesians. At a Beaufort party, it isn't the hand taped like a prizefighter that gets you noticed. It's the lounge suit.

A duty manager trailed me in from the lobby, looking troubled. He caught up inside the double doors to the ballroom and parked at my elbow, coughed lightly and explained that what I'd mistakenly walked in on was an invitation-only, black-tie ball. I was looking around the room. I heard him. Perhaps it didn't show. He tried again, his delivery as clipped as his moustache. "Pardon me, but in the case of someone who does not appear to be bona fide, Mr. Beaufort requires me to inform our house detective."

I left off looking and leaned aside, close in his ear. "If we're talking about your houseman working the foyer, he's Maxie Helmering. Last sent up on two counts of receiving, one of perjury. That was 1940, sentence suspended to accommodate his burning desire to serve in His Majesty's forces. Naturally, the army put him in the pay corps, but it doesn't mean you ought to let him loose in this jewelry store."

I pointed my chin at the table right in front of us, where a tough-looking battle-axe had an armlock on a gin sling and a wrist semaphoring the fleet in six colors every time it caught the light. "Me, I'd start with the bona fides of House Detective Helmering, then pass Mr. Beaufort the name of the born optimist who hired him. There are bracelets in here giving their owners tennis elbow." I opened my wallet in front of his bow tie where he could read my card.

The flat of his palm jerked along his hair gloss. He cleared his throat. "We may be able to find you appropriate attire, Mr. Newman."

"The attire is appropriate. If anybody asks, I'm here on divorce work." I tapped the wallet on his silk lapel. "Why make it uglier than it has to be?"

The band wound down to polite applause. The bandleader exited and his piano player doodled while couples drifted off the floor. I left the duty manager thinking it over and followed a waiter into the crowd, took a glass from his tray and found a table under one of the columns. The ballroom lights dimmed. Electric candlelight burned at every table. A spotlight moved across the dais and followed the bandleader back in. He led on a tallish honey blonde in a satin ivory gown that bared her shoulders and dipped at her back, close-fitted everywhere and split along her calf to let her use her natural stride. Applause picked up. Heads raised out of highballs. The hubbub quieted. Then, while I caught the turn of the blonde's hips and the flash of an earring and waited for her to spin around, the bandleader let go her fingertips and stirred a slow introduction in the strings. He stepped aside, shot his audience a smile, watched the blonde lean into the microphone and gave her the tune.

I didn't move. Watched the singer's forehead wrinkle and her eyes mist, saw her mouth hook down to meet the line and heard nothing. She skipped a small step in tall heels, swayed and stretched the gown across her hips, and still I didn't hear a sound. An eyebrow arched. Her hands pinned around her waist. Long fingers spread at her sides and rose to touch her forehead. Not a thing. The band's reeds swooned and faded. The blonde backed up two paces to lean into the curve of the piano, kicked a calf through the slit of her dress and breathed while the brass took up the reprise. Then she set her head at one side, wandered downstage, wrapped her arms around her shoulders and ran a gimlet eye over her audience. There was a hush. She nodded to herself, lidded the eyes, pressed her lips to the mike.

When she tossed back her head and switched on a smile, I started. Then wild applause broke in, the tables around me got to their feet, she took a bow and hugged a bouquet and I lost sight. Lights went up. The band slipped a gear. Couples moved back on the dance floor. I drained the glass, didn't have a notion what the song had been, was still sitting there stunned when a voice behind me said, "I confess to murder."

When I got to my feet she was leaning on the back of my chair, eyes greener than I remembered, lit up by the performance and the champagne in her hand. The bouquet had been parked somewhere. "Murder?"

"Of a wonderful tune. But I do dance passably well."

I said I could believe it. She set the champagne glass on the table, stepped closer and slid her arm inside mine. Small bumps pressed at the corners of her mouth. "Newman, you're such hard work! I'm pleased with myself and now I should very much like to dance."

"Better ask somebody who was invited, Doctor. It'll be less embarrassing when I get told to leave."

She heeled right around at that and looked puzzled. Then stepped up toe to toe and purred in my ear. "Now see here, I'm the one inviting. And frankly, Detective, if you're trying not to stand out in a crowd it's not working." I stepped aside to let her by, then followed her onto the floor.

She danced a lot better than passably well. Moved taut and light across the crowded floor. Could work soft magic with a dip of her shoulder. I wasn't any match, but I thought I was holding my own when the piano slowed, swerved into *I Could Write a Book* and she leaned away. "You're out of practice, aren't you? What happened to your hand?"

"I jagged it on my magnifying glass. And dancing with the main attraction is making me nervous."

It got me a snort and another toss of her head and we closed up again. "The ball is a Blanche Beaufort charity. They have to applaud or we lock the doors and I begin again. If Blanche were here, she'd tell you the same."

Dancers drifted on and off the floor. The band shifted time. We steered around a couple moving only in straight lines, like marines drilling for parade. I put my cheek back against her hair. "Nonsense. In that gown they'd pay to hear you whistle. And this morning you didn't mention knowing any Beauforts."

"Newman! You admit to noticing my dress." She murmured it, wide-eyed and mocking, but too late. Her waist stiffened under my hand. She made her first misstep. The mood snapped and broke the spell. We were just two people dancing and reeling in a line of conversation, one of them high on excitement and champagne.

I murmured back. "Frankly, Doctor, if you're trying not to stand out in a crowd, it isn't working."

To feel the ripple under her shoulder I swung her back into the crush, past the same tense-looking couple that had got out of the Armstrong, who danced together as if they had to be handcuffed. Then the band worked up another tune and the tide of dancers carried us back where we started, to the champagne glass she left under the table light with its small gold shade. Another, taller drink stood beside it, a cigarette folded in the ashtray, still burning. The owner of both was sitting sullen against the fluted column, wearing black-tie as if he'd been weaned in it. Henry Beaufort slipped another cigarette out of a black enamel case, lit it and squinted through a tobacco cloud. "Am I interrupting, Kathryn? I supposed Newman might be looking for me."

The doctor was already moving off, as if she supposed I might be looking for Henry too. "Nothing we can't continue tomorrow. Won't you call into my office, Mr. Newman? I may have something for you. And even if it was against your better judgment, thank you for dancing with me."

"The pleasure was all mine."

She was turning to leave then checked, long enough to seem surprised. "Did you really think so?"

Henry held the cigarette in front of his nose, between a thumb and a forefinger, watching her move off through the tables and across the room. "It seems I was interrupting after all." We were letting that pass when a bellhop arrived with a silver tray, pulled up and looked over my suit, sniffed and handed me a note. I read the message through, held it out where Henry could read it for himself, then dropped a coin on the tray and told the bellhop no answer. The note was a scrawled, edgy longhand to tell me I was wanted in the Nile Room. It didn't mention my earliest convenience. Henry turned his wrist over and glanced at his watch. "Then my father isn't expecting the interview to last. At ten, everyone will be in the Nile Room for supper. I daresay I'll still be here when he's through with you. Just a little lighter and airier."

The Nile Room was as Egyptian as armadillos. A high, wide oval named for its frieze of the world of mysteries awaiting the well-heeled traveler east of Suez. All of them in shades of green. It was an orient where rickshaws rushed past the Taj Mahal and green flamingos waded in surf, where camel caravans wound through Himalayan passes and where, because the Nile Room aimed for wide appeal, a thousand stars of David made a zodiac across the green dome of night in the light of a green crescent moon. Club chairs and candelabras filled alcoves around the oval. A loaded supper table ran down the center. There was nobody else in the room. I took a piece of toast from under a napkin, started lifting lids on a line of silver tureens and had the toast buried in a black hill of caviar when a compact figure with a pained look and a buttonhole entered through a door at the far end of the table.

"Newman?" Beaufort was a handsome man late in his middle years, with long, weighted features and a complexion that flushed in the light from the candelabras. Black-tie gave him the seasoned look. A flop of white hair swept off a high forehead and added enough of the bohemian so you wouldn't mistake him for the maître d'. I made a mouthful of the folded toast and nodded in greeting. He took rapid steps over, passed me a napkin and started in. "For someone not invited, you not only make yourself at home you make yourself conspicuous. No doubt as you intend. So let me be plain. Commissioner Stearns understands that I will not tolerate my son's questioning by some chancing private investigator. He has given me his personal assurance on the matter. Someone should have spoken to you."

It might have been the secret of his success, to talk straight ahead on anything he wanted done and make it sound as fixed as farm prices. I wiped my chin with the napkin and said, "Somebody did."

"But you choose not to heed a warning. Is that it?"

I looked around the walls at tigers slinking over green sand beaches and swallowed while Beaufort fidgeted his shirt cuffs. "Mr. Beaufort, my talk with Superintendent Littomy this morning covered a lot of ground. He has two vice killings on his hands, a thirty-year-old male and a female closer to fifty. The superintendent isn't sentimental about either of them. In his book, they took risks that go with their trade and came off badly. Still, it doesn't look well, and the idea that it makes his streets appear unsafe depresses him." I ran my tongue along the back of my teeth. "What I'm trying to say is that City detectives aim at all times to make their lives uncomplicated. They don't miss the obvious and they get sensitive about not making arrests. Right now, they hardly have a line of inquiry, except that one of their victims, the thirty-year-old male, kept a signed photograph of your son on his bedroom dresser. Whatever reassurance you got from the commissioner, his detectives will not overlook that fact. And if they have no better lead, sooner or later they'll use it. Count on that, no matter who you telephone or how often. When it happens, young Henry will need a stronger story than the one he has now, because those boys will not only grind him to powder and take him for snuff, they'll do it while they tie their shoelaces."

In the ballroom, the band's clarinets made a run that ended in a high swoop. Faint applause ran over into the next number. While the brass picked up its new theme, I let him give some thought to Henry alone in a room with two City detectives, overgrown, underdeveloped, and ready to make a point. Beaufort dug out his show handkerchief, wiped his palms and gave me a thin, tight smile. "Mr. Newman, leaving aside what exactly you think you're doing here tonight, do not waste your time or mine trying to shock me. It is scarcely possible. My children have long taken it upon themselves to explore the licenses a rarefied upbringing makes available. Those few things they were denied, they sought out for themselves. Doubtless there is recklessness in the blood. I do not complain. Judgment I leave to the better qualified. It falls to me only to shield them from the consequences of their native waywardness, and to that end I will employ the very considerable means at my disposal. You may rely upon it. Now goodnight."

Beaufort straightened his bow tie and wheeled around for the door he came in by. I watched it swing shut and took in the room one last time. There was a pyramid of candied fruit at my end of the table made up in different colored bands. At the foot of the pyramid a sucking pig with an orange in its mouth was stretched flat in a pool of aspic, wondering whatever happened to austerity. I patted it on the jaw, popped a glacé cherry, then headed back to the ballroom. Henry had been right. We were two minutes away from supper.

The ballroom with its lights up was a stale, echoing hangar, using the supper break to get its ashtrays emptied and its spilled drinks mopped. A carpet sweeper moaned at the far side of the room and somebody was putting a shine back on the dance floor under the glitter ball. Henry Beaufort was sitting sideways across his chair at the table where I left him, his head tilted back against the pillar. He was plying another tall drink, his empty glasses collecting in a line under the gold lampshade. "How was the dressing down? The conversation as my father would have it."

I sat opposite. "He doesn't want me bothering you. It makes me wonder what he thinks we talked about this morning."

He mulled that. "I was late for Christmas lunch. He asked me why. I saw no reason to lie."

"That's a fine principle, Henry. Let's apply it. After I left you at the professor's house this morning, you cleared out an item of trash; a winter coat, dark brown, gold silk lining, handmade. Also, blood-soaked. You know the one I mean. Right now, it's with City Police, along with the travel grip you dumped it in. By tomorrow they'll have the grip fingerprinted and the blood on the coat analyzed. Why not try explaining it to me before you have to explain it to them?"

He registered the idea with no show of surprise or any evasion. Three cocktails ago it might have been different. For now, he rolled a mint green bead around the bottom of his glass and pouted. "I was annoyed when you left, so I went to see if Michael had taken an overnight bag."

"To join up with whoever he met at the Raglan? And?"

"He hadn't. His travel case was still there at the back of the closet. But with an overcoat inside it I hadn't seen before, wet through from the weather. Obviously, Michael hadn't left it there. He would never have put it away in that state." He spread his palms on the table either side of his glass, in wonder at his own naivety. "The coat was so wet I thought the color had run. Then I looked at my hands and knew it wasn't dye at all. Beauforts are raised on blood sports. The coat was reeking of it."

So Henry put it all together. From me he'd heard about the small-time hustler who kept his photograph on a bedroom dresser, knew the hustler had been found shot dead near Garfield's abandoned car and that its owner hadn't been seen or heard from since. Then, even though he claimed not to know who his boyfriend met in the Raglan last night, when Henry found a blood-soaked coat in Garfield's closet he'd panicked. It would have bothered me more if he hadn't. The carpet sweeper wound down like a distant siren. The ballroom's bright lights snapped out in sections. I said, "Is the professor being blackmailed?"

Henry's three-cocktail manner bid him au revoir. Tomorrow, in broad daylight, the idea would not only look plausible to him, it would look obvious. For tonight, he needed to write it off as tawdry and ridiculous, strictly for somebody in my line of business. He turned hissing in the flutter of an eyelash. "No, he is *not* being blackmailed. I would know. Throwing the coat out only made things look worse, I can see that. But what would *you* have done?"

His gaze lifted to the entrance from the foyer, to where a couple walked arm in arm at the back of the ballroom. They turned into the aisle behind the columns, strolled around and found a table of their own in shadow and out of view from the entrance doors. From the way she moved, the woman was younger. Or perhaps she was just gayer; dark, handsome in a blue gown, and looking more relaxed than the last couple of times I'd seen her that evening. Her new companion had a reserved, serious look, and an empty right sleeve tucked in the pocket of his dinner jacket. It forced him across and behind her to hold the chair when she sat. When he took the seat beside her, she gave him the small, dreamy laughter her company in the pearl-white tuxedo would never hear. No question, the money that had followed her out of the Armstrong limousine was the husband. The one-armed man getting all her attention was not. Sometimes you don't have to be Freud.

Henry shook off the interruption and lost his hissing fit, decided he needed a dignified exit and raked back his chair. "You know, I might have got to like you, Newman." He got to his feet unsteady, squared up and gave it to me between the eyes. "But you really disappoint me."

NINE

Black cabs plowed by with halos lit around their for-hire signs. Snowflakes side-slipped, so few you could count. I stepped from under the hotel marquee and headed west through theaterland. Its stages were dark Christmas night, but no matter, the Beauforts had put on a gala performance all their own. I'd had the patriarch with the high style who could call in a favor, the college boy who should have been locked in his room, the mystery woman who came alive when she slipped out on her husband, and the friend of the family who knew how to steal a show. In a theater, it would be Coward and manners tighter than a shirtfront. Or Novello and tunes you can whistle, with a hard-gloss heartthrob, a heroine born to play a migraine, and a young blade with a profile and a phony eye for the girls. Not original. And not *King Lear* either. Just the Beaufort ball with better poise and faster dialogue, and a cast that knew how to rehearse.

Streetlights glowed thin and ran ahead along the Strand to Trafalgar Square. I walked and thought over what I'd got. Two unexplained murders. Footprints on a fire escape filling with snow. And an overdue professor, who since last seen might have gone back home and left behind a blood-soaked coat. Added to which I had three nervous men, the boy Reilly, not currently advertising his whereabouts, and an amnesiac nurse with a hearing problem. It wasn't much and it wasn't promising.

The three men were right to be nervous. The first was my client, his civic career threatened by a fruit-for-hire and extortion racket operating from a property he owned. The second was Beaufort senior, aware his son had thrilled to more than the missing professor's poetry and already calling in favors to protect him. As for the third, young Henry Beaufort had grown the not-so-wild idea that his boyfriend could be implicated in a killing. Certainly he'd tried to conceal evidence, but in a way that was so ham-fisted it only looked naive. His problem being that City detectives never yet awarded marks for naivety. Then there was the nurse, who not only failed to hear the gunshot that executed her neighbor, but affected haziness accounting for her time early Christmas morning. According to the doctor, the candles at the crib allowed her forty minutes between lighting them and calling in the murder. Give her ten minutes inside the church, then ten more to decide Jarrett was dead and get to a telephone. It still left twenty minutes unexplained. That is, unless you were acting medical examiner and you thought Nurse Greer could have pulled the trigger herself. It was conceivable she had. But then, what of the footprints on Jarrett's fire escape? Or the bloodied coat in Garfield's closet? And if Jarrett's murderer hadn't left behind either the footprints or the coat, then who?

A taxi horn sounded close by Charing Cross, aimed at a fresh-faced figure in round glasses that recoiled, then retreated under a streetlamp on an island in the middle of the Strand. From there, he surveyed the miracle of the horseless carriage collected all around him, gathered himself and tried again. He stepped off the curb, weaved through a line of traffic and pulled up in front of me at a signboard beside an entrance that read *Saints Fruchtna & Patrick, Catholic Apostolic Temperance Lodging & Dining Hall, Eammon P. Dolan S.J., Bursar.* Below it, another sign said *No Vacancies*. The new arrival planted his feet, twisted and pulled a key fob out of his coat pocket, then aimed a key at the lock over the entrance door handle. He was easing his chin back to get the building in his sights when my nerve cracked. I reached past him and closed my hand over his, leveled his key, slid it in the keyhole and turned, then pressed down the door handle with my free hand and set the door ajar. The young man bent at the knees in triumph, and in a southern-soft accent exclaimed, "Ha! Civil of you."

"Don't mention it. It must have been a heavy day."

His brow clouded in mildest contradiction. "Not the least bit. It is Our Lord's birthday, a day of joy and feasting for all those that do His work. I bid a good evening to you both. God bless."

I acknowledged the admonition and the blessing. "Good night to you, Father." Then went on ahead to the square.

"The Norwegians say they plan to send a tree every year."

The priest would have called it civil of them. For six war years there had been no cutting any down and all Christmas trees were fake, so small they were taken into bomb shelters when the sirens sounded. Some things get better after all. I looked around the rooflines of Trafalgar Square, black against a frost-black night, then up at a tall spruce sparking enough electricity to light a fairground. A clutch of soldiers on a pass yelled and snowballed. Girls in mittens fooled about on the ice in the fountains. The voice at my shoulder said, "You were in Norway?"

My gaze dropped from the star fixed at the top of the tree. "No. You?"

"You might say a part of me still is." The speaker left his gaze on the tree and flicked at the empty sleeve of his coat, tailored into the pocket. "You made quite a splash at tonight's party, Mr. Newman."

"Not intended. I wasn't invited."

"So Guy Beaufort told me. He says you're a private investigator, and was not charmed." He pulled a card from inside his coat and handed it to me. "Edgar Levin, Beaufort Partners." Levin was lean and dark and somewhere in his thirties, less tall than I remembered in the ballroom, with a mouth at a slant, not built for a ready smile. It gave him an odd kind of good looks, geared for a disappointment, and might have been a part of his appeal.

We went on watching the fooling and snowballing until it was too raw-cold to stand around, found we were headed home in the same direction and made for the Whitehall side of the square. Levin flagged a cab there, got in and skewed in a corner. I slid shut the glass behind the driver's seat, took the corner opposite and growled, "Who does charm Guy Beaufort? Tonight, I got threatened with the police commissioner. It was all we had time for."

Levin turned from his view over the square through the taxi's rear window, surprised I needed it explained. His forehead dipped at the City up ahead. "Your answer's there. When the Square Mile rises from the ashes it's not going to be a free-for-all. Government demanded a master plan for reconstruction and the Corporation commissioned Beaufort Partners to provide it. If you're a developer in the City, charming Guy Beaufort is where you start. Don't be too hard on him. He's got a lot on his plate at the moment."

"He's got a train wreck on his plate. He calls it family."

The taxi ran the length of the Strand, skirted the burned-out shell of Clement Danes, then started into Fleet Street. Levin was looking out the rear window again, wondering how much he ought to tell a stranger about his boss's family. "Guy is being protective. His youngest has taken a serious shine to a senior adviser to the Corporation. It puts working relations under strain. Then tonight a private investigator arrives uninvited at his Christmas ball. Guy was unhappy about that. What did you expect?"

The cab ran past the Reuter Building to pull over at the end of a block. Levin got out and stepped across a frozen gutter to the curb. I paid off the fare and followed him to the sidewalk, looking up where he looked, back across the street at a tall spire silhouetted over the rooftops, pointed at a faded star. "You do churches?"

The cab eased out from the curb and back into the traffic.

"Right now, nobody's doing St. Bride's. Someone climbed down into the crater the Luftwaffe left and noticed Wren had built his church over a medieval crypt. Then the archaeologists found the crypt was built on top of something Roman."

"Professor Garfield?"

It brought his gaze back to earth. "Excavating St. Bride's? It's sure to interest him, but the professor has far bigger fish. You've met him?"

"I met his reputation."

Levin made half of a shrug. "Well, the reputation's growing. If only for keeping us planners at bay. But he has a point. There's an entire Roman city buried under the Square Mile and he's got a few fleeting months to excavate it before we start pouring concrete. The professor thinks construction should take a back seat to scholarship and he has the ear of people who matter. It makes him no friends in the City when they're geared up for a gold rush."

Levin said home was at the top of Beaufort Partners' offices on Ludgate Hill, hardly ten minutes' walk away, and we shook wrong-handed and said goodnight. I watched him go then started across the traffic crawl. One side of my door was a cleared bombsite. The Tipperary's saloon bar was on the other, dark as a cloister at an hour when drinking migrates to backrooms like flocks to winter pasture. I put a key in the lock and climbed the stair, went in my apartment and on into the lounge. Streetlight filtered at the windows, enough to find a match and put it to the gas fire at the end of the room. I loosed my necktie, dropped my coat and jacket on the sofa, sat down beside them and listened to the hearth ticking softly, just it and me. My toes touched the bottom of an ocean before my shoulder hit the cushions.

TO THE PAST OBLITERATIVE

The gas fire still ticked and misted the windows on the street. Snow crystals slipped down the outsides of the glass. The telephone was ringing again. I reached around the sofa arm, tipped the receiver off its cradle, heard the connection make and then a subdued voice hesitating before it said, "There's something I should have told you." It's the line that always makes me feel lightheaded, the feeling that one day I'll need it for an epitaph. The voice waited to be interrupted and when it wasn't, went on, "Yesterday when you came to the house, I said I was tidying up, but it was more than that. Someone had been in here. Not Michael. It was a complete mess. I should have said, I know, but I thought..." We both knew what he thought. "Michael still wasn't answering his telephone this morning so I came back to straighten his study. But I think you should see it first. I mean, it's not just that things are out of place." Henry Beaufort sounded close to tears.

I squinted at the darkness outside. "What time is it?"

There was a pause. "Seven-thirty. Look, I don't want to stay here in the house. I'll leave the door on the latch."

The line went dead. I got the receiver back on its stand, groped across the hall and felt for the light-pull. A dull flare struck hard chrome, lit up a mirror and green tile checker patterns around the walls. In purgatory you can enjoy the same bathroom model, only warmer. In two seconds, the sweat was icing on my chest. In ten I had the washbasin filled, my shirt stripped off and my head under the faucet until searing cold jerked me upright. In thirty minutes, I was shaved, dressed and standing in the yard at Cross Key Square.

The janitor was tall and underfed, stooped over the short spears of his breath and halfway to sweeping a path around the courtyard in a dragging gray dawn. He had on the muffler and frayed cord jacket that he wore the afternoon before, straightened at the slam of the cab door and watched me in through the arch. I took the path he'd cleared already, caught whisky on the frosted air as I came up, and made an admiring mouth at his handiwork. We smiled at each other; two members of the same union, who knew what it was to be out and working on a winter day before the sun was up. I looked over at Garfield's house, on the opposite side of the yard. "When did the boyfriend leave?"

The janitor stood with his hands cupped over the top of the broom stale, knees flexed, elbows splayed like a jockey waiting for the tape. His forehead crinkled while he figured it. "After seven o'clock. I was out here clearing snow."

"You saw him arrive?" The question drowned in the moistness of his eyes. I tried again. "Was anybody else in the house since yesterday?"

He brightened at that. "Police, like you said there would be. Two of them last night, wanting the key to Mr. Garfield's house. By eight o'clock they'd gone. Nobody else I saw." He confided, a little shy. "I took to celebrating Christmas myself last night."

I nodded and dug out a photograph. The janitor patted for his wire-rim glasses in a pocket, wound them around his ears and fixed on Jarrett's portrait as the shop-soiled odalisque. He took it in his stride. "He was here a week ago, could be more. Looked at the names on the residents' board

and went away again. People come, people go. I don't ask."
Where Garfield was concerned, he wouldn't need to ask. He
took off the glasses and lifted his gaze across the yard. "You
going in there, Mr. Newman?"

"It crossed my mind." I left him leaning over his broom,
watching me along the path he'd cleared up to the professor's
front door.

I took the same route through the house as the first time, as
far as Michael Garfield's private museum. From there a short
hallway led to the galley kitchen where Henry made tea,
and off the hall a door he'd kept closed. Today it was wide
open, and Henry was right; it wasn't as if things were just
out of place. The study's bookshelves had been stripped, its
picture frames torn from the walls, desk drawers turned out
and the contents strewn around the floor. Whoever had been
looking, there was no way to tell if they found what they
came for. But what they came for was plain. Photographic
prints and negatives lay everywhere. They were emptied
out of cabinets, shaken out of books, turned out of files;
from anyplace the professor had ever stored them or set
them aside or mislaid or forgotten about them. And with
a thoroughness that didn't just look impressive, it looked
frantic. As if Garfield's special brand of orderliness had sent
somebody over the edge, the way a Belgian will feel when he
first sets eyes on Switzerland.

What the two detectives had made of it there was no
knowing, but it was hard to see the bright side for Henry
Beaufort. I sat for a time across the corner of Garfield's desk,
then picked a directory off the floor, found a number, found
the telephone and dialed. A housekeeper's voice answered at
the second ring with an old-fashioned calm, inquired who was
calling, and said if I cared to wait, she'd find out if Councilor
Drake was available. I waited, reached over a litter of typed
sheets with doodles in the margins and lifted a pencil out of an
old cigarette can. The can had a *Sweet Afton* label, primrose
yellow, a dozen upturned pencils, a ball of rubber bands and

paper-tags, a matchbook, sealing wax, pencil erasers. Was it *among* or *along*? I never remembered, pulled the can closer and read the verse on the label: *Flow gently, Sweet Afton, among thy green braes ...*

The line crackled. The same soft, distant voice told me it regretted the councilor was unable to come to the telephone, but said his lawyer wished to see me at his office at my earliest convenience. She read me the lawyer's office address in St. Mary Axe and asked would I also care for a telephone number. When I said there wasn't any need, he could expect me in half an hour, she said, *Very well, Mr. Newman,* and hung up. You could hear the rustle of her curtsey. I took the matchbook off the lip of the cigarette can, wrote the address inside the flap and put it in a pocket, then slotted the pencil back where I found it, point down in the drum.

There was a captured reel of Wehrmacht film I saw once of a German rocket test at a base on the Baltic coast. A switch is thrown in a bunker, the rocket motor fires up, and at a gantry in the forest an early-model V-2 lifts house-high off the ground then keels over, poleaxed like a dynamited smokestack. Next to my knee, the pencil I'd put back in the cigarette can was giving a passable imitation of the rocket test. It eased back up and out of the drum, got to where it turned top-heavy, teetered on the rim and tipped in my lap. I sat watching it, at a loss, until the von Braun in me prodded the pencil back in the slot it vacated and let the performance repeat. Then I snatched up the drum and shook the contents over the desk. Spooled inside the drum, a slim, translucent envelope had buckled where the pencil point snagged it. I got a fingernail under the lip, wound the envelope around a finger and flipped it in a curl on the flat of my hand. Two minutes in Garfield's museum found me his magnifying glass. I snapped on the switch of a floor lamp in a corner of the room.

Inside the envelope was a strip of negative film divided in five frames. At a glance they looked more or less blank, but backlit against the lampshade and magnified under the glass, a small world opened up. It had rail tracks and crossroads and traffic frozen in motion, driving by empty lots on streets blotted with snow. In time, I saw they were five camera shots of the west-center of the City taken from the air, the outline of St. Paul's unmistakable in all five, even in reverse. Not so different in the detail from Henry's wartime barrage balloon drawing, if you didn't count the magic. I slid the strip back in its envelope and pressed it flat in my pocket, put back the professor's lens on his exhibition catalogue and made for the stair. What the photographs meant or who else but Garfield would be interested, I had no idea. Until I did, they might as well be Santa Claus's holiday snaps, taken on a flypast.

A rising wind was shaking the night's snowfall from the branches of the lime trees. I went out through the arch under the janitor's rooms, turned along Little Britain and walked the short, bare strip of Postman's Park. There was an entrance for hospital deliveries across from the end of the park and a salt-gritted path leading around a nurses' residence into the main quadrangle. The path turned aside at a fountain frozen solid, then climbed a ramp into a foyer filled with the smell they bottle just for surgery and painted in shades of the North Atlantic in February; so dismal that if you weren't already dead on arrival you at least could know how it felt.

It was deserted except for an administrator in half-glasses sitting at a desk behind the counter. She was clattering at an Underwood, upright in a Norfolk homespun, gray hair fixed in iron-hard waves to match the décor. At the sound of the opening door she heaved a sigh, peered over the half-moons and took in the tape on my hand. I was standing at the counter, waiting while she tightened the belt around her jacket, when an accent from the heart of Midlothian said, "St. Bartholomew's Hospital treats accidents and emergencies only upon completion—"

I cut in. "It's neither. The name is Newman. I'm here to talk to Nurse Greer."

She went back to hacking at the typewriter, long enough to let me know I was invisible. Then, since it was in her gift, relented. Her mouth bunched and lifted out of her typing again. "Not here."

I gave her my air of surprise. "Isn't she meant to be?"

Her hands lifted from where they rested on the keyboard. She leaned her wrists either side of the machine, eyes closed, jaw clamped. "Mr. Newman, each morning I am sent a list of non-arrivals. Young nurses not being noted for their reliability at this time of year, today's list is longer than usual. If Nurse Greer were not meant to be here, she would not be on my list."

I patted the counter top with the flat of my hand, looked up at the vault of the ceiling, then back at the logician at the typewriter. "But she is on your list."

"That is correct, Mr. Newman. She *is* on my list."

"Not arrived this morning."

"Not arrived."

"Well, Miss …?"

"Hartridge."

I tipped my hat and confided, "I didn't mean to be so hard on you. Frankly, hospitals put me on edge. But if you'll give Nurse Greer a message that I called, I'll know to write her a letter next time. It'll be easier on my nerves. Good day to you, Miss Hartridge. It's been a pleasure."

Her fists clenched and she closed her eyes a second time and let the sounds of my going pour balm on her fraying soul.

ELEVEN

The Trelawne Building straddled a corner between St. Mary Axe and Bevis Marks, a yellow-brick façade with long windows making mirrors of the morning light, pale as tinplate. The street door opened on a silent lobby heady with wax polish, where a waiting elevator glowed behind a wire-glass slit. At one side of the glow, the first rise of a staircase coiled upward around the lift shaft. I shook out some more aspirin from Louis' bottle and climbed the stair.

Buchanan Allynson's offices were on the second floor, off a quiet anteroom. A rosewood desk with a bell on it had a sign reading, *Ring for Attention.* I brought my palm down flat on the button and went ahead to a windowless study furnished in the way of a smoking room at the jockey club; too large to be cozy, too small to be a public library. The kind of room where the trained legal mind has everything in reach to figure out its next percentage. It had a pair of high-back armchairs at an angle to a japanned table, an antique rug in the center of the floor, three walls tiered with numbered legal volumes, and a fourth, between the room's two doorways, taken up by a rustic hearth with firedogs and no fire, only a tall Chinese vase filled with holly berry.

The bell's echo had died before a flat rustle arrived at the far side of the hearth, and following on the rustle an observation delivered in a low, slow throwaway that didn't ask for an answer. "Aren't you late?"

She was five feet and a half of deep-cherry redhead pressed against the door edge, fitted in a costume with a soft chalk stripe. Eyes wide-set, a crimp in her chin and a mouth that made the fall of dark-red hair look incidental. We lingered on her entrance just long enough to consider what else she might add to a winter morning. Then she touched at a silk flower pinned high on her shoulder, gave me the look that says *Welcome* is for doormats and murmured through close, even teeth, "Take your hat off, I'll call my husband." She turned on her heel and took the rustle with her.

I dropped my coat and hat in one of the armchairs and waited. A motor crawled by in the street below, gnawing on a frozen gearbox. It was two blocks off, still spitting out the pieces, when a figure entered at the door I'd come in by and closed it behind him. The redhead's husband didn't waste an introduction either, went directly to a cabinet, poured two straight jolts and brought them over to where I was standing. Without any ceremony he handed one over, stood at a loose attention and raised the glass in his left hand in salute, "*Mea gulper.*" The drink inhaled as if we were about to jump out of an airplane.

I nodded and saluted back. "Christmas."

It was ripe, refined, heady stuff, of an age meant to bring warmth and happiness, but not to the masses. The morning stirred and brightened to the sounds of birdsong, snows melted and leaves unfurled. The lawyer cracked an unexpected gap-tooth grin, took both glasses back to the cabinet and said without turning around, "I believe we're going to get along, Newman. Do sit down."

The brandy settled, spread and pirouetted around the aspirin. I took a seat and watched him freshen the glasses. Allynson looked standard legal fare: slim, medium height, boyish and dressed for sixty-five, in a charcoal three-piece with a watchchain and a squadron necktie knotted with a pipe wrench until his shirt collar buckled. He had a soft, indoor pallor, bad skin and rimless spectacles, and the tight, careful accents that glide around the law in any language, in all places, at any time. But that wasn't how he made an impression. What impressed was the way he didn't keep an unsteady grin in check, or the nervous flex in his step, or a look he had of lolling in the shade of an airplane wing on a grass strip in summer, waiting for the next call to scramble and the short odds it would be his last. It gave him an uneasy appeal, but of the kind you want to see in the other fellow's lawyer.

Allynson fitted the stopper back in the decanter then turned and declared, "It's a damned nuisance about our tenant." As if Raymond Jarrett had been behind with his rent. He set my glass in reach on the table, then lifted the lid of a hammered-silver box and pushed it toward me. I stopped patting my pockets, pried out a cigarette and slewed the box back around. He pulled a wry mouth and tapped his chest. "I'm afraid not. Doctor's orders." Then lifted a lighter from its slot in the box, snapped it and held out the flame at arm's length, as if we were shooting pistols at dawn. "I'll come to the point, Newman. The City is a tightknit community where reputations are as indispensable as they are vulnerable. I speak not only of Councilor Drake's business affairs. He's a Freeman of the City, Chairman of Planning, very likely a future Alderman. Police interest in one of our tenants therefore causes us embarrassment no less than surprise. Your report to the councilor was timely. It allows us to spare the worst of our blushes. You did well. You did very well." Allynson dropped the lighter back in its slot and gave me the grin again, his drink clutched under his chin.

I tipped my glass and said, "That's as may be. But police won't stop at embarrassment. Set aside whether Councilor Drake ever met his tenant, or knew about his record. Raymond Jarrett was using the councilor's property to make introductions for a City clientele, had a studio for camera work and a one-way mirror for blackmail shots. City detectives will take even that in their stride. Their surprise will be that the first the councilor knew about it was Christmas morning, when his tenant took a .38 slug in the back of the head. They'll wonder if it takes Warner Brothers moving in before the councilor asks what goes on."

Allynson folded his arms high across his chest and let himself come to a decision, then raised up on his toes to make me a confidence. "Look, Newman, we're frankly astonished that our property office hadn't the least whiff of this. Naturally, we shall undertake our own inquiry and fully cooperate with City Police, but our priority is to handle this with sensitivity. We shall have a damned awful mess on our hands if we don't." He swallowed the polite third of his refill and reached inside his jacket. "In this regard, I feel certain you can continue to be of service to us. I give you this to include a payment on account."

I ground my cigarette in his ashtray, took the check he handed me and looked it over. Aesthetically speaking, it was a collector's item colored in pastel shades and silky to the touch, watermarked discreetly, made out in a clerical style that had a way with zeros and signed off in a tighter hand that was the councilor's own. A check like that takes a plain, old-fashioned transaction for pieces of silver and makes it a solemn sacrament, mordant as a marriage. You can frame it on a wall and invite in connoisseurs to view. It even smells good. This one, written on a very private bank that ordinarily wouldn't let me through the door, was proposing to pay me four hundred in sterling, in cash if I cared to take it that way, which as proposals go was both pleasing to the eye and satisfying to the mind. I cleared my throat. "Mr. Allynson, what I did yesterday on behalf of your client amounted to less than two hours of my time. This check will buy a month, and that's a lot of investigation. Maybe the councilor can afford to be lavish, but first I need to know how he expects me to earn it."

Beyond making him thirsty, the question didn't appear to trouble him. Allynson emptied his glass again and waved it at me. Evidently his doctor's orders didn't mention brandy. "Your actions so far have been well-judged. Councilor Drake values your work. Continue to assist us in the same vein and your fee will be well enough earned. Quite how you go about that I believe we can leave to your discretion."

He pressed a buzzer at the side of the hearth, the brandy setting light to his eyes as good brandy will. I folded the check in a pocket where it wouldn't bruise, watched him leave and waited. Mrs. Allynson swayed in unhurried, took me through the anteroom to call the elevator and turned on her heel. And did it all as if she'd broken a thumbnail. I lit a cigarette there and wondered where she fitted in. Wondered also since when the councilor had become we in her husband's conversation. It might be a lawyer's royal way with a pronoun. More likely, it was an accessory he'd acquired, like the watchchain and the five-star liquor greeting and the redhead running on ice.

Yellow light waxed in the wire-glass. The elevator hummed in the way of a Tibetan monk, clawed upward, thought about stopping, then passed right by the floor. I dropped the cigarette and hammered the button. But it never works. The light behind the glass climbed on and was gone, like moonrise in a fog.

TWELVE

Bishopsgate police station was as quiet as the street outside. There was an auxiliary at the desk, due a raise for what she was doing to the uniform, who said Dr. Swinford had arrived early that morning, then left, and who knew how long she'd be gone? Not her. And there was no one around to ask. Everybody in the doctor's department was still on holiday. Then again, since I had an appointment, if I wanted, I could wait. She leaned across the counter and explained how to find the medical examiner's laboratory, with a soft, sad smile, as if the last one who went looking never came back.

Halfway along a wide corridor on the fourth floor, a single strip of electric light cut across the linoleum at an open door. The laboratory was somber and deserted. A place where a textbook routine might get a man hanged faster than his wife could give him an alibi. It had no gargling tubes or chalkboards or flasks of smoking alchemy. Only brass-fitted cabinets filled with instruments, and high benches in close, dark lines, closed in a reek of formaldehyde. The examiner's own office was sectioned off a corner, a half-glass affair with regulation file cabinets, a couple of hard chairs and a desk where he could sit and survey his laboratory. Templeton had his name on the door glass, over a list of professional qualifications that took in three continents. His temporary replacement didn't rate a mention.

The door was unlocked. I put on a light, settled in the chair behind the desk, and pulled open a drawer left with its key in the lock, in case I wouldn't know where to start. The drawer had a tired copy of *Smith's Forensic Medicine* inside, some thumbed-over procedure manuals, and under a wad of blank forms and police letterheads, a plain manila file marked for circulation with a name-list. I slid the file to the top of the heap, opened it flat inside the drawer and started reading.

Twenty-four hours on from his murder, Raymond Jarrett's file was thin and mostly filled with police photographs. There were pictures of Garfield's car, outside and in, of Jarrett's corpse stretched across the floor of the church porch, his gunshot wounds taken close up on the slab, and of the blackmail operation he was running in the house on Cloth Court. For the rest, there were statements from Jarrett's neighbors in the court and a stiff envelope with the contents of his pockets and his wallet tipped inside. Clipped at the back of the file there was a page of close typing that looked like notes Dr. Swinford had made for herself concerning her two Christmas Day postmortems. Behind the sheet of typing there was a carbon copy, and the doctor's private visiting card.

If the file held it all, Raymond Jarrett had been carrying as little on him as anybody ever does who arrives at a time and a place they weren't expecting to die: loose change, some folding money, a stamped envelope with the flap ripped off and a check inside, four snapshots, plus the emptied-out wallet. The statements from Jarrett's neighbors you could have written in advance. Until police arrived Christmas morning, they hadn't seen or heard a thing out of the ordinary. More than that, no resident of Cloth Court remembered seeing or hearing anything at all at that hour, except for the nurse's next-door neighbor; a curtain-operator with jaundice in his eyes, who was old and ill and barely slept worth the name.

According to him, the nurse had left home Christmas morning for her early shift at the same time as any other morning he watched and waited. Which made him surer about Nurse Greer's timekeeping than she admitted to being herself. And while it was always possible she might tighten up her story, somehow you doubted it. Either way, her statement wasn't in Jarrett's file. She would have one all her own.

I left the drawer where I could slide it shut with my knee, pulled Doc Templeton's telephone closer and found a line to the switchboard. A slow, burnished drawl answered when the connection made. I said, "The boy who went missing, Louis. You told me he knew a housekeeper in the hotel. Where can I find her?"

He took a second. "That would be Miss Irene, Mr. Newman. But she's gone. The boy came in the hotel yesterday asking for her and made a big commotion. They showed him out and then they fired Miss Irene. She got a girlfriend here in the hotel. If you want, I can ask an address and call back to you."

I said I'd hold the line, heard the open and close of his door to the hotel lobby and lifted the four snapshots out of Jarrett's file. They were a sequence, not good but recent and recognizable, of Michael Garfield on a City street in winter. In the first, he was leaning into a knifing wind, hands deep in his coat pockets and a scarf wound around his chin. In the second, he had a hand raised in greeting to somebody out of camera shot. In the third, they met, the new arrival with his back to camera, in an embrace trying for comrade-to-comrade that just couldn't make it. And in the last, Garfield had turned his friend around and they were walking together arm in arm, Henry and his professor huddled tight against the weather. The pictures were ten seconds' work, blurred at the edges and taken through a car's windshield. Neither of the two subjects had known the first thing about it. I dropped all four back in the file, then pulled the check from its envelope. It was the second of its kind I'd seen in one morning.

This time it was made out to R. Jarrett Esq. in the sum of sixty-five pounds, dated 24 December 1947 and written on the same private bank as the check the lawyer had handed me not an hour before. This time the same crabbed hand that signed it W. I. Drake had also filled it out. Which made it odd on two counts. First, because a day after the check was written, Councilor Drake told me he didn't recollect knowing Raymond Jarrett at all. And second, because as a generally accepted principle of liberal economy, it's the tenant who pays the landlord, not the other way around.

The line clicked and Louis caught a breath. "She's Miss Irene Voigt, Mr. Newman. Her last name I didn't know before. It's not a good name to own in these parts. Lives pretty close." He read out an address in Spitalfields and then asked, "You take any brandy for that head of yours?"

"Every chance I get."

He said he was pleased to hear it and we hung up.

I pocketed Dr. Swinford's visiting card and the copy of her notes, put Jarrett's file back where she left it and sat thinking it over. The doctor had clipped Jarrett's police history at the front of his file, the one she read to me yesterday at breakfast. But she hadn't read it all. Perhaps it had looked too obvious to mention, or it struck her as coincidence and nothing more, but the one and only time Jarrett had brushed with the law, she'd omitted the name of the arresting officer. It turned out McAlester and Raymond Jarrett went back a long way.

When he'd pulled Jarrett in seven years before, McAlester ranked detective sergeant. Now he was detective inspector, running not only Jarrett's murder inquiry but Dillys Valentine's too. It bought him a lot of latitude. His to decide what interested City detectives and what they left alone, what went in and what stayed out of the record, and when and how to improvise wherever he saw a need. If you were McAlester's boss and not prim about his methods, running two murder cases together would have its appeal. Littomy would call it effective policing. The commissioner might buy it. You just wouldn't want to be the citizen without a solid alibi for the first hours of Christmas Day.

THIRTEEN

Christ Church was set across the end of Brushfield Street like a stopper in a bottle, as if it had been put there for the purpose, its spire pricking at a lowering sky. The rest of the building was one more gutted shell standing over a crypt that had been a local deep shelter until the air raids ended. Halfway to the church, a cobblestone lane joined at right, where the iron barrel of a cannon was set in the sidewalk at the street corner. Beyond it a brick row faced Spitalfields Market. The address I had was fourth along the row.

The house was three stories over a wholesale fruit supply, already closed up for the day. It had a light showing at a second-floor window, and between the store's two peeling shutters, a street door with a mail flap. I rattled the flap until the window light went out, then twice again before a chain dragged and the door cracked open. A slight, pale girl was standing sideways in the gap. She might have been seventeen and already looked defeated, wore a thin, powder-blue cardigan stretched across a thinner cotton dress and kept her gaze fixed on her shoes. The fingers of her right hand touched at an ugly, clotted stain under her cheekbone. "Miss Voigt?" She nodded without looking up. "I'd like to talk to you about Terry Reilly." It brought her head level. Enough to show bleak-dark eyes and the right side of a spreading lip; livid, blood-filled and stretched taut as if she had one half of a fighter's mouth guard in her teeth. I handed her my card. "Can I come in?"

She bowed her head to read the card over, wound a dark curl around a finger, and stepped aside to let me through. We took a dim, damp hallway growing mold in stripes, then turned aside to a parlor at rear of the store. The sourness of the room stopped me on the threshold. The girl went ahead. A voice beyond her in the gloom said, "What'd he want?" A heavy-set figure sat like a pharaoh in a sagged armchair at an angle to a smoking fire. He had padded features flushed around the edges, a reddish wad of hair and scratched at a two-day beard as if it bothered him. The shirt under his suit jacket was missing its stud collar. His left hand propped a flat bottle of cane rum on the arm of the chair and seemed satisfied with the work. The girl didn't answer, just walked to a window opposite and leaned against it hugging the cardigan. "Irene!" The voice was a thickened squall, and when it got no reply started rasping with the effort of climbing out of the armchair.

The girl waited till the figure sank back sweating on the seat squab, and in a monotone said, "He's here. Why don't you ask him yourself?" Then to me "Want a cup of tea, Mr. Newman?" I said I didn't want to bother her. "No bother. It'll be company." She pushed away from the window and brushed past me out of the room.

The figure in the armchair followed her exit glassily, peered in the doorway where I stood, then puckered and spat on the smoking coals. "War's over, Yank."

The parlor wasn't flush with furniture. It had a gateleg table set against the wall behind the armchair, a mirror in a horseshoe frame strung above it, a dresser beside the window looking out on a yard and two souvenir dishes on the dresser to help raise the tone. "It's never over, Mr. Voigt. It only moves someplace else." Sometimes you aim to keep it civil and still you know you're not winning the other fellow over. "I came to see your daughter on a private inquiry. But I've got a question for you after all."

"What question?"

I walked up beside him, nodded at the door the girl had left by. "In a year she could be almost half your size and weight. Doesn't she begin to worry you?" His eyes hooded and his forehead worked. Somewhere a dull connection made and gave him an itch. Voigt's left arm pulled fast across his stomach, took aim with the bottle in his fist and swung at my kneecap. That anyway was the idea. But we were past noon already, he'd been leaning on cane rum since breakfast and the liquor was dogging his reflexes as well as his mood. I stepped inside the swing, enough to let his wrist crack against my knee and not the rum bottle, grabbed his belt buckle and hoisted him out of the seat. I twisted the bottle from his grip on his way up, shoved him hard off-balance and pushed the heel of my hand under his chin, breathed deep and heaved from the shoulder. His head snapped back and cracked the plaster wall. The horseshoe mirror jumped its hook, hit the gateleg table and splintered over the floor. His mouth slacked. Liquor drizzled between his teeth. His eyelids shuttered and the handful of shirtfront I had tight around his throat was doing nothing but prop him up. I took a step back and let him glide down the wall in a heap, tossed the bottle in the armchair, straightened my tie and went to find the girl.

Tea stewed bitter on a stovetop. Irene Voigt set two cups on a deal table in the center of a spare, cramped kitchen, pulled out a chair and kept the right side of her face turned away. "He give you any trouble, Mr. Newman?"

"Not this time."

"He will do." The voice the same flat monotone, lisping from the swelling along her mouth. "What's Terry done now?"

"Not a thing that I know of. I'd like to talk to him and I heard he called on you yesterday."

The good side of her lip curled. She tugged a square of handkerchief from a sleeve and put it up to her mouth, sniffed and looked miserable. "Terry turned up at the hotel asking for me, in a worse state than usual. He upset a customer and lost me my job. It's why I got hit."

I looked across at her. The way you look at the magician when he names the card you're holding in your hand. The smudge moustache and the sky-high eyes, last seen exiting the Raglan bar at noon yesterday. And two hours before that, climbing the steps outside the Great Eastern Hotel, absolutely promising to be decorous when he made it inside. It had to be. The same Terry Reilly who arrived to see Miss Irene and made the commotion that got him shown the door. "You've got a picture of Terry?"

She thought about that, dragged the table drawer into her lap, sifted among the ration books and coupons for her identity card, then slid it across the table. A snapshot sat loose inside the card, not recent or in focus but plain enough. Reilly, younger and without his trial moustache, the same dark loop of hair across his forehead and the brooding look he never left off. No mistake. We'd met twice already, we just hadn't been introduced. "What did he want at the hotel?"

"What does he ever?"

"You gave him money?"

"I didn't give him anything. He took what was in my purse and said it was a loan till he saw somebody, then I'd get it back. At least he bothered with a story this time." She sniffed again. "He said he'd got a place in the West End. I told him he needed his head testing, and how was he going to pay for it? He never listens." But we both knew how Terry would pay for West End living. I took a photograph from my pocket and set it beside her picture of Reilly. She shot it a glance. "Who's that?"

"Raymond Jarrett. You don't know him?"

"I know he looks out for Terry. I never saw him. Is that what you want Terry for, Mr. Newman? For being on the game? Can't you leave him alone?" She would have made the contempt louder and clearer if she could have, but the words slurred through her teeth. On the side she kept toward me she was just another growing girl, pretty in the way they don't have to try for, with freckles dotting the side of her eye and running down her cheek.

"I'm not police, Miss Voigt. Not even Revenue. How Terry pays his rent doesn't concern me, but I'd like to keep the photograph. I can promise to return it."

She shrugged, as if a promise ever made a difference.

"Keep my card safe, Irene. He hits you again, call me."

The hand holding the handkerchief lowered to her lap. She swung around slowly in the chair. From her right temple to the point of her chin a dark, soft web was closing her eye, ballooning her cheek and fattening the right side of her mouth and jaw. The freckles had no chance at all. She gave some time to unfolding and refolding the handkerchief, then said simply, "I can't ever tell you anything, Mr. Newman. You know that." I left her sitting at the table, closed the kitchen door and went back into the parlor.

Voigt slumped in the armchair looking bruised, nursing the empty rum bottle for warmth and fellowship. I went over to the window and its view on a hencoop backyard, turned around and said, "Jarrett's dead."

He blinked and stared straight ahead at an ancient calendar yellowing on the wall. Apart from the dresser's souvenir dishes it was the only piece of decoration in the room. Voigt cracked his knuckles one to ten, as if they were the sounds his thoughts made when they fell in place. "So?" He sat hard back, put his hands between his knees and squeezed until his heels lifted off the floor.

"So, you would know about Raymond Jarrett, and when he put a new face on the street, you'd hear Irene had made a friend. Which would bother you. You're a family man, Mr. Voigt. Your daughter and Terry Reilly are one thing, but you wouldn't want her near Jarrett on any account." The air in the room so thick it set my head pounding. "Maybe early Christmas morning, with nobody around, you warned him off and it got out of hand. Your warnings are apt to do that. Or is it all my imagination?"

Voigt's forehead creased. I shook him out a cigarette before he started on the knuckles again. He reached one out of the pack, waited for a match and beat his eyelids against the smoke drifting out of his nostrils. "Irene does what she's told. Why would I go looking for Jarrett?"

"Because she's an age that doesn't stay told. And because you knew Jarrett was playing with fire." I took a cigarette myself and kept it between my teeth, to taste something other than the room. "Jarrett wasn't only renting loose-limbed boys to bank clerks. He had a camera and a line in limited editions and a talent for photographing clients in special moments of distress. Not just any clients. He aimed at the happy few with a reputation to lose and a wallet to try to buy it back with. City money that will pay off because it can and because it doesn't see it has a choice. Jarrett did the homework and made the introductions. His protégés took their tricks back to his studio to get the pictures. Blackmail can look that simple. It can also make unlikely people snap, and in these parts a City bigshot getting the squeeze put on pulls a lot of police attention. You wouldn't want Irene anywhere close."

Voigt concentrated on the cigarette, unimpressed. I hardly liked it any better myself. He could hurt a man and enjoy the work. In the wrong mood, he might even leave him for dead. Except with Jarrett he wouldn't see the need for a gun. I let the idea go and snapped my cigarette unlit in the hearth. "Then one freezing winter night Raymond Jarrett died of exposure to a .38 and your problem disappeared. You're a lucky man, Mr. Voigt."

I let myself out of the house without going back in the kitchen. Outside, small boys from the neighborhood had wheeled a barrow from the empty market and hitched it to the gun barrel at the street corner. They were thin-faced, ragged and pinched with cold, having the best time of anyone I'd seen all day.

FOURTEEN

Smithfield was six acres of vaulted ironwork at the north-west edge of the Square Mile, a meat market high and wide as a cathedral, and by day as silent and solemn. By night it was a wholesale market that fed a city; a deafening, unhallowed vaudeville of selling and buying that decked its halls with gutted carcasses, gaffed on rails as if they'd been hooked as they swam by. So many rails you thought all they ever did was bait a line, throw it in the river and reel in a side of beef. How to make the gods smile? Tell them that every night at Smithfield Market they spill entrails enough to divine yours and mine and all men's futures, then sell them by the truckload for dog scraps.

I stood opposite the south side of the market in early afternoon, on a square wide open to the weather. A public garden made a traffic island in the center of the square, with a ramp at one side spiraling from the street to the market's rail sidings underground. Beyond the garden, the half-timber gatehouse to St. Bartholomew's churchyard. And beyond the churchyard, the porch where Jarrett met his executioner barely thirty-six hours before, with no other place he could run. I was back where it all had started, a hard freeze setting in clear, flat sheets across the City, daylight already draining from the sky.

Behind me, a dozen steps down from the street, the Sesto was a basement diner catering to meat market traders. It was thirty feet by thirty, veiled in a cooking haze under a low ceiling, had four walls dark-stained as if it flooded at high tide, and a single crepe streamer twisted around a column in the center of the room to create the festive mood. Two customers ate at a counter. I took a seat in a booth close by the door and dropped my coat on the bench. A wall clock over the two diners clicked past one forty-five.

The Sesto's patrons relied on its clock. There was no other clue to the time of day. No windows except for one glass half of the entrance door, and a menu that was night and day permanent, lettered across the column holding up the rest of the building. The kitchen door jittered. A solid, sullen figure arrived in shirtsleeves rolled under his armpits, took my order and cleared somebody else's dishes off the table. I watched him go, took the carbon of Dr. Swinford's notes out of my pocket and wondered what exactly she thought she was doing.

The doctor had typed out two paragraphs on a single sheet, then left the sheet in Jarrett's file in an unlocked drawer in an office she hadn't locked either. Even on a floor practically empty for the holiday, it was reckless. The whole building was alive with police. To leave her desk wide open then invite me to call by was borderline certifiable. She didn't know me nearly enough to take that risk. I was interested to find out why she had.

Her first paragraph said Dillys Valentine's murder had been a messy affair that would have been messier still if her heart hadn't stopped beating before she had time to bleed to death. It described how she'd already taken a drink from the whisky bottle she was killed with, how her prints were on the remaining half, and how the rest had been sheared off against the nearby iron stair rail before its jagged end was used for the murder weapon. What was left of the glass bottle had other prints, not good but usable, and excepting those belonging to City Police who arrived at the scene they hadn't been identified. The question was for how long? The City crime laboratory hadn't been introduced to Terry Reilly yet, but the whisky had been his Christmas gift to Miss Dillys and there were short odds that one set of prints would be his. What the boys in the lab had identified was the whisky, a rarity calling itself Buccleuch with a hand-stenciled label that said it was twelve years in the making. In short, a very refined example of high-class liquor, which likely was the last thing in the world Dillys Valentine had expected to die of.

The second paragraph dealt with the topcoat Henry Beaufort claimed he found in his boyfriend's closet then tried to hide to protect him. It was a dark, chocolate-colored wool and cashmere number, stylish and expensive, tailored for somebody slim-built and medium height, and from which the doctor had picked up two distinct blood markings. One, from the right side and sleeve, didn't match with either of the murder victims. The second was on the coat's lower left front, where the blood type matched for Jarrett. The forensic boys had found powder nitrates in the same area as the blood marks and had a theory about that. The powder burns, they said, likely indicated where the killer wrapped the skirt of his coat around the .38 before he fired into the back of Jarrett's head, trying to quiet the gunshot in the echo chamber of the church porch. That was all. Nothing in the pockets, only a label sewed in the lining: *Geo. Bryant & Nephew, Gentlemen's Tailor and Shirt Maker, Cheapside.*

In the heat of the basement the carbon sheet started warming in my hand, sweating the doctor's perfume as close as when we danced. Then a plate arrived at the table, heaped with something grayer than the daylight, and her perfume lay down and died. When I pushed the plate aside, the sound caught the attention of a matron in black pulling a lace curtain across the glass in the entrance door. In stub heels she was a little more than five feet tall, a little less than five feet wide, jet hair shot through with silver and braided in a bun. "You don't eat?"

I shrugged. "I don't have the heart. Whatever it was it deserved better."

The woman had brought a faint, sharp scent of her own from the kitchen. My nose lifted out of the doctor's notes, sniffing the air like a hound. "Are you selling that?"

She pressed her bulk against the end of the booth and leaned across to pull the untouched plate toward her. "You want?"

I nodded. "I want."

She walked toward the shuddering swing door with the dish held in front of her like a sacrifice. When she came back, the woman's coffee was a tablespoon of heavy, dark liquor sitting under the lighter distillation of its oils. She stayed to see how I drank it, hands on her hips, and when it was done I reached in my breast pocket for the matchbook from Garfield's study. I set it on the table, turned it around where she could read *Osteria Sesto*, then snapped Michael Garfield's photograph down beside it like a queen of hearts. "Remember him, signora?" I doubted she forgot anybody who walked through her door.

The woman leaned in to peer at the photograph, caught a crucifix swinging from her bosom and rested the hand that caught it on my shoulder. She pressed hard up against the table, mouth pursed, square as a barn. "Of course. This man is a customer." Tight-lipped didn't come easy to the signora. She just needed to be coaxed. I took a card out of my wallet and put it alongside the queen of hearts, said her customer hadn't been seen for two nights and had a friend getting anxious about him. It was enough. She spread her arms in a gesture that took in all Italy. "Before this war he knows Rome. He comes to here to remind the cooking. Last time ago two days. Christmas Eve. He is very excited."

"Excited about what?"

"About he has pictures."

I asked what kind of pictures and her eyes rolled. "He don't show to me! He shows to somebody with him I never saw before. Somebody who *smow-ked c*igars." She went ball-eyed and puffed out her cheeks for the plutocrat look.

I sat back against the bench, picked Garfield's photograph off the table and eyed the menu on the column behind her. "I was in Rome myself once. This isn't how I remember the cooking."

She twisted around stiffly and flapped a hand. "That I don't know to cook. For that you ask to Stanley."

"I already asked to Stanley. He doesn't know to cook either."

The signora tilted her head and gave me her eye of sorrows. She eased down onto the bench and shuffled along it until we were opposite, then sighed and confessed it was so. Stanley had arrived in Rome with a stripe on his sleeve and fitting his uniform like Mitchum, and even though the uniform was the sum of all Stanley's appeal it was a time and place short on options. So her daughter made a wartime alliance of her own, hooked up with Stanley and brought her mamma with her to a god-forsaken city where the skies frowned, the cooking was lousy and the winters made her joints scream. The signora didn't have all the words. She just looked me in the eye and told her story as if her daughter had been cursed in the womb. We sat in silence, weighing the calamity of it, until she stirred and prodded a finger that dimpled her bosom under the black dress. "To you, I give my *Bocconcini di Coniglio*." Then, the closest she could get to a translation. "Raaaa-bit."

In Italian it sounded like the best offer I'd had all year. I hung a cigarette under my lip and broke out a match from her matchbook. "If the rabbit is as good as the coffee, we could be married before nightfall."

She turned her head to me and tucked her chin to consider the proposition. "You never had a wife?"

"I'd have remembered."

"All right then, Mr. Private Investigator. You make good money?"

"More than is good for me."

A bright light sparked in her eye. She leaned in from the hips. "Ha! You lie to me even before our wedding night. But I hate always to wear black, so therefore I accept." She slapped both hands down hard on the table, tossed back her head and whooped a high, raucous peal at the ceiling. Her two diners at the counter didn't bat an eye.

When she came back from the kitchen, her last customers were gone and the door was bolted on the afternoon. The signora took the same seat. We ate her rabbit stew, drank some more of her coffee and some heady grappa with it, and while the basement went on heating we talked of Rome and I loosed my tie. Two hours later it was only getting harder to leave. I put a hand flat over the mouth of the bottle and stood up, before I got an invitation to dinner.

FIFTEEN

Snow on Snow Hill. No streetlamps. Only office windows lit up here and there on the outside curve of the rise. Inside the curve, a line of bombed-out lots softened by snowfall like a room under dust sheets waiting for spring.

My rental was for one half of a two-room office, sublet from a City commercial agency that kept a desk and a secretary of its own in the other half. We shared a thin party wall and a connecting door behind my desk that stayed unlocked. The safe in her office was mine to use, no charge. She was young, a little bookish behind her glasses, quirky when she took them off, and decided early we'd get along fine whenever I fitted her mood. Sometimes, at the end of a dull afternoon, she'd walk in through the connecting door with two cups, lift the office bottle from my file drawer and pull up a seat. There to instruct me, she said, in how to recognize small talk if ever it should occur in my presence. But today was holiday and besides, what I needed were better ideas, not small talk. I dropped the window blind, wheeled my chair back against the party door, rested my head against the glass as if I meant business and sat in the light spilling from the corridor. Nothing doing. When the telephone rang, I picked up at the first ring. A clenched jaw in a Fleet Street news office said, "Newman, old man," innocent of all irony.

"Carleton Hamnett of the Daily Lama. Does anybody still read it?"

It was the only prompt he ever needed. "Not only do they read it, old man, two murders have wonderfully stimulated our circulation. The *Courier*, as always, follows avidly the exploits of your constabulary *confrères*. Their calling compels a fascination among our readers second only to the weather. I'm a very busy fellow." Carl's pipe clattered against his teeth at the other end of the line. It's the sound the coconuts make in a rumba band. He coughed raucously and went on. "*Apropos* the interests of the *Courier*'s readers, old man, a small bird tells me you happened this a.m. upon the murder of one Raymond Jarrett, otherwise unknown to us. I rather hoped you might have something for me. Professional insight and so forth. The lowdown, so to speak. Off the record, naturally."

"Coincidence, Carl. When I happened by the detective inspector had it wrapped up already. It was snowing. It's about all I can tell you."

There was a crestfallen rasp of breathing. Carl jimmied the pipe stem back in his teeth and grunted. "Quite. But I am imploring, old man. Should you have anything, howsoever *outré*, the *Courier* is sorely in need. The simple *frisson* of *Murder in the Square Mile* will not sate our readership for much longer. Content as Superintendent Littomy may be to play his cards close to his chest, our public relies daily upon us for further revelation. Appreciate a hack's dilemma, old man. Yours truly will be forevermore indebted."

I said I wouldn't forget him and rang off, slid out a drawer from the desk and put my feet across it and went back to thinking in the dark. This time about a sick old man who didn't sleep nights and his statement in Jarrett's police file. The way he told it, he waited every dawn at his window, no different Christmas morning than any other. That being so, he could say positively that his neighbor left home at her regular hour that day, the same as any day she had an early shift. It was hard to argue, and no reason to suppose the old man would lie or make a mistake. But thinking is like putting ice on a hangover; when finally you get around to it, you know you should have tried it sooner. When I thought about it, I knew the neighbor's story was wrong.

I took my feet off the drawer and stood up, walked around the desk, sat down again and took the idea further. The candles she lit said Nurse Greer discovered Jarrett's body before four-thirty Christmas morning. Time enough to return to her house on Cloth Court before she reported it. Why she might do that I had no idea. Only that she didn't stay long. Around four forty-five she left again, this time for the phone booth on the square to call in a murder to City Police. It was when she left home a second time that morning that her light-sleeping watcher at the window saw her, and took it she was leaving for her regular early shift. Just the same, the old man thought, as any other morning he ever watched her at that hour. It was what he would tell police as often as they asked. The exact truth as he saw it. He just hadn't seen the rest. I was still gawking at the ceiling, the way you sit waiting for a dentist to walk in the room, when the telephone rang again. I sat up and crimped the receiver under my chin.

"Mr. Newman? This is Estelle Greer. I'm on duty at Bart's. We admitted a patient an hour ago, an adolescent girl who's been assaulted. She won't give her name or address but she's asking for you. It seems you know each other." Then deep silence on the line, like a well waiting for the falling pebble. I said I'd be there in fifteen minutes.

"You didn't recognize me, did you Mr. Newman?"

Irene Voigt's bloated lips slurred the words, eyes vague with dope, nose taped down to her cheekbones. She had a livid, broken bruise running from her bottom lip along the side of her jaw, her left arm resting on the bedsheet in a web of strapping. She wanted to set me at ease, but couldn't work out how to get the right expression on her face.

"How did it happen, Irene?"

Saliva drooled across her cheek and wetted the pillow. She pushed a finger at the corner of her mouth, too late to stanch it, and winced in dull embarrassment. I took out a handkerchief and folded it in the hand she could move. "He wanted to know where Terry was. I wouldn't tell him." The voice a flat shadow. She had the handkerchief gripped tight in a ball. "He hit me really hard this time, Mr. Newman. If he finds Terry, he'll hurt him worse. He hurts everybody."

I touched the corner of the bedsheet against her cheek. "The only way he can hurt him is if he finds him. Tell me how to find him first."

She wanted to talk but the words gummed in her mouth. "He said he'd be staying in the West End, I told you that. When I asked him where, all he said was Paddy's. Don't know who that is. Don't know any of his friends. I should have told you, shouldn't I?" Her eyes drifted across a thing she couldn't fathom, past needing an answer. A voice behind me said the patient ought to get some rest.

Nurse Greer led down a flight of stairs to a common room with armchairs pulled around a table with magazines. She put on a light, lifted a handbag off of one of the armchairs and found a pack of cigarettes before she said, "It's not as bad as it looks: a broken collarbone, two possible rib fractures, her nose is a mess. The rest is largely bruising and shock. She didn't run into a bus either, did she?"

"Miss Voigt ran into her father. How did she get here?"

"She walked into casualty not long after I came on duty. You seem concerned about her."

"I met Irene Voigt for the first time today. Her father didn't care for me asking her questions. It's why he put her in the hospital."

Her thumb coaxed a flame from a small, nickel lighter. She took the bag to a locker against the wall and eyed her seams in a mirror inside the locker door. "Miss Hartridge didn't care much for your questions this morning either.

Apparently, she's been a bear with a sore head all day. *A verr-ry unpleasant man arrived with the devil's gray eyes and a dimple you could sink a putt in.* You made quite an impression."

You had to hand it to Nurse Greer; the gooseberry mouth, the accent precise and mordant. It was a first-rate hatchet job. She wet a fingertip on her tongue and ran spit along her eyebrows. I went over to the table and dropped a photograph on one of the magazine covers. "This is Irene Voigt's boyfriend. When her father gets to him, he'll make Irene look like choir practice. If either one visits while she's here I need to know."

She left the mirror, stepped across to the table, folded at the knees to pull an ashtray from under the litter of magazines and took in the photograph. Her head tilted to let her lips spin a smoke ring at the ceiling. Not bad at that. "Well, he wears a moustache now, but it hardly makes him Clarke Gable does it? You didn't show me this one before."

I blinked. "You *know* Terry Reilly?"

"No. But yesterday you showed me a photograph of a young man in the Raglan on Christmas Eve, asking after his friend who'd already left. This is the boy his friend left with. I'd never seen him before and didn't know his name. If you'd shown me his picture, I could have told you yesterday." She lifted a loose strand of hair and fixed it at the back of her head inside the cap. "I don't know the names of the other two either. You didn't say. Remember?"

She was right, I didn't say. The faces on a dozen magazine covers looked at each other and raised an eyebrow. They had a point. I'd been running across Reilly's trail for the last thirty-six hours. In that time, I'd advised him on hotel decorum and helped him off a bar stool, talked to people who either knew him or knew of him or remembered seeing him, and caught up with his recent history along the way. All afternoon I'd had his photograph in my pocket. Not only that, I knew Garfield made a chance pickup in the Raglan on Christmas Eve. And still it didn't dawn that the professor was Terry

Reilly's trick that night. Call me Hard-to-Hurry Newman and don't rush me with the obvious, because when it comes to a hot lead, I aim to keep a distance before we're formally introduced. I put his photograph next to Reilly's and took a long breath. "Can we get this straight, Miss Greer? This is Michael Garfield. Two nights ago, he walked out of the Raglan with Terry Reilly. Later that evening, his boyfriend arrived asking for him. The boyfriend's name is Beaufort. And though the names mean nothing and you never saw Reilly before, you're still positive Garfield was his trick that night. Did I leave anything out?"

"I don't think so. Aren't detectives wonderful?" Nurse Greer stubbed her cigarette and said she really ought to go. I picked the photographs off the magazine, then followed out the door.

Miss Hartridge's desk was two flights down, vacated for the day and left at attention. Her pencils were squared, blotter straightened, her in-tray and out-tray clear and the telephone switched to an operator overnight. I reached it across the desk and gave the switchboard the Kensington number on Kathryn Swinford's card, fooled with the pencils until a porter answered, then held while he made the connection. When he put me through, her voice was choking on a level fury.

"Newman!"

"Doctor, I'm sorry. You're rehanging the Gainsboroughs in your bathroom and it's not a good time. I'll call back."

"Stop that right now, Detective," she practically screamed. "And while you're at it, call the fire brigade because Littomy is ready to set light to your career. Some local ruffian presented himself at Bishopsgate this afternoon complaining you assaulted him."

Some local ruffian. I rubbed the corners of my eyes and said, "You're crazy."

"I was there."

"It's not what I meant. I meant you're crazy if you think what I do amounts to a career. What happened?"

"I had a call this afternoon from Littomy to examine someone claiming you intervened, unasked, in a domestic dispute. Littomy wanted to know if the man was genuinely hurt."

"Voigt."

"Yes, Voigt. Who maintains you set about him and then interviewed his daughter, a minor, without his permission. He'll live. Not that the superintendent is likely to lose sleep over an unprovoked assault. His own detectives appear to specialize in it, but you had no witness present to deny it happened, which breaks his first rule of policing. He's hopping mad. Though why I bother to tell you all this I can't imagine."

I closed my eyes, saw Irene Voigt drooling on her pillow, mortified she couldn't find a way to close her broken mouth. The doctor wasn't looking for explanation. I should have let it go, but it was late in the day to start trading politenesses. "Yes, you can. You're telling me because you want to satisfy your standards of fairness. You think there could be more to Voigt's story than he says and in your book that means I get a right of reply. It's gracious of you and you're right, there is more. But tell me something. When you decide my standards aren't up to scratch, what do you do next? Strike me off your dance card?" I flopped on Miss Hartridge's chair, and before she could hang up, said, "Forget I said that. But understand this. Voigt is likelier to join a temperance union than walk in a police station with a complaint. Unless he was told. After you examined him, he went back home to pick up his domestic dispute where he left off and put his daughter in a hospital bed. This time it was her ribs and her collarbone and her nose. She'll pull through. What bothers her more is what happens to her looks next time she gets his full attention, then the time after that. Tell me about standards, Doctor. Lately they interest me."

For a long moment I heard nothing but the creak of radiators and the ticking of my watch. Then a pale voice, speaking close into the mouthpiece. "The man's a louse. For my money, you could have tossed him out of the window."

"We were on the ground floor."

A voice fainter still, hardly more than a whisper along the wire. "What kind of an excuse is that?" Then the line went dead.

I climbed two floors back to the common room, where a single light burned. Nurse Greer's cigarette still hung on the air. Her handbag was still in the locker where she left it. The bag had a flip-clasp and a zipper compartment inside with her purse and identity card, a worn leather key case and a sleek blue pocketbook for 1948, so new it creaked when I opened it. I lifted out the key case, closed the zipper, flipped the clasp and slid the bag back in the locker. Outside, the corridor was brighter than a sunlit sidewalk.

SIXTEEN

My cab crawled down Ludgate Hill and crossed into Fleet Street, the driver muffled like a Greenlander with a chill. Yesterday, Reilly had announced he planned to stay in the West End, gave Irene Voigt a name that meant nothing to her and no address. Today, I couldn't get out of my head a fresh-faced priest celebrating the virgin birth as if it might go out of style. Two hundred feet short of Charing Cross the cab pulled across the Strand, made a U-turn and halted in front of Fruchtna & Patrick's temperance lodging. A customer in a velvet-collar coat exited the building with a spring in his step, sniffed a gardenia in his buttonhole and climbed in the empty cab while I paid the driver. Last night's *No Vacancies* sign had been switched out on the board next to the entrance. Paddy's had a room to let.

There was a hall leading off the street entrance that made a side-step to the back of the building. It had a counter set across the angle and a sliding hatch in the wall behind it, all of it painted mud brown below a waist-high rail that ran along the hall. Above the rail was painted butter cream, for the full Pullman car effect. I'd reached the counter when a slim yellow-blond with slept-in eyes came sashaying along the passage toward me, twirling a key on a ring around his finger like Billy the Kid. Something about him was familiar. Twenty feet away he noticed he had company and slackened pace. Ten feet away he put his tongue in his cheek and asked, "Something I can do for you?"

I grinned at him. "Not unless you're Father Dolan."

Billy sighed and dropped the key on a ledge behind the counter. "It's Christmas, dimples. He'll be on his knees. Why don't you ring his bell?"

He kept on walking, gave no sign we'd met before, took the button mouth and the lidded eyes and the yellow hair licked off his forehead and closed the street door behind him. The hip-swung walk, the soft, high accents, the dress sense that helped a little go a long, long way; it was hard to put a finger on. I leaned over the counter for the register and opened it at the latest arrivals. The hatch in the wall slid aside. A throat cleared and a voice scarcely audible said, "Our register is maintained strictly for perusal by the proper authorities. Please be good enough to return it whence you took it. Do you wish for a room?"

I didn't look up. The hatch shuddered to and a door dragged open farther along the passage. From his pallor, the young priest was still taking his Christmas Day of prayer and feasting square on the chin. He lifted the countertop and installed himself behind it in short, straight lines, raised an elbow likewise and rested it across the register. Cold sober he looked as brittle as a relic, his complexion an unvaried shade of wet gravel. I glanced down the names on the open pages. "Father, we both know this is a work of fiction. And you can take it I'm acquainted with the proper authorities."

The broad, unlined forehead thought that through. "Police? Forgive me if I appear a little under the weather. At this season of the year one indulges the flesh to excess. You're not the officer we ordinarily have our dealings with." His brow knitted. "Have we met before?"

"Not so you'd notice. I worship in a different parish." I put down a photograph on the countertop. "Terry Reilly. He didn't register in that name, I checked. But he's been staying here. Have you eaten today, Father? You look as if you're about to die."

The priest went fish-eyed at the thought of nourishment. "Food is quite out of the question. Thank you." He wiped the back of his hand across his lips, blinked behind his glasses at the photograph. "I really cannot recall the young man. An occasional resident perhaps? What did you say the name was?"

"Reilly. And so we understand each other, Father, he's not a student of anything but older men, and Paddy's has to do with temperance what a bishop has to do with a bathhouse. I can have it closed down and the officer you're dealing with busted faster than the bursar can reach for an altar boy. Take another look."

He fumbled his glasses off his nose and stooped over the photograph. "Well now, perhaps. You may have noticed our board exhibits a vacancy. This young man was away with the lark this morning and a night's room rent owing. I fear the bursar you mentioned will be displeased." I looked around the peeling cream of the walls. The priest straightened up and put his spectacles back on, followed my gaze. "Such unappealing colors are they not? At least when applied to a railway carriage one has hopes the train might leave the station. I have many times called the attention of Mr. Drake's office to the spiritual abyss of our painted decorations."

Deep in the building a door opened and shut. A faint breeze stirred along the passage and shook a flake of peeling paint off the ceiling. I put out a hand upturned, as if we were expecting rain. "Wait a minute, Father. *Councilor* Drake owns Paddy's?"

"The same, I believe. Yes."

The paint flake drifted weightless, see-sawed, slipped and spiraled, then settled rocking in the palm of my hand. And as my fist closed around it, I knew where I'd seen the button mouth before: in a photograph in a bedroom in a house on

Cloth Court, also belonging to the councilor. Billy the Kid had been a full-length study in Jarrett's picture gallery. A pinup on a closet door. The priest gaped unsteadily at my outstretched hand, green-black circles around his eye sockets, skin white as chalk. "Father, inside twenty minutes you'll need food or extreme unction. Better eat." I flattened out my palm and blew the paint flake over the countertop.

SEVENTEEN

The nurse's key let me out of a wind that was freezing tears to my eyeballs, and on to the rug in her red-tile hall. Somewhere down the hallway a coal fire shifted and spat. I listened until it settled, eased shut the door and got a penlight from my pocket. At right, a door opened on a sitting room that ran front to back of the house. At left, the hall led to a kitchen where the coal fire smoked behind a screen, and from the kitchen to a walk-through pantry that had jars and cans hoarded on shelves either side and leftovers put away in a food safe. Beyond the pantry, another door let on a small backyard and an alley running behind the court. Not lavish as city living goes, but par for what a nurse's pay afforded in a peacetime fit for heroes. I flashed the light around it all and went back along the hall to the stair.

The house's top half had stayed boarded off since the blitz firebombing. The stair ended at two bedrooms set back-to-back on the second floor. The smaller bedroom had a washstand in a corner, a bedframe under a window looking over the court, and a closet with some very classy apparel in it for a hospital nurse. On the bedframe, a khaki service Gladstone bag with two initials on its straps sat open and empty. Alongside it, a metal trunk was layered with clothes not for wearing. In one side of the trunk Nurse Greer had put away her wartime Utility fashions. In the other half she was storing what belonged to the officer with his initials on the Gladstone bag: an airman's rank braid, his shirts and collars, a field service cap with an odd, steel-hard bump inside it and a necktie with a squadron badge. I started with the bump in the field cap.

Keeping a serviceable Webley revolver and a twelve-box of cartridges in an unlocked trunk wasn't the best idea Nurse Greer ever had. But I didn't see it as a problem either. For one thing, the airman's sidearm, assuming it was his, was clean and unloaded. For another, the Webley was the wrong caliber for Jarrett's murder, a .45 not a .38, and all twelve cartridges were still in the box. I lifted the revolver out with a pocket handkerchief, broke it open and sniffed at it, then put it back where the nurse liked to park her artillery and moved on.

Her own bedroom faced the backyard and alley. It had an armchair and a tallboy against one wall, with a hairbrush set and a mirror on it and nothing in its four drawers to linger over. On a slim rattan side table beside the bed, there was an alarm clock on a lace runner and a marquetry box for trinkets behind the clock. I squeezed between the window and the bed and hinged back the lid of the box. It had dry stalks of lavender scattered loose inside, the nurse's passport, letters bundled and tied in ribbon. And beneath the letters a snapshot of Nurse Greer, leaning against the iron rail of some foreign promenade with the beach behind her, arm in arm with a boy in rolled sleeves and tennis whites, a sweater around his shoulders, sunburn on his nose and sky-high summer in his smile. Nurse Greer had her free hand holding down a sprig cotton dress billowing on the breeze, and a mixed look of alarm and pure happiness dancing in her eyes. There was more. Under the photograph, in a cheap lacquer frame, she kept a squadron badge of an outspread eagle over a shield, embroidered with the squadron's name and number; and with the badge, a set of thin, official forms folded in the order they'd arrived in. I didn't need to look. I'd seen plenty of the kind before. And looked anyway.

The forms moved through the grinding service protocol that lists a man missing in action, then presumes him dead, and when the time arrives to confirm it, sends out a form for that as well. There was a form to finalize the airman's pay, another from the Revenue doing the same for his taxes, a condolence from his King and Queen, then a list from a wing commander at Central Depository stating the belongings they had in store for the late Flight Lieutenant Charles Irving John Ross. It said the flight lieutenant's effects were there to be collected or forwarded at the addressee's expense. Alternatively, for unwanted uniform items there was a charity, care of Mrs. Jeanne Mayhew of Hatton Garden, London, that assisted fellow officers in cases of hardship. They're thorough at Central Depository. I was thinking they might even tell me what I was looking for when a key grated in the front door.

I twisted off the penlight beam and pushed the forms back in the box, closed the lid and froze while a switch dipped in the hallway and threw a strip of light across the bedroom floor. The front door slammed shut. Feet stamped the hall rug. There was an intake of shuddering breath that couldn't be the nurse because I'd got her house keys in my pocket and she had hours on duty still to go. Quick, light steps went along the hall. A second light snapped and lit cracks in the floorboards under my shoes. The coals in the kitchen range raked over, a woman coughed and dragged out a chair, clicked another switch and Sinatra drifted in from the background static with *Have Yourself A Merry Little Christmas*.

I used a cuff to wipe sweat under my chin, measured the distance to the bedroom door, took three breaths and went through it fast and flattened in the shadows along the staircase wall. The hall light spilled across my shoelaces. No kitchen sounds except the radio. I took a step to the head of the stairs and counted them down, stayed hard against the wall, tried my weight on the inside of a tread, then eased down to the next and then the next. I was four steps short when the woman sniffed and coughed again, snapped shut her handbag, scraped back the chair and started closing up the kitchen range. I stopped breathing and sweated instead, thought about the parlor and didn't remember its layout well enough, then dropped the four steps and glided along the lighted hallway on fresh air. One stretch more took me past the part-open kitchen door and I was pressed flat in the space behind it when the radio shut off. Heels crossed the floor. Sinatra gasped and slid under the surf of cooling valves. Another click and the kitchen went dark. The nurse's visitor pushed the door wide, smack up against my nose, went through it close enough to hear the scratch of her silk stockings and turned out the hall light at the foot of the stairs. Then the street door swung shut and she was gone. I gave her fifteen seconds to let my heartbeat slow, soft-shoed to the front parlor window and peeked out over Cloth Court. Snowflakes stirred in the lamplight. Not a thing else. I let the curtain fall and followed the beam from my penlight back down the hall.

Nurse Greer kept a wood-and-wire letter rack at the back of her kitchen table, some seaside souvenir filled with store receipts and bills for paying, ration cards and reminders. Her visitor had torn a flap off an envelope, penciled a message on it and left it propped against the rack. *The Viaduct Tomorrow. 7.30.* Initialed with a *V.* The time underlined twice. There was a faint perfume I didn't recognize. Nothing else in the room was changed that I could tell. As for the note, it might mean something or nothing at all, but either way it would wait. For now, I had Nurse Greer's house key to put back in her locker and a call to pay on my client that was overdue.

EIGHTEEN

Bartholomew Close ran a curve south and east of the church, unscarred on the church side except for a corner site bombed flat where it joined Bartholomew Square. The other side of the street had been practically wiped out, the few houses left standing twice lucky because they were the ones with the view. Councilor Drake owned a black-brick, five-story town house facing the desolation. It had four tall windows on each floor, a half-basement with a bridge across from the sidewalk, a wide front door at the end of the bridge and a brass bell-push set in the wall. One lean on the button brought a young housemaid, who took my card and my coat and left me in the entrance hall. When she returned, she led along a passage where she tapped at a door, stood aside for me to walk in and without crossing the threshold announced, "Mrs. Willard. Mr. Newman."

The room had sofas arranged around a hearth, and on the walls portraits so dark all I could make out were hands and faces. A floor lamp inside the door was lighting its own shade and not a lot else besides. "You're not how I imagined a private investigator." The voice was flat and thickened and came from the farthest sofa. A woman in a dark silk wrap stretched along the length of it, toes peeking out of rhinestone slippers flashing in the firelight. I hadn't heard the voice before. The face and figure I'd been introduced to at the Waldorf, climbing out of an Armstrong limousine at the Beaufort Christmas Ball.

"You're not how I imagined Councilor Drake."

She took a noisy gulp from a tumbler, wagged a forefinger, then set the empty glass on the carpet. "My father isn't here."

I nodded back at the closed door. "Your maid forgot to mention it."

"She said you were tall, dark and American. And I prefer drinking in company." She waved vaguely at the far end of the room. "Over there."

I crossed to a trolley and upturned a glass, tipped out a slug from a cocktail shaker and brought it over to put in her outstretched hand. A wide silk sleeve slid back along a slim wrist. "The detective isn't drinking."

"I'm here on business, Mrs. Willard."

She shrugged and lifted the glass. "Then here's to business." She draped a bottom lip around the rim, knitted her eyebrows, downed the cocktail and handed me the glass. I went through the trolley routine again. This time when I came back, she was tucking the hem of the wrap around her ankles, pointing me to sit down on the sofa. I guessed she might be thirty, also guessed she'd been drinking all day and that today was much like any other. She had big, dark eyes and darker eyebrows, features getting a little waxed, high cheeks, a small bump of a chin and a mouth wiped with deep red to draw attention from her clouded look. Taken together with her tangle of dark hair and the way she had of rumpling it with her free hand, it gave her an air of floating over the rooftops.

"What's wrong with drinking in Mr. Willard's company?"

I knew the name. There wouldn't be two of them. The figure in the white tuxedo getting soft around the jaw, relaxed as a shirtfront and dressed to make George Raft look down-at-heel.

She put a shushing finger to her lips, a little off-center. "We don't speak of Mr. Willard here. Nor of Drake, Willard and Company. And since the Drakes wish to continue being accepted in polite society, we never *ever* refer to my husband's other business interests. Embarrassment most certainly, acrimony very possibly, are apt to ensue."

"So, you argue. What about?"

"Oh, everything imaginable. Business. Money. Me." She was lonely, flirting-drunk. Sometimes it can be too easy. "I don't *live* with my husband, Mr. Newman. Joseph is not a nice man. After three miserably long years I upped and returned to daddy. Why did the lady stay so long you ask?"

But I hadn't asked. I was thinking about her laughter of the night before, gay with her one-armed man in the shadows of an empty ballroom. "Last night at the Waldorf you were Christmas decoration. Is that it?"

The hem of her wrap lost her interest. She nodded absently and reached for the glass. I handed it over, let her put both feet in my lap and settle back against the arm of the sofa. "Duty called. When Mr. Willard wishes to keep up appearances, Mrs. Willard is available for balls, dinners, garden parties and the like. But"—she took a lift from the drink and wagged the finger again—"things that got worse, can get better. We therefore propose a toast. *To the Past Obliterative.*" The word tripped her. She drained the glass and lurched off the sofa, the wrap pulled tight across her stomach. "God but you pour a bloody awful cocktail. Don't you know you're supposed to shake?" At the trolley she made elaborate play of fixing her own, dropped in ice, shook it clumsily, filled her glass and downed it where she stood, then poured a reserve. She brought it back and sat alongside me, arranged the wrap and nuzzled her chin on my shoulder.

"So why marry him?"

She was silent so long I thought she'd passed out. Then she stirred, snuggled tighter and said dreamily, "Because when the Drakes were being bankrupted by those beastly German bombers, a prince arrived to bail them out, and when the shoe fits you absolutely have to marry the prince. The girl he left behind is in my debt forever." She flapped a hand at her mouth and yawned. "I suppose you think I didn't know what I was doing."

"What difference what I think?"

"Quite. Anyway, the man I should have married went to war and didn't come back. You ask a lot of questions, don't you?"

"It's been said."

She tried angling the cocktail glass to her mouth and fumbled it. Slopped the contents down the front of my jacket, filled my shirt pocket and tipped most of the rest down my tie. What little she had left she emptied over my shoes. Her eyes said it was hopeless. She raised herself on an elbow, registered I was wet through and pawed my shirt. "Your suit—"

"Forget the suit, Mrs. Willard. You wouldn't let it in the house in daylight." I lifted the empty glass from her hand and set it down on the carpet alongside the first, eased her upright and put a cushion on the sofa arm. Straightened out, with the cushion for a pillow, she was more or less how I found her when I walked in the room. By the time I got to the door, she was snoring lightly and rhythmically in the cuff of her sleeve.

The housemaid met me with my coat and hat in the hallway, saw the damage and didn't ask. Just led me to a large back kitchen and started dabbing with a cloth as if it was part of her routine. She did what she could, but Mrs. Willard didn't waste her drinking on small glasses and was generous with what she spilled. I got back to Fleet Street reeking like a bonded store, emptied my pockets, took off my tie and jacket and dropped them on the bathroom floor. Then went to the bureau to get a bottle of my own and stand with it at the darkened window. I liked the night view from there, and in the cab home I'd formed a plan—not sophisticated, but satisfying as far as it went—to plow liquor until the forge hammer eased up hitting the anvil in my head. The plan was on schedule when a car heading east braked hard, the traffic behind honked in chorus and skated to a stop. I leaned my forehead against the sash frame and watched brake lights pop red like skyrockets in the window glass. A Humber sedan had pulled out from a line of parked news trucks and slewed across the center line streaming exhaust, was halfway to Ludgate Circus before it found traction, out of sight before the vehicle horns died. Whoever was behind the wheel was good and didn't care who knew it. Even cops want you to know they sometimes go home and sleep. You just have to remember they don't all sleep at the same time.

A NIGHT FOR GODDESSES

By ten o'clock next morning I was clear-eyed and close-shaved, bathed and breakfasted, my bank credit was waxing on rumor of the councilor's check in my pocket and the cigarette rolling in my fingers smelled of new-mown hayfields in the dew. A stray ribbon of sunlight cut across Littomy's desk. Rime frost sparkled outside his window. I stared into a sky the blue of myth, leaned back in the customer chair as if I owned the lease and ran a thumb around the inside of my shirt collar. The room was hot enough to ripen grapefruit.

Littomy stood gaunt and tall at a line of metal cabinets, raking through files in an open drawer. He lifted one out and walked around the desk, folded in his seat and in the level, disappointed tones of an accountant said, "Voigt." He helped himself to a cigarette from a box on the desk. I leaned over with a lighted match and a pained look. "I can explain."

His hand raised for silence. "There is no need. Voigt is not the reason you were summoned here." Littomy swiveled in his seat, hooked one knee across the other. The toecap of his shoe had the mirror shine of a Steinway. "The man is a disgrace. Our temporary medical examiner informs me of his violence to his own daughter. Also, that the man sustained no serious injury. Voigt has been warned that his attempted complaint was sheer effrontery. For what purpose did you approach the girl?"

"She made friends with a boy named Terry Reilly, two kids each as lost as the other. Jarrett was running the boy on the street, and on the night of his murder the boy went missing. I thought she might tell me something I didn't already know."

"And did she?"

"Not a thing. She'd heard Jarrett's name, nothing else. Voigt, on the other hand, had heard plenty about Jarrett and Reilly both, and didn't like the sound of either. Putting his daughter in the hospital was his way of telling her to keep different company."

Littomy leaned his head back and quartered the ceiling as if he read runes on it. "Indeed. The late Raymond Jarrett. Whose penchant for photography would explain your client's interest in our investigation, would it not?"

I shrugged that it might, but his eyes were floating far over my head. "My client has an eye to high office in the City. This whole affair is an embarrassment. Not knowing enough about who tenants his properties reflects badly on him. The councilor wants no more surprises."

Littomy let out a long breath through his nose. "I daresay. But should Detective Inspector McAlester find that your inquiries trespass upon his murder investigation, he will require you to desist. I could scarcely demur. You have already given him good reason."

As if either of us supposed McAlester needed a reason. "McAlester doesn't know I exist, cares even less, and he can't expect me to take a vacation while he makes up his mind. The day he wants me he'll find me. And nobody called it trespass when I brought in Garfield's coat."

It got his gaze back down off the ceiling. We sat looking at each other along the side of his nose until Littomy said carefully, "Evidence suggests only that the coat was worn by Jarrett's murderer. We do not know it belongs to the professor, much less that he concealed it in his own home, and nothing yet connects Garfield's absence in this holiday season with the ghastly shooting in his car. No doubt when we locate him, he will explain." His attention wandered to the cigarette clamped in his knuckle. "Moreover, it appears young Beaufort has absented himself, let us hope simply out of sheer embarrassment. His actions thus far have been appallingly foolish. McAlester will doubtless return him to the fold 'ere long, but to go to ground when his father has the Commissioner's ear is, to say the least, ill-advised."

Absented himself. I leaned forward in the chair and wondered if I'd heard. Because if I had, Henry Beaufort had promoted himself single-handed to first-grade police suspect. Suspected of what wouldn't matter much, and to McAlester not at all, because Henry had given him license to toss away the rulebook. As bad ideas went, it was up there with trying to lose a blood-stained coat in broad daylight in the middle of the City. A telephone started ringing in the outer office. I heard myself swallow and say, "The topcoat had a label inside." Not for any reason. Only to keep Littomy talking while I wondered how many stunts Henry could pull and still stay out of the tank.

He sniffed and swung his knees back under the desk, pulled his file closer and riffled through it till he found the sheet he wanted. The room went on cooking while he reminded himself. "Indeed. Of a bespoke tailor put out of business by the blitz. The address has been a bombsite since early '41. Our inquiries continue. However, were the overcoat to belong to Professor Garfield, it would be the only item in his wardrobe bearing such a label."

"What about the nurse's story?"

Littomy's eyes lifted off the typesheet. He closed the file in front of him like a sermon, balled his fists either side of it and settled back far enough to get his chin down level with mine. This time he didn't need any aid to recollection. "I have a memorandum here." A pause to flatten a hand over the file, then the ghost of a private smile, of the kind that frightens small children at bedtime. "From Our Lady of the

Immaculate Complexion, in which our deputizing medical examiner notes that Nurse Greer may have lit her votive candles some minutes earlier on Christmas morning than she recalls in her statement. It appears these few unaccounted moments in her story suggest to Dr. Swinford something altogether more sinister." Littomy winced and reached for his ashtray. "For pity's sake, what is the woman thinking? A young nurse falls across an horrific murder, a neighbor shot in the back of the head, his brains spread around the walls. Trained nurse Miss Greer may be, but in the circumstances can the good doctor not permit her a little vagueness about her timekeeping?"

There was a polite tap at his office door. A desk sergeant with apple cheeks stepped half-inside and propped the door open with his stomach. Littomy paid him no attention. I had it all. "We are dealing, Newman, with a gutter dispute turned murderous. Not one iota of evidence suggests otherwise. The nurse is a distraction and young Beaufort will surely prove the same. We must allow Dr. Swinford her inexperience, though some plain horse sense and Templeton's steadying hand would be greatly to our advantage."

The sergeant coughed and interrupted. "A call from Wapping, sir. A body reported on the river."

Littomy squinted at the sergeant through a drift of smoke, stubbed his cigarette and dredged back the private smile. It was no hour to be a messenger. "And our River Police mean us to do precisely what with this information, Sergeant? For crying out loud, man, there are queues forming to jump off bridges at this time of year. They find it a more congenial alternative to Christmas with their families. Frankly, one can understand it as a point of view."

The sergeant's gaze fixed on the wall over Littomy's head. "Inspector McAlester requested to be kept informed, sir. In connection with the missing professor. The launch will put out shortly on account of the tide running. If the detective inspector wishes to be aboard, they say he ought to go right away."

All three of us looked at the wall clock. Littomy lost the acid bonhomie and said as if it hurt his teeth, "Then what delays you, Sergeant? Make a general call, get me Bishopsgate on the telephone and inform Wapping we endeavor to locate our detective inspector." The sergeant backed into the outer office and let the door swing shut. I left Littomy to his sour mood and his telephone call and followed the sergeant out, reflecting on the short odds that McAlester was about to miss the boat. In two minutes I was at the top of Snow Hill on Holborn Viaduct, waving down a cab heading east.

The cab turned down a rattling cobbled alley parallel to the river and let me out at a warehouse fronting on a wharf. Fifty yards along the wharf, a gangway dropped to a pontoon pier chafing between steel piles. Two sleek, green-hulled police launches were berthed alongside the pier, ex-wartime air-sea rescue boats gargling their exhausts as they dipped in the swell. At the jetty, a muffled figure hunched over the head line of the nearest launch, its stern already slipped. I looked at my watch, then across the water at the Bermondsey shore.

Dock cranes tilted against a sky of tinseling blue. A slack tide the uncut color of sapphires was starting to turn. The launch's diesels sputtered and snarled and gulls rose off the mud to soar on a festering breeze. With or without McAlester aboard, in thirty seconds River Police would be gone. I set my hat square and turned down my coat collar, cinched my belt Bulldog Drummond style and hit a purposeful stride that took me out of the alley and brought me in view. Twenty yards out I glanced up long enough to see the muffled figure slip his line, step off the jetty onto the deck of the launch and stoop inside the cabin out of a slicing wind, too deafened by the engine roar to hear me yelling, too bone-cold to look back. Ten yards out, I clamped a hand over my hat and took off for the gangway. I was on the pontoon, still waving and yelling, when the launch cut its motors, stopped dead and drifted back in on the tide, close enough to grab its rail and step aboard while it pitched like a carousel. Somebody inside opened the throttle on the diesels again. The launch shuddered like a shunted train and moved out into the stream. I tipped back my hat and loosed the belt on my coat, jammed my shoulders against the forward cabin and let the beat of the engines hammer the breath out of my bones.

We headed downriver against an incoming tide, made a wide, rolling arc to the south shore, then straightened out along Bermondsey's wharves. The engine note hardened and steadied. The launch pushed flat past a line of freighters riding high at a dock. Then, off Cherry Garden Pier, with the channel widening eastward and open water to stretch out in, they let go the reins. The deck blurred under my feet. Twin screws bit deep. The hull lifted on a creaming pad of bow wave and a trail of fractured blue glass unwound astern for a quarter mile. I grabbed the deck rail, followed it along to the wheelhouse, folded open the door and went in sideways.

There were four River Police standing inside, bulked out in foul-weather gear, peering past a spray-pitted windshield that shook to the pounding of the motors. Air so thick with pipe smoke you could cut it in strips. They held the launch sixty feet off the river margin, worked fast along a string of barges, heading to where the river veered south beyond Rotherhithe. I was braced against a bulkhead when the nearest of the four noticed there was company. He cupped hands an inch from my ear and bellowed over the generator-pitch of the diesels. "McAlester?"

I shook my head. "Couldn't make it."

His boat was eating the distance downriver and didn't allow for conversation. He nodded and turned his gaze back to the wharves and warehouses passing fast along the north shore—New Crane, Saint Hilda, Prospect Wharf—painted on soot-gray sides of warehouses in high white letters. On that morning, under that sky, through a bow spray dancing rainbows off the water, they would never look better. But they weren't where he was headed. Across the fret of flood tide, a half-mile ahead a lighter was swinging at a buoy four hundred feet off a derelict quay. The launch careened to pass around a tugboat, leveled out and made a shallow diagonal for the buoy.

Free Trade Wharf was a blitzed stretch of north shore at the top of Limehouse Reach, where the river broadened in a wide double-loop around West India Dock and the Isle of Dogs. Standing off the wharf was a hundred-yard long disused quay built out into the river on a lattice of heavy lumber. The quay was connected to the wharf by a high walkway over a mud beach, disappearing by the minute under the tide. The launch lost headway to come shore-side of the lighter, stiffened against the breeze and wheeled hard over. It aimed its bow at a concrete slipway at the upstream edge of the mud beach, and when it did that two of the River Police ducked out of the wheelhouse and went aft with a canvas stretcher. I followed and joined them in a ragged chorus line, eyeing the dip and rise while the boat corkscrewed in on the swell. Then on a downswing, as if we'd been rehearsing all week, we stepped over the boat's rail and down onto the slipway and the launch started backing out hard.

From the beach, the quay was a giant's forest of wood supports planted in the river, its decking sixty feet above low water, out of sight. Between the forest and the wharf, the wind sawed through a somber canyon bridged by the walkway, blocked out of the low sun even at midday and slapped by an inbound tide. A sewer outfall spilled from high in the river wall, and in the gravel washout at the foot of the fall a body lay face down in the shadows. When the launch moved up to the slip the body had been twenty feet from the waterline. It was less than half that now. In a race across the beach, it looked evens whether to put your money on the stretcher party or on the tide.

The dead man was meshed in a cat's cradle of steel hawser anchored in the river bed, like a soldier caught in the wire, so swollen that the topcoat he wore might have been bought for somebody else. Forty-eight hours in the water, maybe more, had bloated his features almost past recognizing. The dragging tides had left his limbs dislocated and awry. One of the police squatted down to prize open a loop of hawser making a noose around the corpse's neck, did the same to release an arm and heaved the body over to look at what he had. An eel twisted out of a raw-edged gash in the corpse's chest and fell snapping in the gravel. Four inches below the gash a second hollow pit had a rib threaded through it. The officer scuffed the eel farther off with his hand and said flatly, "We'll lose him if we don't move him." And to me, "He's the one you want?"

They had the stretcher unrolled in the water alongside. Together they tried easing the body from the tangle of cable, saw there wasn't time and dragged it out of its topcoat and jacket instead, left the clothes caught in the wire and heaved the corpse on the stretcher. Thirties. Brush moustache. Well-dressed. A little taller than average. Identifiable, just, from the photograph in my pocket. Forget the fair hair plastered across his emptied eyes or the bow tie skewed like a vaudeville drunk. It was Michael Garfield, stretched in the mud at the river's edge, the debris of a city washed up around him, two ragged gunshot wounds aimed at his heart. I nodded. He was the one.

The launch was edging back into the slipway. The officers hoisted their stretcher and splashed toward it over a strip of disappearing beach. I let them go, went down on one knee in the freezing tidewater and sifted through the stinking mud in Garfield's coat pockets while they billowed on the rising river. The concrete ramp was awash. The police launch stood off again, rolling on the fret with Garfield's body laid across the deck, its stretcher party looking nervous. I got up, waved the boat to get out of there fast, and started wading, clear of the coiling metal and along the submerged beach, to where the sewer made an ugly flowering that the tide was dragging upstream.

At the side of the outfall, fluorescent with weed, a rise of iron staples climbed sixty feet sheer up the river wall, past the open mouth of the sewer to the edge of the disused wharf. I stopped there to look back and get a breath, knee-deep in the clawing flood at the foot of the ladder. Garfield's coats were lost already beneath the water, the launch a speck moving westward, laying down a glittering curve like a meteor tail. A satin blue sash of sky was turning the whole river to ultramarine. Nose clamped, eyes watering against the corrosive stench of the sewer, I lifted a foot to the first staple above water and started the climb up and out of the shadows.

Take away the angles of heavy timber that shored up its streets and it felt as if all of Wapping could keel over and slide into the Thames. Overhead, a mesh of high, iron walkways linked its gutted warehouses. At street level, delivery trucks picked routes through a snowfield where tarpaulins flapped and made pigeons nervous. I tramped tire tracks across last night's snowfall, back along a mile-long reach of river the police launch had covered like an express train. In half an hour I was standing at the head of an ancient river stair, in sight of the police boat station. My ride was tied up at the jetty, its stretcher cargo offloaded and its engines silent, snoozing after its morning gallop. I scraped mud off my shoes at the curb, squeezed river out of the bottom of my coat and walked into the Town of Ramsgate shaking with cold.

The Ramsgate had once been the haunt of a fishing fleet that brought its catch upriver from the coast, its saloon a long, low-lit tunnel set at a right angle to the water. No customers at that hour, only a sulfur blonde behind the bar overworking a tight sweater, pouting in the mirror at back of the counter and painting a wide mouth china red so you wouldn't lose her in a crowd. The saloon had a window bay overlooking the river, a table in the center of the bay, and a coke stove next to the table floating waves of heat across the window glass. The closing door got the blonde's attention back from the mirror. I called for a whisky and hot water and went to sit where I could be six inches from the stove.

When the whisky arrived, I put it down whole and wrapped my hands around the jug of hot water till my fingers unhooked. Then took out the wallet that had been in Garfield's jacket pocket, blotted the river out of it with my coat sleeve and prized it open while the liquor percolated. The wallet was organized in the professor's way with all things: his identity card and reading room tickets, a message off a pad, a restaurant bill too faint to read, and banknotes separated out. I spread the contents on the table, clasped my hands back around the jug and considered my haul.

The note was folded to show a Guildhall crest, and below the crest the words *Telephone Message* all but leached out. I pulled it closer, picked at a corner and peeled it apart. The Guildhall operator had written the message in fat, squat capitals, marked it for the attention of Professor Garfield at four-forty p.m. and dated it December twenty-something, too blurred to make out. The message said the professor's caller wanted to meet him at nine that evening, at a place I couldn't read either. But I didn't need to. Because according to the landlord of the Raglan, Michael Garfield had arrived there Christmas Eve sometime before nine, to wait for somebody who didn't show; a disappointment that left the professor at a loose end until Terry Reilly stepped over to start a conversation, entranced him with brand new possibilities and led him into the night.

Dillys Valentine meanwhile had been staying late at her office when Jarrett walked in the door, expecting Reilly to join him when his trick was through. Turned midnight, when Reilly didn't show, Jarrett left. And an hour later Miss Dillys had a visitor she never saw before. Was it Garfield who'd arrived looking for Jarrett? I couldn't say, and of the people who should know, three of them—first Jarrett, then Dillys Valentine, now Garfield himself—were dead inside the next twelve hours.

I shuffled the contents back in the wallet, dropped it in my coat pocket and left the telephone message on the table. It was my one bright spot. You draw a blank sometimes and you know the questions you're asking are wrong. At other times all it says is you were talking to the wrong people. Asked who the professor went to meet at the Raglan that night, Henry

Beaufort told me he had no idea, and likely was telling the truth. Now, I had a three-word answer in front of me, courtesy of the switchboard at Guildhall. On the message drying out on the table, next to the line marking it for Professor Garfield's attention, the operator had added in the same fat capitals, *From Councilor Drake.*

TWENTY

The housemaid seemed surprised I was back so soon, took my coat and hat and said the councilor was expecting me. This time we went through a door at right of the hall, across a drawing room into a library with sporting prints in the bays between the bookcases. It had two windows overlooking the gardens, Venetian glass in a chandelier, a club chair in front of an elegant fireplace and green plush drapes. The kind of room where you're meant to sit at night in a cravat and a quilted robe reading Kipling by firelight until the Madeira runs out. The maid announced me and waited for instructions, and when she didn't get any, left the room and closed the door without a sound. The councilor was standing on a Persian rug with his back to the fire, short and round in a dark suit and high buttoned vest, drawing on a fat cigar. He cupped a hand to stir the smoke haze he took with him everywhere and motioned at the far side of his library. "You've met already."

Allynson was turned away from us both at a liquor cabinet disguised in the bookcases, prizing the glass stopper out of a decanter. I said yes, we'd met already and no to the decanter the lawyer was waving at me. He shrugged, chimed liquor and soda in two crystal glasses and brought one over to Drake. When nobody spoke, he flashed the strained schoolboy grin again. "Newman. What news?" But what's news depends on what counts and who's listening. The lawyer put the glass to his lips like communion.

"Mr. Allynson, it's more than forty-eight hours since your tenant was murdered. Less than that since the councilor told me he didn't know, or know anything of Raymond Jarrett, let alone the fruit store and blackmail racket he was running from the address you rented him." Drake took the cigar off his bottom lip, rolled it in his fingers and weighed it absently. "You could ask what was there to notice? What does that kind of racket ever take more than a small-time entrepreneur and a select clientele that doesn't advertise its tastes? The answer is, it takes plenty more than Jarrett had. Meaning his small and very private retreat in the City was being bankrolled by somebody with connections." Nobody interrupted. Soda bubbled in the councilor's glass. I turned to him, not to let the conversation get too abstract. "Which is where the problem lies, because not long after I started wondering who could be bankrolling him, I happened across Jarrett's police file. How doesn't matter. What matters is there's a bank check in his file dated Christmas Eve. The problem with that, Councilor, is the check is drawn on your account. You wrote it out to Raymond Jarrett yourself and signed it. He just didn't get chance to cash it before he was killed."

Drake blinked and coughed politely around the cigar clamped in his mouth.

"I thought about how that could be. I even toyed with the idea you could be bankrolling Jarrett yourself. After all, it's something you could lose in pocket change. Except in the end it's not only about the money. The refined part isn't the hideaway or the black-market film, or the boys with moods and haircuts. It's about owning the cops and the muscle that guarantees business stays untroubled, either by the law or by the lawless. And somehow, Councilor, that didn't sound like you."

Coals flamed in the hearth. Drake waited expressionless and laid blue smoke on the room, thick as truck exhaust. Allynson was all bright-eyed attention. I asked, "Have you ever had a religious experience? I used to think they were strictly for shepherdesses short on company. Not anymore. Because yesterday I had one of my own, in a temperance residence at a solid address on the Strand. It's Boys' Town, a house of uplift where well-dressed, older men come and go and a slim-hipped priest is faking the register and racing his conscience to oblivion. Last evening when I checked it out, one of the boys introduced himself, and as we passed the time of day an idea came to me that we'd met someplace before. I just couldn't place where. But then I had a revelation. As a matter of fact, I had two."

Outside in the garden a robin took a dive off the top of a frosted plum tree, landed on a windowsill and started hopping around in the snow. So picture perfect that if he could sing as well as dance, they'd put him under contract at Paramount. "My second revelation was realizing I never had met the boy, only his picture in among a hundred others in Jarrett's bedroom. He was just a face in a crowd and I missed the connection, until out of the blue the priest mentioned who owns Paddy's. And that was my first revelation, Councilor. Because it turns out the owner is you."

Drake's chins were flushing from the brandy and the heat off the fire. The lawyer choked softly on his drink and dabbed at his mouth with his show-handkerchief. The robin had his head to one side looking in the window at the line of hunting prints. There were straight-backed women riding side-saddle to hounds that didn't interest him at all. But one look at the huntsmen in pink had him bouncing up and down, pressed up against the glass with a wild, happy eye. He was making me wonder if I had everything as wrong as he did. "So tell me nothing is the way it looks, Councilor, because when the City's finest put all that together they'll have questions for both of us. You being my client, there'll be some I can't answer and that will go hard for me. But you could help me feel better about it when they're lighting a fire under my heels."

The handkerchief folded back in Allynson's pocket. He put up a tight smile. "Really, Newman, Councilor Drake owns a great many properties in the City. We cannot possibly be aware of every…"

Drake brought his gaze around. His lawyer dried. "Your observations are apposite, Newman. For ourselves, we shall not rest on legal niceties. City Police may depend upon our fullest co-operation." He sucked on the cigar and set on his heels, as if that ought to be enough to put us all in square with the boys in blue. Allynson swirled his glass and emptied it, looking thirsty for the next.

I said, "Councilor, understand this. You're elbowing your way to the top of a police investigation. Not because your tenant traded on your lack of curiosity. Not even because, like it or not, you've been playing host to prostitution and blackmail. This is about fitting you for a murder. Maybe for more than one. Because the question that doesn't go away is who Jarrett made so nervous it got him killed?"

The fire went on shifting. Allynson kept the tight smile. Silence settled over the room like fine ashes. Then the library door opened wide and Mrs. Willard breezed in. She trailed a rustle that started in the drawing room the other side of the door, skirted around the company and pulled up alongside the bookcase that wasn't a bookcase. By way of explanation and without breaking stride, she swept a hand at the doorway she'd walked in and said, "Mr. Newman, allow me to present my always fragrant husband. Which scent are we wearing today, Joseph, *Anemone of the People*?" Mrs. Willard poured a stiff jolt of her own and livened it with a small splash of soda while her husband followed into the room, took in the crowd and let the door close behind him. She brought her drink over and stood right in front of me, close enough to count my eyelashes. "How lovely to meet again. Can we expect regular visits from now on?"

"I doubt it very much, Mrs. Willard."

It was a good time of the day for her. Her cheeks had lost the alcohol flush of the night before, her hair was brushed out, her makeup fixed in morning light and she hadn't overdone the jewelry. The rustle was a satin house robe that fitted down to her hips and trailed along the carpet. In daylight, her eyes matched the dark silver stripe in the robe. She said, "Such a shame," sighed and gave me a small, wistful smile, then went over to her father, kissed him on the forehead and took the club chair in front of the fire.

If his wife's behavior bothered him, Willard didn't let it show. He arrived in the room at a loose-sprung saunter, sleek in a soft lounge suit, loud necktie, two-tone shoes and a cologne sharp enough to scratch diamonds. Added to that, he was good-looking and more or less in shape, a little slack around the middle and the chin but not so much it was fraying his confidence. It might have been practice, but Willard looked more relaxed ignoring his wife in private than dancing with her in public. He slipped a cigarette case from inside his suit jacket, fitted the gold band of a cigarette in the corner of his mouth and talked to me around it. Close up, something about him nagged at me. "They tell me a tenant of ours was shot. Is that what this is about?" The talk styled the same way as the clothes.

"Your tenant was shot and killed, Mr. Willard. This is about something else." He spun the wheel of a gaudy lighter, put the lighter up to the cigarette and flipped it shut with a knuckle weighted with two gold dice set in a jet stone so big the room felt crowded. The knuckle motioned me to carry on. "On Christmas Eve, Councilor Drake met the City archaeologist at a diner in Smithfield. I came to ask the councilor what his conversation was about."

Drake dragged his eyes off the pattern on the carpet and looked perplexed. He hesitated while the library clock hushed the quarter hour. "I remember it. Professor Garfield and I meet regularly to discuss planning matters. Beyond that I recall no detail."

I made a frown. "That's a pity, but never mind. Let's try the appointment you had with the professor the same evening. Chances are you talked about the same things you don't recall talking about in the diner."

"I had no other appointment with Professor Garfield. Is he saying I did?"

"Not exactly."

Willard looked bored, picked a strand of dark tobacco off his lip and asked offhand, "What exactly *does* this Garfield say?"

"Professor Garfield doesn't say anything at all, Mr. Willard. His body was lifted out of the river this morning and my guess is it had been there at least forty-eight hours. So if the councilor doesn't recall having any appointment with the professor, he'd better give some thought to what he did do from around nine o'clock that evening. And in detail. City detectives will be interested to know."

Mrs. Willard took two slow inches out of her drink and cradled the glass in her lap. Her brow clouded, faintly bemused, then she screwed around in the club chair, lost the puzzle in her eyes and looked in mine. "Daddy was here with me. It's a Drake family tradition, father and daughter getting tight and miserable for a Jewish Christmas Eve. Why not join us for the next one?"

TWENTY-ONE

I beat on the basement doorframe of the Sesto and waited, not much later in the afternoon than my visit the day before. The signora pulled aside the curtain behind the door glass, softened her frown and let me in. I took the same seat, watched her back to the kitchen and closed my eyes on a dull ache working its way up from my toenails. When I opened them again, the signora was standing at the head of the booth with two small cups in her hands and the *Courier* folded under her arm. She dropped the newspaper beside me, prodded a sugar bowl and set down the cups, then eased into the bench opposite and butted along it, sighing at the effort. "You don't find Mr. Garfield. And now such a terrible thing."

I was reaching for the sugar, saw the afternoon front page and stopped dead. Under a headline *Professor's Assistant Wanted for Questioning*, was the picture of Henry Beaufort from Jarrett's dresser, with its kisses clipped. Littomy was pictured next to it, looking determined in a handsome uniform, saying his priority was to interview the young man, understood to be the last person to see Professor Garfield alive. The rest was Christmas-killer sensation and some career detail on the celebrated victim. It was the Henry Beaufort angle that bothered me. "I found him, signora. He just wasn't alive."

She wrinkled her nose, resigned. "I am sad for him. To find his *colosseo* and then to die so quick."

I squinted at her over a mouthful of coffee, swallowed and said slowly, "The professor found a Roman coliseum? Here in the City?"

"Of course! He always knows there is one because this city is important and because Romans like to make them. One day he wants to find it and be famous. And now this!"

"Wait, signora. How do you know he found it?"

Her lip dropped in disbelief that I could be so slow. She hunched her shoulders and threw her hands wide. It was nothing personal. Oppenheimer would have gotten the same treatment if he wasn't keeping up. "Because he shows the pictures to the man he brings here. The one with cigars. I tell you already."

"No, signora, you did not. You told me you never saw what was in the photographs."

The hands flapped at me. "I didn't see! But what else can make the *professore* so excited to show to this man?" She was prying herself out of the seat, breathing hard, handing me my hat as if I ought to stop leaving my brains in it.

I slid along the bench and took it. Two nights ago, Edgar Levin had said it was going after the big fish that made the professor no friends. "The man with the cigars, signora. Did the professor give him the pictures?"

She caught up with her breath and eyed me. "Of course no! They are like pictures of his child. After he shows them, he puts them back in his coat, next to his heart." She took two steps, raised up on her toes, put a hand on my coat lapel and patted where my heart ought to be. "My big, beautiful detective who wants to marry. Listen to me. A terrible man is killing my customers. Next time you come, tell me you *catch-ed* him."

It was mid-afternoon. The daylight already spent. From the Sesto, I followed around the edge of the square then walked

Giltspur Street as far as Holborn Viaduct. For a half-mile east, the landscape was an open grid of basements dividing up a snowfield like sheepfolds on high moorland. How it looked before the Luftwaffe arrived I hardly remembered, and if someplace out there under the ruins Garfield had found a Roman amphitheater, then it took more imagining than I had. I waited for a gap in a slow churn of traffic, crossed to the corner of Old Bailey and kept going, and at Ludgate turned uphill and halted halfway, outside a small church still more or less in one piece.

Across the street in the middle of an Edwardian block were the offices of Beaufort Partners, architects, and above them the apartment where Henry Beaufort claimed he stayed on Christmas Eve. I crossed the rise to one side of the main entrance, pressed the buzzer to the apartment and waited. Traffic on the hill passed shadows across the office windows. Downhill a goods train clattered over Ludgate as if somebody was tossing beer crates off the bridge. Passers-by shied from a wind filled with needles, and the church behind me rippled in the plate glass of the Beaufort offices, drowning at the bottom of a pool. Across the surface of the pool the shade of a Humber sedan pulled over from the uphill crawl and coasted to the curb. It was sitting there with its motor still running when Levin answered the door.

Edgar Levin didn't look overjoyed to see me but stood aside to let me in. He led up three straight flights of stairs without a word and turned in through a door off a landing into an outsized sitting room, all-white and as Edwardian as a split atom. It had linoleum the color of gunmetal covering the floor, sofas and floor lamps in a square around a drinks table, and two paintings in the center of each of the blank walls, one gray on white, the other white on gray to ring the changes. They might have been Picassos from his plumbing period, or a layout for steam pipes in an igloo; either way, they gave the room the all-around charm of an automated milking parlor.

Somewhere in the apartment a radio played light jazz. Levin pulled at the empty sleeve of his sweater and didn't want to start a conversation. I started one for him. "We both read this afternoon's *Courier*, Mr. Levin. Boosting Henry for a murder suspect is today's pitch to its readers, but his disappearance doesn't improve the mood of the detective in charge. When he picks the boy up, as he certainly will, his methods are guaranteed to be as ugly as they're thorough. Before that happens, I need to talk to Henry. My guess is you'd know where to find him. If it helps, I don't think he killed anybody either."

Levin eyed me a long moment, then nodded at a drink in a squat glass on the table, not started. "Better sit down. Take the scotch. I'll get another from the kitchen."

I walked around one of the sofas, flopped in a corner seat and reached for the glass. Breathe in a whisky and you hear its whisper. Most often, all it's saying is to brace for firewater and it doesn't mean you lasting harm. Less often, it murmurs a silken promise of soft rain fallen over purple heather, squeezed out, concentrated and waiting in your hand. This one said none of those things. All I breathed was the smell of a cold iron stair in an alley too cloistered for snow. All it whispered of was cheap perfume on a worn raincoat and blood on the air. I sprung a sweat and slid the glass back on the table untouched. When Levin brought the fresh drink in, I was still mopping under my jaw. I watched him put it on the sofa arm and motioned with the handkerchief balled in my fist, "What is it?"

"They call it Buccleuch. Guy goes shooting in the Highlands in season and sends down some cases to make Christmas gifts. Usually from a different small still each year. I don't suppose you'd come across it otherwise."

I didn't suppose so either. What Beaufort had sent south was a straight malt whisky, made for blending with the industrial kind to make something out of nothing. Ordinarily, the natives set some aside as consolation for an arthritic climate. Ordinarily, they don't intend it to travel or move in the circles I move in. But you never can tell. Because the day a Guy Beaufort drives over the hill, with his guns and his dog and the fat-apple appeal of his wallet, *ordinarily* jumps out the window. "Two days ago was my first. For now, I'm more interested in how Professor Garfield might have come across it. Last time we spoke, it sounded as if he didn't make it onto the Beaufort Christmas list this year."

Levin's gaze clouded. "In the current circumstances, I doubt he did. What's your point?"

I gave some thought to my point while he gave some thought to current circumstances. The Buccleuch sparked in the glass like dawn off a peat stream. "On the night he died, the professor stopped by the Raglan on St. Martin's le Grand, got friendly there with a smile-for-hire named Terry Reilly, and not long after they wandered out together into the night. Forget what the *Courier*'s telling its readers today. As candidate for the last person to see Garfield alive, Reilly beats Henry hands down. That was Christmas Eve. Christmas morning, Reilly left some part of a bottle of twelve-year Buccleuch with a friend, and word is he didn't make the Beaufort list either. My point is, where did he get it?"

The door from the kitchen opened behind me. A draft tickled the back of my neck. Slow footfalls crossed the room while Levin frowned and rolled the liquor around his glass. Henry Beaufort sagged beside him on the sofa, ghost-white, and murmured, "It was a present. I wrapped it and put it in Michael's office when we broke up for the holiday. I left my Christmas card inside his diary at the same time. If you'd asked me before, I could have told you."

Questions I didn't ask. It's a complaint I get. Also questions I asked the wrong people, in the wrong places, at the wrong time. In a shamus it's not a recommendation, I admit, but you don't have to let it grow into a complex. "Fine, so answer me this. Early afternoon Christmas Eve, Michael Garfield went into a diner in West Smithfield to show some photographs to a City councilor. My guess is they were taken from an airplane after the recent snowfall, but whatever they were I think he was too excited about them to let them out of his sight. I thought they might be in his pockets when he was found this morning, but I was mistaken about that. I also thought they could be why somebody turned his house over the night he died, and I could be mistaken about that too. What do you think?"

Edgar Levin's gaze swung around. The low electric swoon of the radio fell back on the room. Henry got up off the sofa. "I don't know whether Michael took any aerial photographs recently, but I know the pilot he always flew with. If you want to, we could go and ask."

It was three-thirty. Last daylight was turning the street windows the color of the linoleum. Levin still toyed with his drink and I had no better ideas. I said yes, we ought to go ask.

TWENTY-TWO

We didn't leave by the street door. Henry led out through
a galley kitchen at rear of the apartment, down a back stair
and out on to a cobblestone service road hardly wide enough
for two cars to pass. Outside the exit at the foot of the stair
a low-slung Morgan tourer was parked tight against the
building. He cleared snow off the glass, got the stone-cold
motor started, backed up along the alley and turned the car
around, then nosed out onto Ludgate where the rail bridge
crossed. Two hundred feet up the rise, the Humber sedan was
still sitting at the curb, dribbling exhaust in the gutter.

The Morgan was a straitjacket two sizes too small that
Henry drove hard and flat, north through Farringdon and
Hatton Garden, Clerkenwell and across Gray's Inn Road. He
took byways through redbrick Bloomsbury to bring him out
at Euston, slotted in the early evening traffic running out of
the city and pointed the Morgan west. The car was chill as
a morgue but Henry didn't seem to notice, kept the quarter
lights angled open to stop the windshield fogging and drove
in a trance; out through Marylebone, across Edgware Road,
but always west. On Western Avenue we joined a crawl from
White City to Park Royal, until beyond the Hoover plant

the traffic thinned and up ahead as far as Oxford was open country. Last light drained from a vault of polar cold. The Morgan plowed the mush of tire ridges in its headlights and settled to a low burble of exhaust. Henry spoke for the first time since we left Levin's apartment. "Who's Reilly?"

We were jigging in the glow from the dash, two puppets in a shadow play misting the inside of the glass with our breathing. I had my knees in a bear hug. "Reilly was a chance pickup on Christmas Eve. Nobody Michael Garfield knew. It wasn't the reason he was in the bar."

"Did he kill Michael?" It was a simple inquiry, spoken without rancor while the windshield wipers beat off a snow flurry. The boy was exhausted, thinking through gauze.

"I don't know. I don't think so." No more houses at the roadside, only frozen hedgerows cut out against a moonrise. I scratched at frost riming the side window. "Terry Reilly was working that night. If he was the killer, he didn't plan it or he wouldn't have made his move in a crowded room. Two people behind the bar saw him operating, likely there were others. Reilly as the killer doesn't make sense. Garfield's killer didn't take his wallet; it was still in his pocket with folding money inside. Yet twelve hours later Reilly was broke, went looking for his girlfriend and took everything she had in her purse. It makes him nobody's idea of Prince Charming, but it doesn't make him your friend's murderer either."

"Have you got a photograph?"

I twisted to reach in my jacket pocket, then angled Reilly's picture under the light from the Morgan's dials. Henry's eyes drifted to it for a second, then fixed back on the road. "Somebody else you never saw before?"

Henry leaned to switch off the windshield wiper and peered ahead at a night dancing with frost, his voice flat as an amen. "Never. What did you expect?"

The silhouette of a single-engine Lysander skimmed a fret of trees, silent as a gull clipping wavetops, crossed the Oxford road close to stalling and floated weightless out of a sky dripping starlight. It yawed and dipped over a frozen swell of Quonset huts at the airfield perimeter, adjusted its trim and for a long moment let you hear the whisper of its motor, then glided in over a curling ground mist. It kissed the strip twice lightly, like Proust greeting his grandmother, and when it put its tail down I turned away from the car and followed Henry to the sliding doors of a hangar.

Inside there was a dry smell of cement dust, a string of lights hanging from the beam sections and a cinder block office in a corner. We turned to watch the airplane running on into a flat, dead cold, heading for the evening star until it made a tight turn off the strip at the far side of the field. It taxied a wide arc out of sight behind more Quonsets, then a hundred yards out came bouncing back in view. Twenty yards out and the hangar was echoing the plane's motor louder than a steel mill. Then the roar throttled back, I took my fingers out of my ears and the Lysander's propeller picked itself out of the blur, shuddered and rocked to a standstill.

A hatch swung open in shadow under the high wing and a figure in a flying suit eased out of the cabin and dropped lightly on the concrete apron. The pilot flexed fingers in heavy gauntlets, stomped around on the ground to get blood pumping, then saw Henry waiting hunched under the airplane's wingtip and ducked under a strut to walk over to him. They clasped hands without a word, stood bowed and silent in the light spilling from the hangar, then turned arm in arm toward me. I stepped aside from the hangar door and followed them inside to the cinder-block office.

A kerosene stove reeked in a corner and made the small room swelter. A desk lamp lit its walls, crowded with photographs taken from the air. A hand of solitaire was playing out on the grid squares of a map spread on the desk, split and frayed along its folds. The flyer yanked clumsily at a helmet strap, teeth bared, and worked numbed fingers at the buckle. Henry, gray with fatigue, remembered what we were doing there. "I... I'm sorry. Gerry Fulton, this is Newman. He's a private investigator. He's here to ask about some photographs of Michael's."

Fulton let the chin strap hang loose and thought about that, pulled open a drawer in the desk and set three tin mugs on the upturned playing cards. I leaned against the door, found a cigarette, tapped it on a knuckle and considered Garfield's pilot. Hollow cheeks smutted with engine oil, light hazel eyes close-set, a mouth that pouted when it had the chance and all of it framed in a tight-fitted leather helmet and the fleece collar of a flying suit. From the neck down the suit was a balloon tucked into flying boots, not a lot more than two sheep stitched together inside out. The flyer wearing it was built slender, taut and small-boned. You wondered how often the professor's burning interest in aerial photography had brought him out to visit. Fulton twisted the top from a fresh third of brandy, shared the liquor across the three mugs and motioned me to take one. "Ask ahead." The voice as soft as the mouth, and with a catch in it. Its owner grabbed an earflap to peel away the helmet, then reached inside the fleece collar and shook out a sway of copper-orange hair that bounced around the shoulders of the flying suit before it settled.

I was lifting a mug off a ten of diamonds. My jaw slacked and the cigarette flipped off my lip, cartwheeled into the mug and floated in the brandy like a needle fixing on magnetic north. Pilot Fulton arched an eyebrow for the idiot American in the room. I gave her my rueful look, guilty on all counts, set down the mug and switched to the photographs pinned along her wall. "Miss Fulton, the day Michael Garfield died he was excited about some pictures like those. Henry thinks if he took them recently you would have flown him."

She took a pull from her brandy and let it work under her scalp, put Henry a seat against the oil heater and another alongside it for herself and counted back. "That was three days before Christmas. The snow had stopped and Michael telephoned to say he wanted to take some photographs. There was cloud when he got here but too high to be a problem. We did our usual thing and flew circuits over his blitz sites in the City. Michael was happy as Larry, climbing around the cabin and photographing through the window." She made hopeless eyes at Henry across the top of her mug. "I had to practically yell at him to behave. I mean, the other chap was absolutely green about the gills the whole time."

She drained off the brandy and rinsed it around her teeth. Henry Beaufort blinked. I turned around from her pictures. "There was somebody else in the plane?"

She swallowed and nodded back at me. "A City bigwig Michael brought along. He telephoned me yesterday as it happens. I forget his name." And then, triumphant, "Duck!"

I said, "His name's Drake. Councilor Drake. Did he always go along with the professor for the ride?"

"Never. And he was so awfully ill I can't imagine seeing him ever again. I mean, he was calling to ask if I still had the film we took." She looked up at me, askance.

I went along with it. "And did you?"

"Of course not. Michael never used the plane's camera. He had his own Fairchild. Ex-RAF. Easily as good as mine." She got up from her seat by the stove and unzipped from the flying suit, took out a handful of grips from a flap, clamped them in her teeth and hooked a wad of orange hair behind her ear. "After we landed, it took an hour in here drinking my brandy to get your councilor back on his feet, so completely wretched he obviously hadn't a clue what was going on. When he called yesterday, he actually asked to speak to his pilot, *Mister* Fulton. Well who the hell did he think *I* was, the bloody stewardess?"

Drake. So airsick he didn't notice Garfield was taking pictures with his own camera. Or that when his pilot stood down for drinks, she turned out to be Rita Hayworth with her mouth set in a permanent whistle. Perhaps. But even if the councilor had to be carried in from the airplane, you marveled how his next hour with her could be so hard to remember.

Ground fog settled over the airfield, spread a blanket across the flat acres taking the Oxford road back to the city and muffled the sound of the Morgan's tires. It made the low exhaust sound nervous. I put my knees back under my chin, wrapped my coat around my ankles, slid down the seat until I was staring up at the canvas top and set my hat over my eyes. Then said, "Tell me about Edgar Levin."

Henry was arched over the wheel, straining at a lazy semaphore of oncoming lights. "Tell you what about him?"

"He had a war. Tell me about his war."

And so he told it, in a halting monotone, whispered inside the shake and jar of the Morgan.

According to Henry, Levin had been a Medical Corps reservist in 1939 and got called up early. He wasn't ecstatic about it but he didn't see it as avoidable either; not in the way his boss and his fiancée did. Guy Beaufort didn't want to lose his brightest mind, and had favors he could call in. Levin's fiancée knew it and didn't see why he wouldn't stay out of the fight. Then one early spring day in 1940 their arguing was cut short. The British started out on a six-week disaster that was the Norway campaign, Levin had shipped with it to Narvik and didn't come back.

Henry owned he'd liked Levin from the minute his father brought him to the firm. But it was in the months after Narvik, while they waited for news and scanned the gazettes together, that he'd gotten to know Sybil Drake. By then, Norway read like the military equivalent of Laurel and Hardy putting up a deckchair, destined for calamity from the outset. Sybil Drake had started out tearful, then turned angry at the sheer waste of it, went on pushing officials two long years for information they didn't have and finally decided she had better keep her chin up, understand that Edgar Levin died doing what he thought was necessary and put the whole sorry affair behind her. It was around that time she was first introduced to Willard.

Henry slowed the Morgan for traffic building on the edge of town, sank against the seatback and dropped his hands to the wheel rim in his lap. "You could see why Willard would be interested. The Drakes were old money and well-connected in the City. But *Sybil*? And her father? As a prospective husband and son-in-law, Willard was spectacularly unsuitable, yet they both seemed not to notice."

I glanced across at Henry bent over the wheel, saw he was in earnest and let that pass. Like anything you could name in 1942, suitability had been on ration, and by next summer Sybil Drake was married. The same summer, as it happened, that Edgar Levin's name came up on a wounded list for the first time since he went missing, put there by the director of a Kriegsmarine sanatorium outside the port of Trondheim. The Navy doctor could have signed Levin fit for a stalag long before, even as an amputation case. But he liked his Jewish patient's chances better in the sanatorium, pulled his name from the POW files, and kept him permanently on a recovery ward. It wasn't until summer of '43, when he'd gotten notice of a Red Cross exchange of wounded, that the doctor put Levin's record back in the file, added him to the discharge list and told him he was going home.

When the exchange went ahead that fall, Henry had been stunned seeing his friend as good as return from the dead. Likewise, Beaufort senior, who couldn't believe his luck at getting back his best talent. But he also had qualms. How Levin would take to the fact of the new Mrs. Willard there was no telling. But after three long months of matrimony, Mrs. Willard's distaste for her husband was already undisguised, and how she might take to getting Edgar Levin back was aggravating Beaufort's ulcers. By the close of 1943, the City was looking ahead to the end of the war, the Corporation had two hundred and fifty acres of flattened, high-grade real estate waiting on reconstruction and Guy Beaufort was its chief adviser on a master plan that took the breath away. Having his star architect seen around town with the planning chairman's lately married daughter was not what his doctor ordered. Henry noticed his father was upping the milk in his nightcaps.

The Morgan crawled past Euston in a swirling snow that blotted out the rail station arch, then got in line to re-cross Gray's Inn Road. Henry was craned permanently over the steering wheel, using the flat of his hand to wipe off the screen. He hadn't spoken since his Levin story ended. "I've been thinking. Michael's office at Guildhall." He faltered, as if he'd forgotten how to swallow. "I'd like to go there. I've got a key."

The car rolled past a phone booth and halted again. I stretched to find if I had any sensation below the waist, felt under my armpit for the lever, sprung the door and got out. Sleet drizzled in fingers down the back of my collar. I put my head back in under the canvas top. "On a night like this nobody will stop you. Wait there for me." I slammed shut the car door and stepped across the gutter to the empty booth.

TWENTY-THREE

Kathryn Swinford was working late in the glass office. She reached in a drawer and said offhand, "Take one of these. They're yours."

She emptied the contents of a manila folder on the blotter in front of her. I put the cigarette I was lighting back in its pack and sank in the chair opposite. "Mine?"

Her nose wrinkled. "If you really want me to, I'll explain. But give it a moment, I know you'll remember."

The lump on my neck felt ready to crack open and hatch a chick. I put a hand to it, shut my eyes and breathed the coffin smell of Sun Street Passage. On the blotter was a crumpled pack of Passing Clouds, cocktail-hour pink.

"Where else are you hurt?" Her gaze settled on the dressing taped around the ball of my thumb, then watched me shrug the question off. "You really don't trust me, do you? You ought to you know." She didn't wait for an answer, took an envelope from a wire tray and tossed it in front of me on the desk. "Garfield's postmortem. The reason you telephoned. But we'll come to that. There's something we need to talk about first." Her fingernails tapped the edge of the desk. "When I left you my working notes, they said the only prints identified at

Miss Valentine's murder were her own. So they were. But this afternoon I had what I expect you'd call a hunch and did some identifying of my own."

I pulled my hand off the throbbing behind my ear and thought, why not? Everybody has hunches. Night or day I get a hundred of my own and one in a hundred that gets close to being a long shot. Probably it was as good an average as the next genius, and no reason to suppose Dr. Swinford was having a better than average day. I gave her the grin through my teeth. The one that charms at the same time it breaks down defenses. "Doctor, any other prints likely belong to City Police at the scene. They tramp all over out of pure enthusiasm. Leave it to the boys in the lab. They can tell the difference."

She gaped at me wide-eyed in disbelief. Not all of it was theater. "That was cheap of you, Detective. I have prints I take to be yours on the wax candles from the church crib; that can be checked. But in any case, they match with others taken from this packet of Passing Clouds. Miss Valentine lit one of them before she was killed. The rest of the packet was found tucked in the cuff of her sweater." She took a pencil from her lab coat pocket. "For goodness sake, credit me with some sense. And give me due for not passing this on, at least not yet. I was there when you were brought these. Remember?" The end of the pencil turned the cigarette pack around. "But they weren't for you, were they? They were a Christmas present for Miss Valentine. After you left the Great Eastern it was her you went to see. An hour later an anonymous caller reported her body at a location scarcely a quarter of a mile from here, less still from the hotel."

She looked past me to the darkened laboratory outside her office window, then leaned in, voice lowered to a hiss. "Look, there was blood on her coat and skirt, and on the ground around her body that wasn't her own. As of now, so help me, my report says it was probably her killer's. But there's no evidence, none whatever, that she fought him off. So tell me the blood isn't yours or tell me what happened." She prodded the crumpled cigarette pack in my direction. "Because these say Dillys Valentine was alive when you arrived and dead when you left. Which is not ideal, Detective, now is it?"

Her chair scuffed hard back and she walked to my side of the desk, reached for my wrist and spread my palm. Her thumb pressed hard into the wad of gauze and tape until my eyelids floated. She said flatly, "There's glass still in the wound." Pipes cracked. Low-watt lighting hummed and flickered. No other sound in the room. The doctor went back around her desk and took the faint, sharp mortuary smell of ether with her, stood with her hands deep in her pockets and waited for answers with a look I wasn't meant to like. I looked at my wristwatch. It was past seven o'clock. I picked up the envelope with Garfield's postmortem inside and said, "All right, but first I need a drink."

She nodded, went over to the stand by her office door, swapped her white coat for her outdoor and collected her hat and umbrella. "Not any more than I do."

The Viaduct was a quarter mile east of the bridge that carried Holborn in three iron spans high across Farringdon Road. It was a saloon bar left over from a Victorian gin mill, set on a corner opposite the Central Criminal Court. Any Saturday night it had cadet nurses from Bart's spilling from its doors, off-duty, loud and fried. On a Saturday night between Christmas and New Year all that was added was a sea of colored streamers, tinsel and balloons.

The saloon took up the quarter circle of the street corner, with three sets of double doors at intervals around its frontage, all three opening into the single barroom. I had one of the swing doors pushed open while the doctor shook out her umbrella and surveyed the crush. She sucked in a breath, dipped a shoulder and shoved for the bar through the press of bodies. I stepped in behind and trailed in her wake.

A counter ran along one wall, tall gilt mirrors along the other, with paintings in fake marble frames in the spaces between. I leaned in close to the barman's ear to call two drinks and steered the doctor to the only right-angle in the room. She turned there, put her back to the corner and peeled off her gloves. I kept my back to the party. It got us the one place in the Viaduct where we could talk without a loudhailer and gave me a mirror view of all three entrance doors.

Kathryn Swinford was wearing the same cream coat as Christmas morning, with its button cuffs and a high collar turned up around her ears. Tonight she wore it differently and I liked her better this way: tired and a little frayed around the edges in a felt hat with a slouch brim, swallowing warm whisky in a place she didn't want to be. I watched the liquor hit the pit of her stomach and sink with all hands, saw her nose wrinkle again and the line of her jaw relax. She took another sharp breath and frowned.

I said, "You're taking a big risk, Doctor."

She rolled the glass between her palms and summoned up her bright tone. It cost some effort. "By leaving you Jarrett's file to read? Don't tell me you disapprove."

"That depends why you're taking the risk."

Her eyes slid around to where they could watch the buzz and the high jinks going on over my shoulder. She talked past me, near enough to scent the liquor on her breath. "Well, I can't sit on my hands and do nothing. Blanche Beaufort has spent the past two months in a sanatorium, not nearly well enough to be told how idiotically her son is behaving. Much less that Littomy talks to the newspapers as if the boy's a fugitive from justice. It's cynical and dangerous of him. And Garfield's postmortem isn't going to help things one jot." I said nothing and watched the color fade from her cheeks. She shrugged an eyebrow. "You see, you were right. I do have ideas about fairness. I've told Guy about you, and that you're not jumping to conclusions the way Littomy is. That being so, I thought you ought to have whatever help I can give you. *Are* you jumping to conclusions?"

"You'd be the first to know. Tell me about Garfield."

It wasn't good. Her postmortem showed two gunshots fired from a .38. What was almost certainly the first one had smashed through the professor's upper left arm and ribcage before the bullet lodged in his right shoulder socket. It was damage enough to kill him anyway, but the killer hadn't left that to chance. A second gunshot had punched a hole in Garfield's chest and exited his left shoulder into the night. There was no water in his lungs. He'd been dead when he hit the river, and not less than forty-eight hours before he was found. His wristwatch said more like sixty; the water had stopped it minutes before eleven and the doctor judged that to be eleven at night on Christmas Eve, not later. She drank and winced and shook her head. "In short, Garfield couldn't have killed Jarrett. He was already dead six hours before. And there's more."

The wall mirror behind her caught a new arrival. The farthest street door pushed inward on the crowd, and when it opened wide enough, a nurse in uniform slipped through it brushing wet snow off her cape. The nurse stopped there and turned to someone who followed in through the door, masked by the slant of the hat she wore. Then she started for the bar with her company in tow. I lost sight of them both and pulled my gaze off the mirror. "It was the same .38 that killed Jarrett?"

The doctor was unbuttoning her coat, slacking a silk square knotted under her chin. "It seems likely. I'll have something more definite tomorrow. But that's not what I meant. It's that the second bloodstain on the coat in Michael Garfield's closet, the one Henry tried to throw out—"

"Is Garfield's."

She nodded distantly, drained the whisky and looked past me again at the crowd. "The same blood group. Meaning if Littomy really wants to, he could bring Henry in on suspicion of a double murder. In which case, I've become an accessory to a complete mess." Her voice had the same note as her first telephone call two days before, as if she saw a calamity coming and didn't know how to duck. But even calamity comes in degrees. The whisky bottle that ground the life out of Dillys Valentine had prints on it that hadn't been identified yet. The day somebody thought of checking them against Blanche's boy, Littomy would have a candidate not just for two, but for all three of his murders.

I pointed at her empty glass, and when she shook her head, said, "When Henry didn't find his boyfriend home on Christmas Eve, he stayed the night in the family apartment on Ludgate Hill. Next morning, he went back to Cross Key Square. Still no professor, or any sign of a break-in, but overnight the house had been turned over and a bloodstained coat left in a travel grip at the back of a closet. So says Henry, and if you've got reasons to believe him that's dandy. But Littomy hasn't any reasons and your postmortem will tell him Garfield was already floating on the tide. How else would he see it but as a double murder? You're an accessory to regular police work Doctor, let it go at that." I looked for my two hats in the mirror. For Nurse Greer with her wayward dark waves pinned in a starch-white cap, and for her companion in the slantwise fashion number who'd let herself into the nurse's house, broke out the kitchen fire, turned on the radio and left a message to meet at the Viaduct tonight.

"Well thank you for your interest and concern!"

My head jerked around. Kathryn Swinford's lips drawn so hard across her teeth they could barely form words. "Newman, what on earth is the matter with you? I simply want to know how to stop this getting completely out of hand. Who would you have me turn to?" She had a fighter's reflex for a fast combination: the feint with the unreasonable and then a fast cross with the unanswerable, before you got a chance to step inside.

I twisted the glass from her grasp, set mine in her hand and snarled at her when she demurred. "Take it and listen. The boy might be telling the truth. It's hard for me to tell. But if you want him out of this jam, start asking smarter questions about Dillys Valentine. The night Jarrett died she ran into somebody who was out looking for him. Nobody she ever saw before. Not Garfield because he was already with the fishes, but if it was Garfield's killer, maybe Jarrett's too, he knew she could identify him. Which is motive for her murder. But there's better."

Balloons started popping like firecrackers. A wave of cheering broke out. Then wild applause. In the mirror, a patron with a thirst was cutting glassy-eyed across the crowd, aiming directly for the bar and making uncanny progress, the throng opening up ahead to let him through like Moses headed for a margarita. My two hats were in his way. Nurse Greer eased aside like everybody else who saw him coming. In the angle of the mirror, her companion made a quarter turn and did the same. The drop of her shoulder, the curve of her throat, the high cheekbones that gave her the wild-pearl look were unmistakable. Then the crush closed around her and she disappeared again in a welter of damp faces and squealed conversation. "Did it occur to you that Jarrett had charmed relations with the law? He made an entire career hustling in the City and only once got the hook dropped on him. After that his police record is white as snow. Sure I went to see Dillys Valentine that morning. I wanted to hear how Jarrett stayed invisible for so long to City Police. She was ready to explain when somebody cut her short and left me a warning to lose interest."

The anger around her eyes turned fugitive, then tried for disbelief, and finally settled for confusion. She took a lick from the glass and touched a knuckle at the corner of her mouth. Pale and startled she said, "You think Miss Valentine was killed by police? Are you serious?" She churned the thought as if I'd broken the news that there are fallen angels.

"Jarrett could be protected by just two or three officers. It's all it takes. Only one of them had to decide Dillys Valentine was better dead than talking to me. And who else needed her dead right there and then? Garfield's killer? He would have waited until she didn't have company and used the .38 he'd used twice already. Unless you think the sound of gunfire was beginning to fray his nerves."

She squinted at the idea as if the brightness of it troubled her, then began working through it in a murmur, like long division. "So, when you arrived unexpected at Jarrett's murder and took too close an interest in the victim, it made them nervous. Worse still, you went looking for Miss Valentine, who could name police who'd been shielding Jarrett for years. You're saying one of them followed you there, aren't you?"

Working the thing out for herself wasn't what took time, any more than deciding a patient had whooping cough or swollen ankles. What she needed time for was believing where it led. Her pale green eyes widened at the possibilities. I said, "When Littomy decided he had two related vice killings on his hands, it put some of his detectives on edge. They knew a murder investigation would trip over vice rackets they were a part of themselves. So they needed a different version. One that spared Jarrett's history. Two days later, the professor was dragged from the river and they were gifted one. It says Henry shot and killed his boyfriend who was cheating on him, then gunned Jarrett down hours later with the same weapon. In their version, Henry tried to hide the coat because he'd been wearing it himself, complete with bloodstains from both his victims. They even have Jarrett's wallet with its photographs of Henry and the professor to back up their story. Then Henry going missing this morning gave the detectives their best break yet. It put Littomy on the front pages and leaves Jarrett's history in the shadows where it always was; nothing but a rumor."

She frowned at a headlong rush of low behavior that left her feeling giddy. "If knowing Jarrett's police connections was what got Miss Valentine killed, then what about you?"

"Dillys Valentine died because I led somebody to her then asked questions that made her look dangerous. Nobody tried to kill me. Not even when they had the chance. It would have made them a problem when what they wanted was to solve one. I got a warning. They'll wait to see if the warning takes."

It was one more idea the doctor had to make room for, but she'd stopped looking shocked or even surprised. The Saturday crowd at the Viaduct was guaranteeing no awkward silences. In the end she said simply, "Will the warning take?"

The directness of her own question made her blush. It shouldn't have. By leaving me out of her report on Dillys Valentine, the doctor was staking a lot more than her career. She was entitled to know what it bought her. "Littomy fed his line to the press because his detectives told him they'd got Henry cold on two counts of murder. And because the commissioner will sleep better on the news. Whether it adds up isn't his concern. What are you asking me, Doctor? Do I believe Henry's story? I said I might. Was leaving me out of your report the upright thing to do? That's for you to decide. But if what you really want is a reason for keeping me out of a police cell, then it's this. I'm the best chance Blanche Beaufort has of seeing her boy grow old. I might be her only chance."

Neither of us moved. Then the room drowned again in shrieks and liquored laughter and jolted her out of her thoughts. She got busy with the coat buttons, pulled on her gloves and smoothed them along her fingers, set her hat brim and threaded around me and out through the crush without a word.

I put down another whiskey while the two hats finished their conversation. When they pushed for the exit together, I let them go. If I needed either one, I knew where to find her, and the whisky was dulling the screeching in the room. I bought myself another, then another that pricked at the back of my eyeballs. When I walked out on the street, the cold slammed me like a wave against a sea wall.

TWENTY-FOUR

This time I went into the hospital by a different route, avoided Miss Hartridge's reception bunker and arrived in the fountain courtyard at a door heavy with brass work. The door opened on a high, silent hall out of an age of elegance and surgery without anesthetic, and a grand stair that mounted wide and shallow around three more floors. The staircase had a chandelier the size of a zeppelin floating high in the shadows, with only a handful of bare electric lights sparking in a thousand glass prisms on account of the power shortage. Add the reek of ether and walls hung with dark-painted canvases in dull-gold frames, and the hospital's grand hall was giving a fair impression of the high style in outer Transylvania.

I took the stair two floors, cut out at a high-lit corridor and followed along it to the common room I visited last night. A window blind was still drawn against the cold. A thin tobacco haze stirred in the warmth off an electric heater and I was thawing there, still a little jagged from the liquor, when Nurse Greer walked in for her next cigarette. She took three steps, pulled up when she saw she wasn't alone and pressed a hand flat against her midriff. I said I hadn't meant to alarm her.

She put the hand to her cheek and a bright nervousness in her voice. Her uniform crackled as she let out the gasp. "Not alarmed. I've been trying to telephone you. If you came to see Miss Voigt she's not here."

"Not here since when?"

"She had a visitor this afternoon. I wasn't on duty but I think it must have been the boy you told me about. Apparently, she got dressed and just walked out with him. Miss Hartridge is furious." An electric wall clock ground the intervals like fine sand. Her jaw unknotted and she frowned at my bandaged hand. "I'd better take another look at that." I walked over and she took my wrist, peeled off the tape and the gauze pad gummed with blood and rolled the dark eyes.

There was a treatment room along the corridor, with a seat either side of a metal trolley and a chromium tray of instruments that glittered as if they'd just been minted. She brought in a basin of warm water, sat opposite and soaked off the rest of the bandage, cleaned out the mush in the center of my hand and then reached a small hooked probe from a sterile cabinet on the wall behind her. She laid the probe across the corner of the chromium tray and we squared off again.

The room had a day bed in a corner, with a screen pulled aside and an anatomy chart framed on the wall. Nurse Greer spread out my hand and buried the point of the probe deep in the muscle at the base of my thumb, and while she sat working under an angle light, levering out small jewels of glass splinter, I started counting: the folds on the screen, the creases pressed in the bleach-white sheet on the day bed, the vertebrae in the spinal column on the anatomy chart. Then I started counting them over again, until my eyes filled and the wall went out of focus and the chart was just a blur. I wiped a knuckle down the ridge of my nose. "How many vertebrae does anybody have?"

"Thirty-three, why?"

"Does it depend which end you start counting?" The hook felt as if it was scratching out a garden patch to plant tulips.

"If this is hurting you ought to say so."

"I wouldn't want to make you nervous."

When she was done she bathed the wound again, and while she inspected her handiwork asked casually, "Do you think the police will find out who killed Mr. Jarrett?"

It brought my gaze up from the raw, spreading pit in my palm. There hadn't been anything remotely that casual about Nurse Greer since the first time I set eyes on her. I said, "Don't bet against them."

Her wide eyes lifted. The hand she held cupped around mine loosed its grip. "How can you be so sure?"

"It's this way, Miss Greer. Sometimes a murder is a random, solitary affair. Two people who never met before collide one day like hermits in the desert and only one of them walks away. Police look for a motive, an explanation, reasons why their paths might have crossed, and don't see any connections because there aren't any connections to see. All it took was a place, a time, a flash in somebody's brain. It might as well be a murder on Mars." I shrugged. "Whatever else Jarrett was, he was no hermit. His murder was no random affair. There were reasons why and none of them will be pretty. For now, everybody who knew him is clammed up because they think it's their way to stay safe. But they're wrong. In the company Jarrett kept nobody is safe. Sooner or later, in a bright room with two City detectives, somebody will be persuaded of that fact and the detectives will have their lead."

It wasn't the answer she wanted. She said nothing, just pushed away the angle light and listened to the humming quiet of the ward curling in under the door. It lapped around our shoes and crept up the walls until we floated on it. "Miss Greer, River Police pulled a body out of the water this morning, making three murders in three days, all of them connected. How many more are you waiting for?"

The metal probe slipped from her fingers and clattered onto the chromium tray. She watched it, mesmerized until it stopped spinning, then collected herself. "Can you come back when I'm off duty? I have to make a telephone call first. Now I really must get back to the ward." A line of fresh blood was oozing around her fingers and inside my shirt cuff. She laid my hand back on the trolley and opened it out again as if she meant to tell my future, then reached in the cabinet for a dressing and split open a fresh roll of gauze.

TWENTY-FIVE

A freeze was falling out of an arctic night ragged with ice clouds, hammering on Gresham Street like the back of a shovel. A single streetlamp glowed a hundred yards ahead. I took aim at the lamplight, unbuttoned my coat as I went, and flattened my hand against my stomach like Napoleon marching on Moscow. Ten-fifteen struck close by. There was nobody else on the street to hear it.

Past the streetlamp was the shell of Saint Lawrence Jewry wide open to the sky, sour with the permanent smell of charred timber that never leaves a blitz site. At its east end was the drive-in to Guildhall Yard. What survived of Guildhall was a long white-stone frontage roofed over in tin, three stories high with a carriage entrance in the center of the block. A bomb had taken out its entire east wing. Its west wing had two office floors over a disused courtroom, all still in one piece. Henry's Morgan was the only vehicle in the yard, parked outside a lighted doorway in the angle of the courtroom. The only other light showing was at a second-floor window at the end of the wing, overlooking the bombed-out church.

The doorway opened into a stone-floored arcade, where wall lights burned and flags of City liveries hung limp at intervals along the vault. A night porter slept behind a glass hatch, close up to a stove, arms folded across his chest and an alarm clock posted on the counter. Past the porter's hatch a narrow stair climbed to the floors over the courtroom. I cut out at the second, found the spilling light at the farthest end of the passage and went in.

The light was from a floor lamp behind a high-sided couch in the corner of a two-room office. A desk in the main room faced a window onto Guildhall Yard and the church. Henry sat hunched and ashen on the couch with two books balanced in his lap. The only sound was his long-drawn breath before he said, "Homer and Horace." They were two volumes from an edition with the same fancy binding, one of them open at a page of verses, the left-hand column in Latin, a translation on the right. I waited for an explanation. "Two poets. This one is Roman from the first century BC. The other is Greek, and centuries earlier. This is how they were when I got here. Horace next to Homer. The *Odes* next to the *Iliad*. On the same shelf, as if they were alphabetical. Can you imagine that? *In here?* He looked wild-eyed around a room so hushed you could hear him blink away the tears. "The only thing we ever quarreled about was how stupidly fussy Michael was. Greeks and Romans are on different walls. Don't you see? Someone's been here."

I lit a cigarette and waved out the match, tossed it at a wastebasket at the side of the couch and watched it bounce back at my shoe. "The door was locked when you arrived?"

He dabbed at the tears with the cuff of his sweater and nodded. I talked with the cigarette on my lip. "Henry, there are yards of books in here. One out of place doesn't mean the room was searched. What does it give you anyway? Unauthorized entry by somebody who thinks Horace was a Greek? Now we're really getting somewhere. That sound you hear is my bloodhound licking his lips." The room was twenty feet square of dark wood and worn carpet that smelled like a pipe rack. The door to the second room was letting in a strip of pearl-white light. "Maybe the cleaner put it away and doesn't know there's a system. Or her attention wandered because Horace and Homer were two GIs she met on victory night."

Henry shook his head. "Not the cleaner. She hasn't been in here since before Christmas." He motioned at the wastebasket to make his point. A loose-rolled sheaf of manuscript jammed slantwise across the rim. I gave him the weary look and lifted the pages out, fanned them and dropped them in his lap to get us off the subject. "Something else in Greek. What does it say?"

Henry thought about an answer then got up from the couch. He was inside the doorway to the other room before it occurred to him to tell me what he was doing. "It's easier if I show you."

The adjoining room was windowless. A room without books and half as big again as Garfield's office, lit from behind a pearl glass ceiling panel that made it perpetual high noon and with no furniture except for a single, heavy table at its center. It was bigger than a pool table, and laid out with a detailed model of a walled town on the north side of a river crossing, so different from the town and the river I knew that I hardly recognized them. This town was a grid of narrow streets beside a waterfront, set behind a protecting wall with gates to the wild country beyond. It had fine buildings and a central market square. Dogs slinked in its backyards. Legionaries marched broad avenues in column. There were bathhouses, storehouses, barracks and bordellos, and a fat-hulled trading ship loading at a dock where merchants tallied cargo. I tipped back my hat and squatted down to look along the rooftops.

Henry sighed behind me. "Michael loved this. He said it let him walk in Roman London and watch the passersby. Some of the buildings we're certain of, others are guesses. Roman towns repeat the same patterns, so we know what to expect and even where to look if we ever get the chance." He swayed with the effort to concentrate. "You can't possibly understand what it meant to Michael, to know there was an entire Roman city beneath our feet that he thought he'd never see." Under the ceiling light, Henry could have passed for a cadaver. I straightened up to call a halt and tell him to go home and sleep, but he'd stopped noticing he had company. "Before the war, Michael would take his students down to the platform at Aldgate tube and tell us we were as close as we'd ever get to the street level of Roman London. Then came the blitz and in two nights of bombing a third of the City was left in ruins. Hundreds of acres where you felt you could reach down and almost touch the Roman streets. The possibilities for excavating were endless. It was his chance of a lifetime." He rocked on his heels, lost in the idea, then remembered what we were doing there, pressed both thumbs hard in the corners of his eyes and leaned over Garfield's model to show me.

It wasn't complicated. From where we stood, the Thames ran left to right along one side of the table to where a bridge brought in a highway from the south. From there, a wall enclosed the town in a half-circle north of the river. Henry's finger traced the line of it and paused when it got to ten o' clock, where the wall made a right-angle sidestep before it continued its arc. "The City's medieval wall is built on the Roman wall's foundations. We see it on old town plans and they all show the wall making this same sidestep at Cripplegate. Until Michael excavated there, no one realized the maps were showing the corner of a Roman fort. It was a tremendous discovery, but in the worst possible place."

I glanced at my wristwatch. We were close to midnight. I thought, Blanche, don't worry. They'll put your boy on the stand and by the time he's through answering nobody will remember what the question was. I said, "Henry, there's a faster way to do this. I can leave now, learn a dead language, come back and read this myself."

It went over his head. The boy was alone with himself in the room, slack with fatigue. He caught my lack of enthusiasm and his voice grew smaller. "But I want to tell you about Michael's coliseum."

Sometimes it can be hard to put a finger on why you're interested, or why you think you ought to be. But there are words you've been getting by without for a lifetime, then suddenly everybody is using them in conversation and you know somewhere along the line there was something you missed. First it had been *colosseo*. Now it was *coliseum*. First it had been the signora and now it was Henry, and both of them inside the last eight hours. I took the cigarette off my lip and motioned him to go ahead.

Henry stood hugging himself, trying to find a way to explain that could possibly be simple enough for me. It took a while, but he got there. "Look, everyone thinks of games and gladiators, I know, but a Roman amphitheater was meant for drills and parade, close by the garrison fort and always outside the walls where they could site a large arena. So when Michael found the fort at Cripplegate, he knew his coliseum must be nearby. And that was the problem. The Corporation had bought up the whole area for reconstruction long before the war ended and already had plans for building everywhere Michael wanted to excavate. And the worst of it was, they were my father's plans. We didn't know whether to laugh or cry." He laid Garfield's manuscript soft on the edge of the table. "This is Michael's draft for a report to Drake's committee, his reasons why the Corporation should call a halt and let him excavate outside Cripplegate. It was hopeless. What we needed was something new and spectacular to make them sit up and take notice, but we didn't have it. When the snows came and ended our excavations for the year, Michael said he'd write something I could type up after the holiday. This is it. He said his ideas were better when he had them in Greek." Henry was staring straight ahead at some vision he saw on the wall. "I suppose when the weather cleared, he couldn't pass up one more look from the air."

Maybe. But Michael Garfield wasn't the only one not passing up a chance that day. The councilor had pinned on his medals for airsickness and gone along too, and got his reward two days later in the Sesto when the professor showed him the photographs. My guess was they were the something new and spectacular Garfield needed for his report. It would at least explain why he canned his first draft. But there wasn't any point asking Henry. His eyelids slammed shut while I watched, then his chin hit his chest and jerked him awake again. The boy was dead on his feet. I turned out the lights, walked him into Garfield's office and put him on the couch, rigid with exhaustion. It wasn't the Ritz. Just less far for him to fall.

St. Sepulchre was working through its chimes at midnight when I walked in the Thornburgh. I took the elevator, went straight through to my neighbor's office and locked Garfield's wallet in the safe, then came back and put on a light and sank in my chair as if I had a leg in plaster. The building hummed to keep itself awake. I hadn't any idea of sleeping either. In the drawer at the side of the desk I had a china teacup, a jug with a teaspoonful of water left in it and a flat quarter of Whyte & Mackay. I emptied the jug in the cup, dipped in two fingers and dabbed the corners of my eyes, drank the rest of the water and then half-filled the cup from the Whyte & Mackay. I sat breathing it, let it work behind my nose like smelling salts and thought some more about Garfield's office.

Either I added Horace and Homer to a dozen other things that didn't explain or I allowed that Henry could have been right. But if somebody really had gone looking in the professor's rooms in Guildhall, the puzzle was still who and for what. The liquor wrapped the puzzle in warm, yellow light, then hardened it in clear blue flame. Sleep pricked my face like soft rain. I wiped a hand across my eyes, dizzy with the brainwork, and went out as if I'd been given a needle.

I was walking a dog along a line of bookshelves—a waddling, liver-colored springer—reading off titles as I went, until the dog moaned and dug in its heels, put its weight against my leg and flopped on my shoe. I was ruffling his throat, looking into soft brown eyes as round as chestnuts and telling him that big and old and lard-tub that he was, I'd put him in a dogs' home if he didn't get off my shoe. Somewhere a boiler fired up. Heating pipes started snapping like flags in a breeze. I woke with my tongue fat as a herring, late already for an appointment I'd wanted to keep.

TWENTY-SIX

Dawn was hours away. Streetlight washed the hospital entrance on West Smithfield. The market's night-time circus was already winding down. In the middle of the square, two tall iron gates stood at the entrance to the garden, wedged open in drifts of snow. At the center of the garden under a bare canopy of plane trees, a life-size statue of a goddess was raised on a plinth. She wore a plaited crown of cornstalks in her hair, trailed a branch of olive at her side and reached one hand to a high, pale moon. A figure was sprawled across the steps at her feet. The steps were bloodied as a butcher's stall.

There is a compressed quiet you hear between the flash and rumble of distant heavy guns, like swimming underwater. I walked in through the gates, saw three figures standing aside from the body in the snow and heard it again. Miss Hartridge was looking rumpled, with hair wisped around the edges of a black tam-o-shanter and her jaw puffed with too little sleep. She wore black zippered bootees and a long wool coat thrown over a dressing gown in a hurry, like a down-at-heel duchess. A hospital intern was standing beside her blowing on his knuckles, shaken and shaking with cold. The same giant from Christmas morning looked up, decided I held no interest for him and went back to the intern. He said calmly, "You reported the body, sir. There's nothing more you can do. Better wait indoors." And when the intern didn't move, took his elbow and walked him toward the garden gates.

I went over to where Miss Hartridge sagged in the freezing air, breath flaring at her nostrils. "Miss Hartridge, Nurse Greer was planning to make a telephone call before she went off duty. Who she talked to could be important. If your operator connected the call she might remember. Who was at the switchboard?"

Miss Hartridge smelled liquor on me, stiffened and pulled her coat tighter across her throat. "In the first place, Mr. Newman, we have two nighttime operators, both gentlemen. In the second place, if you refer to a personal telephone call, Nurse Greer would not have made it from hospital premises. Our rules do not permit." She turned on her heel to pick a way back along the gravel path between the trees. A truck ground past the markets holding a low gear, snarled as it dropped downhill to Farringdon and headed for the river. I turned around to the body.

Nurse Greer lay on her back along the steps at the foot of the statue, her right hand tucked behind her hip, left hand flung outward, one foot lifted and crossed behind her knee, as if she died dancing a reel. No disorder in her clothes, except where her cape lifted in a swirl and made an ink blue halo on the snow. Soft curls tricked along her starched white collar. Her mouth took the nervous twist it always had. More than that I couldn't tell. A gunshot aimed point blank at the bridge of her nose had filled the cavities of her eyes with blood, clotted in blank, black tar pools by the freeze. It gave Nurse Greer a look of being masked for an end of year ball, and left her barely recognizable.

The nurse's outstretched hand grasped the leather fold that held her house keys. Her handbag lay across her stomach, its clasp sprung and its contents spilled in the snow. I squatted down, prodded aside her lipstick and cigarette lighter and picked up her brand-new pocketbook. It had a monogram blocked in silver on a dark blue cover, pages thin as a traveling Bible, a ribbon for marking her place. Two nights before, there hadn't been any entries in it. Nothing was changed. Nurse Greer hadn't written in any telephone numbers or circled any dates or added any names or addresses.

A shower of ice crystals shook off the branches overhead and powdered her ink blue cape. They were sparking in the moonlight when a sedan entered the square fast from the south side, slewed over and pulled up at the gates to the garden. I fitted the pocketbook back in its mold in the snow and got on my feet. A car door slammed. The sedan dowsed its lights and left its motor idling. Low voices carried and a City Police photographer came sliding along the gravel path loaded with equipment, two steps ahead of the giant. We saluted each other as we passed, the officer looking grave, the photographer red-eyed and breathing hard with a look of somebody suffering for his art. You sympathized with him. In his part of town, the murder rate was skyrocketing.

Outside the garden, a Humber sedan sat at the curb with its windows misted and its motor running, shuddering under its skin like an animal asleep. I got in the back seat behind the driver and clicked shut the door. The motor wheezed gently far ahead, mixed with a closer rasp of breathing. A camera flash lit up the statue in the garden through the trees. From where I sat, McAlester blocked most of the car's windshield, his right arm jammed against the side window and his frame heaving faint and slow, sucking the air out of the car's interior with every heartbeat. He wore a dark homburg square on his head, and his head square on shoulders so wide they might have built the sedan around him. The rasp interrupted and formed itself in passing conversation. "Another day, another body."

McAlester had talked in whispers since a wartime brush with a US Army Ranger in transit, celebrating a birthday with some drinking laureates from his unit. The City bar they ended in was having trouble breaking up the party and closing for the night. The bar owner had called for assistance, and when

McAlester walked in the trouble looked nothing but routine. Only two of the GIs could form whole syllables, the rest were catatonic. The birthday boy, his thoughts fugitive at the end of a long night of companionship, was slow to appreciate that the officer reining in his celebration was not only not military, he wasn't even American. It was when that thought occurred that the detective sergeant found himself flat on his back on the bar counter, with the barrel of the ranger's Navy Colt so far down his throat it bruised his instep. No question, the ranger made a big mistake. Just not as big a mistake as his next one. Overcome by hauling McAlester's two hundred and fifty pounds onto the zinc counter and liquored enough to keep him sedated all the way to Casablanca, the ranger keeled over, loosed off a round from the Navy Colt and shattered the mirror wall behind the bar in flying, fractured diamonds.

The ranger was still slow to grasp the nature of his predicament. The detective sergeant was not. While the bar owner got the rest of the party out the door, McAlester dabbed his fingers in the glass cuts across his face, picked the Army Ranger off the floor and beat him to death, slowly and methodically, with the crosshatch grip of his own Navy Colt. In a city at war it hadn't been an incident to harm McAlester's police career, but it added to his temperamental mistrust of his fellow man. And left him permanently hoarse. I fitted a cigarette in my teeth. "The nurse could be more than just another body. Your stand-in examiner thinks she might have put the bullets in Jarrett herself."

McAlester looked out the window, as if the scenery had better things to offer. "Littomy was never interested in the nurse. He likes Beaufort."

"Then the superintendent's a lucky man. He can take his pick. As of now, he's got four killings. Which one would he like Henry Beaufort for?"

A hand scrubbed across the misted glass. "Any of them." Another camera flash in among the trees. "All of them."

"So here's a thought. Why not quit following me and go look for him?"

The massive shoulders twitched. "Littomy says you're interested in the boy. He says stay with you, you'll find him. I say Newman wouldn't find which end of a bottle to piss in, but he's the boss."

McAlester might have had a point, but the Humber felt like the inside of a diver's helmet without oxygen enough for both of us, and he didn't need me to agree. I let myself out on the curb and slammed the door shut with my shoe. The sedan racked into gear, reversed out fast from the gutter, bought some traction in the ice ruts and slewed off around the empty square while its exhaust still trailed at my feet.

I crossed to a streetlamp against the hospital wall, put a light to the cigarette there and wondered what ought to be the big surprise. That you can be so blind to a thing at the first time of asking? Or that at the second time of asking, the exact same thing is unmissable? Two nights ago, I'd taken Nurse Greer's pocketbook out of the bag in her locker, looked over and through it and saw nothing at all. Tonight, even before I lifted it out of the snow, I knew where I'd seen its monogram before; in an anteroom to a study lined with law books, on a desk with a sign saying you'd arrived at the office of Buchanan Allynson, *Ring for Attention*. The lawyer's initials were made in flourishes, tangled like creeper, and because Allynson was a believer in publicity, for New Year he'd had the same initials put on the cover of a pocketbook, the kind anybody can get given when they're not fast enough with an excuse.

Across the garden in the square, the Sesto was putting up a thin glow from its basement. Strong men would be sitting apart at the tables there, leaning on Stanley's breakfast while the signora catnapped in her back parlor dreaming of goats and olive groves. I snapped the cigarette at the gutter. A quarter-mile ahead, the dome of Old Bailey pressed flat against the sky, and above its dome a gilded goddess weighed justice in her scales. It had been a night for goddesses. This one was catching the moonlight in gaps between scudding clouds, flashing off and on like a sign in Piccadilly.

TWENTY-SEVEN

I put a cushion on the sofa arm, sat with the telephone in my lap and dialed, then stretched out while the gas fire warmed the room by inches. It took a while before the connection clicked through. A rapid, shallow breathing came down the line. I said, "Mr. Beaufort."

"Who is speaking?"

"Newman."

There was a pause while the voice steadied its flutter. "Mr. Newman, were your reasons for calling at this hour of any importance, Commissioner Stearns would already—"

I cut him off. "We don't have the time for this, Mr. Beaufort. Your son is about to get taken in for reasons the commissioner won't even know yet. When it happens, I can promise you will not get a call." I reached in my jacket for a cigarette and waited.

The snatched breathing evened out. At length the voice said, "Go on."

"As of two hours ago, the commissioner has four unsolved killings on his hands. He needs an arrest so badly he wouldn't care if Littomy pinned it on National Velvet. But the superintendent can do better than that. His detectives are telling him Henry is a natural for two murders, and they're working on the others. Me, I'm supposed to give them everything I know and let Henry take his chances. What I'm not supposed to do is keep wondering why they don't look anywhere else for their killer. Do I have your attention?"

"Why are you telling me this?"

"I'm not telling you anything, Mr. Beaufort. We haven't spoken since Christmas Day. Your son is in Garfield's office in Guildhall holding a wake for his dead friend. Get him out of there and do it now. The night porter is out cold with an alarm set fifteen minutes before his shift ends. Take Henry and put him somewhere City Police won't fall over him."

"Mr. Newman, I still fail to understand your interest in my son."

"Just collect him, Mr. Beaufort. The commissioner will sit by and watch him hang. There isn't anything else to understand." I cut the line, sank back on the couch and tried thinking, one small step at a time, about the dark-haired nurse who died tonight in a moonlit winter garden. I saw her wearing a high-class dress for Christmas dinner, a tortoiseshell comb pinned behind an ear, the frown she had on call for any occasion, and heard the edge in her voice. *You have no idea how hard you are to like.* But it was as far as I could get. The eyes that fired up when she said it, I didn't see at all. Not even the color.

I lit another cigarette as the telephone rang in my lap, picked up and heard Henry, distant and hesitant as if he were talking in his sleep. "I read Michael's report after you left. The one he threw out. I think you were right, he did see something in the aerial photographs that we hadn't noticed before. He'd put a red line through the final pages and written in some references instead. But there's nothing to say what they mean. Probably they were the last thing he ever wrote." He started choking on the ache of it.

I got off the sofa, kicked the trail of wire clear and took the telephone to the window. "Henry, listen to me. Unless you stay out of McAlester's way all this will go for nothing. He has enough on you already and your prints are everywhere, even if he doesn't know it yet. A jury would convict Gandhi on less, and he's vegetarian." Thin lights burned in newspaper offices across the street. I took the prosecutor out of my voice. "Your father knows where to find you. He'll be there soon. Take the report, leave with him and stay with him, and don't try doing this any other way. Do you understand?"

Only silence. Then, in the same hollow murmur I hear in bad dreams, "There's someone outside in the corridor." And the line went dead. I left the telephone on the bureau and walked to the bedroom, stretched out on the bed, pulled the blanket over my head and slept like a mummy.

THUMBED-OVER SOULS

I woke to a voice too low to hear distinctly, as out of place as it was familiar. I rolled toward it. The voice was saying, "I said you look awful and you'd better drink this. It's all I could find in your kitchen cupboards. Don't you keep tea?" Kathryn Swinford held out a cup on a saucer. She was sitting on the edge of the bed in a glaze-green costume that crackled when she moved, her gloves and clutch purse and a dark astrakhan in a heap at the foot of the bed. I squirmed up against the wall, drank and couldn't tell what, turned around the watch on my wrist and wondered where she'd found a saucer. It was barely ten o'clock. "Not indoors. How did you get in here?"

She cast a glance around four blank walls stenciled with bunches of violets and at a thin wedge of daylight at the bedroom door. "Well, obviously not through the window. You didn't answer your doorbell. The lady cleaning in the bar downstairs said you hadn't long come in. She gave me your door key."

"Bridget? She wouldn't give even the Holy Virgin my key."

She reached for the clutch purse, opened it and tossed the key on the pillow. "You're confusing me with someone else.

And the world still turns while you sleep, Detective. I had two urgent calls this morning. The first was Guy Beaufort. The second was to perform a postmortem on the young nurse who so fascinated you last night in the Viaduct. I know you'll remember her, because the minute she walked through the door was the minute I lost your attention." She jerked the cup out of my hand and set it down on the night table. "Shall I tell you what I think? I think you knew perfectly well Nurse Greer would be in the Viaduct last night. I think you already knew she was in danger, and since I can recognize a hospital dressing when I see one, I also think you saw her after I left. So now I want you to listen to me very carefully. After you telephoned Guy this morning, he called to ask what I thought of you, which is no easy question for me to answer. In the end, I said all we could do was trust your judgment, because I had absolutely no idea what you meant to do or why. But be clear about this. I will not—*will* not—do that for you ever again. I will never again cover for you or give you the benefit of the doubt or be party to what you do, when you always and deliberately tell me nothing." She was pounding her knuckles in my chest, leaning on every syllable until her hair tangled in my mouth. The effort made her hiss. "Do. You. Hear. Me?"

I heard. But the way she smelled of a walk in a cottage garden was beginning to make my teeth ache. She let up on the chest while she got her breath and I said, "Doctor, my judgment lately doesn't recommend itself to anybody. Nurse Greer died this morning because I wasn't there. Dillys Valentine died Christmas Day because I was. What do I do next time? Toss a coin? But what I know is, Blanche's boy didn't murder anybody; not the professor or the nurse or the nurse's neighbor, and not Dillys Valentine either. Take it from me. I was there and it wasn't Henry who sapped me. He doesn't have the wrist. I called Guy Beaufort because my knowing it counts for nothing. Henry is short on alibi and Littomy will put him up for every murder he's got available. There's another story in there. There has to be. I have no idea where it begins or with who, only that somebody is burying it deeper with every passing day. Keeping Henry out of a police cell buys me some time, that's all."

She hooked her hair behind an ear and stayed where I could see the whites of her eyes, then snapped upright, smoothed out her skirt and stood up. "My preliminary report on Nurse Greer is in your sitting room. Littomy won't receive his copy till later this morning. I can't delay it any longer. We recovered the bullet and it indicates the same gun that killed Jarrett and Garfield. I imagine it's what you expected."

I swung my head off the pillow and my heels off the blanket and stood up, lifted the astrakhan off the foot of the bed and helped her in it as if we were leaving for the opera. While she pulled on her gloves I gave some thought to what I might have expected. Whoever murdered Nurse Greer had got as close to her as he got to Garfield and to Jarrett. Close enough to point a .38 between her eyes and squeeze. The sight and the sound and the smell of it might have sickened him, or merely raised his pulse. Or both at the same time. I said, "Jarrett almost got away. It taught his killer that a bullet in the head is the way to be sure. One more life just proved it."

She stiffened at that. "Two more lives. Read my report." The air went out of the room. I put a hand out to the wall, steadied against it and thought back to a candlelight nativity and a crib in the straw, and a nurse who spelled out what she was doing there in case I could be dumb enough to miss it: *As a matter of fact, just lately I light two.* Kathryn Swinford wheeled around, her head tilted to one side, the astrakhan collar bunched in both hands under her chin. She gave a small gasp of surprise. "You really had no idea, had you? Nurse Greer was going to have a little girl." The tip of her tongue put a smudge in her lipstick, her forehead cleared and she started unbuttoning the coat. "I'll boil some water. You need to shave."

TWENTY-NINE

Smithfield market was already shuttered for the day. The City trembled beneath a sky of pounding blue. A police officer shifted foot to foot outside the garden in the square and had nobody to turn away. I went through the gatehouse to St. Bartholomew's churchyard with a razor wind under my eyelids, squeezing out tears with a thumb. In a niche over the arch the flayed saint looked as if he ought to be freezing to death.

Both hospital switchboard operators said Nurse Greer hadn't telephoned anybody overnight. One of them remembered putting through an incoming call before five a.m. but nothing about her caller. To walk home all she had to do was follow the high wall along the hospital side of the square, pass by the churchyard entrance and turn into Cloth Fair, then turn again into Cloth Court. Instead, with the air freezing hard and an ice rink underfoot, she'd crossed to the garden at the center of the square and walked in through the gates before dawn. The late morning editions said nobody had seen the nurse exit the building or heard the shot that killed her. The hospital gateman was still talking to City Police. As for the intern, he'd overrun his shift, left the hospital late and saw the body lying in a heap in the snow. It was all I had. Not much more than anybody else who read a newspaper.

The church porch was showing no signs of a murder, the walls and floor had been scrubbed clean. I hadn't any idea of going back inside, then smelled incense on the air, pushed on the door and walked toward daylight angling through the shadows. I followed the same squat columns I'd followed three mornings before, passed by the Christmas crib and went along the line of the wall as far as two wrought-iron gates open on a lady chapel behind the main altar. It had rows of straight-back chairs set facing an altar of its own, and at the end of one of the rows, sitting pressed against a heating pipe running under a high window, a woman in a black velvet coat wrapped close around her calves. She sat with her head bowed and a glove stretched taut between her fingers, her wrists rested across a black patent bag in her lap. A kneeler lifted her toes and high-heels off the chill of a stone-flagged floor.

There was a glass cabinet against the north wall of the chapel, draped either side with an RAF standard and a Union flag. I moved over to it. It had a notice under the glass that said *London City Squadron* and a typed committee letter inviting donations to a memorial plaque for its airmen killed in action. Below the invitation ran the names of the dead. I read down the rollcall and found the one name I recognized. A voice behind me caught softly and said, "Charlie." I turned around. "Estelle always seemed to hold a fascination for him and vice versa." And when I didn't answer added, "Estelle was my sister. Isn't she the reason you're here?"

The woman at the end of the seat row left it at that. She wore her dark red hair caught up in a hat of wide, black velvet, with a veil so fine it floated on her breath. We looked at each other for long seconds. Then she shivered extravagantly and I sidestepped along the row behind and put a hand under her elbow. "Mrs. Allynson, sitting in here

is a ticket to pneumonia. Why don't we go to the house?"
She thought about that and nodded, put on her glove and
got to her feet and moved along the row. And if she was
taller in heels than I remembered, the walk hadn't changed
at all.

Inside five minutes we were standing in her sister's kitchen
on Cloth Court, thin curtains drawn aside on the backyard
and daylight cutting stripes across the room. Mrs. Allynson
brought an electric heater over to where we stood, dragged
two chairs from under the kitchen table and lit a flame under
a kettle on the stove. She lifted her veil with both hands and
took out a pin, slid out from under the hat and touched her
hair back in place. I was halfway to sitting, watching two
short creases knit across her forehead, when she said, "If we're
to talk about Estelle, please let's not be maudlin about it. I've
spent two hours with policemen already this morning." And
then, "Is something wrong?"

Not wrong. Only that Mrs. Allynson had her sister's glossed
brown eyes, so dark they were practically purple. So exactly
the same that the last five hours peeled away with her veil and
I was back in the garden on the square again, hardly able to
breathe. The nurse still danced her reel there in the snow, teeth
parted, cheeks hollowed, her bottom lip dropped in a look of
mild surprise. No different. Except now she had eyes to gaze
with, up through branches glittering with frost, in blank wonder
at the throbbing constellations on a night as clear as glass. I
shook the apparition off. "I was... wondering."

"Wondering what?" She stared and waited.

I asked the first thing that came to mind. "You knew the
flight lieutenant?"

"Charlie Ross?" Her lips squeezed and weighed what they
ought to say, then said it anyway. "Both of the Greer girls had
a crush on the flight lieutenant. What girl didn't? We shared
practically everything, but Charlie was smitten with Estelle.
Did you know he flew with my husband?" She dropped her
gloves and hat on the oilcloth on the kitchen table, then went

to a corner cabinet by the window. "No, why would you? My husband was older of course. Always the lawyer, but he'd flown before the war. Quite early on his lungs were burned in a bad landing and he never flew again. Charlie, on the other hand, seemed indestructible, until one day he went chasing buzz-bombs over the Channel and didn't come back. Or were you asking out of politeness?" She was up on her toes, reaching at the back of the cabinet. "I don't intend making tea, by the way."

You guessed she wouldn't. Mrs. Allynson brought over two tumblers and a quarter of cheap rum, poured two slugs and made the kind of conversation anybody will make when they're dressed for deep mourning and the highballs are under par. "My husband found this house for Estelle. I was never sure whether she liked it or simply hated it less than the nurses' residence. Drake & Co. owns most of the court apparently." She carried the kettle over to the glasses and filled the room with the scent of thin liquor.

"So Nurse Greer had to get over the flight lieutenant. What then?"

The question bought me a sigh. "Oh, do please stop this. Charlie Ross can't possibly be interesting to either of us." She took the seat opposite, her glass held against her lip, and watched me pull the nurse's letter rack across the table. I riffled through for a torn-off flap of envelope with a message written on, and when I found it, flattened it on the oilcloth where she could read *The Viaduct tomorrow.*

"Mrs. Allynson, from the time she found her neighbor's body your sister was running scared. Scared of what or who is something I have to guess at, but you would know. You just said how the Greer girls shared everything, and the two of you talked last night."

Two hours of police interview is meant to show. According to Mrs. Allynson it had left her feeling ragged, but she was making it hard to tell. She wore a sketch of powder on her nose, a soft bow of red on her mouth, fitted black silk and blacker velvet from the toes on up, and a wave of dark-cherry hair that brushed her cheek every time she gave me the quizzical look. She unbuttoned her coat, cool and untroubled, and let it fall loose at her sides, blinked long lashes and waited for what came next. "You don't want to seem disloyal, so I'll make it easy. Your sister's story about what happened Christmas morning didn't make sense then or now. After she found her neighbor's body and before she called the police, she came back here to the house. Leaving out that small detail gave her fifteen or twenty minutes unexplained, so she stretched her story to account for them. It was a cockeyed thing to do, a lie that put her in the frame for Jarrett's murder, and even though she pretended not to notice, her timings still didn't fit. I'm hired by your husband's employer, Mrs. Allynson. What was scaring your sister is something you're supposed to tell me."

She slid one knee across the other, breathed the rum to clear her head and shifted in her seat. "I really don't know what to tell you. She was upset when we met last night, hardly making sense." She took another deep breath for both of us. "All she would say was that there was someone else there when she came out of the church. In the darkness Estelle didn't see who, and anyway he was gone before she understood what had happened." Mrs. Allynson looked up and made astonished eyes. "I admit I was angry with her! How could she be so idiotic not to tell that to the police? When I asked what she intended to do, all she said was that she wanted to talk to you. I told her if she thought you might help, then for goodness sake do it quickly." Mrs. Allynson put her elbows on the table, crossed her fists under her chin and let sisterhood churn in her eyes.

"You told all this to McAlester?"

"Not that Estelle wanted to talk to you. It only seemed to complicate things. The rest...well, yes."

"So, at around four-thirty Christmas morning your sister falls across her dead neighbor and sees his likely killer escape. She can't identify the mystery man, but he doesn't know that, and it makes her so nervous she leaves him out of her story, right up until last night in the Viaduct. By that time there are two more murders and finally she's so scared she admits to you she's been lying. Is that what you told McAlester?"

The question knit across her brow. "Something of the sort, yes. But I think you're being very harsh."

A dull glow from the heater itched at my shins. I got up and moved to the door, stopped there and put my back against it. "The flight lieutenant was killed three years ago. Who did your sister know since?"

She turned the question over and decided it was shop-soiled. "In the way I think you mean, no one I knew of. We had no secrets from each other." As flat as that, as if the Greer sisters had shared secrets as easily as they might have shared Charlie Ross, or whatever else there wasn't enough of to go around.

"Mrs. Allynson, later today McAlester will get a postmortem report telling him Nurse Greer was going to have a child. So best give some thought to the men in her life, because when he's through with the report McAlester will be back, asking the same question I just did. Tell him your sister didn't have any men friends—not in the way you think he means—and harsh will not begin to describe his manner."

She touched the wave of cherry hair across her cheek with a look of frank amazement. Up until now she'd been good—better than good—in a repertory that had stretched from ice-cool untouchable to concerned big sister leveling with me across the kitchen table. But this was her best yet. The purple-brown eyes switched from shock to bewilderment to disbelief and back again. So seamless, it might have been for real.

THIRTY

The telephone began ringing before I shut my office door. I raised the window blind and reached across a shaft of daylight cutting the room in half. A voice asked, "Mr. Newman?"

There was a faint lisp in it, hesitant and unmistakable. I said, "Hospitals get touchy when you walk out on them, Irene. Where are you?" I sat across the corner of the desk and looked up past the rooftops at ice clouds five miles high.

She let the question go. "Terry says he'll talk to you, Mr. Newman. I said he had to. Will you see him?" And to clinch it, "He paid me back the money he took." She gave me an address in Soho and waited for an answer, but I was looking over at the figure that just walked in my office, fists deep in the pockets of a long outercoat, permanent homburg worn square. McAlester crossed the room behind me, parked in front of my window and blocked the daylight as if somebody moved a closet there. I said all right and to give me an hour and chopped a hand down on the connection. Irene would see to the rest. She knew the answer anyway before she dialed.

I found a cigarette, lit it and inhaled. At length a whisper said, "Littomy was right." I waved smoke out of my eyes and listened for what Littomy had been right about.

McAlester wound his shoulders up around his ears, went over to the connecting door to my neighbor's office and opened it, satisfied himself I didn't have him surrounded and went back to blocking the view. He relaxed there, pulled a licorice candy from his coat pocket, prized it out of a gaudy paper twist and slotted it in his cheek. Then shrugged and struck the conversational tone. "We put a watch on the Beaufort place when the boy went missing. For twenty-four hours nothing. But Littomy says be patient, junior will telephone home. Then early this morning house lights go on all over." The candy wrapper rolled tight in a ball between his palms. "It's a lot of lights." I felt the same airlessness around McAlester I always did; the urge to put a chair through the window before the walls closed in. He stopped rolling the wrapper and sucked on the licorice. "Ten minutes later, Beaufort drives out as if he's been called to a fire. The detective on duty follows. Twenty minutes and Beaufort's in Guildhall talking to junior in his professor's office. Then I get a call."

The candy cracked in his teeth. I snorted absently at a picture of McAlester walking in on Henry before dawn with four unsolved murders in the air. Call it a late-arriving part of Henry's education, useful for his future understanding of police method. But that depended on him having a future. The idea stuck my tongue to the roof of my mouth. I swallowed and said, "It makes sense. A milk-fed City detective comes face-to-face with Henry Beaufort, thinks he could be too tough to handle alone and sends for you. What happened to his old man?"

McAlester left me his rueful look and made unhurried for the door, his teeth blackened by the licorice. "Left before I got there. Drove off to see his friend the commissioner." His disappointment in a fellow citizen so touching you wanted to console him. Then a flat and final shake of the head. "Big mistake." My cigarette began tasting of cold ashes. McAlester looked me over with infinite regret. "Your big mistake was calling him to the fire."

THIRTY-ONE

Soho was so empty it might have been in quarantine. Windows strained daylight out of the afternoon and held it captive. Snowdrifts hid a sealed-off air raid shelter in the center of Golden Square, and along a soot-brick street on its east side an electric sign flashed over the sidewalk. It showed a large, green bird with its wings folded, a long, curving neck and a bill the size of a hammock. The bird was preening in flickering neon. Below it in red-lit letters the sign said, *Pelican Club. Private. Members Only.* I climbed the steps to the entrance and went in along a low-lit corridor. A straw blonde was sitting alone at a hatcheck at the head of a stair, winding a curl in front of her ear and reading her star sign in a magazine. By the time I got to the hatcheck we already had an understanding; if she didn't have to break her concentration, I didn't have to be a member. I walked on past and took the stair to the basement.

The Pelican was a regulation poison-well for the lower excitements. A place where bubbles will sink in the champagne and a deal from the top is novel, where the hop is less reliable than a second thought and a girl with a permanent and a hard, straight smile will empty your wallet faster than the Marshall Plan. It traded to thumbed-over souls in tastes unsullied by refinement, didn't advertise or give any guarantees, overpay its taxes or entertain the principles of union labor. In Soho, you wouldn't pick it out in the crowd.

At two in the afternoon, the clientele it ministered to wasn't breakfasted yet. Business was slow. The basement stair opened on a bar with a piano wedged in a corner and a tallish cadaver propping the back wall. The cadaver was posted at a closed velour curtain, reaming a fingernail with a toothpick and eying the only two occupied tables. At one of them, four US Navy officers were fixed on their hands of blackjack and paying me no attention. I paid them no attention back, sat down at a table tucked in the curve of the piano and lit a cigarette. Terry Reilly hunched there, sunk so far inside his coat the epaulettes made wing-flaps for his ears. His bottom lip wrapped over the pencil moustache to boost his next thought. "You took your time. I didn't have to wait, you know."

"Sure you didn't. But things being what they are, you waited anyway."

The boy stroked the rim of an empty glass, confounded. "What things?"

A barman pushed out through the curtain next to the sentry, carrying a tray at his shoulder. Reilly caught his eye. I said, "Pimps and professors. You're democratic with your dalliances, Terry, but they're dying on you. Garfield? There are witnesses to say he left the Raglan with you Christmas Eve, making you the last person he was seen alive with. Jarrett? Murdered hours later with the same handgun as Garfield, and you're the last known to see him alive too. Call it coincidence. Police will call it a pattern. Meaning if they decide you killed the professor, they'll take you down for the pimp as well. Or vice versa. You won't notice the difference. Meanwhile, Voigt is looking for you, and you make yourself so memorable how hard can that be?" The drunk scene Christmas morning at the Great Eastern; the Raglan in a midday crowd; checking into Paddy's and quitting next morning. All inside twenty-four hours. I eased in the crook of the piano. "You sold something Christmas Day, Terry. Who was buying?"

The barman set a glass from his tray on the table and went back through the curtain. The sentry was gone. Reilly made a slow, deliberate, knight-takes-pawn to replace the glass in his hand with the one at his elbow, wetted his lips, put his head back, shut his eyes and tipped the gin down his throat like raw eggs. I counted the seconds until the gin hit, then watched the startled eyes flutter. When he landed the empty glass on the table he was flying on instruments, the voice a sullen lament that all its luck had run out at one time. "I never heard of Garfield till the papers said. He was just a trick in his car in the docks, that's all. Then the car door opened and somebody with a gun took him across the street toward the river. I don't know who. Nobody even spoke." The boy was sweating seventy percent proof, his face and hair damp on a tide of alcohol, lucid as a drunk gets before he passes out.

"So you didn't know him. Tell me how he looked."

Reilly's mouth slacked. "A coat. A hat. How do they ever look? I was trying to see. I got out of the car and followed them. Then I heard two gunshots. I even saw the flashes." The idea pulled him up. "So it can't have been me doing the shooting can it?" In his gin haze it might have looked like an ace to play, and you saw what he meant. It just wasn't the alibi to try out on a jury. Light faded from his eyes like dusk in small windows. He watched himself backing away from the gunfire, getting in at the wheel of Garfield's convertible and driving out of there fast. "I never thought there was going to be shooting, Mr. Newman. I..."

But you knew what he thought; that the turned-up collar, the turned-down hat brim and the .38 loose in the hand were nothing but props in the theater of the rackets, like the lace handkerchief D'Artagnan will flounce in the face of some no-account count. "Then you're innocent of two murders. It's not what I asked." One of the Navy card players yelled and clapped hands. Reilly twisted around as if the commotion broke his concentration. I stubbed the cigarette in the empty glass, reached across and cupped a palm under his chin. "Over here. Look at me."

The boy was leaving the planet, his eyes floating dark and unknowing as spawn in a pool. I walked to his side of the table, put a hand under his armpit and hoisted him off the chair. He swayed, breathed thinner air, looked around the basement as if it was another country and let himself be steered across the room, out through the velour curtain into a small, dim vestibule. At right was a deep-button door with *Club Dining* in brass letters and low murmuring behind. At left a door with a closer, its paint worn bare around a push-plate. I shoved Reilly through the left-hand door, felt for a light switch and set the catch. The air weighed with the rank, corrosive pall of a field latrine.

It was a single cubicle, close and peeling, with a pitted mirror over a washstand and a light over the mirror fluttering as if it had a moth trapped inside. I held Reilly upright, ran water in the basin until it brimmed, then grabbed a handful of his hair and pushed his head underwater. I held him there until he gagged, lifted him to get air, then ducked him again, and when he started flailing stood him up and let him grip the edge of the washstand. He spluttered over the wall mirror, wiped his face with a coat sleeve and started taking an interest in his surroundings. I leaned back against the door. "I'm not the one to convince, Terry. I know you didn't murder Garfield. Or Jarrett either. But Jarrett was so contagious people are dying from his acquaintance and you know you could be next. It's why we're here. So tell me something that makes sense, because Garfield wasn't just a trick you met in the Raglan and you didn't get his name from a newspaper. He was set up. It couldn't have worked any other way. You got to talking, let him buy you a drink. You told him where to drive his car and where to pull over, and after he was hauled out of the car at the end of a gun you got out too, not to miss the excitement. What else?"

The door handle pressed and turned in the small of my back. A customer outside in the vestibule made a low groan.

Reilly rested his head against the wall mirror, coughing, wet and miserable.

"Nothing else. Jarrett had been watching Garfield around the bars for weeks, for Mr. Willard. That was nothing to do with me. I only did the pickup because I was told, and Jarrett didn't say anything about a gun. I never wanted any trouble."

But you don't have to want trouble, you just rub up against it and it multiplies. I nodded, but not encouragement. "Well that's grand. So now Garfield is dead, you're driving his car away from a murder scene and before the night's out his house gets turned over by somebody who has a key. I think the professor's keys were in the ignition of his car, Terry. I also think you knew his address, and from the river you could drive there in fifteen minutes."

Reilly moaned and rolled his forehead over the mirror, his biggest problem always to explain the simple things. "I never knew his address. I only drove his car back to Jarrett's and I didn't take any keys. All I took was his case off the back seat."

The latrine floor was a sump for the water slopping out of the washstand. The soles of my shoes were trying to blot it dry. But you can't always have your moments of clarity over sherry in the library. When Henry went away for the holiday, he'd left the Buccleuch as a present and slipped a Christmas card in the pages of his boyfriend's diary. Christmas Eve, Michael Garfield had carried them home from his office in the briefcase Reilly took from the back seat of his car. For Reilly, the Buccleuch would look like a gift-wrapped Scottish miracle, put there to settle his nerves. But when he showed his haul to Jarrett, it wouldn't be the liquor that interested him. I said, "Go on. Police searched Jarrett's house. They didn't find any briefcase. Or Garfield's diary inside it."

The door behind me rattled in the lock. A Popeye voice whined from the other side. "C'mon will ya? Hang it up in there!"

Reilly gulped at the rotted air. "When Jarrett got back, I told him what happened at the river and he started screaming at me. He said the diary was good, Mr. Willard would want it, but where I left Garfield's car was stupid and he'd have to move it."

It was the truth. On a blitz site two hundred yards along Cloth Fair, the convertible was a liability. It needed dumping far off and soon, and since Reilly was likely too hopped, Jarrett went himself and died so Reilly could live. Which was poetic of him. Reilly pressed his face flat against the mirror, gasping through his teeth. "I was watching from upstairs, waiting for Jarrett to come back, when the nurse walked into the court with somebody. It was snowing hard and I couldn't see his face, but when she went indoors and left him standing there, I knew." His cheeks gray as wax paper. "I knew it was the one who pulled the gun on Garfield."

So Reilly panicked for a second time that night, grabbed the briefcase and put Garfield's diary back inside, and the Buccleuch along with it because he wouldn't want to risk sobering up. He left by the fire escape, walked the City till daylight, then found a phone booth and left a message for Willard and got an answer right back. It told him: one, to stay away from Cloth Court because Jarrett was dead; two, that as of now he had a new address; and three, to be at the Raglan bar at noon with the briefcase and Garfield's diary. It left Reilly with the rest of Christmas morning on his hands. He made it sound like purgatory with no remission. Part of the morning he'd passed with Dillys Valentine and gave her what was left of the Buccleuch for a Christmas present of her own. Next, he looked up Irene at the hotel and took a loan to pay his bar bill while he waited at the Raglan. Then came his biggest holiday surprise of all, when Willard arrived at noonday to make the collection in person, on account of his close interest lately in the professor. A thin, clear, stream trickled from the corner of Reilly's mouth to the point of his chin, then pattered in the water in the washbasin. Outside, Popeye was hammering the door with the flat of his hand. "Jesus! You in there! You gotta problem?"

Reilly heaved and steadied himself. "Mr. Willard took the briefcase. He gave me money and said to stay at Paddy's because of what happened to Jarrett." He clamped his mouth shut, his features contorted in the glass.

"Go ahead. Make room for breakfast."

For two seconds you could hear the mold crawling up the walls. Then the boy's frame stiffened and convulsed into the washbasin. I slid a hand behind my back, loosed the door catch and stepped out into the vestibule.

A petty officer bristled in past me, short and solid with bulging eyes. At the threshold to the cubicle he halted abruptly, heeled around to look me up and down, then turned back to where Reilly was retching over the washstand like a trout taking a fly. The officer's mouth looped around a fat, wheezing chuckle. "Well, good afternoon lay-deeez!" He shouldered into the cubicle, unbuttoning. "Pardon me, sweetheart, but dis is oygent."

The hatcheck blonde was fixing her stocking run with nail varnish. At the head of the steps from the sidewalk, the Pelican's street sign lit green and red shadows under the porch. I stood breathing air again while the bird jigged on the sign overhead. Smoke trails lifted off chimneys that still had coal to burn. In the west, a winter sun was clipping the rooftops, turning snowdrifts liquid gold in one last flare of afternoon so bright it glued my eyelashes together. Just to feel the warmth on my face, I stepped to the corner of the porch, leaned back against a column and looked straight into the light. Sunset swam. A roman candle showered sparks behind my eyelids like metal pouring. Then knuckles cracked and a voice behind me, familiar and easy, said, "Red sky."

I twisted around, put a hand in front of my face and saw nothing but a dazzling, rippling crimson lake, and between it and me, three long, heavyset figures dancing in a row.

The first blow came high across my temple and bounced the side of my face off the stone pillar. The next and the next were put in low on my left side before I had chance to breathe. Three of them; one to take my wrists from behind and snap my arms back around the column, one to beat slow time into my ribs, deliberate as a swinging axe, and a third who only spoke two words and cracked his knuckles. They made unhurried business of it, strictly in a day's work, and when the beating alone was enough to pin me, the one behind let go my wrists.

My mouth filled with blood. My chin wedged in my collarbone. My knees locked and jammed me upright until the one doing all the work straightened up and sighed, discouraged by the monotony of it. He put his palm against my forehead, pushed my head up to look in my eyes, then grunted and turned away to straighten his necktie. My legs folded. I keeled and twisted sideways, pitched forward and went down scraping plaster off the column with my chin. Paint flakes rained on the ground around me, like confetti at a wedding. It was the last thing I remembered.

DISTILLATION OF A CORDIAL PROMISE

I was lying face down on a beach in a shallow pool, shivering and listening to the dragging tide. Above or below high water I couldn't tell, and what interest I had was theoretical because I was going no place. My left side had been worked over by somebody who practiced, I had a mouth and nose full of blood and grit, and I hadn't figured out how to spit yet, let alone crawl.

There had been haunted hours of the same chasing dreams, twisted shadow plays of scratching rats and witches' bedtime stories spinning in halls of mirrors, strange, unfriendly and impossible to grasp. They brought with them a smell of night at an ocean's edge, a lift and crunch of footfall, a voice fractured and dissolved beyond understanding, talking without letup in my ear. Then the footfall scuffed around me on the shingle, a hand scooped under my shoulder and shook it hard. The soft, crazed voice leaned closer and still made no more sense to me than weeping in a madhouse. No use. I was slipping sideways again, spiraling like a seashell in a rock pool. Not touching bottom but falling through mile-wide spaces I didn't know existed, in between wet grains of sand.

When I surfaced, I had my coat tucked under my chin for a blanket and a fire was cracking lazily nearby. The heat licked at my cheek and a sound of soft, low keening was making me curious. Not that curious, but enough to lift an eyelid and take a look around. Wide acres of a warehouse floated in the light from the fire. A plantation of cast iron columns stood shadowed in close rows. A roof pitched over studded beam sections stayed the weather directly overhead. The rest of the burned-out building was shattered and open to the stars, jittering under a hard frost. At the limit of the firelight a figure was sitting on the edge of a mattress, lean and hollowed, knees pulled up to his chest. He was tugging the ends of a blanket across the shoulders of a ragged blue suit, writing with a pencil stub on his shirt cuff one slow mark at a time. His tongue worked along his teeth as he wrote. Spittle trapped in the stubble under his lip. And from some Ypres or Delville Wood or Vimy Ridge or Paschendaele, every restless atom of his limbs danced the perpetual St. Vitus of shellshock. I lay watching him for a time, then looked around at the rest of the building.

A bonfire flared in the center of the floor where the old soldier camped out. In the shadows beyond, a line of blown-out windows hung high in a wall. At the foot of the wall there was a heap of charred planking, dragged out of the weather for fuel. A skinny mongrel with a tiger-stripe was snuffing around in it. Except for the three of us, what was left of the warehouse seemed deserted. Whatever company he kept in daytime, it was likely the soldier passed his chafing nights in solitary. Nobody would get any sleep otherwise. Not for the last thirty years. I lay back, started counting the pulses of a high, blue star beyond the roof ribs, and drifted out over the dark edge again, effortlessly.

There are spilled hours before dawn when the air tastes of tinplate. The shuttering blue star had set. My ribcage only hurt when I breathed out or breathed in and I was waiting for daybreak, sitting propped against an iron pillar in front of the dying fire. Each time I stirred, the soldier put away his pencil stub, picked up a rag and came over to squat down beside me. He had a can sunk in the embers at the edge of the flames, ready to reach out with the rag. We had a routine already. The soldier knelt down, wiped a thumb across two holes punched in the rim and put the can in my hands; condensed milk, warmed-over, thick enough to lay bricks with and sweeter than molasses. I held it on my knees in the rag, waiting for the metal to cool, one eye on the soldier's dog flat out on his side with his paws crossed. Tiger twitched an earflap now and then to show he'd got me covered, but I'd been around long enough not to bother him anymore. I tried working out how long.

Two days' growth on my chin said I'd lost thirty-six hours; making five days since Jarrett was murdered, three weeks or more since he began following Michael Garfield around the fruit bars on Willard's orders. Yet on Christmas Day, when Willard already knew Garfield was likely dead, he'd been interested enough in the professor's diary to meet Reilly at the Raglan himself. The dead don't blackmail. It followed that whatever Willard had in view, Michael Garfield wasn't the target. I drained the can. A halting dawn was bleaching out the heavens. "It's getting light, soldier. Better show me where we are." The soldier looked up from writing on his cuff, crossed the blanket tighter across his chest and got up from the mattress. He stooped to pull the coat off me, put it over his arm, slid his free hand under my elbow and lifted me up in one clean, unfussed move that knocked the breath out of me. I leaned hard against him, let him set the coat around my shoulders and feed my good arm in a sleeve and button me in. The other he let hang loose at my side. When it was done, I nodded at the twisted metal frame of a window sixty feet away. "Over there. Let's take a look." The dog stretched and yawned and uncrossed his paws, decided I was too sorry to worry about, then heaved on his feet and followed over anyway.

The window was a pallid square of dawn looking out to the river from the north shore, six floors up and a few hundred feet downstream from the Tower. Derricks moved over the wharves across the water. The malt taint of a brewery carried on the breeze. In the middle of the river, a tugboat worked at keeping a freighter steady while the bridge raised, and on the bridge approach a line of vehicles waited and cut their motors to save gas. It could have been any grudging daybreak between Christmas and New Year, and not more than a couple of miles south and east of the Pelican Club. I sank into the soldier's grip under my arm. A hundred feet below, uncovered by the tide, a small bay of gravel sand ran wet along the river wall. I asked, "That's where they left me?" The hand tightened around my arm, pulled away from the view and manhandled me across the angle of the building. We skirted rubble from the wrecked end wall, moved along a line of iron supports, got to the last window on the east side of the warehouse and stopped there, scuffing splintered glass across the floor. Below us stretched the three connecting basins of St. Katherine's Dock, its lock gates spilling tidewater back into the river. And round about the dock, twenty more acres of burned-out warehouses like the one the soldier called home. On the December night the Luftwaffe put a match to them they'd been filled with raw rubber. The fires had set a low, stinking pall across the City, blotting out daylight for a week. Every brick in every warehouse and rubble heap around the dock still oozed the smell of it. A dozen ragged shadows had arrived with the dawn, circled the bonfire behind us and set a pan to boil. They looked over without interest or surprise. I followed the soldier's gaze across the view and shook my head. "Not here, soldier. You didn't pull me out of the water. There was shingle. I remember a beach."

The soldier stared out across the desolation with me and lurched his free hand toward the window frame, his index finger crooked to point at what I was missing. I peered out over the sill and down. Right there beneath the window, sitting low in the water, an abandoned river lighter was tied up in the lock, its deck level with the foot of an iron ladder climbing down from the dockside. A low ridge of gravel ballast filled the open hold. I tasted grit in my mouth again, smelled tidewater slopping in the dock, heard sluices spraying inside the lock gates and saw my shingle beach. No lights down there. The dock would be invisible from that window after dark. But no vehicle could get anyplace close, and they'd been dumping a deadweight. The soldier wouldn't see, but he might hear them hauling me, get curious and go looking. I turned around. He had his teeth clenched, his throat strained taut as piano wire, chin jutting at the shadow figures in the firelight. The wild labor of finding a voice shook his whole frame. "Strairr-rrr. Strairrr-tch. *N-N-Nggggh.* Strairrrr-tch-tcher." The effort left the soldier quivering like a watch spring. His dog fidgeted and whimpered.

I put a hand over the hand steadying me. "Easy. Take it easy. I know what you did." From where I was dumped on the ballast in the lighter, there wasn't a chance he could get me up six floors. Not unless he organized the shuffling ghosts from the campfire into a stretcher party before they left him for the night. They would oblige. There wouldn't be a way to tell him no. And while we looked out the window and let the soldier settle, I gave some thought to Voigt. Not Voigt in his own house and on his own time, averse to company and shy of social graces, but Voigt who could take instructions, stay sober and dress for work, so sure he was untouchable he couldn't help but introduce himself. *Red Sky.*

I reached for the soldier's free hand, took his wrist and slid back his jacket sleeve. There were no words written there. No numbers or letters. Only pencil marks from a Rosetta stone, pressed deep in the flannel of his shirt cuff. We looked each other in the eyes. "I'll be back, soldier. Write it down." I patted the hand he still had on my arm, prized out of his grip and moved in the direction the ghosts around the fire had appeared from.

THIRTY-THREE

I pulled a clean shirt and necktie from the chest of drawers at the foot of my bed, slid the drawer shut with my knee and nudged the light off with an elbow. In the bathroom I peeled down to the waist by degrees, ran water on a hand towel and dabbed around the dark hatching covering my left side. Then I shaved and buttoned into the shirt, knotted the tie in a noose and looped it over my head, pulled up the loop one-handed and folded down the soft collar. I stepped back from the mirror to take the effect. Not bad. My jaw was advertising its brush with the Pelican's porch, the ripe plum behind my ear was toughening into a prune, and if I kept my left hand propped in my jacket pocket I could pass for Dickie Mountbatten. I turned away from the glass, walked to the sitting room, picked up the telephone and dialed. "Good afternoon, Doctor."

A small catch of surprise came like static down the wire. Kathryn Swinford said brightly, "My goodness, we haven't spoken in ages! There is *such* a lot to tell you I hardly know where to begin."

"Then listen. I heard Blanche's boy ran into McAlester. Does he still walk?

"What? Oh no, no he doesn't. But would you mind awfully holding the line?" I dropped the receiver on the sofa and went to the kitchen, found Louis' aspirin bottle and carried it back. I had the telephone clamped under my chin when a low, fierce whisper broke in. "Newman? Oh, for heaven's sake!"

"Here. Company gone?"

"Yes."

"And Henry?"

She hesitated. "I was called in late on Sunday afternoon to make an examination. There are fractures, all sorts of bruising, possibly internal hemorrhage. He'll survive, but McAlester is an animal and what he did frightened even Littomy. So I did some frightening of my own. I told Littomy Henry needed immediate hospital attention and he had him sent to Bart's within the hour, with a police guard at the door. It's an outrage. Where on earth have you been?"

You were always searching for English she would understand. "A pressing engagement came up. I need to talk to Guy Beaufort." I chewed aspirin while she took it in.

"What good would it do? Guy is so appalled he's ready to believe you set up the whole thing for McAlester. I've told him it's ridiculous, but I doubt he'll listen to you or anyone now without his lawyer present. I imagine that's not what you had in mind."

I had a picture of her seated on the edge of Templeton's chair, forehead knitted, serious in patent shoes, the telephone cord wrapped around a little finger and her shoulder parting her hair where it fell. On the desk in front of her a crystal paperweight with two crossed hockey sticks, *Truth* engraved on one of them, *Beauty* on the other. I said "Doctor, Henry's about to go down for a killing spree. If you're there, Guy Beaufort will listen."

I saw her finger the paperweight, chewing the corner of her lip. "Guy hasn't been going into the office. When do you want to see him?"

Early afternoon. The room already in twilight. I switched on a lamp beside the sofa. "I can be at his home in an hour. There's something I need you to do first."

What the Beauforts called home was a picture out of a nursery tale, the one about the lady hedgehog who put on her bonnet and mittens to go visiting, then left her basket behind and just knew it was going to be that sort of day. Sharp-pitched gables and shingle roofs, tall chimneys and creeper, spread wide against a framing acre of box hedge and beech wood. Rhododendron-edged lawns dropped to a high brick wall at the roadside, and across a one-car lane it overlooked a part of the heath rolling toward Hampstead, deep in snow.

Kathryn Swinford's car swung in through the entrance and climbed the drive to the front porch. I stepped out from behind the gate post to trail it uphill, and by the time she cut the motor I was level and had the door open, breathing hard. Her calf stretched across the running board. She got out and tucked a purse under her arm, looked along the house frontage while I slammed the Austin's door. "I telephoned Guy. He's not ecstatic but he's expecting us." Her glance took in the side of my face. "Do you know, every time I feel like socking you on the jaw, I have to remind myself there's a queue."

A manservant wearing a black necktie and a long dustcoat opened the door, saw the doctor standing there and brightened his smile. She called him Ernest and walked ahead with him to the end of a beamed hall, where a frowning retriever filled a rug in front of a log fire. Ernest turned and waited to take our coats. He was attentive, answered her as if she still wore ribbons in her plaits and braces on her teeth, and when she told him she would announce herself to Mr. Beaufort he said he would show me in the study and bring some tea. "With lemon and sugar, Miss Kathryn?"

"Thank you, Ernest. Mr. Beaufort and Mr. Newman will both take a straight whisky."

He said, "Of course, Miss Kathryn," and the retriever sneezed and beat dust out of the rug with its tail.

Beaufort's study had the English look of being put together by a color-blind eccentric; broad and long, accommodated with faded chairs, scattered with old magazines and musty with the smell of beeswax and pipe tobacco. Set against the wall by the door was a workbench with chests for storing plans at either side, a drawing board angled in the center of the bench and a high chair turned aside from it. The shade of a desk lamp was pushed flat against a drawing on the board. In the wall opposite, a brick hearth hissed with wet logs and kept the room warmed over. I walked to a pair of French doors at the long end of the study and parted the slats of a blind. Out beyond a glass conservatory, a stand of beech cut the failing daylight from the room. A tall clock ticked off seconds in the gloom behind me, weary for the excitement of the quarter-hour.

Henry Beaufort had gotten his build and his looks from his mother. Her portrait hung full-length in a recess beside the hearth. It showed a fashionably dazed young beauty from the roaring years, sparking jewelry everyplace she could find a pulse, languid in a shimmering red ball gown and up-tilting a wishbone chin. Two vertical rows of photographs at left and right of the picture frame only helped make her look more ethereal. They were group pictures taken at around the same time, of pale company men and ascetic bankers rigid in black-tie, keeping a yard of daylight between them in case easy fellowship might be contagious. A younger, brasher Guy Beaufort was in every one, gazing directly at the camera, looking so cocksure of himself he was risking being blackballed.

"Guy will be down in a moment." Kathryn Swinford shut the door behind her, looking uneasy and fingering a brooch on the collar of an olive-green tailor-made.

I nodded at the portrait on the wall. "Blanche is the real McCoy."

She glanced at the painting and gave it a faint smile. "Blanche is the real Delaware. They're a soldiering family. There was a Delaware with Marlborough at Blenheim, another with Wolfe at Quebec; they charged at Balaclava and were chums with General Gordon in China. Not to mention excelling in two first-rate world wars."

She settled in an armchair at a cartwheel table in the recess. I moved to the workbench and pushed the desk lamp aside from the drawing taped on the board. It showed a clean, wide cityscape where tall blocks of residences stood weightless in acres enough for a deer park, and where whoever toiled with their hands or sweated over a machine was making sure to do it someplace else, because at the foot of the residences, down among the ornamental lakes, there were only passersby strolling in eternal springtime and old men sitting under shade trees patting small children on the head. A box stenciled in the bottom right corner read, *Cripplegate Area Development, E.W. Levin for Beaufort Partners.* I said, "Blanche married an architect. Where did it all go wrong?"

From where I stood, she was invisible, wrapped in the wings of the armchair. "You really shouldn't underestimate Guy. He's very well respected. Those may be Edgar Levin's designs, but even before the rubble was cleared it was Guy who persuaded Corporation bigwigs they had to modernize. I think the whole idea still rather petrifies them."

I went back over to the French doors, looked out past the beech trees swaying in late afternoon light and wondered aloud, "Why would they worry? They don't expect to be moving in there any more than the Beauforts do. From here they'll walk out on Hampstead Heath and those towers won't even be a cloud on the horizon."

"Newman!" She hissed the word. Then as if we were thumbing through a Corporation press announcement, "Cripplegate will have its own concert hall, art gallery, schools, a theater. It's all going to be rather splendid." I dropped the wood slats and turned around, to where Guy Beaufort was holding the study door open and Ernest was pushing past him with a trolley, his dustcoat swapped for a linen jacket. Beaufort looked short on sleep, rumpled in a high-buttoned suit and a bow tie. Kathryn Swinford patted an armchair to have him sit beside her. The retriever waddled in behind him and flopped at his feet. Ernest switched on lights around the room, set a tea tray on the cartwheel table and brought over two large whiskies from the trolley. The doctor squeezed lemon in her teacup and looked around the party as Ernest ghosted out the door.

I picked up my glass, raised it an inch to let the liquor catch the fire glow, and in the way of a toast said, "Twelve-year Buccleuch." Kathryn Swinford sat slowly upright and turned in her chair. Beaufort's chin came up off his chest. "Until four days ago, I never heard the name before I read it in one of Dr. Swinford's files. I didn't know it was this year's Beaufort Christmas gift either, or who got sent a bottle and who didn't. But it hardly matters. Only one bottle is a problem. The night Professor Garfield was murdered, he took a passing interest in a boy named Terry Reilly. The law about that being what it is, they drove down to the river in Garfield's car to get to know each other better. From there on, everything that could go wrong, did. The professor was murdered, Reilly drove the car back to the City in a panic, and when he got there took Garfield's briefcase off the back seat. One of the things the briefcase had in it was the professor's diary. The other was a bottle of your twelve-year Buccleuch that Henry gave him for a Christmas present." I put the glass down on the table. "Next morning, a sometime streetwalker named Dillys Valentine was murdered with a sheared-off bottle of Buccleuch whisky. Miss Valentine was a friend of Reilly's. He'd visited her that morning and left the whisky as winter comfort, with no more idea of handling a murder weapon than Henry had when he took it to give to his boyfriend. But that won't save your son, Mr. Beaufort. As of now, he's not only under police guard, they've got his prints on the bottle. They don't know that yet, but when they do, they'll decide the whole story is a wrap: Henry caught his boyfriend cheating with Raymond Jarrett, put the whisky in his pocket for morale and went on a murder spree. Facts that don't fit, evidence they don't have, will be nothing but inconvenience."

Guy Beaufort leaned forward in his armchair, hearing how it would sound to a jury. His dog heaved out from under the seat, put his chin on the squab and listened with him. "Mr. Beaufort, you took time out of your Christmas ball to warn me Henry was off-limits and how one call to the commissioner could put me out of business. Maybe it could have, but it started me wondering what made you so nervous. Then I learned Willard had been having the professor followed and photographed for weeks, and by the night of the ball he even had his diary. Henry featured in it all. I think Willard told you that and gave you the chance to keep a lid on the boy's indiscretions. The question is what he wanted in return. You could tell me what, here and now, or we could all finish our drinks over small talk about this weather we're having, forget about Henry's prints being at the Valentine murder and count on forensics not noticing. Which is it to be?"

A green log spat in the hearth. No other sound than the lick of firelight. Kathryn Swinford's voice, fainter than the light in the room, murmured, "Guy, I knew nothing of this. I'm really very sorry."

Beaufort blinked as if she'd snapped her fingers at him, then sank the contents of his glass, dabbed a knuckle at his lip and said, "Mr. Willard wanted Edgar Levin to stay away from his wife. He advised me to speak to him about it at once. Nothing more."

Put that way, it not only sounded uncomplicated, it sounded reasonable. Beaufort only had to take his star partner in hand and Willard would put the pictures and the diary on ice. With the boy's name and future at stake, Edgar Levin would do the decent thing. He wouldn't see he had a choice. And coming from Willard, the idea was a lot subtler than having Levin's good arm broken. I shifted in my seat, raised an eyebrow at Kathryn Swinford and we both stood up. She stepped around the table and rested a hand on Beaufort's shoulder. "Ernest will see us out. Remember me to Blanche when you see her next." Ernest already had the study door open and two coats over his arm. You doubted his boss noticed anybody was leaving.

Kathryn Swinford pulled the Austin over at the edge of Hampstead village in front of the single, rusted pump of a motor garage. The forecourt was closed up, the heavy wooden doors of a repair shop nailed shut with a sale board. She stopped the motor and left on the car's sidelights, shivered in the silence and pulled a silk choker up under her chin. The Austin's engine clicked as it cooled. An underslung moon was rising on the late afternoon.

"Please pass my gloves." I looked along the dash, gritted my teeth and shuffled around to search the back seat. "Try the glove compartment." I twisted around, paused to get breath and opened the glovebox, took out a pair of dark kid gauntlets and handed them over. Salt sweat trickled in the corner of my eye. "Not much of you still works, does it?" She leaned across me to close up the lid. "Where did it happen?"

I turned half toward her, my shoulder wedged between the seatback and the car door, cradling the arm. "A Soho flytrap called the Pelican. I found Reilly there and ran into somebody else who was looking."

"Someone with a name?"

"Voigt."

She wrapped the skirt of her coat around her ankles. "What would Voigt want with Terry Reilly?"

I watched her busy with the gloves, fastening them at her wrists and flexing her fingers as if she were next man in to bat. "Reilly was around Jarrett. Enough to know who supplied the clients and the blackmail targets, the picture studio and the protection. Willard put him in a safe place, but the boy understood that being in Jarrett's circle can be life-shortening. It made him restless. So he skipped and went looking for a friend, who happens be Voigt's daughter. She's gritty, determined, also persuasive, and she called me to say Reilly would be at the Pelican, ready to talk." I eased upright in the seat until my head hit the roof lining. "So we talked. Then outside I walked into Voigt. He hadn't come alone."

The doctor tilted back against the side window looking serious, green-lit in the glow from the dash. "Voigt arriving at the Pelican can't have been coincidence."

I didn't think it could be coincidence either. And the tall cadaver taking so little interest had to be a phony. "Word was out. Reilly had been marked before I got there. I'm guessing McAlester told Willard to get the boy off the street and Voigt was sent to collect him. Running into me was cream in his coffee."

Kathryn Swinford sat up abruptly, an elbow crooked on the wheel. "Willard sent Voigt because McAlester told him to? Why would he?"

"Because the only way McAlester can take Henry down for four murders is if everybody forgets about Terry Reilly. Remember him? He's the one who knew all four victims, the last to see two of them alive. And still it's a name nobody raises in police time. The last thing McAlester needed was for some vice detail to pick him up by chance, working a late bar." Headlights swept around the bend behind us, spangled the frost on the sale board, turned the insides of the Austin into a fishbowl and passed on. I watched them around the next bend. "Reilly can connect Jarrett to Michael Garfield. Also to McAlester, who likely recruited Jarrett the first time he ran across him, seven years ago. Added to that, he can connect all three to Willard. Now that Willard has him back, running out a second time will not be in his stars."

"And where does Littomy stand in all this?" Her breath misted the windshield while she thought her own question over. Moisture pricked beads on the cold metal dash. "We'd better go, before I ask why you waited to tell me about this damned whisky bottle in front of Guy. That was below the belt Detective. I thought we had an understanding about things I'm entitled to know. How naive of me." The starter motor cranked, teetered and gave out in a dry cough. She flipped the choke and tried again, and then a third time, groaned and sat back. Her hand dug in a door pocket for Garfield's cast-off report to the councilor's committee. "You were right about these. Henry had them with him when he ran into McAlester. They were at the back of his file. I daresay no one had the least idea what to do with them. My Greek's too rusty. How's yours?" It wasn't an inquiry. The words ground between her teeth while she squared the sheets and dropped them in my lap, her gaze held flat on the windshield. "Next time you need assistance with police matters, write to the commissioner."

Her left hand yanked the starter-pull again. The car shook on its springs. I folded Garfield's report and opened my coat, got the narrow, translucent envelope between the tips of two fingers and flipped it out of my pocket as the Austin's motor heaved and caught. Kathryn Swinford's brow melted. She sat back again, puffed out her cheeks and let the motor hum at a fast idle. I propped the airplane film on the dash in front of her. "I need these made into prints, Doctor, large and clear." Slowly and without enthusiasm, the way she would open a can of whale meat, she slipped the strip of curling negatives out of its envelope, flattened it on the hub of the steering wheel and held it up against the dashboard light. Her nose pinched, her mouth set in a pressed white line and her eyelids shuttered as if she saw her soul burning in hellfire. I said, "Better do it for Blanche."

The motor gunned. She grabbed her purse off the seat between us and flipped the clasp, pushed the strip of film inside and snapped it shut. Her wrist worked at finding a gear. "And the prints her son left on a murder weapon? What am I supposed to do about those?"

But if either of us had an answer to that, we wouldn't have been sitting freezing in her car. "You'll think of something."

The clutch bit hard and slammed me against the door, clawing at my shoulder. She circled the Austin tight around the garage forecourt and swung it back up the hill into Hampstead.

THIRTY-FOUR

Bunny Lush's Academy leased the floor over a commercial laundry in Bride's Alley, a cobblestone passage that took a dogleg off the south side of Fleet Street, ran eighty yards and found it had no place else to go. He kept the Academy spare: a regulation ring with benches for spectators around three sides, speed balls along the fourth, floor mats frayed with sweat and rubbing alcohol and heavy bags strung from the ceiling in front of a whitewashed window. More than that Bunny said was decoration, and he didn't need to tout custom. He was right. Lush's Academy was flypaper for any fighter aiming to train in the warm glow of silk stockings and gasps of admiration. It was a haunt of showgirls and hangers-on, and it did no harm at all that Fleet Street was just a sports writer's stumble along the alley. Not that the fight pages made a difference to Bunny. He hadn't read them in thirty years. He said for his money, sports hacks one and all could kiss his ringside seat and go spit on somebody else's floor.

Boxing had been good to Bunny. Very likely it also saved his life. In 1915 Kitchener's army had been all-out for recruits, but when it found one with a pig iron jaw and a right cross that could stop a light truck, there wasn't the ghost of a chance his service career would be wasted fighting Germans. Instead, Lance Corporal Lush passed his army years in a depot kitchen in Palestine, boxing middleweight for his regiment and collecting the two outsize ears that earned him his nickname. He'd also collected agoraphobia, a forty-two-inch waist, flat feet and a rare and unsightly form of venereal disease known only to Bedouin. But that was all right by Bunny. He'd seen what else Palestine had to offer, and was relieved when his army chaplain told him it had already been promised to Abraham. What he didn't expect was that it would be the agoraphobia that called time on the fights. A kind of paralysis set in when he left his corner, so that in a strange ring under bright lights it was like being back at the edge of the desert with the ropes dancing in the afternoon heat; so mesmerizing, he was taking knockdowns before he could raise a glove. So Bunny quit the ring, and decided a training gym was his only way to carry on breathing canvas, sweat and resin. The way he saw it, the army had taught him two trades, and no civilian on six continents was going to pay money for his cooking.

The street door to the Academy led up a single-rise stair, twisted right and passed a glassed-in office and a thickening in the air. Beyond a locker room was a ring under a haze of overhead lights. In the out-of-hours of a winter afternoon there were no onlookers, only two men in shorts and undershirts cuffing at each other and raising dust with their footwork. Bunny Lush was the one with no expression and a nose spread across his cheekbones, a military back-and-sides and a forty-pound advantage. He was back-pedaling in a lazy circle, elbows pinned either side of his stomach and flat on his feet, taking shots from the other man on the heels of his raised gloves. Once in a while he looped a low right under the other man's guard, careful not to break sweat. The figure following him around the ring was twenty years younger and not any prettier to watch. He pushed awkward, straight lefts into the waiting gloves, crowded in each time to catch his balance, then got back up on his toes to throw another left. I walked to the ringside while the two men took another turn around, clinched, broke off and touched gloves. Bunny turned and ambled to the corner where I stood, climbed out through the ropes and stepped down next to me with the bounce of a sandbag. He put a gloved thumb up to my chin and took a professional look at the side of my face. "Anybody I know?"

"Anybody you know would have made a better job."

Bunny's tortured nose crinkled. He flipped my chin aside, turned in the direction of the glass office and said, "Next time make him lead. Stay in shape."

I watched him go and thought, in shape or not, I had four inches height and reach over Bunny and the only way to put him on the floor would be to shoot him. A voice behind me said, "You're here to talk to *me*?" Edgar Levin was leaning over the top rope, looking around the deserted gym for any other possibility. He had a limp towel draped across his shoulders and a mouth guard hooked under the thumb of his glove, his head lolling and his chest still heaving from the ring work.

I glanced up at him and nodded. "About Willard. Your office said to try here." Levin blinked in the lights and waited to have it explained. "I already talked to Mrs. Willard. She doesn't flatter her husband, but her story doesn't add up. I think you would know about him." The staleness of the room itched at my throat.

Levin steadied his breathing and said, "Born Benjamin Josef Wilhardt. Quite right, I know about him." He spelled out the last name and followed with the history of an East End Jewish boy with a bad lung, who made a mark in the rackets and then climbed the ladder catering to more expensive tastes. Along the way, Wilhardt became Willard, a club owner passing for legitimate if you didn't have to be rigid about it, with a grade of associates and interests that made him hoodlum aristocracy even before war broke out. The lung that caused him to miss the shooting held up well enough. It let him move in on the City's black market and cut out a share all his own. By 1942 he had an interest in every freight shipment north of the river, and owned a string of burlesque and clip joints magnetic to the US Army dollar. It was no secret. So when Willard introduced himself one night in the blackout, when the councilor and his daughter were dining at one of his tables, they already knew the score. Mrs. Willard had admitted as much. But then a family need arose at a time when she wasn't in a mood to care, and she went ahead and married him anyway.

"For that," Levin said, "you can blame me." He caught up both ends of the towel in his fist, dried under his jaw and hung his arm out over the ropes. I turned his glove over, unlaced it and pulled it off, then dropped it on the canvas and stripped the bandage off his hand and wound it around my fingers. The way Levin told it, by 1942 Willard was already looking beyond the duration, to a time when he would dress in quieter suits, live on an elegant street and even pay some income taxes. Setting eyes on Councilor Drake's handsome, distracted daughter that night had filled out most of the rest. When he introduced himself and she looked straight through him, what he recognized in her was class, and buying some of her kind of class was a part of Willard's plan for peacetime.

I thought about Mrs. Willard, drowning in the cocktail she was shaking with the devil, slipped the roll of bandage off my fingers and tossed it beside the glove on the canvas. "Why would I blame you? The lady doesn't. According to her, the councilor lost everything in the blitz, Willard stepped up to rescue the family fortune and marriage was her part in the payoff."

A ceiling fan flapped. Dust eddied in the lights overhead. Levin spread his hand, flexed the stiffened knuckles and snorted. Not as if the idea amused him, but as if the notion of Drake getting cleaned out by the bombing had something ridiculous about it. "I've heard her story. Her father was and is a land speculator in high political office. He didn't need rescuing, then or now. On the contrary, the blitz turned the City into a vast construction site, ready and waiting for the councilor to make his next killing. Drake lied to his own daughter. I have no idea why."

I dipped the center rope. Levin held the stub of his arm and climbed down from the ring, dropped from the apron and stepped to where the heavy bags hung off the ceiling. He set himself square to one of them, put in four hard, short lefts, then leaned in with his right shoulder like a bird trailing a wing. He twisted around with the bag to keep balance. I shrugged. "Maybe not, but promising to stay away from her would be sporting of you. And not only for getting Henry off a hook. Garfield was on the Corporation payroll and Willard's pictures of him fritzing his young assistant would make them a scandal. You know they owe you. You also know it won't mean a thing come the day City Police take Henry down for murder. Drake's committee will back away from Beaufort Partners in the blink of an eye."

Levin steadied the scuffed leather with his hand and sagged against it, breathing hard. "Oh, come on, Newman, keep up. Drake has already backed away." He put in another crabbed shot, higher and harder, hissed with the effort and lined up the next.

I took a step and swung the bag aside before he broke his hand on it, waited while he wiped sweat out of his eyes and asked, "Why would he do that?"

Levin dropped his arm at his side and sighed as if I ought to start writing some of this down. "Out of the blue Drake telephoned Guy on Christmas Eve, with news that Garfield might have made another big discovery and we were to stop all work." He went over to claw the glove and the bandage off the canvas. "Quite a Christmas present. Who knew what Garfield might turn up? Another find like his Roman fort would delay us indefinitely."

Except now Michael Garfield was dead, and the radio talks, the columns in the press, the high-society arm-twisting, would all die with him. Drake's committee never would see his report, and if the councilor decided it was business as usual, who was there to argue? Levin moved off across the gym headed for the locker room. From his office, Bunny was switching out the lights row by row. Just to stir the flyblown emptiness, I said out loud, "Business as usual." And waited on the echo, *business as usual …as usual …as usual.*

THIRTY-FIVE

I hailed a taxi on Fleet Street and headed east in a freezing
mist that smeared the lighted office windows and followed
me inside the cab. At Ludgate the cab made a left into
Farringdon, along the same crawl of storefronts Henry had
followed in the Morgan, then ran under Holborn Viaduct and
swung left again into the jewelry quarter. Streetlights thinned,
the goldsmith and gem trader lockups were already closing for
the night. The taxi slowed and made its next turn. I dragged
a sleeve across the side window and took in the stores on
a street I didn't recognize at first, then lunged at the glass
behind the driver's head and hammered for him to pull over. I
sat crouched forward, recalling the frontages the cab had just
driven by. There was the charred brick facade of a fire-bombed
charity school, a canvas blind flapping over a shuttered café,
a silversmith, name and initials etched across a rubbed glass
window that turned the light inside the showroom to a sodium
glow. And then there had been an outfitter's shop behind a
curved window set back from a step, with a slim mannequin
on show inside the curve: trim cardigan, silk blouse, pencil
skirt; dressed for a manor house on a fall afternoon. I paid off
the cab and let myself out on the street.

Right inside the outfitter's shop door there was a second mannequin, another county type sporting an Eden moustache and plus fours, a bow tie, a newsboy cap in plaid and scarf to match. He had his hands cupped in front of his stomach holding a card printed with snowflakes that read, *Selected Seasonal Sportswear for the Discerning Countryman.* Gaslight puttered in glass shades along the walls and soured the air. Except for the discerning countryman promoting his plus fours, the store was as empty as the street outside.

The outfitter's was a single room with a counter of glass cabinets running front to back along one side. The wall opposite had a tall cashier's desk with a high chair under it and framed advertisements for garment manufacturers strung beneath the gaslights. Behind the glass counter, a wall lined with shelves had a library step for reaching down merchandise, from the years when the store had merchandise to reach. Scarcity being what it was, all the seasonal sportswear it could muster was ranged along the countertop in plain, flat boxes labeled for size. I lifted the lid off the nearest while the doorbell went on tinkling on its spring.

In time, a white-haired old lady drew aside a curtain in the store's back wall and peered out. She was spare and a little stooped, handsome in a loose-fitting two-piece and a string of garnet beads, smiling faintly out of faded blue eyes behind her half-glasses. Once she spotted me the novelty of a new customer seemed to surprise her, but she took it in stride, closed the drape and moved unhurried to stand behind the cashier's desk. She stroked the high chairback with knotted hands, ran her eyes over the side of my jaw and cleared her throat to help her concentrate. "From a Scottish woolen mill and not your size I'm afraid. I always tell the manufacturers they must think everyone is built like a crofter. Anyway, I imagine they must be terribly itchy to sleep in and I'm quite sure you would find a cotton nightshirt much more comfortable."

"Mrs. Mayhew?"

I put the lid back on the box, slid the box back where I found it and took off my hat. She gave me a smile of exquisite tenderness from a serener world. "Yes indeed. But I am sorry. Nowadays I have no memory at all for faces."

A receipt pad lay in among the patterns and magazines on the glass counter. I picked it up and flicked through. At the head of each one of the receipts a couple strode out arm in arm across a bracken moor in matching tweeds, and under their feet the same legend I'd seen from the passing taxicab lettered across the shop window. I opened out the pad and took it over to where we both could read it. *Mayhew's of Hatton Garden, Outfitters to Gentlefolk.* "We haven't met before, and it might be coincidence, but in wartime there was a Mrs. Jeanne Mayhew who ran an officers' charity. I was wondering ..."

She gave me the surprised, faraway look again and went on stroking the chairback, pleased to be found out. "Why yes of course, that was me. We were a small charity assisting with uniform. With the approval of the services, naturally." I nodded, naturally. "It was such an expensive item for young officers to buy. Then there were the families whose sons and daughters had been killed. We were a go-between trying to help both. The whole thing has entirely wound down now, thank goodness. But is it really what you wanted? An officer's uniform?" Her lips pressed together in a small mischief. "One does have to *be* an officer to qualify, you know."

"Reduced to ranks for impersonating one."

She crinkled her eyes and made a high, soft mewing in her throat. "Untrue, I'm sure. Now what uniform had you in mind?"

I said flight lieutenant, on hardly more than a hunch. In a trunk in a spare room in the house on Cloth Court, Nurse Greer had kept a private collection dedicated to Flight Lieutenant Ross: his squadron necktie, braid and field cap, and his service shirts pressed and folded alongside the dresses she wore for him once. Just not his uniform. Even though Central Depository had listed it for return. It was all the hunch amounted to; Charlie Ross's uniform had been sacrificed to a good cause, otherwise it would still have been there in the trunk, along with the rest of her collection.

Mrs. Mayhew touched the beads at her throat and maneuvered into the cashier's chair, lifted out a ledger from a drawer and slammed it square on the desk. Her teeth gritted with the effort. "Every item donated was written in here quite religiously, therefore anything not crossed through must still be in our storeroom, mustn't it?" She took out a flat wooden rule from the drawer, then opened the ledger at the first double page, dropped her eyeglasses on their silver chain around her neck and bent over the entries one line at a time, recollecting as she went. "One has no idea where these things will lead. Our eldest grandson was so very young when he was killed, and it seemed terribly morbid to let his uniform simply rot away. Better offer it to another young officer, we thought, without the slightest idea so many others would feel the same way. The response was so overwhelming we soon registered as a charity."

It took a while. Mrs. Mayhew was past halfway in her ledger when she came across an entry she paused at, then let out a small squeal of triumph. "Well, can you believe it? According to our records we do still have two tunics, a dress cap and a raincoat. Not quite your size either, alas, but all of them kindly donated by…" She put the glasses back on and leaned away from the ledger to get the name in her sights. "a Mr. Greer."

The hollow drum of a passing truck rattled the street door in its frame. Her finger tapped an entry at the foot of her page and she read off an initial and address. For no reason except to set her record straight, I said, "*Miss* Greer. She was a nurse at Bart's hospital."

Mrs. Mayhew checked a note pinned at the side of the ledger. "Well, if you're sure. But I shouldn't have thought so. You see, if it were a Miss Greer, our ledger says she purchased an overcoat from us at the same time. We made an alteration to it. There." She drew out the pin to show me her instructions, and a line of hand-blocked capitals that read,

Bryant Overcoat. For Collection E. Greer. "A Bryant is not a lady's overcoat. Mr. Bryant and his nephew were exclusively gentlemen's tailors, bombed out of their premises years ago. Such a shame, though some of their items were quite undamaged, and when they were put up for sale, we bought several. Ordinarily of course we would not expect to sell townwear, but in those days I employed a young assistant who thought we should make an exception. It was so beautifully made, and anything other than the dreadful Utility wear was scarcely obtainable." The pale eyes became distant. She gave her idea some more room. "Miss Greer might have bought it as a gift for a gentleman I suppose, but really, it would have taken so many of her clothing coupons. She must have liked it very much. And here am I, not able to remember a single thing about her. It's too bad of me."

Mrs. Mayhew twisted around a bracelet, slack on her wrist, to squint at a tiny watch face getting tinier with every passing year. When she had it in line with the bridge of her nose, her mouth made a loop. "Gracious, it's six-fifteen! Please forgive me while I shut up shop. Young assistants, I'm afraid, are quite a thing of the past." She put away the ledger, got on her feet and dragged the library step to the street door, took a long moment peering at the last passersby and turned the *Closed* sign on its cord. Then she climbed her step and drew the blind level with her shins.

I let her climb back down and park the step before I wondered out loud if we were too late to wrap up the plaid scarf. She reached it on tiptoe from around the dummy's shoulders, with the secret smile that said she knew it was sold the minute I walked in. It was string-tied, paid for and receipted before I asked, "Mrs. Mayhew, the Bryant overcoat Nurse Greer bought. Do you remember its color?"

She rested her wrists on the edge of the desk like a small bird at a birdbath, looking frailer than when I arrived, her mouth trembling from the adrenalin of making a sale. "Such an elegant dark chocolate, lined in gold silk, how could I forget? It's so maddening that I can remember the coat and not the lady who bought it. I do wish there were another like it to show you. I'm quite certain it would suit you wonderfully."

I pulled a disappointed mouth. "I'll keep a lookout. Maybe there were other outfitters buying when the Bryant stock got sold off."

The notion amazed her. She touched her fingertips over her heart to calm the flutter, then aired her serene smile on me one last time and explained how there wouldn't be another like it for an outfitter to buy, because Bryant & Nephew were bespoke tailors, and no matter what garment, they never would think of making two the same. Mrs. Mayhew thought she could speak for his nephew just as well as for Mr. Bryant, "I don't believe..." She tried her hardest to imagine. "No, I really don't believe Bryant *ever* felt the need for mass production."

The window with the mannequin snapped into darkness. I stepped out onto the street. A cold, steady rain was setting in, drifting needles past the streetlights and making an empty cab as likely as a sleigh ride. I had less than a mile to walk, pushed my package of selected seasonal sportswear inside my coat and moved off along the sidewalk, thinking a riddle:

A stray from a Heinkel hits a tailor's shop in Cheapside.

An outfitter to gentlefolk breaks her rule on outdoor wear.

A flight lieutenant gets too cozy with a doodle-bug.

And a wing commander recommends a charity.

All so a nurse will see a winter coat she can't really afford.

So who did she buy it for?

THIRTY-SIX

A row of red-brick houses ran the west side of Mecklenburgh
Square, saw-toothed where high explosives had taken bites
out. At the center of the square, in the sidewalk around
a railed garden, a line of tall elms shooed off a drizzle of
icing rain. I stood under one of the elms opposite a gray
Armstrong parked at the curb mid-row. The house with the
Armstrong outside had four double-fronted stories and kept
its grandest windows for the second floor. A housekeeper
in a white apron was drawing curtains there, to shut out
the freeze. Three steps up from the sidewalk a lantern lit
a shallow porch, and at either side of the steps some fine
wrought iron fenced off a basement, the same as at every
other house in the row. Live on Mecklenburgh Square and
nobody tells you they plan to take away your ironwork to
melt it down for a war.

I stepped from under the elm, detoured around the
Armstrong's hood, climbed to a doorbell, leaned on it and
waited. The limousine's hood had been stone cold. A sleet
squall was washing the square when the front door cracked
open on a dark gloss chin with a small crescent scar where the
beard didn't grow. The Armstrong's chauffeur, short and slim

and trussed in a light-gray double-breasted, looked me over without interest and glided the flat of his hand along a side part. I said, "Mr. Willard."

Scarface gave me his right profile and a look of studied tedium. "Mr. Willard is elsewhere."

He was already closing the door when I reached for the handle and snapped it down hard, then snapped it up out of his grasp and stepped inside. The chauffeur backed against a wall, his mouth working and his wrist tucked under his armpit. I heeled shut the door, used my hat to brush the weather off my sleeve and kept the arm inside it stiff in my coat pocket. "His car isn't elsewhere. I'll wait."

The entrance hallway had a telephone on a marble stand, a lighted chandelier hanging at the foot of a sprung stair, and on the stair a hurry of arriving footfalls. The housekeeper in the starched apron at the second-floor window, large, smiling and a little breathless, was looking from the chauffeur to me and back. "Mr. Willard is expected, Sidney. On such an evening as this we can hardly turn the gentleman away, now can we?" Then to me, "I'll take your coat and bring you to Mrs. Willard in the meantime." She was in a style Willard wouldn't recognize or know how to hire. Probably she came with the house before he noticed. I gave her the smile back and said if it was all the same to her, I'd keep the coat. At that, she turned and got set to take another run at the stair, and while Sidney nursed his wrist and eyed the hall telephone, we climbed the first long oval rise. We got a second wind there, turned toward the back of the house along a corridor of striped walls and wine-colored carpet and halted outside the last door on the passage. The housekeeper put out a hand to the door handle and then checked herself. "Mrs. Willard will be taking cocktails at this hour. Is there something...?"

"Not a thing. Mrs. Willard will be taking cocktails for both of us."

The housekeeper looked away and bit on her tongue. "Of course. Whom may I announce?"

I took her elbow and pulled her to the middle of the carpet, her bosom still heaving from the exercise. The climb had put a moist pink bloom in her cheeks. Close up she smelled of flat-ironed linen and lavender. "There isn't any need. Mrs. Willard and I are acquainted. But if Sidney wants a name to give the boss you can tell him it's Newman. Then again, you might just want to let him sweat."

She thought about that, put a hand to her mouth to stifle a short gasp of mischief. "Well then, Mr. Newman, if it's all the same to you, we'll let Sidney perspire for the time being, shall we?"

There was talk the other side of the door, but not conversation. Mrs. Willard was curled in the crook of a sofa and wrapped in a quilted robe, a pair of satin-heeled sandals tossed on the seat cushion beside her. She didn't notice she had company. Not even the empty glass in her hand. Only the flickering story playing out on a screen drawn down against a wall, and the fast, clipped commentary scratching along with it, hard to hear over the clatter of a cine-projector. I leaned back against the door and watched with her. It was a British Movietone newsreel from a fall day in 1943. An ocean liner with Red Cross markings edged into Leith Dock under a leaden sky, with three thousand returning POWs lining the ship's rails. *Everything considered*, the commentary cut in, *after four years in a stalag, our boys are in fine spirits and pretty good shape.*

Mrs. Willard rocked in the angle of the sofa. A cigarette burned in an ashtray on the floor. The film cut to pale figures on a mess deck dressed in brand-new khaki. Then to crowds cheering and waving on the quay. Then cut again to a military band playing *Roll Out the Barrel* before it panned back along the returnees filing down the gangway, dazed and disbelieving. Can it be? *Could* it be? They gazed around the dockside wanting to be convinced, until one fixed and final certainty began to dawn: no argument, no question, no doubt about it; no place else on God's green earth could ever look so ordinary. They were home.

The newsreel cut again, this time to a platform set up on the quayside and a figure standing at a microphone surrounded by Saltires and Union flags. The Lord Provost of Edinburgh, a solid-built Churchill lookalike, pushed his fists deep in the pockets of an army greatcoat, let his audience taste the moment, and by way of introduction began, *Those of you who are Scotsmen will appreciate very much how warm the welcome we want to give you.* A weighted pause. *But those of you who are not Scotsmen...* He purses his lips, takes time to scan the mass of upturned faces and measures for effect. You can hear three thousand tears roll down a cheek. *Those of you who are less fortunate...* The crowd roars as one. Home!

As if the sound of cheering squaddies was more than she could bear, Mrs. Willard looked away and registered she wasn't alone. She took a long moment to compose, lifted a lock of hair behind an ear, cleared her throat and said as if we were there for elocution, "Would you be so kind?" The empty glass held aloft like *Liberty Leading the People.* I straightened up to find the projector switch and turn it off and while the newsreel wound down carried her glass over to a liquor tray that glinted on a table by the fire. I smelled gin on the glass, added some more from a bottle showing wear and floated ice in it from a silver bucket. "Were you expecting one of my husband's films?" Her voice was thick with liquor. She wiped her tongue around her lips and concentrated on taking the glass. "He has a collection to satisfy most tastes, for the appreciation of distinguished visitors and their escorts. But you're not distinguished, are you?"

I let that pass. When the newsreel cut to the men on the mess deck it had lingered on a one-armed man with a strained smile, who smoked a cigarette while another POW tied his bootlaces. I motioned at the darkened screen. "It was how you found out he was alive?"

She shrank back against the sofa, the flat of her hand across the top of her glass in case the liquor might take off. "One wet afternoon in the Astoria on the Charing Cross Road. It was too ridiculous." She frowned at telling a story she hadn't expected to, about an RKO feature that had Ginger Rogers married to a Nazi aristo when one day Cary Grant came along. It being Hollywood, when Ginger discovered the truth about her Nazi, she ditched him. In the movies it can be that simple. But the too-obvious parallel, so far as it went, had made the new Mrs. Willard feel miserable. She noticed the glass in her hand, took a lick out of it and grimaced. "I expect I would have sat through the whole wretched film again, feeling utterly dismal. Then in the interval they showed their newsreel and there he was. Edgar. Maimed, I could see that, but alive and on a troopship home. It was all too much for me. I ran out of there bawling, and kept on practically to the Tottenham Court Road."

The Willards hadn't heard there was a coal shortage. The room was stifling. I hung my hat on the back of a chair and considered what exactly had been too much for her. One part might be realizing she wasn't going to shake off her husband over breakfast the way Ginger shook off hers. That's RKO. But the main part would be knowing her marriage had been more than just a terrible mistake. From the way she acted that afternoon in the Astoria, she already knew she'd been tricked and betrayed. Not only that, she knew why. "You ran because you knew sooner or later Edgar Levin would ask why of all men you had to marry Willard. And because when he did ask, you were going to give him the same lie your father gave you."

Mrs. Willard shaded her eyes with her hand, took another inch from the gin and grimaced again, as if she couldn't stop hitting her thumb with a small hammer. "You've been talking to Edgar."

She was sitting up, steeling herself to drain the glass. I stepped over and took it out of her hand. "Will you stop that? You don't even care for the taste." I carried the drink to the hearth and emptied it on the coals without any protest. "Mrs. Willard, I'm tired of these games we play. We both know the Drake family didn't need rescuing. The councilor never was going broke. He had a history. Willard knew it, and when you were traded it was for silence not for money. That was the deal you were a part of, and when you finally learned the truth of it you knew it had to stay strictly in the family."

There was a soft knocking at the door, the housekeeper moved into a wedge of light from the passage and Mrs. Willard said in a gravel voice, "What is it, Rose?"

"Mr. Willard will join Mr. Newman in the drawing room presently, Ma'am, and wishes to remind Mrs. Willard that she has an engagement this evening." Rose eased shut the door. The room folded back in firelight.

"For a time, I wondered how you worked out what you really were traded for. Then I realized you wouldn't need to, because one happy day your husband would be big enough to explain it himself. Good night, Mrs. Willard. Better get dressed." I let myself out. Rose was in the corridor, ready to go back in. At that time of day, the lady of the house would always need help with a zipper.

The Willards' drawing room was on the same floor as their private movie theater. It had an elegant plaster ceiling, pocket doors dividing it in two, heavy drapes at its windows on the square and two large chesterfields facing across a low table in front of a hearth. A dozen wall lights livened the shadows. Up against the pocket doors there was a card table, and in a corner in front of the windows, a lighted Christmas tree that touched the ceiling, sparking with clear glass icicles as if it had just been brought in out of the frost. Willard was at a sideboard opposite the hearth, sluicing soda in a glass. "This is unexpected, Newman. Join me?" When I said not, he slotted the siphon back in among the crystal, carried a brandy across the room and helped himself from a dish on the table. In black-tie he looked slimmer and taller, shirt cuffs opal-studded, chin close-shaved, hair as glossed as his patent shoes. As if it had nothing to do with anything, he asked, "You're here to talk about our late tenant? What was his name again?" He settled in one of the sofas, shelling nuts and pressing them between his teeth, rinsing with the brandy.

I played along. "That and the late Professor Garfield, and a jailbait named Terry Reilly who was helping your late tenant pay expenses. For all I know, he could also be the late Terry Reilly by now. He's been working at it." The glass icicles trembled on the tree at the end of the room, as if they caught the wake of a passing specter. Willard looked over the work on my face, but not as if it interested him. I said, "The thing is where to begin. Why not take it from where you had Garfield tailed and photographed with his latest crush, up until Reilly handed you the professor's briefcase in the Raglan bar? That was around twelve hours after Garfield was shot dead and dumped in the river. The rest we'll get to."

A fairy with a wand was bobbing at the top of the tree, putting the room under a complicated spell. Willard tossed empty shells in the coals and watched them flare. "Reilly told you that?"

"About the Raglan? He wouldn't need to. There was a noonday Christmas crowd, but it didn't make any of us invisible." The wry salute from the figure in a camel coat, caught in the mirror behind the bar before I passed out.

Willard reached for the dish on the table and rooted in it, leaned his head back and tried recalling his Christmas Day. "You were *following* Reilly?"

The fire spat nutshells back in the hearth like firecrackers. Sparks drifted up the chimney. "Not Christmas or any other day. Forget Terry Reilly. He's not the problem. But the lowdown you had Jarrett collecting on the professor is evidence in two murder inquiries. That could be a problem." Willard's gaze flickered. He shrugged, but not enough to put a wrinkle in his shirtfront, then looked past me and his gaze congealed. I turned around.

Mrs. Willard had pushed open the pocket doors to stand right behind me, unsteady on her satin heels. She wore the quilted robe still, buttoned to her calves, a bath towel piled in a turban and a cold cream mask gouged out around her mouth and eyes, her expression behind the mask unfathomable. Willard slid an arm along the back of the chesterfield and composed the look of somebody who could handle his wife. It took him time, and cost him his nonchalance. He put on the cool, honeyed tone of a *capo* who calls over the waiter to send back his dessert. "I pay a maid to see you're dressed and ready. What the hell does she think she's doing?"

The remoteness of what her housekeeper might be thinking of left his wife wide-eyed. Willard observed her from a distant planet, emptied a handful of nut shells on the table and dismissed his own question. He unwound from the sofa, touched two fingers on his show handkerchief and pointed one of them my way. "See me later at the Garden."

Mrs. Willard pulled her robe tighter and swayed on the sounds of her husband's going: his light, fast tread down the stair, the help-on with his coat in the hallway, the street door's open and close. She remembered the cold cream and wiped across her chin with the towel. "I... You'll need a taxi. Rose will call one."

We heard the Armstrong's starter motor flutter. The slick of its tires from the curb. "On a night like this there aren't any taxis, Mrs. Willard. When the snows come they fly south with the ducks. I'll walk."

THIRTY-SEVEN

The Paradise Garden was on Charlotte Street, in a low-rent quarter at a distance from the bright lights. Far enough from the West End to thrill its patrons with the idea of crossing the tracks, not so far that their drivers wouldn't know their way back. Outside it might be cold war, where high-living felt as permanent as bubbles. Inside, the Garden still blossomed, kept refined prices, a French kitchen and good-looking waiters and liked to call itself exclusive. Tonight, it was so exclusive it had tables reserved for Eskimos. The street lay under a polar cold. Pink neon flashed *Paradise* in the night, then *Garden*, then both together against the coal-black emptiness of the spheres. In daylight you might walk right by and not even notice an entrance. But on a night like this, its lights glowed solitary in an icebound waste, whispering promises to the frozen soul. The whisper was the sum of all its charm. In the foyer, they had the heavy-set choirboy they always have, who thinks conversation is for ballerinas and gives you the look twice-over because it's all the exercise he gets. He jerked a thumb at the hatcheck and a tawny-blonde in house uniform followed me over. She wore a cool, private smile, a matador jacket with gold braids and epaulettes and a walk that doesn't teach. In back of the counter, looping my coat on a hook, she fumbled the check ticket and watched it land at her feet. The matador swore softly under her breath. You saw why. Under the clip jacket she had on a yellow-sequin dress that fitted like snakeskin down to her ankles. To try picking the ticket up she hitched the dress past her calves and flexed at the knees. When that didn't work, she grabbed at the hem and started rucking it higher, and when I couldn't watch any longer I stepped inside the counter. "Don't do that. It's not good for me."

I kept my ribs stiff and stooped for the ticket, got it between my fingers and stopped dead. Slotted under the counter, in a line of bags and umbrellas, there was an air force khaki Gladstone with a metal initial fixed on each strap. The matador was eyeing me, wrapped in a scent as tight as her yellow dress. "Well, what do you know. You take somebody for a customer and it turns out he's a gentleman. What a flutter-brain cluck!" I put out a hand to the countertop and straightened up. "And I took you for drum majorette. We're both flutter-brain clucks."

It got me the cool smile again and she walked me to the back of the foyer, where a sign over two swing doors flashed *Welcome to Paradise* in electric-green loops. The blonde lifted her chin at the enticements within. "No drum majorettes in there either, Galahad. Watch your step." I thanked her for the advice and said I would do that.

On the other side of the doors was midsummer night in dreamland, set on the terrace of a Riviera villa perched high above the sea, where stars twinkled, high cloud drifted and sailboats made specks of china-white on a calm, moonlit bay. The terrace had palms in giant jardinières, waiters gliding around them in long aprons and cutaways, a scent of mimosa and a concert grand playing soft as the gurgle of a fountain. It even had a handful of diners making low conversation over the tune. But on a night when it was marooned in a frozen city, in limbo between Christmas and New Year, the Garden's restaurant could have raised dahlias sooner than a party mood. It was barely a quarter full.

At right of the diners a trellis trailed a wall of fake bougainvillea and vines. Two wide steps climbed to a veranda built to catch the sea breeze, and on past the veranda to a sundowner lounge, with slow-beating ceiling fans and a couple in a corner sitting over daiquiris. There was a bar on the veranda, with a line of high cane chairs to give a view over the tables on the terrace. I took one of them and pointed at a bottle behind the counter. The bartender slid a glass between my thumbs, reached for the bottle and uncorked it, then poised it over the rim of the glass. "What else?"

It lifted my chin off my chest. "Tell Willard I'm here to see him."

The bartender's hand stayed poised, mouth pinched in a bow as if his gums hurt. He had years left yet to grow into his shirt collar. "Tell him *who's* here to see him?"

I looked past him through the bougainvilleas to the diners under the starlight. There was a table for six, its occupants frosted by the same winter mood as everybody else in the joint. Willard and the councilor and two guests ate and talked. Allynson fussed with a napkin. The seat next to him was vacated. I got my left arm by the wrist and lowered it in my jacket pocket where it ached less, then looked from the still empty glass deep into the bartender's eyes. "He knows who. Did they show you how to pour that or only how to point it?"

He tipped the bottle as the seat beside me dragged back. A hand rested lightly on my sleeve and I turned aside. Mrs. Allynson had on a black satin gown, too chic for mourning, too long for a swimsuit, that covered her arms and shoulders in a gauze so fine you wanted to brush it off her skin. She leaned an elbow on the zinc counter and pointed the cigarette where I could light it. Her head tossed. The fingers flexed to wave away a cloud of tobacco smoke. She pouted and leaned in toward my cheek, confidentially. "Otherwise respectable people are losing their shirts in there. Why don't we join them? I might like to see you lose yours."

Her eyes were bright and she was slurring a little, the smile she lit was meant for diving into and it was a line in conversation I hadn't been pitched in a month of Sundays. I followed her gaze past her shoulder. At the end of the bar, standing either side of a door that blended in the wall of the veranda, two more choirboys sweated gently in tuxedos, hands rested over their stomachs. The barkeep had left without a word when she sat down. Now he was setting a shallow glass on the counter, stem so slender it might snap in a breeze. A green olive cradled at the bottom of the glass. "Then again, your husband might not. Or did he already give permission?"

Mrs. Allynson eyed the yellowing putty connecting my ear to my chin and started prodding in her drink with a cocktail stick. "You think I was *sent* to talk to you? Don't be silly. I don't run errands. Joe's guests are an awful bore so I excused myself. Oh, these things are detestable." She had the olive spiked and levered out of her martini onto a coaster. I reached over and put it between my teeth. She said, "I suppose we may not have so very much to say to one another either. Though you might tell me where you got that awful bruise." It took her two seconds to think better of it. "No, don't. Tell me instead what a private investigator does in daylight, and whether you're any good at it."

The martini olive had been pickled in kerosene. Mrs. Allynson watched me pucker, raised an eyebrow, prodded the coaster with a long fingernail and didn't say a word. I spat the pit in the coaster, made a paper screw out of it and dropped it on the counter. As for her question, it was one I'd been asking myself lately. "Opinion differs. Before the war, I worked insurance cases at Lloyd's for an investigative genius name of Maurice Lynagh. I thought I was pretty good at it, but it turns out I was a minority. After Poland fell, he got drafted to run an army unit chasing down supplies fraud and said I ought to join him, because as far as he could see I had no future in the City. When I asked what he meant, he said I didn't have any esprit de corps—imagine that! —and not to take it to heart because where he planned sending me it would help me fit in. Nobody there had any esprit de corps either."

She asked, "Which was?" And made it sound illicit.

I said, "Washington, DC." And made it sound hush-hush.

She kept her quizzical look, so I explained. It got us off the subject of what I do in daylight.

It was December 1940. The fighting had hardly begun. Roosevelt had just announced the United States was the *Arsenal of Freedom* and the British were already in hock for a billion dollars of war supply. Just to last another year out they needed plenty more and fast. Meanwhile, some of their American suppliers were betting that the British couldn't fight Hitler and still find time to check their billing. They weren't wrong. It took them a while to catch on. Then some clerk in Whitehall noticed deliveries were shy of payments by a country mile, and next day Lynagh was called to the Cabinet Office. His orders were to question the military, the Americans, their suppliers and contractors, find out what the British had been paying for and follow the money where it led. And as money generally does, it led everyplace: to truck motors shipped to Lima not to Liverpool, to oil stores nobody could find on a map, to Long Island estates billed as production lines in Los Angeles, and sand tires for tanks. For some patriots, the war in Europe had been their biggest break since Prohibition. But that was before they started supplying the US Army for a war in the Pacific. I said, "I got a telegram. Lynagh had it from my file that I was raised by a great-aunt in Washington. His wire said to stay with her and save the army a hotel bill. I wired back the great-aunt had died, and anyway my file said Wenatchee, Washington State, which his map ought to show is three thousand miles from DC. Then I got another telegram: *You joined Supply Fraud not Intelligence. Get a hotel.*"

She registered polite amazement. "You were an officer in the British Army?"

As if in 1940 it was a club so exclusive you needed Herbert Marshall's accent to get in. I tipped a salute. "Major. Lynagh's Light Inventory. Motto, *Don't Shoot! They Might Shoot Back!* I came here after the '29 Crash and didn't go back. America wasn't in a war yet. And you're the second person who asked me that tonight as if I owed the military an apology."

She let a smile light up, emptied her glass and called for two more, then let the smile die even before the bartender glided them back across the counter. She put out the last of the glow, watched her next martini pour and said a little nervously, "Estelle will be buried tomorrow morning. I suppose I wanted a professional opinion about why anyone could possibly want to kill her. I still don't understand, and Inspector McAlester told me nothing." Nurse Greer's murder had been only three days ago. Mrs. Allynson watched me count back. "The police hadn't any objection so the coroner released her body. Do I take it there's nothing new?"

I lifted my glass to where it caught the light. "Not a thing. Unless you recall your sister buying a classy winter coat three years ago. You might. For a nurse it would be an expensive item."

She turned again to look me over, her forehead knotted with the effort at understanding. "No, I don't recall. And I don't follow. Even in wartime she would need a warm coat, and Estelle would hardly buy one she couldn't afford."

"Maybe she wouldn't, but Nurse Greer didn't buy it for herself. This was a man's overcoat, chocolate-colored with a gold silk lining. Custom made by a firm of City tailors." Mrs. Allynson twirled the stem of the martini. I shuffled on the bar seat so we could both look uncomfortable. "Look, Mrs. Allynson, this isn't only about your sister. Crime editors don't get this excited about a string of incidental killings. They scent four murders joined up in a single story and each editor has a million readers waiting to be told how. They could be right. There were already three victims before your sister died. The blood matches say that when two of them were shot dead their killer was wearing the custom coat she bought. It's the only one of its kind."

The bartender arrived back behind the counter, cut a glance at the diners and dropped the corner of his mouth. "Boss wants to see you."

Out on the terrace, Willard and his lawyer had left their guests care of the councilor, their places at table taken by two tough-looking hostesses in tight-spangled dresses. They were already occupying themselves. A body wearing long ruby earrings was rubbing lipstick off her teeth in a powder mirror. Her friend was emptying a champagne bottle around five glasses the way a lumberjack dowses a campfire. I stepped down from the counter. Mrs. Allynson sat slim and very straight, slotted another cigarette between two lips that trembled, and aimed it at a flame the bartender held out, so shaken you didn't want to break her concentration. At the end of the bar one of the choirboys patted down my jacket with the back of a hand, then led me through a door that slid aside like entrances in fairytales.

The Garden's greenroom was a chain of baize islands set in a shallow pit the size of a paddling pool in the park. It drowsed on a handful of players, and on the distillation of a cordial promise that in the cloistered hours, when the late crowd is gone and the fast money stirs, any game of chance you cared to play could be accommodated, for as long as the night lasted and your nerve held. It was a promise for keeping later. For now, the tables were cleaning out their scatter of patrons from nothing but force of habit, and the two hardshells in spangles had the fast money all to themselves. My chaperone led me around the edge of the pit to where another tuxedo heavyweight loitered at the far side of the room, guarding the foot of a stair.

Willard's office was at the top of the stair, behind a black-lacquer door with nickel trim. A room so much wider than it was deep it should have been a corridor to someplace else. The room was soft-lit by shades along the walls, stale with talk in whispers. It had a presidential desk at center, a davenport at both ends, each face-on to a broad window with slatted blinds. One window gave a view on arrivals on Charlotte Street. The other looked over the diners and the bar. The greenroom would have its own window someplace else. From all three together a practiced eye would figure a night's take from first principles, know whose pocket it went in and whose percentage was getting clipped. The door clicked shut behind me. I stood motionless inside it, waited and watched. Willard lounged behind the desk, his right hand out of sight and his left hand splayed. The slab of polished jet he wore for a finger-ring was drawing off the light from a shaded lamp. He drawled, "Talk in front of the lawyer. Where were we?"

Allynson sat in a wing-chair at right of Willard's desk, rigid behind a tight smile and black tie. He said nothing, only lifted his wrists an inch off the chair arms, in the gesture that asks what can a man do when he's only the hired help? I stood—hadn't been invited to sit—sighed and said, "We were getting to Garfield and how Jarrett had been following him around for weeks. How a Cinderella named Terry Reilly rented out to the professor the night he died, and how you ordered Reilly out of circulation until the cops fit Garfield's boyfriend for his murder. What's wrong with *you* remembering where we were?"

A muffled piano tune broke in from the other side of the blinds. Allynson cleared his throat and put his palms together between his knees, gave the room his strained, gap-tooth grin and hesitated as if he were about to start on a proof of Euclid. Willard swung back around, picking at the gloss on his fingernails. He motioned one of them at his lawyer. "He's anxious to hear your point."

Allynson swallowed aloud. I looked along Willard's office, at the dark, heavy furniture a racketeer will order from the catalogue to give himself a personality. In a room like that, they can put an arm around your shoulder, be grave and wise, offer you the fruits of their philosophy and experience, then tell you to fall in line or get all your toes cut off. I gave Willard the long, wearied look that comes with free advice. "Last night, McAlester took the boyfriend in for questioning and damn near killed him. Think about that. He knows who the Beauforts are and the influence they can call on, knows they're so select they even get the Willards at their Christmas ball, both at the same time. And still he went ahead and made a hospital case out of their son." I loosed a silent whistle and turned for the door, awestruck. "McAlester in that mood is nobody's idea of protection. Worse, he's a liability. Let him have Reilly and it'll be plain murder. The point is, why be an accessory? You don't need it. Ask your lawyer."

I picked up my chaperone outside on the stair, went ahead of him down to the tables and out through the same thin crowd of players to where I started, at the bar with its view over moonlight on the bay. Mrs. Allynson was gone. The hostesses on the terrace had the fast money wrapped and sold, their breath so hot in their faces it kept their teeth bared. The lumberjack's client leaned over to mumble in her ear. Across the table the councilor sat out the end of a fat cigar. And then the hilltop villa's lights dimmed outside and in. Electric starlight guttered and fizzed overhead. There was a flat, hollow snap like a stud popping and the whole Riviera blacked out. Liquored groans rippled through the darkness then a muted squeal. I bumped against one of the high stools at the bar, edged around it and put my back against the counter. A chair scraped. A glass shattered. Voices called between the tables and the maître d' asked for calm. Catcalls started. Then one, then another, then every cigarette lighter on the terrace rasped in turn to make jittering rings of fairy lights around a couple of dozen diners. A scatter of applause broke out.

The Garden's lights stayed off. In ten unhurried minutes every dinner table had a wax candle butted in a wine bottle, the veranda bar lit up a line of its own, and the last cigarette lighter flicked off. I pushed away from the counter, cut through the stalking shadows to a table at the far side of the room and pulled out a vacated chair. The girls had taken advantage of the blackout to move their clients on. The table was a litter of unfinished drinks. Drake sat heavy-lidded and alone, tilting an empty glass at the candlelight. "Your guests are otherwise engaged, Councilor. Can we talk?"

He made a wry smile. "Mr. Willard's guests.HeMy presence this evening, you will observe, was entirely unnecessary. What do you wish to talk about?"

I lit a cigarette off the candle flame and took the chair. "About a trip Michael Garfield took a week ago in a light plane out of Northolt aerodrome. It had been snowing, and after a snowfall you sometimes see things from the air you missed on the ground. Even if you're City archaeologist." The councilor's ebony cane lay across the table like a hand on a ruined clock face. The half-smile took leave of his mouth. "But you don't need that explained, you were in the airplane. Your pilot, Miss Fulton, thinks you could be the world's worst flier. How would you forget?"

Drake caught a shallow breath. Just thinking about being airborne was giving him vertigo. "Indeed. Miss Fulton was most considerate. What is your object?"

"On Christmas Eve, a caller left a message with the switchboard at Guildhall, gave your name and a time and place you wanted to meet Garfield that evening. You'd met Garfield once already that day, at the Sesto, to look over photographs he'd taken from the plane. Pictures so sensational the professor assumed you wanted to talk about them some more. So, at nine o'clock he went to a bar in the City where the message said to meet, and when you didn't show somebody new caught his eye. They left together. An hour later the professor was dead in the river. In short, Councilor, he was set up." I looked around the Garden's endless imitation nights, turned cool and starless in the gaps between candlelight. The piano was playing with a soft pedal. Palms on the terrace made their shadows on black. Waiters moved around invisible, waiting on a handful of diners who'd liked the mood better and stayed on. "There's something else. The morning Garfield's body was found, Miss Fulton got a telephone call, also from someone who gave your name. The caller asked to speak to his pilot—*Mister* Fulton—and when they got that one straightened out, he asked if she still had the plane's film from three days before Christmas. Miss

Fulton thought you must have been so airsick you hadn't any idea what went on. Otherwise, how could you miss that Garfield was taking his own photographs that day, with his own camera? Miss Fulton never did have the film. She straightened the caller out on that too."

I rubbed the cigarette in a champagne glass and gave him time to think. First, about a train of killings that started with somebody using his name, and how awkward that could prove to be. Second, about who else would care what Garfield saw in his airplane pictures in the snow. Maybe the councilor could tell me who, but even if he couldn't, when it's your client you want him to try, just to hear how it might sound in court. "Councilor, at the Sesto that afternoon Michael Garfield showed you photographs that could stop City planning cold. Somebody who couldn't let that happen either killed him or had him killed just hours later, took his photographs and then went looking for the negatives for insurance." A draft swayed in the umbrella pines and guttered the candle on the table. "So tell me who else he might have shown them to."

Drake lifted the edge of the linen tablecloth, ran it under his lip and called over a waiter to take an order. He took the silver-top cane and levered up on his feet, pulled a watch from his vest and sprung it open. "You will excuse me. My car is waiting." He looped the watch back in his vest pocket, set his shirt cuffs and turned on his heel. A whisky arrived from the private bottle and took care of the next quarter-hour. Then I left the Mediterranean behind and walked back out onto Charlotte Street.

The Garden's marquee flapped under a quilt of low, wet cloud the color of sump oil. Charlotte Street was oblivion so black you blinked to see if your eyes were shut. Far back along the street, two headlamps flicked on and lit a faint trail. I stepped out from beneath the marquee and started walking. The auto with the headlamps came up behind me at the pace of an expensive funeral, drew level before I heard the motor ticking, passed by and became a silhouette in its own rear lights. Fifty feet ahead, it braked and pulled over, opened a rear door wide across the sidewalk and waited. When I caught up, a voice from the back seat said, "Get in, Newman. We travel in the same direction after all."

The Daimler moved off in gears of spun silk and headed south to Oxford Street, like a warm bath with the lights out and soft rain beating on the windows. Drake was a shadow talking at his reflection in the quarter light. His car's insides smelled of new shoes. Warm air from its heater was lapping my ankles and crawling up my shins. For my money he could talk to himself all night. We moved in a hush through a full-scale blackout while the councilor gave me his introduction to civics, as if I should have asked before. He said Garfield had the gift for persuasion, but that his radio audiences and broadsheet readers and even Churchill himself were just the professor flying a kite. When it came to City planning, the people he needed to convince were the committee members that voted, and the committee had other things on its mind. The councilor spread a fat hand on a fatter armrest. "Professor Garfield saw the City's devastation as an opportunity for his own advancement. My committee saw the vital needs of our banking and commerce. It fell to me to reconcile their differences."

It hadn't always been a problem. Until last spring, the committee hardly knew it had a City archaeologist, let alone who or how he filled his days. But that was before the professor found his Roman fort under the rubble and made headlines saying he wanted to go looking for more. The editorials called it a national disgrace not to let him. Their cartoonists had a field day. One of them showed a pack of hyenas labeled *City Money* tearing apart a carcass labeled *Reconstruction.* It put the councilor in a tough spot. His committee had promised a masterplan and the Corporation needed to see progress. It wanted to hear how the City could get back to making money, not another highbrow lecture on the radio. Drake's driver slipped past a line of buses into Charing Cross Road. I said, "The masterplan was Beaufort's."

The councilor's eyelashes ruffled. "Quite. I sympathized with Professor Garfield, but in order to consider any delay to planning we needed more certain evidence than he offered." Then ten days ago the snows turned the landscape to sugar icing, and when the weather eased the councilor got his invitation to an airplane ride. As committee chairman, he said he felt obliged to go up and take a look. Which was heroic of him when you considered he could have stayed in his office, waited until New Year and read all about it in the professor's report. But Drake hadn't spun a City fortune out of waiting to read a thing in print. If it put him a step ahead, he would have climbed out on the airplane wing that day. Airsick if he accepted Garfield's invitation, heartsick if he didn't. We made a battleship turn, joined a line of traffic into Trafalgar Square, passed by the flank of the National Gallery and slowed for St. Martin's Lane. The car's wipers shunted sleet in the corners of the glass and gave the windshield eyebrows. "I next met Professor Garfield, as you say, two days later on Christmas Eve. He showed me photographs, spoke of making another monumental discovery and was plainly exhilarated. As always, he wanted to investigate further. It was our final conversation. I left him no telephone message. Whoever might have been using my name I have no idea."

I dropped my hat on the armrest between us. The Daimler nosed around a cab rank on the Strand as if we were on rails. Three days back, in his library and in front of his lawyer, my client claimed to recollect no detail of his last conversation with Michael Garfield. Now the memories were flooding back. Such things are heartwarming. "Fine, but after you left the Sesto that afternoon you called Guy Beaufort, told him about your talk with Garfield and put Beaufort Partners' work on hold. If we're still interested in sparing blushes, you could tell me who else you called."

Passing headlights set Drake in profile, padded in the fox-collar coat and derby, holding a strap in front of his ear. He let go a small, sad sigh. "Beaufort I informed as a matter of courtesy and trust. I spoke of the matter to no one else, though Professor Garfield may have. His enthusiasms were not easily contained."

Drake went back to window-gazing. The limousine ran on past Aldwych, lit up black drifts of snow, skirted the burned-out shell of Clement Danes then straightened up for Fleet Street. Newspaper trucks were backed up for blocks, waiting out the power cut until the presses restarted. I leaned forward to slide the glass partition, said to let me out and closed it again. "Councilor, what I think is that Garfield's pictures were his proof of a Roman coliseum buried under the City. What I know is you wouldn't have got in the airplane unless he promised to show you something special. So far you didn't say where."

The Daimler eased over and pitched to a standstill. Drake's hand dropped from the strap, took the ebony cane and rapped the side window. "My dear Newman, the photographs were merely an exhibit. Professor Garfield was subject to the fiercest professional rivalries. It is inconceivable he would reveal a location before he published his report. Not to his colleagues, nor to his intimates one suspects. Most certainly not to me." Drake's chauffeur had my door open, standing at attention in the gutter in a sleet shower. Fleet Street was colder than the bottom of a loch.

The Daimler pulled out around lines of delivery trucks parked nose to tail both sides of the street. Offices were deserted. The presses stilled. Every newspaper's night shift camped out in the bars until the lights came back on. The Tipperary was buzzing, kerosene lamps yellowing its saloon windows. I was standing in the recess of my street door, jigging a key in the lock, when a voice behind me said, "Newman?" I spun around. At an arm's length across the shallow recess a low moan switched to a stifled spasm of coughing. A shadow-figure slumped inside a corner of the entrance, wrapped in a thin robe and wet through. There was a gasp and then the head lolled and the figure started buckling at the knees. I shoved hard in his chest to pin him upright against the wall, kicked open the door, took away my hand and dropped on a knee and let him pitch forward over my shoulder. We went in through the street door that way in a fireman's lift, backed up to click shut the latch and got a balance, then started on the stairs. My side felt as if a road gang was hitting it with shovels.

Kathryn Swinford was dressed like a country vet come to sit with a sick heifer, in riding boots and breeches and a heavy sweater that rolled up under her chin and flopped around her shoulders. Her patient lay curled under a hill of blankets, shallow-breathing and bright with sweat. She put away a syringe in a physician's bag at the foot of the sofa. "It's as well you called me. He has pneumonia. I've given penicillin and something to make him sleep and he'll need to stay warm and rested. How on earth did he get here?" As if all you ever do is sprinkle shamus dust and the police suspect of the year floats in.

But Blanche's boy hadn't needed any magic. He just took his chance and didn't see what he had to lose. While lights blacked out all across the City and his police guard went to check with the night staff, Henry had walked straight out into the freeze wearing a hospital robe and slippers. He'd taken a bad beating from McAlester, understood that he was prime for a murder rap, and knew while the blackout lasted, he could be invisible. The gas fire burbled in the hearth. Night shifts drifted back out of the bars. Lights were switching on all over Fleet Street. I looked away from the window and said, "Running out on City Police won't improve Henry's chances with a jury."

"Hardly. But if I take him back to Bart's, what chance he'll ever go home again, innocent or not?" She pulled a stethoscope from around her neck and coiled it, already decided. "Anyway, he plainly can't stay here. Help me get him downstairs and I can promise the Beaufort family will stop making such an utter nuisance of itself."

It was an attractive idea, if a little late in the day. But it had everything wrong with it, and the truth was there had been everything wrong from the minute I carried Henry in at the door. Still, it would take some explaining to the doctor. When you're raised on the playing fields of England a losing hand is just another opportunity for a magnificent gesture. "It's gallant of you, Doctor, but lately I have the full attention of City Police. Leave now and we could all be picked up before we get to your car. Besides, Henry hasn't been here. I called you in because I'm getting dizzy spells. Your records will show you gave me a sleeping shot and penicillin, and you stayed the night because you're a regular Florence Nightingale." I went over to the cabinet and poured two stiff nightcaps. "Wait till morning and my police tail will leave with me. Take Henry out of here then and you can put him wherever you want. All you have to promise is to keep him there."

Kathryn Swinford had been staring beyond the window, at a vision playing out against the night. It might have been a grandstand view of her career slipping beneath the waves. Or she was looking for one good reason why we still ought to do things her way, not mine. Whatever she saw, when I turned around, she was standing on her toes on the tile hearth, warming her back at the trickle of gas flame, the stethoscope draped on the sofa arm and her boots kicked off across the rug. I brought over the two glasses and put one in her hand, level with her eyelashes. She sighted me across the rim. "There was someone who asked you to dance with her in the long, long ago. Remember?"

"I remember."

"Well, that wasn't Florence Nightingale, Detective."

TAKING THE HEMLOCK

I got out of a taxi on Liverpool Street bathed and shaved, in a clean shirt, a dark navy suit and a tie I didn't remember ever seeing before. The entire outfit had been laid across the foot of the bed, and on the seat of a chair beside it a pair of black leather Oxfords with a sock rolled like a soused herring inside each shoe. When they expect to see you suited up for breakfast that way, you don't want a dinner invitation from the Swinfords.

She had come to lean against the bedroom door while I dressed, arms folded, ankles crossed, eyeing her work with a bandage as if we ought to put in for a prize. I was sitting on the bedside, working out how to bend and tie my shoelaces, when I saw her standing there. She had on one of my shirts without a collar and a pullover wound around her shoulders, breeches tucked in a pair of long wool service socks and her hair tied back as if she'd wandered in from my fruit orchards. On her it not only looked fine it looked everyday, and better yet the effect entirely passed her by. Then Henry moaned in a drugged sleep on the sofa and she left to go check on her patient. I finished up the shoelaces and knotted my necktie single-handed. There is no end or limit to Newman's accomplishments.

Under my shirt, I was strapped in a bandage that looped around my side and made a bandolier over my shoulder, Mexican bandit style. It left me a lot less sore. It also left me climbing out of the cab as stiff as Mrs. Mayhew's window dummy. I paid the driver, took four steps across a broad, wet sidewalk and entered Louis' barbershop. The doorbell tinkled bright as sleigh bells.

Louis was seated in the barber's chair reading a morning paper in front of a mirror in the center of the wall. He eyed me in the mirror, got out of the chair, dropped the newspaper on one of his waiting seats opposite and stepped up to take my coat. "You're not looking so good, Mr. Newman. And you look set for a funeral." He helped me out of the coat sleeve, seemed out of joint himself and started on what was upsetting him before I settled in the chair. "A funeral can hit you hard. Only yesterday I went to see where they laid Miss Dillys to rest, and I don't mean to judge for none of us is blameless before the Lord, but I was unquiet about how that lady ended her life." A cotton cloth shook out. Louis moved behind the chair and prodded my chin on my chest. "I had trouble even to find her because they didn't put a marker on her grave. I don't know they ever will. But do you know what? Across the ways there was a tree letting fall the prettiest pink blossoms on the snow, spread around her just like flowers from an admirer. I was most glad to see them. It made me hope I was too quick to fear for her soul. You think I was too quick, Mr. Newman?"

The door opened in from the hotel lobby and Louis broke off. Measured, easy steps moved to the seats along the wall, halted to pick up the newspaper Louis had dropped there and then walked up behind him. I raised my head. The mirror had both of them framed; McAlester twice as wide, twice as heavy and a head taller, conservatively speaking. I let go a long sigh and nodded at the headline rolling in front of his stomach. "It's fifteen below freezing in a socialist winter, Bevin still sends boys down the mines and electricity is decadence. They call it news."

The newspaper twisted in McAlester's fist, his features gray dough under his hat brim, eyes the gloss of wet sand, his eyebrows two shades lighter. The blank eyes pitied that I always had it wrong. His mouth hooked at the corners and his patent on a whisper said, "Bevin is front page. News is inside. It says the Beaufort boy went missing last night in a blackout. They call it unexplained but what do they know? What I know is, three hours later Newman gets a visit from the Beaufort family doctor and we don't see her leave. So what kept her spitshine? Did you have a heart attack? Or does she get the sweats when you start talking politics?"

I caught Louis' eye in the mirror and nodded him to go on with the haircut and talked with my chin back in my chest. "Henry Beaufort? I read about that. How City Police wanted him for interview and the boy tripped and fell on a question. Now he barely walks. So they took him into the hospital, set a guard on the door and still they lost him. Coming from anybody else it would be a letdown, but City Police say not to lose any sleep; they put a full-time tail on me so they know their streets are safe." I pulled aside to find McAlester in the mirror again, lips pursed as if he'd found a loose tooth. Sometimes you start the regrets even before you know what you're going to say. "I needed a doctor. You would know why. I keep running into people who act like they think they're police."

The rolled newspaper lifted inches, chopped down fast and hard across Louis' knuckles, jumped the scissors out of his fingers and left him watching them skitter across the shop floor and under the row of seats. McAlester's neck was a livid purple band lapping his shirt collar. His voice strained at the leash that choked it off the way it always did, like a yappy dog that never learns. "Beaufort's a lucky boy. He was going nowhere last night unless he found a doctor who doesn't ask questions. I think he found her. I think she patched him up. Her problem was where to send him next. So she went for advice to the only shamus she knows." There was enough truth in it not to argue the detail. The leash eased off his throat and let him breathe again. "She's out of your class even in daylight, but at one in the morning she makes you a house call that takes all night. So tell me she stayed for your big blue eyes. Because the thing is, Newman, you don't look that sick to me." He tossed the newspaper in my lap, turned away and quartered Louis' glass shelves with their patent scalp rubs and shaving sticks, hair oils and bay rum. "Littomy says be in his office at six. Disappoint me and be there." McAlester flipped his collar and left by the street door, hunched against a slow, icing drizzle and joined the passersby. The doorbell stopped chiming. Louis didn't move.

I said, "The detective inspector can be excitable."

Louis twitched his moustache and collected his scissors from across the room, then took a seat to let the electricity out of the air. "I know it. I met him once before."

He waited for McAlester's ghost to follow him out the door, then got back up to finish the haircut. We were done, I was getting change from my pocket and asked, "Met him when?"

Louis flicked a brush over my jacket and didn't need to think. "That was Christmas morning, Mr. Newman. You went out of here into the hotel. Sometime later the gentleman walked in from the street and asked where you went. The truth is I didn't know where, but he saw there was a door through to the hotel lobby and didn't wait for his answer. I think the inspector didn't know you could leave that way."

I went over to the street door to pull it open. Louis was standing at his cash till in the window, writing down the sale. He tucked the pencil behind an ear and looked up. I said, "Never fear for Miss Dillys's soul, Louis. She'll get by. Fear for the soul that killed her."

THIRTY-NINE

Hampstead cemetery was a snowfield gridded with pathways across the side of a hill, freighted with monuments and wintering trees and cut in two by a poplar avenue giving a view south to the city. It was situated off a quiet-money neighborhood of high-pitched roofs and tall brick chimneys, wood smoke and diamond-leaded glass, where children toboggan down private driveways cutting through broad, sloping lawns and even the snowmen wear derby hats.

My cab let me out at a gatehouse at the entrance to the drive, snow-cleared as far as a mortuary chapel halfway along. A stooped priest in a black beret waited at the doorway shaking with cold in a cloak that reached to his shoes. I ducked inside, took off my hat and made my way to a seat. A lamp flickered in a corner. Gray-glass windows fought off the morning light. The silhouette of a mourner sat bowed and alone beside an aisle. The chapel's only other occupant sat bolt-upright in a pew in front of me, her lean frame fitted in a long, plain coat, an iron permanent under a black felt hat, balancing a handbag square on her knees. I leaned forward, close enough to murmur in her ear, "Where is everybody?"

Miss Hartridge stiffened. We sat there cheek to cheek, her jaw knotted and her gloved fists balled on the handbag. Without turning her head, she arched backward over the pew. "As no doubt you are aware, Nurse Greer was with child. She was also unmarried. In view of our rules, we could not encourage the attendance of young nurses. I am here to represent the hospital."

I looked both ways along the empty rows and sat back. "Nobody better."

Nurse Greer's sister and her husband hadn't encouraged attendance either. The *Courier*'s photographer, waiting under the poplars in the snow, was going to be disappointed. Motors cut. Car doors slammed on the drive outside. The doors to the chapel flapped open and four bearers scuffed in on the wet tile. Miss Hartridge got on her feet, ramrod-straight, the Raglan's landlord turned in his aisle seat, I pushed up off the pew an inch at a time, stiff as Lazarus. We were five mourners, not even a quorum for a secret society, and one hollow-eyed priest who patted a handkerchief at the corners of his mouth and kept the talk about Providence as simple as it ever is.

Carl's photographer leaned against the empty hearse taking pictures of the family at the graveside with a long lens: of the lawyer standing loose at attention, his pallor white as lime-wash, and of his wife looking weightless as her veil in the breeze. Behind the photographer, the poplar avenue followed the ridgeline as far as the gatehouse, past where a Humber sedan had pulled under the trees thirty yards inside the gates. The committal over, the priest muffled in his cloak and stood aside. The landlord of the Raglan, blind with tears, grasped his hand and stumbled after Miss Hartridge. I watched them climb the path back to the chapel, then crossed to the fresh-turned earth of another burial, where almond blossom scattered over the last snowfall.

"I suppose we can expect to see our pictures in every newspaper."

I hadn't heard her footfalls, looked from Dillys Valentine's grave to the cars parked uphill in front of the chapel then along the drive to the Humber waiting under the trees. There were no agency photographers. Or any photographer at all, excepting Carl's.

I said, "You can count on them being in one."

Mrs. Allynson lifted the veil on a hat I hadn't seen before, wore a coat cut to pinch at her waist and swell at her hips, black velvet gloves, and tall heels that made her stand tiptoe in the snow. You wondered just how much black she kept by for mourning. Her shoulders drooped. A sigh of frustration spun a frosted cloud on the air. "It was perfectly obvious the funeral was meant to be private. Do you think we could ask them not to print their photographs?"

It was a novel idea. "Appeal to the editor's better nature? Only if you've got something he wants more."

She folded back the veil and bit her lip. "I'm sorry. By private I didn't mean... It was good of you to come. I expect the older man was Estelle's employer at the Raglan. He seemed terribly upset. And the lady who looked so stern?"

"Miss Hartridge is a hair shirt, here to pay the respects of the hospital. She has to act tougher than everybody else or it doesn't work. It wasn't personal. She thinks Job gets treated with kid gloves."

She made a taut smile that emptied her eyes. "Then the service might have offended her, I suppose."

"There were two funerals just now, Mrs. Allynson. The padre only knew about one of them. What offended Miss Hartridge is that he didn't have all the facts. Not setting him straight was a big effort for her." She wrapped her arms around her shoulders and cast around at the blossom at our feet. I motioned with my hands inside my pockets. "Miss Valentine was buried here yesterday. Until the freeze lets up, there's nowhere else they can break ground. Hampstead isn't a place she expected to pass a lot of time in."

The horizon was closing in so fast you could reach out and touch it. Her eyes leveled along the almond trees while she registered the name. "Still, it might have pleased her, mightn't it? And the blossoms could be her special mark of grace. Didn't the padre say that in the end each of us receives what we're deserving of?"

It didn't need an answer. It wasn't even meant for conversation. We were passing words at a graveside to save on the silence, signifying nothing. The day being what it was, I should have let it rest. But what with the priest and his mysteries, Miss Hartridge and her book of rules, the funeral talk and the trees dripping petals as if a thaw was setting in, the morning was giving me a nose bleed. I followed her gaze to a line of low gray cloud hemming the south of the city. "Mrs. Allynson, I don't have the gift for thinking in signs and symbols. For all I know the padre could be right. But what if he's wrong? What if there is no grace and there are no just rewards and the blossom falls where it falls because a wind blows in the night? Who gets to put Dillys Valentine's murderer in the dark and lonely place where he belongs?"

She turned her cheek as if she'd been hit and took a moment to recover. Then pirouetted on her toes, traced her own footsteps in the snow and climbed the almond walk to where her husband waited. Allynson was standing at the open rear door of the funeral limousine, bent back at the knees like a strung bow, taking a long, steadying pull from a hip flask, as if he'd climbed out of the clouds onto a mountaintop and saw there was no place else to go but down.

Beyond the rows of headstones, down at the farthest edge of the cemetery grounds, a strip of bare woodland glinted in the slow thaw. Past the copse, a street of garden-city dream homes ran at the foot of the hill, made a right-angle to a bridge crossing some rail tracks and ended where it met the highway back into the city. I'd had police company all morning. It was time to part. I put my head down and took off in a straight line downhill for the trees, plowed in between lines of headstones and kept going, went fast down a snow slope, waded knee-high across a last, flat eighty yards and pulled up in the shelter of the wood, breathing hard. I sank on my heels there in thick brush, and took the view back up the hill.

A quarter-mile off, the funeral cortège was riding out through the poplar avenue to the lodge gate at the east end of the ridge, passing by the Humber sedan pulled over on the verge. It had passed the Humber's driver already. He was the one running flat-out along the drive in the opposite direction. Say what you want about City detectives, they're game. This one sprinted as far as the mortuary chapel before he thought of quitting. Then he took one look at my tracks down the hillside, and another across the city spreading all around him to the horizon, stopped running and started thinking. Not about me. Not even about what his next move ought to be. It wouldn't be his pressing concern. Right now, his only thought was how to explain to McAlester that his tail job had given him the slip, on foot and in broad daylight in the middle of Hampstead cemetery.

FORTY

The Sesto's basement ran beneath a row of store fronts off the north-west angle of West Smithfield. At the street corner there was a record store closed for lunch, with a sign over that read, *Old Time Favourites, Swing, Hot Jazz, Popular, Classical, Opera and Foreign.* The rest it was leaving to the competition. The shuttered markets on the north side, the hospital through the plane trees on the square, the street running west to Farringdon past the walk-down diner; from the record store's front step, I saw it all. A mother and her small daughter tramped the sidewalk toward me, muffled and hand in gloved hand, both of them hooded like Hudson Bay trappers. Ten feet away, the mother drew aside to look in a grocery, but her daughter wasn't interested, wriggled out of her grip and scuffed through slush to the record store window. She put her nose up against the glass, where a dog with its ear in a gramophone horn was advertising new arrivals. The girl's mouth worked at the sales line handwritten on the poster. "Hhhh. Mmmm. Vvvv." She took a breath and tried it again. "Hhhhmmmm. Vvvvv."

I had my back to the shop door, looking out across the square. The small frame next to me went rigid and readied for another lungful. Concentration was sending her cross-eyed. I said, "H.M.V. His Master's Voice. It isn't the name of the dog."

The girl clammed shut her mouth and backed up from the window to give me the squint, then squeezed two steps sideways and climbed up on the step so we were standing toe to toe. She sank her fists in her hips, rocked back on her heels and mouthed in case I was deaf as well as stupid, "I know how to *spell* it. I only don't know how to *say* it." Out of nowhere, her mother grabbed her arm, rolled eyes at me over her daughter's head and dragged her off.

A truck crawled up the ramp from the rail siding under the markets. Somewhere out of sight a locomotive huffed. A taxicab pulled over at the Sesto's entrance and Kathryn Swinford got out and hurried down the stair. The sidewalk had emptied. The garden in the square had been chained since the nurse's murder. I quartered the area one last time and followed the doctor into the basement diner.

The Sesto's tables were busier than before, thick with the blue smoke that was the marvel of Stanley's cooking. Kathryn Swinford sat in the booth by the door, dressed the way she'd arrived to fix up Henry, looking as much at ease in the company of meat market traders as at breakfast in the Great Eastern. She had the physician's bag at her side and her coat draped over her shoulders, her fingers pushing the sweater collar up around her ears. Before I hit the seat, she was saying, "Could we find another table? I sat here because you said to but it's absolutely freezing so near the door."

I sat opposite and looked for somebody to take an order. "From here I see who comes in."

Her alarm bells rang. "Why? Were you followed?"

Not unless Littomy was recruiting six-year-olds with mittens and snub noses and scarves crossed under their armpits and tied behind their backs. And the mother's style was too refined. I pulled a mouth that said no, I didn't think I was followed. "But I suppose *I* might have been. Shouldn't you be able to tell?"

I sagged and shuffled back around to face her. "Doctor, there are a million things I should be able to tell, but for insurance I put your shoes outside the bedroom door last night and my trusted valet turned the heels around. Anybody trailing you here in the snow will think you already left. How do you tell when a patient doesn't have a cough?" She was staring past me, not answering. I twisted around. The signora stood wheezing at the corner of the booth wearing the black dress she always wore, a thin black cardigan buttoned at her throat, black stockings, flat black shoes. She had a bright metal tray pressed across her stomach and a wounded look. "The lady doesn't drink coffee, signora, and I need something stronger."

She tugged the cardigan across her bosom, left without a word and pressed back through the diners to the kitchen. Kathryn Swinford watched her go, looking puzzled. Her voice lowered to a murmur. "It all went the way you said it should this morning. Bridget telephoned for a taxi and between us we got Henry downstairs and out through the rear of the saloon bar. I didn't go into my office and I haven't been home yet either. My car's still parked where I left it last night." She paused to reflect. "Bridget didn't ask any questions. Has she done this sort of thing before?"

The signora squeezed back up to the booth with a tray, set down two small wineglasses and a saucer with two sugar almonds. She filled the glasses with honey-colored wine, set gimlet eyes on me and rested her weight on her fingertips on the table edge. "Vin Santo. To make you more holy." She gargled on the H, took the bottle and her tray, and left.

I prodded the saucer across the table. "Bridget is safer than the post office."

Kathryn Swinford fooled with the saucer, weighed something she had on her mind and picked off one of the sugar almonds. "Good, but there's something I ought to tell you. I mean about where Henry is."

"For now, I don't have to know. When I do, I'll ask."

She blew out her cheeks, as if it always made such slow work because I never could grasp the basics. "Yes, I understand that. But if this all goes horribly wrong, I may not be here to ask." She nibbled at the sugar tip of the almond. "You're the private investigator, I know, and you're used to finding people, but where I took him..." I lifted the glass, took a mouthful and let the syrup coat the back of my teeth. There is no legal way to stop a high-bred Englishwoman telling you what she thinks is good for you. She leaned in across the table as if we were rehearsing for her first prison visit. "Look, Sir Bernard Hirst is a senior judge and a Master of the Bench at the Temple. He's been reviewing the courts in East Africa since the war ended. The point is, Henry was in no state to travel this morning, Sir Bernard's private rooms in chambers aren't being used and the Temple was a two-minute taxi ride away." She moved the stem of her glass in a tight diamond on the table. "It's awkward of course, but there really was nowhere else close at hand and Sir Bernard is my uncle. On my mother's side." As if that side of the family ought to swing it for me.

I sputtered wine back in the glass, reached for a handkerchief and dabbed at my chin. "Doctor, understand this. There are things not even Women of Good Family can square. Awkward is if they find young Henry hiding out in the Archbishop's skirts. This is way more special. What did you do? Make a shortlist headed *Large Buildings Crawling with Lawyers?* It's Littomy's backyard. He knows it better than you know Debrett's. How long do you suppose Blanche's boy can last in there? Meanwhile, a senior judge and knight of the realm is harboring a murder suspect you put in his chambers without his knowledge or consent. Do you have any idea what you've done to him? He might as well take the hemlock now. Because out there on the savanna, where Uncle Bernard sits in his grass skirt swapping learned opinion with the natives, one unholy mess is about to fall on him out of the African sky. He might not have caught it on the wind yet, but believe me, when it happens, he will not fail to notice."

Kathryn Swinford looked from under her eyelashes as if I were pitiful. "Must you always treat me like an upper-class idiot? Of course I understand the risk, and when this is all over I shall own up. What else would you have me do? Guy is desperate, Blanche knows absolutely nothing of what's happening and their son has been assaulted in police custody. I hate all this cloak and dagger, but I work for people who are trying to frame the boy for murder. To let it pass without lifting a finger would be shameful. Anyway, the Temple is absolutely the last place police will think of looking, and lawyers are only ever interested in other lawyers' fees. They won't have the faintest idea what's going on." She snapped open the bag beside her, drew out an envelope and laid it on the table, set a key on the envelope and slid it all my way. Her tone honeyed, the way you talk a dog into letting go a ball. "The key is to Sir Bernard's rooms. I really do think you should take it. And those are the photographs you asked for. I meant to give them to you last night, but events rather took over, didn't they?" She popped the last sugar almond and raised the wineglass. "Anyway, don't be silly about the archbishop. Henry's a good Catholic boy. It's the first place they'd look."

The signora had her wine bottle hoisted over the heads of her customers, pushing through the tables. The doctor saw her, wagged a finger over her glass to stop her pouring more, then checked and slid along the seat toward her. "We've not been introduced. I'm Dr. Swinford."

The signora blinked and eyed the physician's bag at her side. "A real doctor?"

"A real doctor for policemen, and I can see that something's upsetting you. Why not sit down and tell me what it is?" She put a hand to the signora's elbow and guided her into the booth. It was all the invitation she needed. "You don't see the newspaper? Of the dead nurse who is so young? It is very, very bad."

There was something in the way she said *very, very bad*. Kathryn Swinford heard it, turned to where she could search the older woman's eyes, then took both her hands and balled them in her lap. "You knew her, didn't you?"

The signora looked under stones for words she wasn't born with. "Of course I know her! She comes here with her man who dresses good and don't talk so much. Without her, I think he don't come no more."

Kathryn Swinford was already taking a card from her bag and writing. "But perhaps he will. And if he does, I want you to telephone Mr. Newman at this number. Will you do that? It really is important you should." The signora looked the number over, then gave it the shrug-off my success rate was due. She slipped it in the bosom of her dress, shuffled along the bench, filled my glass again from the bottle meant to make me holy and went back with it to her kitchen. I added a memory for telephone numbers to the doctor's many wonders.

FORTY-ONE

When I walked into the Thornburgh lobby it was past three in the afternoon, back among people who'd put in a day at the office already. Regular people, decent people, reliable people who answered their mail and returned their calls, had a line in conversation and a smile they didn't need to practice in a mirror. People who'd put in another solid day toward another solid week, would take the same bus tonight they left on this morning, and go home more or less satisfied. All things considered, I thought they might be on to something. I had my office door pushed open, heard footsteps hurrying along the corridor, turned to see the post clerk and stepped aside. He went straight in ahead of me, stirring a new perfume on the air, unmistakable. I caught his elbow. "Hold up, George. Since when are we wearing *Texas Dew*? There are cops in this town who don't need that kind of excuse."

George was three months in the job, fifteen years old and passing for twelve. Ordinarily, he went around the building in a cloud of *Dixie Peach*, and what was on the air today was not it. He dropped the mail on my desk and coughed in his fist, then glanced past me at the line of chairs in the recess outside. I craned around at a visitor seated in a corner, peeling off her gloves and dropping them one at a time on a package in her lap. I patted George's elbow and nodded him to leave.

Mrs. Willard was dressed for noticing, had a purse tucked tight under her arm and a wide-brim hat set over one eye, a fur that started up around her ears and cut in below her calves, so orange it would have looked gaudy on the fox. I raised the window blind on the last of the daylight, then went back to invite her inside. She handed me the packet on her way in. "*Texas Dew* hardly sounds flattering. Ought I to ask?" I sat her in the customer chair, leaned back in mine with the packet unopened and said probably not. But Mrs. Willard wasn't ready yet for any other kind of talk. She set her purse and gloves on the desk, touched a stray wave of hair off her cheek and asked anyway.

It had been the winter of 1944. Four months after the Americans landed at St. Tropez. Three months after a Seventh Army NCO introduced himself to the madam of a cathouse behind the old port in Marseille. The NCO was from Wisconsin, with access to a supply of aviation spirit liberated from a navy seaplane base, forty miles along the coast. The madam was from the hill town of Grasse, inland from Cannes, where before the war they made the finest French perfume sold on Fifth Avenue. The NCO and the madam agreed on a trade, Guerlain for gasoline, and turned her basement into a depot for both. It meant the girls were entertaining daily on top of sixteen thousand gallons of high octane and perfume racked in US Army jerry cans, likewise liberated. Mrs. Willard picked at a fold of the fur and let it fall back on her knee. "Such an interesting war you had."

"Marseille? I was in transit. Two days before I got there the cathouse had blown sky high and not a German in five hundred miles, only the NCO with a lighted cigarette, checking inventory in the basement. It was Sunday morning. The girls were all at mass. At any other hour of any other day, he would have taken an entire company of infantry with him.

When the aviation spirit burned off, the air in the old port was filled with *The Blue Hour*—the perfume you're wearing—and Marseille never smelled so good, before or since. The GIs kidded it was the smell of oilfields in early morning: *Texas Dew*. The locals said it was the smell of a miracle and they'd better believe it."

She watched me hook a finger under the brown paper wrapper on her package. "You make it sound like Götterdämmerung."

"Who's she?"

"It's an opera by Wagner about a country boy out of his depth in the big city. He meets a bad end. Everything goes up in smoke."

"That's it?"

"More or less."

Mrs. Willard's package was half the size of a shirt box. I had the wrapper loose at one end when a handful of photographs slid in my lap. At a glance, they were more of Jarrett's work, as dull as blackmail pictures ever are and dynamite for anybody who could use them. Mostly of Henry cozying with his professor in the flounce bars and private burlesques where they supposed they were among friends. I tore off the rest of the wrapper, put it in a desk drawer along with the pictures and turned to the other item in the package. It was a diary for 1947 with a marbled cover, filled with names and appointments, telephone numbers and addresses, and the journal entries Garfield crammed tight against the margins in the same dead languages that had stopped being a surprise to me. I riffled through the pages then closed them up for some other time. Mrs. Willard waved a manicure over her gift. "My husband's interest in Professor Garfield seemed important to you last night. After you left, I went looking in his room. I daresay he'll notice eventually, but when he does I won't be there. I thought I owed you more than just an explanation for the way I've been behaving." She slammed shut her eyelids. "I'm sorry. This... might be more difficult than I imagined. Is there a drink in the house?"

Her hand dropped in her lap. She sat straight and took deep breaths. The explanation she thought she owed me looked a long way off. "It isn't necessary to do this now, Mrs. Willard. I can call you a cab."

"But it *is* necessary. I simply can't do this by myself any longer and there's no one else I can tell, especially not Edgar. I don't know where to begin, but if I don't begin at all I think I shall start screaming."

I weighed that, went around her to the file cabinet, pulled out a tumbler and broke the seal on a fresh bottle and half-filled the glass. The rest I filed back in the drawer and put the drink in her hand. "Begin with how the councilor met Jarrett. Whenever you're ready." She nodded and took a sip for appearance's sake, sat back and closed her eyes again. Her mouth softened and her cheeks took on a bloom. I went back to my seat to give her time to put down whatever she needed, and when I got there, she was dabbing a handkerchief at the corner of her lip. The glass was drained.

The way Mrs. Willard told it, she'd gotten the real story from her husband soon enough. Her marriage had been poison, Willard was brittle and she learned fast how to rile him, up until the day he snapped and acquainted her with two new facts of life. One, that the trade their marriage had been a part of was never for money, but only for the coverup of a single, sordid rendezvous; and two, that however tough she might try to make life for her husband, it wouldn't even get close to the misery he could promise to arrange for her. Mrs. Willard didn't recall which of the two hit her hardest at the time, only that she'd gotten good and tight before she went to brace her father for an explanation. Drake had listened, couldn't deny what his daughter had already heard, sat her down and filled out what had happened.

The councilor had long had an unsafe fondness for young hustlers. Raymond Jarrett was merely his introduction to the problems that can arise: a late-night pickup at a cab rank that had played out on an operetta stage at an address in Cloth Court and—as such things go—had ended in the third act, when two City detectives dropped by. For Jarrett it had been all in a night's work. For the councilor, it was his first acquaintance with a police shakedown and the sainted look of two vice detectives eyeing his birthmark and his silks tossed in a chair. The irony being that Drake owned the address where the detectives pulled their shakedown, and didn't know it at the time any more than they did.

The councilor's interview in the bright room with City Police had taken place sometime in New Year, 1943. By then, he'd already met Willard in the way of business and had even introduced him to his daughter once, though like everything else since Edgar Levin went missing the occasion had passed her by. Then or later she hadn't any idea that Willard was taking an interest in the Drakes. She thought her father hadn't any idea either. So that in the dead hours with the two detectives, cold-sweating through a night of dark wonders, the biggest wonder was when Buchanan Allynson arrived in the bright room with the look of a man late for an appointment. It was no courtesy call. As things stood, Councilor Drake was two hours away from an appearance at morning court on a gross indecency charge, at which point he might as well start waving goodbye to his commercial interests, his name and his standing in the City. When news got out about the court appearance, they would all be gone. What puzzled him was why Willard would send his lawyer in the middle of the night to tell him what he already knew.

Allynson operating wasn't hard to picture: the permanent smile of apology, the consoling that even the worst nightmares are ones you wake up from, the urging that for two more hours the councilor still had a choice, and that a public humiliation was avoidable. Willard had sent him with an alternative on offer. Take it and what had passed overnight would be nothing but a forgettable inconvenience. It was guaranteed.

When the councilor walked back out onto Snow Hill, it was winter dawn. A gray Armstrong limousine idled at the curb, waiting to bring him home. The rest followed as Allynson predicted. Drake's appearance at morning court dissolved in broad daylight. There was no entry in the Snow Hill desk log.

City Police had no record of an interview, or of any late-night call two detectives might have made on a rented property in Cloth Court. By way of return, next day saw the councilor announcing not only a new business partner, but the marriage of his only daughter, and the future Mrs. Willard began sporting an engagement diamond bigger than her knuckle. As for how to explain the hurry to the bride-to-be, Willard let Councilor Drake decide that for himself. Mrs. Willard rolled the rim of the tumbler across her lip in a reverie of chances missed. "I daresay that all sounds terribly harsh of me. My father knew a court appearance would utterly destroy him."

I went to sit closer, across a corner of the desk. "Mrs. Willard, homosexual importuning would get him nothing but a ten pounds fine at morning court. The magistrate is a man of the world. He expects the defendant will give a false name and occupation and then apologize, or better yet his word to go see a doctor about these unsocial urges he's getting lately. That's all. Court was never the problem. The problem was Allynson making sure a court reporter would be primed. That was his message from Willard. Now better tell Levin what you just told me. It'll make you both happier."

Her mouth buckled. The eyes glazed and looked in mine. "How can I tell Edgar when he won't even see me? I really don't understand why not. What difference can it possibly make now?" The guileless, desolate look, deep enough to drown in.

I handed her the purse and gloves. "Go talk to him. You'll find a way. And tell him you brought me what your husband had on Garfield. He'll like to know." I lifted the telephone and ordered a cab to take her wherever home was.

FORTY-TWO

The *Courier*'s offices took the whole of a Victorian block, across the street and less than fifty yards east of the Tipperary. I paid a cab under its corner clock then climbed the shallow steps. A florid usher waited sentry at the entrance, dressed for the Prussian cavalry and complete with curled moustaches. It was after four-thirty. Inside was a lobby where gilded columns ran around pink marble walls. A wide stairwell climbed from its center, and running upward through the well, rising and falling like slow pistons, a line of elevators inside a wire mesh shaft. A small painted sign said *No Staff*, and next to the sign an attendant lounged beside an open cage door. He folded his copy of the evening edition, stepped in the cage behind me, clattered shut the gates and slotted a brass lever on the control box. The cage shuddered up through the floors while the *Courier*'s employees overtook us on the stair.

The sixth floor hadn't heard about gilt or pink marble. I arrived opposite a door that had *Marge!* handwritten on a card taped at eye level, knocked and got no answer, tried the handle and walked in. The room had a radiator hammering from overwork, tobacco haze stiff enough to cut through a head cold and a tray of tea steaming on an open rolltop desk. I unbuttoned my coat. There might be reports coming in of Red Army tanks rolling down Pall Mall, but Carleton Hamnett of the *Courier* was sure to be back before his tea cooled.

Carl had been Royal Navy and knew how to organize in a tight space. His office amounted to the rolltop desk and a set of file drawers inside the door, reference books running around the three other walls and an extra chair he could stand on to reach them. An outdoor coat hung beside the file drawers. Rubber overshoes warmed against a heating pipe behind the desk. There was no window. The only decoration was a framed picture on top of one of the cabinets of a sleek navy frigate edging into Malta's Grand Harbor. It was barely creating a bow wave, on the kind of hot June afternoon that can make even a warship look serene. The office door rattled open and Carl stepped inside, threw back his shoulders, stood extravagantly at attention and saluted with the file he was carrying. "Newman, old man! How the devil are you?"

Carl was gangling, in a dark blue gabardine suit missing only the stripes on the cuffs. He wore a Service tie, crooked a thumb outside the side pocket of his jacket and kept a clench on the stem of a straight briar pipe, rigid in a slot in his teeth. You guessed he bathed and shaved with it there. He laid the file on the rolltop and shut the door behind him, pumped my hand as if the water in the hold was gaining on us and said, "Ah, that." He nodded at the Grand Harbor photograph in my other hand. "Days of brine and poses. Showing the flag and taking photographs with tremendously pretty girls. After VE, it was all they asked of us. Can't interest you, I suppose?" Carl levered the unlit pipe out of his mouth, slipped it in his breast pocket and lifted a squat brown teapot in both hands. He made circles in the air with it, as if it helped his divining, then poured black tea in a cup and added milk from a jug. The heel of his hand wiped across his forehead, he rolled out the swivel chair from under his desk, stretched out in it and tilted back his head and asked, "*Don't Forget the Bootees. How does that strike you?"

I looked down at him slowly. He had his elbows planted on the arms of the chair, the saucer and cup level with his chin and his lips pursed ready to blow. I got a coy, sidelong glance straight from the wardroom. "Marjorie, old man. *Vox pop* tells us our distaff readers have no wish to be lectured about isobars and dew points as they ponder their day's attire over breakfast. No indeed. They want down-to-earth advice. When Marjorie says *Take a Mackintosh*, she tells our lady reader all she needs to know. Plain talk, you see. Well then, the weather chaps inform us temperatures are on the up, whereupon the appalling white stuff will turn to something still more ghastly. Well and good. But the question is, what does Marjorie say?"

Carl brought his gaze up from the tea and saw my wonder.

"She's a cartoon, old man. Well upholstered, tight skirt, nice legs; inside-back page under the racing form. You must have seen her. There is manifest research showing our representative male appreciates Marjorie not one whit less than the ladies. In fact..." He gave me the confidential eye. "I am reliably informed that until he read the *Courier* on the afternoon before D-Day, Eisenhower himself was entirely unconvinced by his boffins' weather prognosis. Opens to our back page and what does he see? Marjorie! Saying, *We're Off to the Beach Tomorrow!* She made the decision of his military career for him. Not a technical chap either, I gather."

I was still gawking at him. "You mean *you're* Marjorie?"

Carl sketched a deflated frown. "She is but one of the editorial functions I perform loyally for this august sheet. And insofar as I may be the judge, by no means the least. *Vide* Ike, old man. I rest my case."

He was reaching a pouch of pipe tobacco from his desk drawer. Not a week ago, Carl had been begging for anything at all on Jarrett's murder and calling it an hour of need. Since then, his newspaper had reported three more City killings, and still he hadn't asked what I was doing in his office. I leaned against his bookshelves, wondering where he was getting his news. "The *Courier*'s photographer was at the nurse's funeral this morning. Her sister meant it to be a private affair. What will it take to pull the pictures?"

Carl slid his cup and saucer back on the tray and swiveled around, scented a high card in his hand and gave me his artless look. "Of course, I'd like to help old fellow, but our readers ever clamor for more murder mayhem and we're frankly scraping the barrel. Omit our graveside pictures of the victim's family and yours truly would risk defenestration from a great height. Candidly, I would need to show exceeding good cause." He buried the bowl of his pipe in the tobacco pouch, squared up in the seat and squinted off in the distance.

"Carl, you're right. Your boss will want to know what gives, and all you'll have instead is a story to light a fire under City Police. Forget I asked."

Carl bared his teeth around the pipe stem. The idea bubbled behind his eyes. He looped a leg over his knee, set the tobacco on fire and chopped a hand at the rising smoke signals. The room relaxed with him. He grinned, seraphic. "Say on, old man. I truly am all ears."

FORTY-THREE

Littomy's office was hot as ever, its air thick enough to spoon. Four homicides had left him looking parched around the eyes. There was plenty for him not to like. Investigations were taking some of his detectives places they didn't care to revisit, his officers' conduct was getting the close attention of the press, an unsolved murder spree added no luster to City policing and mistakes were tarnishing his reputation. McAlester stood in a window bay overlooking the hill, white-lipped and wall-eyed, his features arranged in slabs. I took the customer chair at the desk where Littomy sat. He leaned back, fixed his eyes on the ceiling and thought out loud to the room. "This is not our finest hour, Newman. Three days ago, McAlester here brought in young Beaufort with a hand so heavy we were compelled to move the boy to a hospital bed. It is no small embarrassment that from there we contrived to lose him. Simply put, our invalid walked out of his hospital room. The officer on duty will assuredly never wear the uniform again. Of greater urgency however, is our need to find the boy and return him for questioning. Every hour we fail to do so makes us appear more inept. It also leaves a suspected murderer at liberty on our streets."

McAlester was a flat cut-out against the window glass. Littomy put his hands together as if he might be about to lead us all in prayer and eyed me past the tips of his fingers. "Tell me again of your interest in the Beaufort boy."

I gave him the bored look and put the edge in my voice that goes with it. "I already explained I don't have any interest. My client either. If it's what I'm here for we're all wasting our time." Littomy blinked and waited. No sound except the distant hum of the building, like radio valves warming in the basement. I fingered the necktie the doctor had picked out, wonderstruck at my eye for line and color. "You're way off base. Henry Beaufort didn't chalk off his boyfriend. The three other victims he didn't either know, or know of. They died because Garfield's murder unraveled and no other reason. Jarrett because he was hired to hustle Garfield in a City bar and drive with him down to the waterfront. Dillys Valentine because she knew Jarrett too well. The nurse because she was in the wrong place at the wrong time and witnessed Jarrett's murder. Your killer ends a life whenever there's a need, and for that there are thousands on your streets better qualified than Garfield's latest muse. Men who were six years in uniform, taught how to kill and handed medals when they showed more talent for it than the rest. Henry Beaufort doesn't make sense as a murder suspect, even if you had the weapon. Without it he isn't even a theory."

McAlester hadn't noticed the temperature in the room, stood with his topcoat buttoned and his hat set square, staring at the wall over Littomy's head, indifferent. He twisted a piece of his rock candy out of its paper into the palm of his hand, put his palm to his mouth like the wise monkey and let the wrapper glide to the floor. It got him everybody's attention. "Newman ties his guesses in ribbons. They're still guesses. Henry Beaufort is a sister jilted by his boyfriend and no alibi for Garfield or any of the others. The .38 we can find."

Strange the way you always wanted to clear your throat on his behalf. I looked over at where he blocked the window bay. Then at Littomy. "Well that's swell. Only Garfield's killer wasn't jilted, wasn't jealous or even in a rage. Just somebody with a problem two murders could have solved if Jarrett had died on the waterfront with the professor, where he was supposed to. But Jarrett didn't follow the script. He sent an edgy kid named Terry Reilly in his place, and when Reilly heard the gunshots that killed Garfield he panicked and drove his roadster back to the City. It left Jarrett on borrowed time. The nurse and the hooker were innocents who got in the way. Or does the detective inspector think they all jilted Henry Beaufort on Christmas Eve?"

McAlester parked the candy in his cheek. It was the sum of his interest. Littomy's chin veered round. "And what of Reilly?"

"Reilly is gone to ground, smart enough to know he's your next corpse when Garfield's killer finds out about him. But that wouldn't be Henry Beaufort. The professor was murdered because he was City archaeologist, not because he chiseled on his boyfriend."

Littomy's nose was built for a profile on old coins. He sighted along it. "How so?"

"The professor thought he'd found another major Roman site in the City. There was a lot at stake. If he could convince the Corporation, reconstruction would grind to a halt." I shrugged. "It didn't happen. Garfield was murdered before he could show what he had."

The nose twitched and let out a long breath, tuned to the basement hum. "And this gets us where exactly?"

"It gets you murder for money, not for a jealous mist. Reconstruction in the City is a long game, played by the well-heeled and well-connected, a collective enterprise of that happy band that bought itself a piece. By now, they have eye-watering amounts riding on Corporation planning. Every delay trims their percentages and disappoints them one and all. But Garfield wasn't killed for a clipped percentage. He was killed by somebody so far in over his head that murder could look like deliverance. Take the professor out of the picture and construction wouldn't miss a beat." We let the idea find its own level. I smoothed my necktie and put shades of loss and sadness in my voice. "When this is over, it won't be losing Henry Beaufort that makes you look ridiculous. It'll be how you mistook him for Jesse James."

McAlester snorted. The candy cracked in his teeth like a plank splitting. Nobody spoke or moved. Littomy noticed his telephone was ringing, reached for it and asked some questions, then rang off and keeled back in his chair again. He took the same level tone he'd used on his caller. "That was the *Courier*. They plan to run an item in their late edition, from a source undisclosed. They have it that young Beaufort suffered no mere accident while being approached by police for questioning. He was, they say, so severely assaulted by a senior City detective, that in last night's blackout the boy absconded from our care, fearful of further violence at our hands. The *Courier* will print detail of his injuries. The commissioner has been invited to respond. Should I wish it, they will be good enough to give my own reply due prominence in an edition on the morrow." He stretched his neck over the chairback and shut his eyes, sucked in what oxygen the room still had left and breathed, "Good. Christ. Almighty."

I left Littomy reflecting on his upcoming interview with the *Courier*, took the stair down and went out onto Snow Hill for some reflecting of my own. Dress it how you wanted, the long view on 1948 wasn't stellar. Italy and France might go commie, and when the Americans decided red wasn't the color of money, we could all be back in uniform by summer. I thought the hell with the long view. The old year still had five more hours to run and I wanted to see them through without another corpse. Five hours free of committee politicians and crooked lawyers, racketeers and oversize cops, and free of clients with lives so far out of joint they thought only a private eye would answer. A handful of hours didn't seem a lot to ask. I turned into the Thornburgh thirty yards up the rise, collected a package and a bottle of rum out of the file drawer in my office and rode the elevator back down to the street.

There was a small newsstand on Cheapside at the entrance to the Central Line subway, two hundred feet from the east end of St. Paul's. It faced across the sidewalk, side-on to a north wind, had an oil drum brazier to keep the news seller from frostbite and chestnuts blackening in a skillet over the fire. Just to stand there and inhale was worth the price of a newspaper. I walked over, picked up the latest edition of the *Courier*, pointed at the pan in the brazier and put down a coin. "One day Clem Attlee's going to walk by here, Harry, and when he smells these he'll want to nationalize you."

In winters before the war, Harry had kept a pool of hot grease in the fire all day long, frying eggs and bacon and bread in wedges thick enough to tile a roof with. Not anymore. Going into 1948, eggs were powder, bread was on ration and bacon wasn't even a rumor. As for *Fruits of Victory* they were a menu item, just not in any restaurant I dined at. He stooped under the counter for a square of newsprint, made a cone and filled it with chestnuts, wearing so many layers under a long straight coat you didn't see his knees bend. "Mr. Newman, if it gets me out of this weather, Attlee can pasteurize me."

Harry blew on his knuckles, felt for change in the satchel at his hip and wished me Happy New Year's. I wished him the same back and put the chestnuts in my pocket next to the bottle, got in a cab going east and started on the headlines in the *Courier*.

Mrs. Allynson had gotten the privacy she wanted. The *Courier* covered her sister's funeral in a notice as bare as a telegram, about a City nurse killed three days before and buried today in Hampstead cemetery. It was lean fare for devotee readers of high crime: no photographs of mourners, no pictures of a burial in the snow, no purple editorial about a young woman caught up in the cold-blooded slayings of a heartless Christmas killer. Carl had been as good as his word. He could afford to be. The late evening edition had bigger news, and a lot easier to find.

The *Courier* had run its Henry Beaufort story on an inside page, four columns to give room to develop a theme. The story began with a City officer assaulting the scion of a prominent family, ended in Henry's flight into the night. In between, it detailed his injuries sustained in questioning, asked what had gotten into the heads of City Police, and said whatever it was it had taken over the place where they used to keep their brains and decency. Littomy's picture was there under the headline. It showed the same thin smile, the lifted chin, the level gaze of probity, and the knowing eye of a superintendent who always got his man. They printed it bigger this time, in case you still couldn't put a face to the name.

The cab let me out at Tower Bridge, where a line of bombed-out warehouses ran downslope to the river. I turned east there along the waterfront, left the streetlamps behind, and in three hundred coal-black yards came on the disused ship entrance to St. Katherine's Dock. A low slick of cloud looked as if it might start raining oil.

Nothing was changed. A dead tide dribbled through the sluices. The lighter still rusted in the lock. Wrecked storehouses around the dock basin still leached their scent of wet, fried tires. I found the warehouse I wanted, and its doorway without a door, climbed the same stair I used when I left last time and worked up six floors to the top. Then, across ranks of cast iron pillars, past the section of blown-out roof, there was a glow of campfire and the soldier silhouetted, seated on a heavy beam and mumbling under his blanket like a medicine man. At four paces, Tiger twitched an eyelash and gargled low in his throat. I squatted and ruffled between his ears, then squeezed the soldier's arm under the blanket and sat down beside him.

It was the way we passed New Year's; the soldier locked in a room he let nobody inside and giving no sign he cared for company. From time to time, he got up and put wood scrap on the fire, and in the spaces between we had a one-way conversation about whatever came into my head: the slow thaw in the weather, the *Courier*'s latest on the City murders, some talk of the town. Harry's chestnuts cracked in the ashes. Water for the liquor steamed in a can. The soldier sat and listened, and sometimes his eyes lit up, just not in the places you expected. But you can't have everything, not if you don't want to drink alone. Tonight I needed sane company, even if he didn't.

We had a party and ate the chestnuts. The soldier found me a can for the hot rum. And at midnight, when the City church bells cut in one by one, we drank to whatever the New Year might bring us both. It might be that the shell shock that always plucked at him let him sleep sometimes. If it did, I never saw it. He stayed wide awake, and cold sober, and as the fire died and the liquor ran out, I got Mrs. Mayhew's package out of my pocket and unwrapped her plaid scarf. I wound it around the soldier's neck, tied it under his chin and pushed the loose ends inside his jacket. He had the military bearing still, and if things had turned out differently, he might have worn it along the high street in some county town and looked very fine. I crossed the blanket over his chest and got up off the beam to leave. Tiger didn't move a muscle. The soldier didn't look up. He had the string untied from the package and wound around his fingers, the brown paper flattened on his knee, folding it in small triangles that opened out in stars. No doubt about it, Mrs. Mayhew's parcel wrapping was his New Year's present for a rajah. I never did tell whether he liked the scarf.

The walk back through the City took most of an hour in a sleet as fine as sugar crystals. What was left of the night I had to myself and I was in no hurry. Not for any original thoughts I might have about four unsolved murders, but because at three in the morning Fleet Street would be a circus. New Year's with the soldier had better suited my mood. As the quarter hour struck I was past the south side of Saint Paul's, on the down slope of Ludgate Hill and right across the street from the Beaufort offices. I stepped in a doorway out of the weather. Levin's apartment was in darkness, high in the office frontage. Even from where I stood, the news offices were burning so much electricity you could smell it on the air. It flashed in the signage, ran along the wires, setting and printing column inches as if tomorrow they might go out of fashion. Tonight, they had a currency acting like the Titanic and a war in Kashmir, Gable and Goddard romancing in Hollywood, and Hogmanay pretty much everyplace else that counted. It was no contest. Kashmir wouldn't get a look in. City Police brutality would stay on an inside page. As for Marjorie, the *Courier* had got her syndicated until the A-bombs rained.

I put my head down and picked up the pace. In ten minutes I was alongside a line of trucks loading from the presses, tail lights running red in the gutter. In two more minutes I had my key fitted in the lock, checking corners to see I was alone. No fugitives from justice waiting in the shadows tonight. No clients or nervous lawyers or steam-shovel cops. I counted it as progress, went in and closed the door, cut the traffic noise in half and climbed the stair. Inside was chill enough for penguins.

WITTGENSTEIN'S EIGHTH PROPOSITION

Daylight scratched at the window. Traffic was building in the street. The gas fire burned and left its smell of dead matches on the room. I eased upright against the arm of the couch while the telephone went on ringing, lifted it off the floor and heard Willard's voice. "Get in the car. I want a collection made from the lawyer's office. Now."

He was hanging up when I said, "Wait." I got off the couch and trailed the wire to the window. The gray Armstrong was at the curb, parked under the same streetlamp as the councilor's Daimler a week before. It's not that you don't expect the talking tough, the limousines and their drivers in fancy uniforms or the everlasting *I want*. It's that a racketeer doesn't have it in him to disappoint. Sidney was prowling the Armstrong, rubbing the nickel trim with the cuff of his hourglass jacket, getting the office girl vote while traffic backed up. I slotted the mouthpiece under my chin, put my nose against the window and craned to see the clock at the corner of the Courier Building. It showed eight twenty-five. I said, "Can't be done. Councilor Drake is my client already. Send one of your wallflowers, they work for less."

Willard sighed. "What concerns the councilor concerns me. Talk to Mrs. Allynson." The connection hummed. I listened to it the way you look skyward on a rainy day, as if it changes anything. I was still listening when Willard cut the line.

The staircase of the Trelawne Building had the dry echo of a mausoleum. Six days ago, the second-floor door to the lawyer's anteroom had been wide open. This time I had to push it ajar. I stepped in sideways, heeled the door shut behind me, then went through to his study. The high-back armchairs were set at the same angle, side by side. The japanned table shone dull under a hanging light. Decanters glittered on the tray in the recess and holly still filled the vase in the hearth. So far as I knew, *Crown versus O'Shaughnessy, Volume IV, 1752* was on the shelf where it always had been, and in the anteroom the sign said to ring for attention, just as it did before. But there wasn't any need. The lawyer was waiting for me.

Allynson was folded over the arm of the nearest chair wearing the working suit he always wore, his right leg tucked so far under the front edge of the seat he was almost kneeling. One heel splayed at a wild angle. His right shoulder jammed in the seatback. The left hand twisted and cupped on his hip and his cheek rested along the arm of the chair. It gave me his left profile, gaze fixed on his shoe, the rimless spectacles slipped in front of his chin and his shirt collar filled with blood. On the side of the lawyer's head, a scorched and ragged wound gaped, as if a white-hot bar of metal had been forced through the cavity of his ear, spilled the insides of his skull over the shoulder of his suit and passed on through the wing of the armchair. At his left, a liquor glass had pitched unbroken on the carpet at the foot of the bookshelves. Across the carpet pattern a dull rain of blood radiated, as if the lawyer died at the center of a cloudburst.

I let out a long breath between my teeth and went over to the chair, reached for his wrist and lifted it, ice-cold already. A .38 Enfield revolver pointed at me from under the table.

I pulled a handkerchief from my top pocket, squatted down to reach it by its trigger guard, dragged it out and broke it open and sniffed. The cylinder held one spent cartridge. Its five other chambers were empty. A shot had been fired, but not recently, and the lawyer had been dead for hours. It fitted well enough. All things being equal, the .38 ought to have Allynson's prints on it. Likewise his overturned liquor glass. You wouldn't necessarily want to believe them, but it would be a beginning. I sat on my heels and snapped shut the gate of the .38, slid it back under the table, then went around the lawyer's chair and stooped to touch the carpet, damp where his drink had spilled.

One thing that feels cheaper than going through a dead man's pockets is doing it when you know there isn't any point, then finding nothing there to prove you were wrong. That apart, I left him the way I found him: doubled over the arm of the chair, hair tousled and his clothes awry, looking younger in death than I ever saw him in life. Maybe younger than on any day since they dragged him out of a burning cockpit and laid him choking in the grass. Dead, he had an air of letdown I hadn't appreciated before. I liked him better for it. Some people leave it late to make their best impression.

I quit the room by the door Mrs. Allynson had walked in the first time I visited, went through a shoebox office for a typist, then along a passage that arrived at a corner suite at front of the building, dim in a crawling winter dawn. Mrs. Allynson was sitting between two windows that overlooked the street, behind a desk that cut off the rounded angle of the room. She was dressed in the chalk-stripe she wore for a workday in the City, her hair loose around the collar of a lilac silk shirt. On the desk in front of her, a metal deedbox with a carry handle, and in her lap, one of those chromium-plated calendars the office cleaner flips so the boss will know what day it is. I moved to the corner of the desk and sat across it.

Mrs. Allynson didn't look up. Just went on flipping dates on the calendar, humming to herself and rocking in her chair, as if we were on some fairy lawn under the moonlight making daisy chains. The kind of thing, if you're a paid-up psychologist, you can snap somebody out of with a slap across the mouth. I lit a cigarette, leaned over and put it an inch from her lip and waited for smoke to get in her eyes; then when she blinked and slipped the cigarette from my fingers, let her take two deep, shaking lungs-full before I said, "You called Willard?"

Her eyes flashed their small purple lights while the question percolated. She fumbled the cigarette to an ashtray on the desk. Her head still didn't lift. "No. Joe calls my husband every morning before business. I hadn't long got here. When I told him what had happened, he said there was a box he wanted from the safe and not to call the police until you collected it. How could I say no?"

She noticed the gadget in her lap and put it back on the desk. I nodded Willard could be hard to refuse, then said, "There's a gun on the rug in your husband's library. Is it his?"

Her eyes rounded. "Whose else could it be? Doesn't it look that way?"

I reached over to grind out her cigarette still burning in the ashtray, and thought about how any dead husband will look when there's a lately used handgun and a brand-new widow close by. "Mrs. Allynson, you don't have a secretary today. The way it looks is you were the only one arriving here this morning. Let's take it you knew your husband wasn't home last night, and since that obviously didn't alarm you, let's also take it you assumed he'd worked over and his not coming home wasn't unusual. Your husband was a war veteran, invalided out, and they can find it tough being civilians again. But you didn't think his problems were serious, and even if you knew he'd kept his service revolver, you had no call to think he might use it on himself. The shock of finding out how wrong you were might explain why you didn't call police right away." We listened to traffic slowing at the crossroad below. "Any City detective will see how it looks two minutes after he walks through the door. They get the practice. When they turn the place over and start asking questions is when it gets rougher. They have the men, they have the time and they're thorough, and they'll stick with it until they're satisfied that the way it looks is no different to the way it was." One long breath let her get accustomed to the idea. Then I asked, "*Was* it any different?"

She looked out past a misted window while she made up her mind. "I suppose not. Not so very." At that, she clamped a hand over her mouth and her eyelids squeezed shut. Tears welled along her cheekbones and turned her fingers sticky.

"Call the emergency operator, Mrs. Allynson. It won't wait. And when they get here, try talking to the detectives as if they know what they're doing. Generally it helps." But it was wasted. Darwin says somewhere that the fittest to survive will always be a recently widowed redhead with brains and looks and style. Any door will open for her. A car will collect her rain or shine. She will never need to light a cigarette or dine alone or carry folding money. And for one wild, dark glance a policeman will make her allowances he makes for nobody else, because she brings out the Walter Raleigh in him. Daylight hardened in the windows. I pulled the deedbox off the desk and left. Whatever Mrs. Allynson might need to get her through the rest of her day, advice from me wouldn't be it.

A back stair dropped from the shoebox office to the lobby and brought me back out on the street, thirty yards from where Sidney had reversed the Armstrong into a tight alley, out of sight. I turned my back on it, went fast around the corner into Bevis Marks, found a phone booth and dialed the Bishopsgate police switchboard. When Kathryn Swinford came on the line her voice was guarded. "Newman, this might not be the best—"

"It isn't the best. I'm in a jam. Have you ever used a public telephone?" There was an indrawn breath. I cut in before she could get started. "There's a line of booths outside Liverpool Street subway. Call me from there. Do it now and take some loose change. They don't take a check or put calls on account."

She took my number and hung up. I left the receiver under my chin, jabbed a thumb on the cradle, closed my eyes and watched her leave. I saw her grab the purse beside her chair, put on her coat and hat from behind the office door, walk out through the laboratory without a care in the world, then pick up her stride along the corridor. She took the stair down to the entrance hall, put her shoulder to the swing door, stepped right over the sidewalk and off the curb and let the Bishopsgate traffic honk. From there she had less than two hundred yards along one side of the rail station, a cut across the frontage of the Great Eastern Hotel, a sidestep onto Liverpool Street and then the phone booths at the head of the subway stair. At that hour, one ought to be free. I had her still clipping the front of the hotel steps when the connection clicked in my ear. My thumb snapped off the cradle. Coins clattered in an empty bucket at the end of the line and she said, "I'm here. Go ahead."

Not even out of breath. You wondered if she'd saddled up and taken the bridle path. I looked both ways along the street. "Doctor, this is important. In an hour you'll get a new customer, name of Buchanan Allynson. Willard's lawyer until sometime last night. Right now, he's in his office looking like a suicide, next to a .38 Enfield his wife will say is his. When word gets out, the press will tag the lawyer as the City killer and write off Henry as a sad mistake police made along the way. Don't buy it and don't let Henry buy it. He made McAlester trouble he won't forget. Until this is over, he needs to stay care of Uncle Bernard."

She said *All right*, but without enthusiasm. Then, "Do you think it's the .38 police have been looking for?"

"The thought occurred to me."

"But if Allynson's revolver was used in three killings and he took his own life with it, how can McAlester still be interested in Henry?"

"I didn't say he took his own life. I said it looks that way, and it's a gift horse. For the front pages because neat answers make good copy. For McAlester because it can shut down every one of his murder investigations. For Littomy because by now he'll take anything that squares him with the commissioner. All Henry has to do is stay out of McAlester's way and not give him any better ideas."

She said *All right* again, as slowly as the last time. "So you found the body? Is that the jam you're in?"

"The jam is if and when McAlester learns I was anywhere near. Tell Henry to stay where you put him." Passersby were leaning into the weather and holding on to their hats. Taxicabs plowed wet snow. I cut the line and stepped back out on the sidewalk and made a circuit of the block, came level with the Armstrong and got in the back seat before Sidney looked up from the racing news. He folded the newspaper and tossed it, then took a studied interest in the blank wall of the alley. I slid aside the glass partition behind his ear. "Boss wants to see me."

Sidney eyeballed me in the mirror. He'd had a tough morning. The idea of driving me for any more of it was weighing on his bonhomie. "Wants to see you where?"

"Wherever you left him." He didn't answer. The Armstrong edged out of the alley and onto the street. At right, a hundred feet away, a Humber sedan had pulled across the sidewalk outside the Trelawne Building, where its driver had left it in a hurry. Sidney saw the Humber, pressed further back in his seat and peeled the Armstrong left. I wound my hand around the glass partition, reached for his newspaper on the ledge behind his head and opened it to the inside back page. I was interested to know how Marjorie saw the rest of the day panning out.

Inside ten minutes, the Armstrong was crossing over London Bridge into Southwark, went left on Tooley Street, doubled back along the river and drove the quarter mile to a converted block of offices between the cathedral and the wharfs. The block was four stories, empty lots both sides, shored with heavy timbers and slicing a stiff, chill wind off the water. It had an entrance set back from the weather and a board listing tenants. Drake, Willard & Co. occupied the whole third floor.

No elevator, only a stair climbing to a door marked Reception and an office with a low wooden rail across the center of the room. There was a gate in the rail, opposite an inner door, and a secretary seated at a desk guarding the gate, pert and pretty with her hair cropped in a fringe, fragrant as a warm breeze.

She was bent over a heavy-duty typewriter, the Willys jeep model, her bottom lip clamped under her front teeth and her chin tucked, trying to feed it a sheet of paper when what it wanted was a pulp log, whole and raw. I peeked at her around the side of the machine. She glowered back across a dozen fans of crimped paper scattered across her desk, said Mr. Willard was expecting me and to go on inside. Then she started pumping the roller feed again and the Willys spat out another paper fan. She squealed and snatched at it as I went through the gate. I had my hand on Willard's door and heeled around. "Why not climb in? We could try to jump start it." It lifted her chin out of the typewriter, far enough to give me the bleak look. Then she put her lips together, spluttered into the keys and broke out a grin from her best collection. I grinned back and went through the door.

Willard was standing at a window with a view across the river, turned my way when the door closed and watched me across the room. I put the deedbox flat on the desk between us where he could open it and moved to a window of my own. A tugboat hooted mid-river and poured soot on the water. Willard found a key and used it on the box, sat down at his desk and began reading in a slim file he took out. Each time he turned a page a lump hardened in his throat and his mood clotted. He twisted in the chair and rapped a knuckle on the file. "Mrs. Allynson says what about this?"

The click of a typewriter started up on the other side of the door. "Mrs. Allynson was in the nursery cutting out paper dolls, probably because her husband was in a room nearby with his brains in his lap. It didn't help conversation, and besides, my mind was on other things. As for instance her upcoming interview with City Police, and the guarantee that if they learn I was in Allynson's office ahead of them, they'll first stand me in hot coals and second put me out of business. I mean for good. No more private inquiry ever. You already knew that when you sent me there, and one small part of me is curious to know why. Every other part thinks I ought to break your ankles."

It got me the elegant, irritated look. His perfume so heavy on the room you wanted to open the door and let it run down the stair. He dropped the file beside the metal box, settled the stud in his tie and wound his wristwatch as if my time was his money. "She says her husband killed himself last night. What do you say?"

Wall lights burned low in the corners of the room and only made the day seem darker. I said, "Consider it his New Year present to City Police. What's in the box?" Willard leaned forward in his chair and told me what, in the listless, detached way a dealer will announce the house just lost, the better to conceal the heartache. Snow White can sound like conspiracy if you tell it that way. It wasn't what bothered me. What bothered me was why Willard would be telling me at all.

He said what was in the box were sale contracts on four City properties, bought by his late lawyer for a private company Willard owned. What else his company owned he didn't say. Only that on the last day in December Allynson had added a wholesale dairy, an industrial coal yard, a small brassworks and a produce warehouse, lately used by a dry goods distributor. But only in a manner of speaking. Because none of the four properties had been a going concern. What the lawyer had bought were four joined-up bombsites in the City, where even the rubble had been trucked away. Four lots that cost their new owner nigh a million US dollars, in hard, straight cash. American dollars because, owing to a range of services rendered to United States personnel in wartime, Willard had greenbacks to bathe in. Also because sterling was in a crisis that could make it stage money before long, and the dollar talked. I lifted my chin at the view over the river. "You bought four empty lots. So cut the grass and learn tennis. What's wrong with them?"

All he said was, "The date."

According to Willard they were deals he'd had his lawyer working on for the past two months. Then, come the week before Christmas, Allynson had arrived to get a signature on four contracts, ahead of making the transactions between Christmas and New Year. He'd left with the deedbox, carrying dollars enough to float a banana republic. It might be sixth sense. Or it might be overactive glands. But when the commercially gifted brush up against an unsound investment it can break them out in a rash. Willard hardly knew how to explain it himself, only that days after he signed the contracts he had a change of heart, called his lawyer late afternoon Christmas Eve and told him the deal was canned. Just like that. Willard considered the matter closed and hadn't given it another thought until a little more than two hours ago, when Mrs. Allynson took his daily call and explained why her husband wasn't answering the telephone this morning. The news had rocked him. And in her time of loss, Willard's thoughts had naturally gone out to the king's ransom in hundred-dollar bills locked in his lawyer's office safe. He didn't want it distracting City detectives when they arrived at the scene of a suicide.

Willard needn't have worried, because all the box now had inside were four separate contracts, making him owner of some high-priced fresh air in the bombed-out heart of the City. The money was gone. The lawyer who could explain where was dead. Making two inconveniences, both of them in the past, when Willard was only looking to the future. Pale sunlight ghosted the water. Tall buildings glinted on the north shore. Willard gave me the blank, bored look that passes in the rackets for an exchange between minds and took up the file again. He read me the four addresses in the City and the names on the contracts as if they gave him heartburn, tossed the file back in its box and with the level reasonableness of a New Year's resolution said, "I want to know who these people are." Then slammed the deedbox shut like a train door. The typing in the outer office stopped dead.

I nodded at the broken skyline. "Sure you do. Noblesse obliges if somebody took you for a million dollars and left your lawyer dead as a calling card. On either count, if they don't end in the river you lose your sense of worth. So ask McAlester. It's work he enjoys."

I turned, made across the room and opened the door to the outer office. The secretary shot a nervous glance from under her fringe. Behind me, Willard said, "Last time you called McAlester a liability." I waited. He read off the four names like a catechism. "Boyd, Ralston, Seeley, Irving. Find them. I can guarantee you stay in business."

A racketeer's largesse is Maundy money. You get tossed something you didn't ask for, it doesn't change your economics in any way whatever, and still you're meant to tip your hat in gratitude. Down on the street, the Armstrong was waiting with its windows misted and its motor ticking, burning gas enough for a small village. I left it sitting at the curb. The addresses Willard had given me were just a walk across the river. As for the names on the contracts, they could wait. We were already acquainted.

I crossed back north on Southwark Bridge, leaning into an upriver wind that cut strips off my chin. Two hundred yards downstream, a solitary locomotive steamed in the opposite direction above a tide roiling past the bridge piers in lumps. I took a straight line across Cannon Street, turned west onto Cheapside and walked halfway to St. Paul's, then went north again on Wood Street. From there, a vista opened that might have been Rotterdam or Warsaw or the outlook from the Brandenburg Gate. I stepped in the shelter of a boarded-up storefront, put my back against it and took the view.

East and north of St. Paul's, the street grid cut through a checkerboard of snow-covered basements. Nothing left standing but a scatter of shored-up ruins in a wasteland of empty lots, nothing moving but a drift of traffic with no reason to stop. Up until a week ago, Willard had been ready to pay a dollar fortune for just four pieces of it. Now he owned them and there was no disguising his sense of loss. Sixth sense to one side, you wondered what or who had changed his mind. I held onto my hat and moved out into no-man's land.

Away from the river the wind had dulled its knife-edge and a thaw was crawling out of the ground like waking spiders. I followed telegraph wires that marked out the through streets, as far as a City block that ended at Aldersgate and had Bart's hospital along its west side. On its south and east, the block ran to the edge of Cripplegate. In between it had been bombed flat as tulip fields and you saw its appeal. Forget rolling blue hills or hay carts or fat cattle fording water meadows. If you plan to buy and develop it, not paint it in oils, there is no landscape easier on the eye than a city block blitzed to rubble.

Cripplegate. Henry had shown me it was once a gate in the Roman city wall. Centuries later it was a Jewish quarter, and later still the neighborhood where Milton spun lines of *Paradise Lost* when he was old and blind and republican enough to get himself arrested. The night it was fire-bombed it had been a close-built factory quarter. Hardly anybody had lived there for a generation. Now, all it had to show was the rat-run pattern of its medieval streets pressed in the ground like a mold in sand. That, and the street names. They hadn't changed either. Not since before the time they tossed Milton in the slammer.

By Christmas 1940, the Luftwaffe's bombers had been working the same shift for months, took a few days' break for the holiday and came back rested. Then one night before New Year's—eight years ago almost to the day—dropped a hundred thousand incendiaries in a single raid and started a firestorm. Somewhere in front of me, a coal yard, a dry goods distributor, a brassworks and a dairy had gone up in flames. Exactly where the buildings had stood was impossible to tell. I didn't see it mattered much. What mattered more was a kind of alchemy. On that one night alone the bombing turned a third of the City to brick dust. Every day since, the City Corporation had been working at turning the brick dust back into gold. The same alchemy had gotten Councilor Drake airborne, flying circles over the City while Michael Garfield took pictures from the cabin window. And two days later, on Christmas Eve, it was alchemy that brought the councilor to the Sesto to see the results for himself. The signora had seen the light in Garfield's eye that afternoon and had an instinct he'd found what he was looking for. She wasn't alone. The councilor had an instinct about it too, and when he left the Sesto he'd called Guy Beaufort to tell him so. I turned west and headed to Smithfield.

The slow thaw was putting a gloss on the tire tracks. The path through the churchyard had boiler ashes underfoot. Snow was slipping off roof pitches and piling in the gutters around the church. Nowhere outside of Littomy's office had been this warm in a week. I pushed inside from the porch along an aisle I'd taken twice before, through the same pulsing quiet, the same veil of incense, as far as the wrought iron gate to the lady chapel behind the altar. Gray daylight drifted in overhead. The chapel swam in the waters of a cold ocean, filled with dates and histories, verses and valedictions, on its walls and on its floor and in its window glass. Everywhere crowded with the dead. If they hadn't pulled him out of his burning airplane with his lungs on fire, Allynson would have been there himself, at the head of his squadron's honor roll, in company with Charlie Ross and a score of others. I read through the names behind the glass again. It was illustrious company. The lawyer just hadn't been destined to keep it.

FORTY-FIVE

It was one of those midwinter afternoons where the sun comes wrapped in high fog, and hangs by a thread so fragile you're ready to put out a hand to catch it. I was on New Bridge Street, walking south to the river at Blackfriars, the sidewalk had a spring under my shoes and the sun was on my face for the first time in days. Two hundred yards before the bridge I turned aside into a street blocked in shadow, buttoned my coat to the chin and left the top hat and tails mood behind. Tudor Street was as dank as a fish cellar.

The street ended at a gatehouse on the east side of the Temple, a part of the Inns of Court that reached west halfway to Waterloo Bridge, and from Fleet Street south to the river. Temple Inn alone was the size of a city park, an ancient warren of lawyers' chambers and residences where trained legal minds deliberated on the statutes the way a clam deliberates on an ice age. Until the Luftwaffe's bombing opened up the view, it had looked much the same way it looked to Dickens. King's Bench Walk was a Georgian brick row looking out over the parkland, leading down to the river from inside the gatehouse arch. There were frayed and blackened gaps in the row. But out there in Africa, sitting under a shade tree in his safari wig, Uncle Bernard didn't have to worry. His chambers stood in a section the blitz had skipped by. I went in under a lantern set beneath the hoop of an iron gate, climbed a short rise of steps to the door, let myself into a narrow hallway and put on a light. The hallway breathed the scents of silk and old port that high court judges' dreams are made of.

Sir Bernard's private rooms were closed up and shuttered just the way he left them. Dust thickened in the parlor. Clocks had stopped. The air was stiff with the smell of animal hides. Walls, tables and all spaces in between were stuffed with a colonial's collection from darkest Africa. The judge had enough fly whisks and native drums, antelope rugs and witch doctor masks to fit out a high-class bordello in Bulawayo. Through the parlor, there was a study with a coal stove set in a corner. At one side of the stove, a screen gave some privacy to a daybed where Henry lay in a heap under the covers. I pulled up a chair. Henry shifted, looking feverish, blinked and waited to get me in focus, then croaked, "I thought you were Kathryn."

I poured water from a decanter by his pillow, got him sitting upright and passed him the glass. "It's hard for her to get here. City Police know she's a friend of the family and she can be followed. Besides, she's got another body to work on." He took a sip, set down the glass, and bunched a blanket under a jaw still ballooned from his run-in with McAlester. Add his curls and sickroom pallor and he could have been Shirley Temple acting the mumps. "A lawyer named Allynson—Drake & Willard's lawyer—was shot dead in his office last night. It might have been suicide or it might not, but either way a .38 revolver was found next to the body. Pretty soon, City Police will know if it was the same gun that killed Michael Garfield, Jarrett and the nurse. If it was, and if McAlester decides the lawyer killed himself, he'll fit Allynson for three murders straight off, find a way to make Dillys Valentine the fourth, and close his files. It will be fast, clean and his suspect is already in the morgue. So don't complicate it for him. Stay here, stay out of his plans and let him make his play. Understood?"

Henry sweated and shivered at the same time and tried to make sense of it. "Why would the police think Drake's lawyer wanted to kill Michael?"

Good question. How to tell him it was nothing but convenience? Convenient to Littomy because he had a policing disaster on his hands. Convenient to his detective inspector because he needed better press. Convenient to a commissioner desperate for a success to dine out on, and convenient to every Fleet Street crime editor scouting for something fresh. I dragged a chair where it put me in his line of sight. "Henry, they don't need reasons. It's one policeman's arithmetic, and if you're not a part of his calculation then take it as a gift. Either that or tell me who else but you in this entire city doesn't have an alibi for any of five killings. Then tell me why McAlester would care."

He pulled the blanket across his mouth and folded in a racking cough, and when the fit ended went slack as if he'd been hit in the stomach. I leaned closer. "You want to know who killed your friend. I want to know too because the arithmetic is making me unwell. So listen to me. Michael Garfield's airplane pictures were enough to grind City planning to a stop. Around lunchtime Christmas Eve he met Drake to tell him so. Eight hours later, the pictures got him killed by somebody with too much at stake to let him chase a dream." I was emptying my pockets, setting what I had on the bed cover: a draft report Garfield had dumped in his wastebasket, an envelope with the airplane pictures he took, his diary written in languages out of fashion for a thousand years. What the professor wrote I couldn't read. What he'd photographed I didn't understand. For what it had cost it wasn't much return, and without Henry's help it was nothing at all. "The diary was in the professor's briefcase on the back seat of the roadster. The photographs were likely taken from his pockets after he was murdered." I shook Garfield's pictures out of the envelope. "But his killer couldn't rest without the negatives and he had the professor's house key from the car ignition. He walked the quarter-mile to Cross Key Square, ditched his blood-soaked coat in the closet where you found it and took the place apart. And still he missed the negatives that printed these."

Henry's eyelids flickered while he worked at a problem. "If Michael's killer couldn't find the negatives, how did you?"

"The way I find everything. I hear voices. Like Joan of Arc." His eyes shut and he nodded, as if he thought so all along. "Henry, there's something special in those pictures. It's a longshot, but the diary might say what. I want you to read it for me." But I'd lost him, his face buried in the covers, snorting like a seal. I dropped his two keepsake pictures with the rest; Henry and his professor photographed one hot summer afternoon in the dapple of a summer lawn, before either of them knew they had a care in the world.

The telephone had started ringing in the hallway. When I picked up there was a faint catch at the end of the line. I said, "He sleeps, Doctor. Even jungle drums won't wake him."

Kathryn Swinford's voice cut through, low and pressing. "I need to see you, but not here in the office. I can take my lunch break and we can meet by the Countess of Albemarle. In half an hour?"

"I'll find it. But it's getting near closing time."

I heard her eyes roll. "It is not a public saloon, it's a painting in a quiet room in the National Gallery. You do know we have a National Gallery?"

I put the receiver under my chin and felt for a cigarette. "We do?"

"Yes, we do."

"Then I'll be there."

She said *Good* and hung up.

The Second Countess of Albemarle was a Georgian society widow with a pallor and time on her hands. The portrait showed her busy at her lacework in a black-edged bonnet, and a shawl covering a blue silk dress. She was forty years past her prime, not overjoyed at having a new likeness taken. She needn't have worried. The painting hung in a room so out of the way only the guard ever saw it. He was standing outside in a corridor with his arms folded, flapping at a yawn. Having him there for company wasn't improving the countess's mood. "She's a relation?"

Kathryn Swinford said, "Distantly. Why? Is there a resemblance?"

I considered the idea. The Second Countess had been a beauty once. "The nose."

She stiffened at that. "What's wrong with my nose?"

"Nothing's wrong with it. I like it. It's just that hers looks as if it doesn't want to be here either."

We stood shoulder to shoulder at one side of the picture, two swells admiring the brushwork on the flesh tones. She had her coat belted, a fine wool scarf tied at her throat. The gallery was a refrigerator. "The Earl left the Countess in debt when he died. She didn't stump up for the portrait until years later." Then, offhand, "You found Henry."

"What I found was the source of the White Nile. Henry was in the next room. I said to stay where you put him, but the advice might not take."

The guard lifted a watch from his vest pocket, swayed on his heels and headed off to find another crowd to marshal. Kathryn Swinford waited till his footsteps died, then turned her back on the countess and watched the entrance to the room, small talk over. Her voice lowered. "I saw Allynson. McAlester telephoned soon after you did and insisted I should see the body before it was moved. How did you come to be there in the first place?"

"Willard called, wanted a collection made from his lawyer's office and didn't say what. He also didn't mention his lawyer had taken a bullet in the head. I walked right into it. Was it suicide?"

A rain squall started beating on the roof lights. Shadows in the room turned to sick yellow. "Hard to say. He died between late evening and early morning from a single gunshot, very close, that entered behind the left ear and exited into the chair frame. His prints are the only ones on the revolver and on the glass he was drinking from, though they're not the best. Against that, there was no suicide note and the powder nitrates pattern isn't that convincing. Mrs. Allynson's prints are everywhere of course. Other prints will take time to check against his secretary and known visitors. Yours will be among them, I suppose." Her eyes lifted to the drum of heavy rainfall on the skylight. "Meanwhile, McAlester seems to have decided that Allynson took his own life, with the gun he's been looking for since Jarrett's murder. I doubt the lab report will contradict him. It will at least be better for Henry this way. You think it sounds all too neat for words, don't you?"

She said *neat* and made it sound like an allergy. Maybe she was right. Since my first call from the councilor and my first interview with Littomy, there were things giving me an itch. Things that passed in shadows, unasked, unanswered and unremembered, as if the asking and remembering would break a spell. Hoodlum or harlot, policeman or politician, the spell had cast across the City and marked whoever it touched. Last night it had touched Willard's lawyer, and McAlester planned to call it suicide as if I wouldn't know or care. "So the lawyer's prints were on the gun and on the glass. Which hand?"

It got her attention back from the weather. "Left-hand prints on both. Why? Wasn't Allynson left-handed?"

I nodded. "Yes, he was. When the .38 was fired point blank he had the glass in his left hand. It hit like a steam hammer, the glass jerked over his left shoulder and ended at the foot of his bookshelves. The rug behind his chair was still damp from spilled liquor. Meaning he didn't shoot himself. He was shot. Not even a lawyer will hold a stiff drink in the same hand he shoots himself with. It's how it looked when I got there. Also, how McAlester saw it when he arrived."

"But it wasn't on the floor..."

Everybody does it the same way, more or less. They go back over a room in their mind's eye, move around in it and place the things they can recall. Some are more reliable than others, some are even photographic, but it's rare, and Kathryn Swinford wasn't one of them. She had to fit the lawyer's study back together one item at a time: the legal books on the shelves, the holly in the vase on the hearth, and the lawyer curled over the arm of his chair as if he'd been searching for something he dropped. Fitting it together wouldn't be the hard part. The hard part would be realizing McAlester had been two steps ahead of her, and that Doc Templeton's classes ran short on police method. She shook her head at the low humiliation of it. "When I arrived, Allynson's drink was unfinished on the table. McAlester saw the same murder dressed up as suicide that you did, but he meant it to stay that way. And if the glass and the revolver both had the lawyer's left-hand prints on them, then obviously suicide wouldn't wash if the glass was empty on the floor. So he tidied up. He put the glass back on the table, poured another drink, then called me to the scene before forensics arrived. I'm his corroborating witness, aren't I? He's made an utter fool of me."

Being set up by police is like a summer rain; by the time you smell it on the air, you're already caught in the storm. You wonder that you didn't see it coming and tell yourself next time you'll be wiser and stay dry. But you're wasting your breath. Because the truth is, police sit at a high table where the rules are their own, and honest or dishonest is just a matter of who they're working for. Kathryn Swinford's cheeks colored and her eyelids sprung open. "Damn him for it! What do we do now?"

I'd been thinking about that. For one whole week McAlester had kept his investigation on a leash so tight it was choking; neglecting a trail of payoffs and shakedowns and five-star police protection that would finish more careers than his own if he let his detectives loose on it. Fixing Allynson's suicide would square it all, no question. But it was a big risk. To fit a dead lawyer for the City murders, McAlester had to be very sure the killing was over, and if it turned out it wasn't, he had no way back. Another homicide would give the press a field day, certainly end his rank, necessarily leave him worthless to Willard and likely take Littomy down with him. You wondered how he could be so sure. But the doctor was right about one thing. It ought to see Henry Beaufort walk free. Likewise Terry Reilly, assuming he still lived. I looked over at the blue countess. "What do we do? The dead lawyer gives us a widow of our own, and her money troubles are only just started."

FORTY-SIX

For a one-client lawyer, Allynson had kept an elegant brick row house, four floors with white stucco detail around the windows, on the north side of Lincoln's Inn Fields. Its entrance stepped up off the sidewalk, set back inside two lime-washed pillars. From the second floor, three tall windows overlooked the treetops in the park, which would make satisfying viewing on this or any late afternoon, even if you had company. And there was company. An Armstrong limousine was parked right under the windows, polished as a button on parade and sparkling from the last rain shower. Sydney sat limp behind the wheel, wrists rested on the spokes, his neck arched over the seatback and his eyelids hooded against the smoke from a cigarette slotted in his teeth. I walked up on the Armstrong's blind side, stopped at its rear door and brought my hand down flat and hard on the roof over his head. Sidney jackknifed, bit through the filter of his cigarette and buried his chin in the roof lining. He had one hand clamped across his nose, the other batting out the cigarette burning in his lap, when Mrs. Allynson answered her doorbell. She lifted her eyebrows to tell me I wasn't expected, then invited me inside.

Grief takes people in different ways. Mrs. Allynson's had moved her to change her chalk-stripe costume for a soft, blue housedress that fitted in her waist, fell loose along her arms and clung from her hips down. The blue was livened by a string of cut stones of a lighter shade, a dark silk flower pinned high on a mandarin collar, high-heeled matching slippers, straight seams and a scent of jasmine blossom in her hair. We didn't speak. She seemed a little out of joint. Following close behind her to the top of the stair was work you don't expect to get paid for.

At the second floor, she led directly across a hall to a sitting room on the grand scale, furnished in old gold and dark crimsons and low-lit along the walls like the lounge car of a night express. It had easy chairs in corners where you could be solitary, and a maps collection in the spaces between the wall lights to stroll by and study on a foggy day. A quiet hour alone in there would have appealed right then, but you never can have it all. Willard was sitting at a low table with his back to the last of the daylight, wearing a suit cut wide at the shoulders and a silk tie louder than the room could bear. He had a cigarette pinched in a knuckle while he tipped a powder in a glass of water, swirled it, swallowed it and winced. He set the glass on the table, hooked the cigarette in one side of his mouth and talked out of the side he still had available. "What brings you?" The cigarette jounced as he talked in the hard-boiled manner they practice in a mirror until they can scare themselves to death.

Mrs. Allynson sat across from him and knitted a frown. I said, "News concerning your late lawyer, but don't leave on that account. It ought to interest you both." The afternoon was giving up, exhausted, turning the room's windows to mirror-glass. Night clouds rolled by so heavy they bumped against tall chimneys on the roofs. I took a chair and started before I hit the seat. "City Police are deciding Allynson killed himself at some time last night with his own service handgun. It was near his body and likely the same weapon that killed Garfield and Jarrett and the nurse. No gun was involved in Miss Valentine's murder, but they'll work on it and take him for all four."

Willard snapped a thumbnail between his front teeth. "Why would they do that?"

"Because it appeals to their sense of economy. Also, because they can make a case for it faster than you can lose your headache. None of us has to believe it. They don't even have to believe it themselves."

Willard pulled the cigarette off his lip, dipped it in the water at the bottom of his powder glass and let his eyes dull with poison. "There are harder things to believe. Take our widow here. She can't think what kept her husband at his office overnight. Or why he signed away a million dollars of mine before he died to people I never knew, for something I didn't want. The widow says she never knew them either and their names don't mean a thing. Isn't that so, Vivien?"

For somebody at the center of a conversation, Mrs. Allynson had been preoccupied since we walked in the room. She sat with her chin tilted at the prowl of traffic on the square. I raised an eyebrow for mild surprise. "She knew one of them." Her chin swung in my direction. Willard's lip lifted off his front teeth. I said, "Boyd. Ralston. Seeley. Irving. The counterparties to the contracts your lawyer made. You read me their names in your office this morning, and any one of them alone probably wouldn't have meant a thing to me. But all four together? Not a mile from here there's a memorial for a fighter squadron and they're listed on its honor roll: Flying Officer Walter *Boyd* Headley Hammond DFC; Pilot Officer Edwin Rollo *Ralston* Walcott; Warrant Officer Owen Evan *Seeley* Ryle; and Flight Lieutenant Charles *Irving* John Ross. Names like that stand out in a crowd."

Mrs. Allynson stiffened and sat up with a look of wild, unvarnished disbelief. "Charlie?"

Willard hooked a patent shoe over his knee and contemplated her like a boat cut adrift from the shore. It isn't enough that they dress like Robert Taylor, they have to act like him too. "You *know* these people, Vivien?"

I shuffled for a cigarette while she sat and looked hollow. "Mrs. Allynson knew Flight Lieutenant Ross because her sister was his girl once. It's irrelevant. What's relevant is her husband knew them all. They flew together, and by summer '44 he was the only survivor. The others were lost in action. They're names Allynson pulled out of the air. Their signatures are make-believe. Your title contracts are a fraud. And it still doesn't tell you how your lawyer died." A pulse started fluttering in Willard's cheek. I put in the cigarette and talked through it. "If Allynson shot himself it's because he skimmed on you and knew there was no disguising it any longer. That makes it not pretty. But if he was shot, it means somebody set you up in style. And that makes it a problem."

Mrs. Allynson started as if I'd stepped out in front of a tramcar. Willard dropped the contemplative air and got to his feet. When I arrived his mood had been corrosive and the powder hadn't done a thing to lift it. He was halfway to the door when he spun around. "Be at the Garden tonight, Vivien." Then to me, "You've got a loose mouth, Newman. Don't let it be the way you're remembered."

Mrs. Allynson didn't move until the street door closed, then unwound out of her chair. She took the cigarette off my lip and walked along the room with it, lifted a lighter from the mantel over the hearth and steadied it in both hands. It flamed till she heard the Armstrong pull from the curb, then snapped shut. "Did you have to be so brutal?" She had her thumb pressed against her temple, watching the curl from her cigarette climb to the shadows on the ceiling. It gave her a fragile look I didn't know she owned.

"Willard? He's adjusting to being on the wrong end of a shakedown. It's unfamiliar territory. Let him adjust. He thinks you're not leveling, and if I give him nothing at all his next stop will be McAlester, in which case brutal will not be the word. Besides, he's right. You're not leveling." The coal fire flickered and put dark red lights in her hair.

Sometimes you talk to somebody half a room away and they might as well be in another country. "City Police still have to decide who shot Jarrett, but you would already know. It was the conversation you had with your sister at the Viaduct."

Vivien Allynson didn't argue or show any surprise, just stood a long, still moment, let the heat from the coals burn pink in her cheek, then glided back along the room to stand behind my chair, slotted the cigarette under my lip again and rested her hands on my shoulders. "Of course, but what could it matter now that Estelle heard the gunshot from inside the church? Or that when she ran into the porch it was my husband she saw standing over Jarrett's body? The little fool was trying to protect me. If she'd told me before, we'd have gone to the police together and she might still be alive." Her hands ran around the back of my collar and squeezed, close enough to feel the sway of her necklace. "She knew you never had believed her story and wanted to explain. She thought you'd know what to do. I said I thought so too. At least it was something we agreed on." Her grip loosed and pulled away. "Then next day she was dead and what was I supposed to say to the police? That Estelle had been lying all along? That I was so sick with fear I couldn't bear to be near my husband? Or that when I found him this morning the only thing I felt was relief? Who else but you can I say that to? Not to Joe. He thinks if his lawyer cheated him then his lawyer's wife had to know, though what he imagines I can tell him I have no idea." She went back to her chair at the window, toying with the buttons on her cuff. Evening was crawling up the sky. The room sighed and stretched out along the rug.

"Since when did you know him?"

Her eyes wondered if I'd been listening, then decided they could humor me. "Since the summer of '41. At about the same time he met a new lawyer—a flyer invalided out—and promised him the law would never be dull again. Joe made an impression, as he does. We saw a lot of each other. Then he was introduced to a councilor's daughter and soon they were married. Not long after, so was I. Consider me the lucky one. I already knew more about Joe Willard than anyone should." A line of moisture was glossing the top of her lip. She touched the back of her wrist there, as softly as a moth lands. We left it at that.

FORTY-SEVEN

George had put two items under my office door. I put on a
light and read them both. The first was a telephone message
to return a call. The second was an envelope, hand-addressed
and hand-delivered. I dialed the return number and ripped
open the envelope flap while the line connected. Inside was a
note from Carl Hamnett, wanting to explain about the picture
in the afternoon edition of the *Courier*. I took my copy out
of a coat pocket and dropped it on the desk, already folded
to a headline, *Lawyer's Suicide Link to City Murders*. Below
it, a fuzzy portrait of Allynson showed him looking cold and
miserable, cropped out and enlarged from a long-shot taken
in Hampstead cemetery. The *Courier*'s editor had decided
the picture was a gift, and Carl was contrite because we
had an agreement. Our agreement had gotten Carl his scoop
on Henry Beaufort's run-in with City Police. In return, the
Courier was supposed to lose its photographs of a private
funeral for a murdered nurse. Strictly speaking, his editor
had kept Carl's promise. The *Courier* hadn't printed the
funeral pictures, which was all I asked. But Carl felt shabby
about it, and the reek of his black tobacco on the notepaper
was like having him standing there in the room, shamefaced.

The receiver picked up at the end of the line. A wheezing voice steadied itself. I flattened out the Allynson item on the desk and cut in. "You called me, signora. You read this afternoon's *Courier*."

The signora dredged a sigh and said she had. She was calling because the lady police doctor said to if ever she saw the man again who used to dine in her restaurant with the nurse. Didn't I remember the lady doctor? I said I did, but she sounded doubtful. "I never think to see this man again, and now he is a picture on a newspaper. Ev-ery-body is dy-ing."

I commiserated on another customer lost and pulled the lawyer's portrait closer. "Signora, are you certain the man in the newspaper is the man the nurse came in with?" We had a second's silence while she caught her breath. Then she blew a fuse and cut a high squeal, called on Mary and all the saints, told me how the nurse always looked, what her friend in the photograph wore and what each of them ever ate at her table. She knew her customers. Did I think she needed glasses or did I think she was losing her mind? I tried to tell her neither, that it was just something I was supposed to ask, but the chance never came. We went around her grievances until her breath gave out, then she cursed and slammed down the phone. In Italian it passes for conversation.

While the signora ran down her oxygen supply a silhouette had drifted past my office door. Half a minute later it came back and stopped to read the letters on the glass, as if they were instructions for opening. When my call ended, I got to my feet and went over, yanked open the door and nodded at the gilt letterwork. "It says *Private Inquiries*, and you're meant to use the buzzer."

Edgar Levin peeled off his hat and used it to brush rain off his gabardine, looked sheepish, stepped inside and closed the door. "Yes, of course. I'm sorry. This business of calling on a private detective is new to me."

I never yet had a client who said it wasn't. Not unless they came to argue expenses. Levin slacked his raincoat, took the customer chair and hooked his hat over his knee. I settled opposite and let him find a cigarette, flared a match on my thumbnail to help him with the mood, and asked, "Why would you want to start now?"

He leaned across the desk to dip at the flame. "I had a telephone call this afternoon from Henry Beaufort." The lighted match licked at my finger. I shook it out and tossed the stalk on the desk, sank back and said to go on. "He was barely able to talk, but he said you'd asked him to go through Michael Garfield's diary and photographs. He gave me a list of things he needs for reference from the professor's office at Guildhall, and if you can credit it..."

I credited it. "Garfield had his best thoughts in dead languages. I know."

Levin's dark eyebrows lifted. "Then how long can you wait? He sounds all in." I sat staring at Levin, wondering why Henry Beaufort not acting on advice should surprise me. Next time I'd put a gag on him, rip out the telephone cord and leave him tied in a chair. For now, it was something else added to my long history of omissions.

Henry had telephoned to Edgar Levin. Edgar Levin had called on me, and if McAlester still had me watched, a City detective would tail Levin back to Guildhall, then to Temple Inn. After which, Levin might as well stand in line with the City's acting medical examiner and her distinguished Uncle Bernard, put his head between his legs and kiss his career goodbye. I eased up in the chair and turned the *Courier*'s headline around where Levin could read it. "He is all in. He also wants to know who killed his boyfriend. As of this morning, City Police are working on it being Willard's lawyer, who they say killed himself with the same handgun he used in three murders. It's a blind, but the *Courier* says Littomy likes the theory so much he's put all his detectives on it. Which is where you're in luck, because it ought to mean you won't have a police tail when you leave here. Maybe you're right. Maybe I can't wait that long. And maybe nothing Garfield ever wrote in Greek or photographed from an airplane will point at his killer. Without Henry there isn't a way to find out. If you need to, you'll talk your way into Garfield's office faster than I can. So go get our boy what he needs and do it now, while City Police have higher things on their minds."

Levin looked startled at the idea of being shadowed by the forces of law and order. Then acclimatized and went through the one-handed maneuver that got him on his feet. He was buttoned in his raincoat, standing square in the doorframe and batting his hat against his knee, needing to get something off his chest. "About the diary Sybil brought you. She really had no idea how Willard was using it."

"When I thought about that, I didn't expect she had."

His hand motioned with the hat, satisfied. "What will you do with the diary?"

"That depends what Henry finds in it, don't you think?"

He nodded, then his mouth slanted in the closest I ever saw him to a grin. You thought he ought to try it more often. "I also wanted to tell you I'm leaving Beaufort Partners."

I sat up and gave him the grin straight back. They can be infectious. "If that means with Mrs. Willard, better head for Tasmania, and soon."

"California. We're sailing in the morning."

I said California ought to be far enough and wished him luck. We might have managed more, this side of gushing and the other side of a handshake, but the phone started ringing.

FORTY-EIGHT

It had been five nights since I last stood in Guildhall Yard. A lot had happened in between. Five nights ago, Nurse Greer had been distracted and unhappy but still alive. Five nights ago, Joe Willard still had a lawyer with a fortune locked in his safe. And five nights ago, it hadn't been obvious to me that the nurse and the lawyer even knew each other, let alone they were related. My visit to Guildhall that night had ended in a lecture—Henry Beaufort on *Roman London: The Luftwaffe and Opportunities it Created*—things that ought to improve my conversation over dinner but didn't explain why anybody would want to murder on account of them. At least not until you added in Henry's boyfriend. Because Michael Garfield hadn't only been brilliant, single-minded and well-connected, he'd been a hard-driving publicist for his cause, which made him admired by some but also threatening to others for just the same reasons. Threatening enough in the end for somebody to want him dead. As for the lawyer, Littomy's detectives would be working to wrap up their case on him before anybody blinked. It didn't necessarily mean they had the wrong man. There was something to connect Allynson to every single one of the City murders. But that was strictly by the way. The City had its police, its crime laboratory, its overtime and its taxes to put to whatever end it had in mind, and at New Year 1948 what it had in mind was cleaning house. The lawyer was just a convenience, a rag they could wipe the slate with.

There were cars reversing out of the parking lot around Guildhall Yard. Lights going out in office windows. Secretaries wrapped against the weather were starting home. This time, I could walk up to the porter's window, say I was expected and count the buttons on his uniform while he wrote my name in a register, gave me directions to Drake's office twice over and pointed me at the stair. It can be easier getting inside a building when you're invited, just not always quicker. This time I climbed a floor higher than before, to an oak-paneled corridor out of the somber-deluxe school. It had a shaded light beside each door, a carpet sprung like a trampoline, the City coat of arms set in lozenges on the ceiling and a line of offices for City grandees overlooking Guildhall Yard. The side without the view had committee rooms named for Corporation big-shots too ancient or too dull to have enemies. It was the kind of corridor where you can make an entire career out of advice off the record, get counted a success and still not know what year it is. I turned left along it and checked the nameplates on the office doors.

Drake's secretary had left her desk tidied and her door unlocked, and enough perfume on the air to make the room feel human. I didn't knock or put on a light, just walked inside and followed the sounds of an orchestra that came and went in waves so canned and hollow they might have been playing between decks in a submarine. Across from the secretary's desk, another door spilled light through a round window at eye level. I peeked in.

There were drapes drawn back at windows looking on the yard, life-size portraits hanging in the spaces in between, and eyeing me from their frames in powdered wigs and knee-breeches, a row of Lord Mayors long deceased, weighted in chains of office like Marley's ghost. Drake was seated facing me with the windows and portraits at his back. He was slumped at his desk in the kind of chair a robber baron will dine alone in, his chins folded in his collarbone, vest riding high over his stomach, hands upturned in claws on the chair arms and his necktie skewed under one ear as if he'd been cut down from a lynching. I shook a handkerchief out of my top pocket, used it to twist the doorknob one half-turn and went in without breathing, got halfway to his desk on my toes when the councilor's shoulders heaved and eased back in the chair. One of the claw hands twitched, tugged at a flap of his vest and moved to straighten the tie. His other hand motioned at the orchestra playing behind me. "If you please." I sank back on my heels and put away the handkerchief, went over to a radio set flush in the oak panel lining the walls and clicked off the broadcast. When I turned around, the councilor was pointing the end of a fat Havana at the seat in front of his desk, the cigar lit up and smoking like a mill town. Except for a high-volume copper ashtray, the desk was clear. His chins had settled back on his shirtfront. "A brief interlude of repose from this most regrettable business."

I took the seat. "Your lawyer's regretting it no end."

"Indeed. I summon you here because your work is done. City Police have their man, and such understanding as we have of his designs we owe to your enterprise and persistence. We are indebted to you, Newman. Mr. Willard appreciates your efforts no less than I." Drake breathed his stomach in, inched open the desk drawer and slid out a check, poised it on its edge and stroked it with his thumbs to feel the pedigree. From where I sat, it looked pretty much a twin of the one I still carried in my wallet, for purposes of spiritual renewal. He laid the check flat, turned it around and prodded it where I could see my name written out on the line that matters.

I looked along the portraits on his window-wall and at the pattern on his carpet, at the club chairs set around a licking coal fire where a bottle waited unstoppered on a liquor cabinet. It was a room versed in how to hush for quiet words under low lights, the pat on the arm and the payoff. I left the check where it lay. "As for my time, it's already paid for, there aren't any extras. As for Mr. Willard, he never was my client. I explained how working for both of you couldn't be done. Remind him, he'll remember. Then give him this back." I twisted the check full circle and slid it between his thumbs.

Drake said nothing, raised an eyebrow to register disappointment, pursed a lip around the end of the Havana and rocked it between his teeth. We sat watching each other while rain pitted the windows. He pulled the cigar off his lip. "That might be unwise. There are things it can be better for Mr. Willard to believe he's bought."

I stood and walked over to the liquor, turned two glasses and lifted the bottle to let its contents catch the light. It was my first of the day. I didn't want to hurry it. I said, "The check isn't in appreciation Councilor, it's payment on account. A backhand warning that in the past week I got to know more about Drake, Willard & Co. than is good for me. Which is progress of a kind because the last warning I got ended on a gravel heap in the docks." I built two large glasses to keep the conversation oiled, and went back around Drake's chair to put one in his hand. "It's a week since you called me out of the blue, wanted a job done and told me practically nothing about it, then or later, that I wouldn't have to work out for myself. Two days on I got introduced to Willard and it was the same story. Days passed. Things got more complicated. Innocent people were killed. And always they pointed back at Drake & Willard, at the rackets it operates, at the police it corrupts, at the lives it squeezes and rolls over. Allynson opened Pandora's Box, and at the end of a long, nervous night in the Snow Hill tank you discovered his boss had set you up and life was about to change, one way or the other. You could put in an appearance at morning court and get blackballed from all the City's best clubs, or you could take Willard's offer and walk right out of there, name and reputation unharmed. Your choice. All you needed to add was a cockamamie story for your daughter about the Drake family going broke, to explain why she was a part of the bargain."

We lifted glasses to each other. Drake took a lick of the kind that takes practice. "My dear Newman, don't be naive. You can have no more idea what was being threatened than did Allynson himself. One does not suborn a daughter to marriage merely to avoid the consequence of an indiscretion."

The hand with the cigar motioned from the tip of his coat lapel down to his shoelaces. It took in the loose-fitted, square black jacket with its buttonhole, the watchchain and necktie with its crest, the gray-stripe trousers and handmade shoes with toecaps and a high black shine. Even on Drake, the outfit was roomy. It's the City way. They get sent away for schooling at an impressionable age, in uniforms meant for growing into. The habit never dies. "We are a closed community, Newman. In the City we live by rank and badges. Some more desirable than others to be sure, but if we know each other at all it is by our guilds, our leagues, our associations. An appearance in court would have been difficult for me, and no doubt an end to public office, but not ruinous. It would simply have marked me out as a member of quite another club; one with many distinguished members. No indeed, the prospect of ruin lay elsewhere." In the portraits behind him the wigs-and-breeches brigade sat up and cupped a hand behind an ear. "It was wartime. Some in the City, as we both well know, were more at war than others. Even while our armies fought and died, our bankers were open to business with Nazi Germany at the highest levels. Permit me then, if at the time I doubted their finer impulses. When Allynson arrived that night the calamity in prospect was not simply a court appearance. The calamity was to be Jewish at a time when one's bankers had Nazi sympathies. The Soviets did not invent the nonperson, Newman. Bankers perform the same function every day simply by withdrawing one's lines of credit. Had I been identified in court, there were those who would have destroyed me entirely, in an instant and with satisfaction."

Drake leaned for the ashtray and parked his Havana with the butts from the rest of his afternoon. He looked mildly surprised, as if we were touring in country he hadn't expected to visit. "Unlike his lawyer, Mr. Willard had the advantage of also being Jewish. He therefore understood exactly what he threatened. Given time, I trust my daughter will understand that his method left me no choice."

I nodded she might but doubted she would. Yesterday she'd given a fair impression of a mind made up. "Willard's method? It was trademark. You had control over construction and he had money to burn. How could you lose? Square your daughter to marrying him and your City bankers with a Jewish problem were a thing of the past." I took my glass to one of his windows and looked down into the yard. The ebb of cars had slowed. Walkers hunched under umbrellas. A steady rain was turning the snowfall to mush. "Your airplane ride with Garfield never was committee business. Neither was the afternoon at the Sesto when he showed you the pictures he took. Sure you put in a call to Guy Beaufort, but your first call was to Willard. You'd already told him the professor could be a problem, and as insurance he'd set Garfield up for blackmail. It's his way. But that afternoon you warned him off all real estate until Garfield's report came in, and he passed word to his lawyer. Too late. By then, Allynson had bought four lots on his own account with company money, laid a trail of phony contracts and booked a million-dollar resale to his boss. He thought he was home free. Then out of nowhere Willard cried off and lit a fuse that left Garfield a corpse in the river. Everything else followed."

You can grow old reminding clients about the things they failed to mention when they hired you. I swallowed the councilor's brandy, left my glass on his desk and made for the door with the porthole. I had a hand on the doorknob when the drawer in the hand-carved desk slid open again. Dull metal clicked in the way it sometimes will when your back is turned. Drake's wearied voice said: "Professor Garfield died because a lawyer's greed had the better of his judgment. You take a tragedy, Newman, and make melodrama of it."

In my circle, letting a client get the drop on you is hard to live down. Getting shot by one is enough to put you on the tourist map. I took my hand off the door, flattened my palms and raised them and eased around very slowly to face the click. Drake stopped what he was doing and upturned the doleful eyes, nonplussed. He had his next Havana pointed at me, lined up to a cigar cutter the size of a flat iron. I let in a breath through my teeth and put my hands down. If I didn't get out of there soon, I'd be jumping at the rain showers scratching the windows. I said, "Greed got the better of both of you, Councilor, but Allynson was out of his depth. You knew it the first time you set eyes on him." I reached across to switch his radio back on, then turned it to a murmur for one last question. "Two detectives shook you down that night you spent in the tank. One was McAlester. Who was the other?"

Drake's mouth turned down either side of the cigar. He struck a match against the ashtray and shrugged heavy shoulders while it flamed. How would he know? McAlester wouldn't introduce anybody but himself, and when you're in the councilor's league you don't trouble with the name of the clerk. I turned up the volume on his broadcast and let the door take care of itself.

FORTY-NINE

A wad of fog sat on the rooftops in Charlotte Street. Fine, steady drizzle slid down the night. It slapped at the darkness like wet sails, made the Paradise Garden's neon glare grow brighter and slicked the coachwork of the cars on the street outside. I walked into the foyer on the tail of a party crowd, got ahead and crossed to where a trim brunette swayed to a tune of her own at the hatcheck. I said I didn't want a new ticket, she could put my coat and hat with the bag she already had, the Gladstone with initials on its straps. The brunette stepped back from the counter to look along the line of checked bags by her toes. "C.R.?" It was all I wanted to know. The party crowd already had us surrounded. I backed up through the crush, turned and headed for the exit.

Out on the sidewalk a doorman waited on arrivals under the Garden's marquee. He was strictly theater, hired for a solid build and costumed in crimson and yellow to let the patrons know they'd arrived at the races. But business was slow tonight and he had no audience, so he'd stepped aside in the fog, lit a cigarette in the lee of the building and didn't appear to care who was checking, so nonchalant it made me curious. I swung out through the entrance and bent against the rain slanting under the awning. The doorman killed his cigarette, curbed his native geniality and watched me out without a goodnight.

The Paradise Garden didn't have its employees arrive on Charlotte Street. The help went in with the kitchen deliveries along a service lane that cut through the block forty feet from the Garden's flashing neon. The lane ran the depth of the building to a cobbled yard cleared of snow and ice, where a truck could unload. For the kitchen entrance, all you did was follow the reek of stale booze and rotted garbage across the yard, to a fire-door wedged open with a beer crate to change the air. I pulled down my hat brim and stepped in over the crate, as if I had some business being there.

When you climb in a pit with the snakes, the snakes are supposed to notice. But not at the Garden tonight. Nothing happened. Not inside the fire-door or in the passage it led along, past a line of storerooms and noises from distant kitchens. No voice called out. No hand pressed my shoulder. No shadow stepped in front to push an arm at my chest or a gun in my stomach. All it took was a sense of direction, some wrong turns and dead ends, a switchback of stairs and service corridors and I was standing outside the black lacquer door again, uninvited and without a chaperone. For somebody who kept a small private army on his books, you wondered where Joe Willard was using it tonight. I pushed on the door's nickel trim and let myself in.

Willard's room was in darkness, lit only by the stab of pink neon through the street window. I left the door wide, used the flashes from the street sign and moved along the wall to the davenport at the far end of the room. The window there was doubled to cut down the noise, the blind angled so that if you stood up close you could take in the dining at one side and the veranda bar at the other. It was early yet for the Garden's night crowd. There were empty tables under the palms, a girl show hoofing in smiles and spangles and a band blowing hard to keep up. Then a slow murmur of applause arrived out of nothing, the girls were making curtseys and the band began doodling around a fresh tune. The clarinet was still teasing out a line when Willard stepped through the flush door at the back of the veranda bar, paused there to fix his cuffs and take the view, then headed for the two wide steps down to the terrace. He moved on through a scatter of diners, paid them no attention and ignored the waiters who stood aside to let him by. I got up on my toes and pulled down a slat of the blind.

There were three men seated at a table at the far edge of the room, solid-looking citizens who might have been company directors meeting over drinks and dinner. Willard walked up behind one of them, rested a hand on his shoulder and got introduced to his two other guests. Then he cast an eye over arrangements, summoned the maître d', and left with a word to each man in turn as a waiter wheeled in champagne on ice, set down three glasses and popped a cork.

The arrangements were impressive. They also explained why the Garden was left wide open tonight. All its available muscle had been fitted for white tuxedos and ranged at intervals around the edges of the floor, like a cordon thrown around a prison yard. I was counting how many when the black lacquer door snicked shut behind me. There was a silk rustle. The Garden's neon lit up a silhouette against the window overlooking the street, and a figure that didn't need to put on a light moved easily across the room, side-stepped Willard's desk and dropped an evening purse in his chair. A drawer pulled open. A decanter clinked against a glass. I let go the slat on the window blind and said, "Make it two."

There was a small, high gasp. The decanter thudded on the desk. The figure waited on the next flash of the street sign, and when it came gasped again. "Newman!" Vivien Allynson let out a long, fluttered breath, fumbled at a clasp to the fur around her shoulders, laid the fur next to her purse and took a second glass from the drawer. "I'm here to see Joe. I have to wait, apparently. As you see it's making me nervous."

I nodded past the window blind at the diners on the terrace. "You're both nervous. Councilor Drake is down there entertaining the commissioner and his superintendent, and Joe's handling it as if they both might get up and start shooting. But at least it gives you time to decide."

She carried two drinks around the davenport and stood in front of me to take a look through the blind. Then she swung around, close enough to let me feel the rustle of her dress. "What do I have to decide?"

She was back in black satin, off-the-shoulder mourning, as fitted for widowhood as for embroidery classes. I took the glass out of her hand. "Two hours ago, the councilor called me into his office to say my job was through and that Willard meant to pay me off. Which is odd considering he was never my client, but then that's not the message. The message is that Willard doesn't want me around for what happens next." The band's new number drifted in on us, too pale to guess at what it was. "No matter what his police report says, when McAlester arrived in your office this morning, he saw what I saw, and the inspector doesn't get paid to keep his thoughts from Joe Willard. Your husband was panicked last night about the fix he was in and used some brandy to calm his nerves, but he didn't turn a gun on himself and it was no professional hit either. Sure, Joe mixes in circles that would relieve him of a million dollars. They might even gun down his lawyer. But they wouldn't get delicate trying to fake a suicide and a double-cross."

She stirred her sidelong look. "Meaning?"

"Meaning your husband didn't try to get out of his chair. Meaning he was killed by somebody who could get close without making him more nervous than he already was. Meaning it was you who pulled the trigger. One shot. Point blank. You put his prints on the gun and went home, then made sure to be back in the office this morning to pick up the boss's regular call."

She could have stopped me there or thrown a fit, tossed off the whole idea as ridiculous or tried pleading for an even break. But it wouldn't be her style, and she did none of those things; only wrapped her arms around her bare shoulders, touched her glass to her cheek and became intent, as if the conversation fascinated her. "After you talked to Willard this morning, he called me, then called McAlester to tell him to be first at the scene when you telephoned City Police. Willard understands you killed your husband, Mrs. Allynson. That isn't what bothers him. He'd have ordered it done himself if you hadn't saved him the trouble. What bothers him is the money he was eased out of by four dead men, and he wants it back. He thinks the money would be the reason you murdered his lawyer."

How do you ever know what makes a difference? Maybe it was the part about never having worked for Willard. Or that tonight at the Paradise Garden she was staring at a busted flush, ready to take whatever help she could get, even mine. She took a sip from the glass. The tip of her tongue peeked between her lips. "If you can believe it, I never did consider my husband and Estelle. I have you to thank for enlightening me. There were his absences of course, but I didn't ask any more than he cared to tell. Yet when the police said Estelle was dead, I knew my husband had murdered her as certainly as I knew he'd murdered the others. From that moment I understood I could never be safe. By the time of Estelle's funeral I'd had days and nights to think about it. I was scared half to death, until I decided no one has the right to terrify you for a lifetime, no matter what you have to do. Now Joe thinks that if I killed my husband it had to be about the money. Isn't that what you're thinking too?"

Imagine that. The lights are out. A handsome widow in a tight black dress is pressed so close you can look into her soul and she asks what's on your mind. The last person who really wanted to know was great-aunt Wilma in Wenatchee. Anybody asking since was just checking on how far ahead of me they were. She had her forehead rested lightly on my shoulder, wearied by all the talk of money and murder. "What I think doesn't matter. What I know is you're not here tonight to talk to Willard. You're here to collect the bag you left at the coat check two nights ago, the one with Charlie Ross's initials. Leaving it in Willard's front yard for safekeeping was bright of you. Less bright is thinking he'll let you walk out of here, with or without it. We ought to start for an exit before the councilor's law and order party breaks up."

Her head lifted slowly until her eyes leveled on the knot in my tie. But not to ask what I could possibly mean by the bag with the flight lieutenant's initials on it. She put a hand flat against my chest and her gaze dipped back in an ocean, then surfaced again, dripping its dark purple lights. "*Is* there an exit?"

I took her wrist and held it down by her side. "The same way I came in. Take a cab someplace there's a crowd and be in my office by midnight. I'll bring Charlie's bag there. Tomorrow, you can go take a first-class cabin, put a slow boat between you and Willard and rent a palace somewhere in the hot sun. Or did you plan to stay on and discuss your future with him?"

The choice didn't overburden her. She sank the liquor and handed me the glass with her lips still wet, then turned on her heel toward Willard's desk. Her back made ripples in the satin like water in moonlight. Her finger hooked under the fur and let it trail. "Joe's hardly going to be thrilled. And you're taking an awful risk. Are you so sure I deserve it, or are there conditions attached?"

I set the glasses on the sofa arm and followed to where she stood, lifted the fur and draped it around her shoulders. "No conditions. I don't have to thrill Joe Willard and I wouldn't know what you deserve. McAlester says your husband killed himself, the commissioner is dining out tonight on a case closed and I can't prove either one of them is wrong. Besides, when you murdered your husband you saved somebody else's life and for all I know it balances out, one life for another. Ask the padre. He understands the bookkeeping."

She fastened the clasp to the fur wrap and thought about that, found her purse on the chair and opened it and held up her check ticket between two fingertips, as if we were trading for her room key. "If I saved a life, shouldn't I know whose?"

I reached around her to take the ticket and said probably she should, and how it all went back to a past-his-prime hustler her husband had hired to make a Christmastide trick. The band tailed to silence. Another scatter of applause passed around diners on the terrace, faint as paper tearing. "Jarrett knew the professor's tastes ran young and didn't follow his instructions. He sent a boy named Reilly in his place, and Reilly was so green that when the professor got hauled from his car he followed the excitement. He trailed Garfield and his killer to the river, saw the shooting start and took off in the car." I slipped a hand inside her arm, her dress so sheer I could count the goose bumps. "Your husband didn't leave loose ends. Sooner or later he was going to find out about Reilly. The boy doesn't know it, but he owes you his life. We ought to go."

We left the Paradise Garden the way I went in, its backstairs still deserted and the click of her heels along the passages the only sound, her dress cutting her stride so short she practically ran. We moved fast, went out through the kitchen door to the yard, then followed the service lane through to the other side of the block. Headlights drifted by on the street ahead, across a last twenty yards of frozen wheel ruts guaranteed to break a heel. We halted there, breath hanging on the air, waited while she hitched her gown and held on my arm and took the tire ridges on tiptoe as if we were trying not to wake the neighbors. When I waved down a cab and she climbed inside, she pulled down the window, perplexed. "I suppose I must be crazy thinking I'll ever see you again. Isn't this where you kiss the lady goodbye?"

She was looking up from under her butterfly lashes, lip pinched white under her front teeth. I reached in the window, tilted up her chin and ran my thumb across her mouth. "You're not crazy and it's not goodbye. Be in my office. Look in the book under Boy Scouts." I slapped a hand against the side of the cab and watched it move ahead, lost its tail lights in the traffic, then turned back into the lane. The fog was still falling. For the second time in one night I was planning to step into Willard's office uninvited, starting not to care for the odds.

It was ten o'clock. Littomy and the commissioner and the councilor were through dining. The Paradise Garden was beginning to stir. No girls were invited over. No one in the party moved on to the greenroom or the veranda bar. The three men got up from the table and filed to the exit, looking cordial. By the time Willard stepped into his office, their table had been re-laid for a foursome.

Willard put on lights as he entered, closed the door and walked up to the window I was at. He glanced out over the diners with a strained look, flopped on the davenport and loosed the stud behind his bow tie. For greeting he looked at the ceiling and asked, "Why would you be here?" I went over to his desk, poured a fresh drink, brought it back and put it in his hand. He tasted it and eyed the glasses on the arm of the sofa, one lip-red around the rim. "Where is she?"

I shrugged. "Mrs. Allynson? An hour ago I showed her out of here and put her in a cab. The cab went south."

A cloud passed across Willard's face. He sank back and gave me the tight look he practiced when he cut himself shaving. His glass lifted to where soft lights made the liquor glow. "She couldn't just walk out of here. You took some trouble. Why?"

"To get your undivided attention. First to hear how to bring her back tonight, along with the money. Then what I want in return." I moved in front of the window, where I had his eye. "When McAlester arrived at your lawyer's office this morning, he saw a counterfeit suicide with enough wrong about it to make the widow his murder suspect. But most of all what he saw was opportunity. Fix the detail, let it go as suicide and he could close down a string of murder inquiries right there and then. Reason enough by itself for cleaning up the evidence. Then again, maybe the corkscrew police work was just a sideshow."

"Sideshow to what?"

Diners were filling the tables. The band took a pause. Moonlight softened the view on the bay and a shooting star skipped across the heavens. Give it another hour and the Garden would be afloat until dawn. "McAlester finally got it through his head that the City killings were fallout from a fraud gone wrong and every new corpse was steering him closer to the money. This morning in the lawyer's study he was so close he could smell it, and what he saw didn't only put Mrs. Allynson in the frame for murder it made her a part of the fraud. Overnight she'd become a seriously rich widow, but only if McAlester played along with her story about her husband's suicide. Did they talk? You could try asking McAlester. Or do this my way and you'll know. If the detective inspector threw a loop on her, you can take it he no longer has your best interests at heart."

The maître d' arrived at the foursome's table while a waiter flapped a napkin at the linen. The strong-arm presence around the terrace had evaporated. Willard considered a thumbnail, to denote his lively interest. "What's in this for you?"

I turned away from the view. "I get to see Terry Reilly."

His eyes hooded, dazzled by the notion. Then, as if it was my idea of a private joke, *"Reilly?"*

"Since you had him taken out of circulation, being the last person he was seen with is making me nervous. Show me Reilly still lives and Mrs. Allynson can be in my office tonight with the money. Give me two hours, send McAlester to collect her, have him tailed and let him make his move. If they talked, you'll know it. If I'm wrong, what can you lose?"

There is a moment the emperor takes deciding to like or not to like while the courtier watches, holds his breath and sees his future drifting by like a boat on a slow stream. Willard twisted the jet ring on his finger and put the tight look back in his eyes, and while he thought it over, I leaned against the wall and asked, "Where'd you first run into her?"

It was to end a silence, not to start him reminiscing. But when he thought about her Willard eased up on the bleak look as if he hadn't considered the subject in a long time. His jaw softened. He set his glass down on the sofa arm in line with the others. "Vivien?"

Even a racketeer will own to a past when he's the one telling it. He said Vivien Greer had arrived at the Paradise Garden one night late in 1940, on the arm of a film producer after an air raid all-clear. Nobody at the Garden remembered ever seeing her before. And they would have remembered, because she was all her own work; an ice-cool redhead with looks to stop traffic, a put-down in every nerve and a walk Chamberlain would have jumped the barricades for. She'd drawn a crowd that night around any table she moved to. That much was real enough. The film producer was a blind. Vivien Greer had made an impression in a handful of forgettable British pictures, but that was before a war began. On the night she walked into the Paradise Garden her screen days were over already. By 1940 the scripts had turned to home-front heroines, ration book romance, and a new style in pert that wore uniform and flat heels. Nobody doubted she could set a screen alight. She just wasn't cut out to play Mrs. Miniver. Willard relaxed into the seatback, musing. "The calls from the studios dried up and she didn't see herself as an army nurse like her sister." As if it exhausted the possibilities. "So she stayed around the Garden. The arrangement suited us both."

"Until the day you noticed Councilor Drake had a daughter."

Willard eyed me to consider if I was out of order. When he couldn't make up his mind his tone hardened anyway. "I didn't hear her complain."

I nodded and lit a cigarette, dropped the match in the lipstick glass and watched it gutter. "Sure you didn't. You made a new arrangement and had her marry your lawyer. What suited her this time was the home on Lincoln's Inn Fields, a wardrobe out of MGM and the highlife no regular lawyer could afford. You gave it to her because Allynson knew so much about your operations you needed him watched from the inside. And since it was no affair of the heart, she made it expensive. What did she ever give you that wasn't?"

Willard got up off the davenport, the glow gone from his reminiscing. He crossed to the desk and leaned his knuckles on the edge. "Two hours. McAlester will be in your office, alone but not alone. Mess this up, Newman, and your credit won't buy spit to shine your shoes." He used a buzzer to call the nursemaid forever on hand. I dropped my cigarette in the glass alongside the dead match, the air so full of mutual understanding there was nothing else to taste.

We didn't leave the building. From Willard's office there were unfamiliar stairs, a walk along a gaudy corridor spilling glaze-eyed girls and their clients and a heady mix of colognes, and then more stairs to a passage in an attic story closed to the paying customer. It ran ahead in the dim-lit pitch of the roof with small pent rooms on either side, dank and unlit, until we halted outside a wide-open door bleeding yellow across the bare wood floor of the passage. Inside there was a cot pushed up against a wall in a corner, and stretched out on the cot a gaunt figure wrapped in the greatcoat he never left off, gazing blank at a skylight in the pitch of the roof. The rest of the room amounted to an unshaded light, looped over a card table on a threadbare rug, and a second figure seated at the table, playing out a solitaire with an electric heater angled at his knees. The figure was suited tonight, slicked and close shaved, with the look of a man who thought keeping watch over Reilly was work beneath his grade.

Voigt glanced up at where I stood in the doorway, did a double-take and let fall the deck of cards. He kicked the chair back hard, moved fast to one side of the table, then noticed I had company. The chair bounced off the wall and spun around. My escort snorted and jerked his head for Voigt to leave. Voigt looked sheepish, trawled for a cigarette and clamped it in his teeth, then found the swagger to stroll up to the doorway, close enough to rub noses while the tuxedo looked on. He snapped a match alight on the wall behind my ear, hooked the cigarette up between his eyebrows, lit it and filled his lungs. The trick tickled him. Probably it always tickled him. Then he snuffed the match, patted me lightly on the jaw and moved off along the passage in a gurgle of good humor. I heeled shut the door behind him and went over to the cot. Reilly hadn't taken his eyes off the skylight.

If Terry Reilly owed one of his lives to Mrs. Allynson, he owed at least one more of them to Willard. Since the first time they met in the Raglan Christmas Day, Reilly had been riding his luck. His history with Jarrett made him a risk from the start. Ignoring a direct order to stay where Willard told him made him look halfway between unpredictable and insane. Yet somehow Reilly's luck had held, and now a dead lawyer was framed for four murders and the boy was past being a threat. So he still lived, and in one Christmastime had used up more lives than anybody ought to rely on. When Voigt hauled him out of the Pelican his only trouble would have been keeping the boy vertical. Then and now, Reilly looked like death: so sick-yellow around the eyes he glowed in the dark, so still on the cot you doubted he knew or cared where Voigt had brought him. But it wouldn't be his whereabouts that were laying him low. What currently sapped the boy's vitality was an unplanned reacquaintance with the ache of being junk-free and cold sober, both at the same time. For the rest, so far as I could tell, he was in one piece.

I dragged the chair where he could see me, leaned close where he could hear and said I had one question for him only, and not a lot of time. His gaze pulled off the ceiling and gave me the baleful look that comes with being three days on the wagon. It had been one whole week since Reilly waltzed Michael Garfield into the docklands and became accidental witness to a murder. And saw what exactly, more than a gun pointed in the shadows, a silhouette behind a tipped-down hat and the turned-up collar of a coat? Take away the gun, and on that night, at that hour, what Reilly had described would fit any adult male still outdoors. Yet hours later when he saw the nurse walk into Cloth Court, he could identify the figure walking with her as Michael Garfield's killer. So sure of it he took off and ran till dawn came up. That had been Reilly's story in the Pelican. I leaned closer, where he could read my lips across a yard of gauze that was separating him from all thought, feeling, light and color. "Here's the question Terry. The night Garfield died you were so far inside the bottle Jarrett had to go dump the roadster himself. And still, from an upstairs window on a dark court in the middle of a snowstorm you recognized a murderer whose face you never saw. Tell me how you did that."

For a time, his eyes wandered over the tilted ceiling, lost in the mystery of why I would need it explained. His chin sank deeper in his coat and muffled his answer. "I just know, don't I? I have to know." It was what I thought. And all I was likely to get. The strain of entertaining me was killing him. I left Reilly with his shakes, left my chaperone in the foyer, traded Mrs. Allynson's ticket at the coat check, and walked out onto Charlotte Street carrying Charlie Ross's bag.

For two weeks, the cold had been brushing aside the winter fog like a curtain at daybreak until it left you feeling light-headed. On a good day you might see a horizon. At nighttime, even a star. And then last evening the *Courier* had forecast a rise of two degrees, and made it sound like the difference between north and south Siberia. Today, Carl's cartoonist had put Marjorie in a parka peeking out of an igloo, explaining to a shivering polar bear, *It's a Heat Wave!* but hadn't said anything about a fog. She ought to have. Tonight a wand had waved and made a city disappear in a broth at the bottom of an ocean. Streetlights floated in a fog of the kind that rims your eyes red, fills your mouth, and coats anything you plan to touch or breathe or swallow with a slick film of sulfur grit. A regular London fog.

Traffic was thin. The city stole back its bleak midwinter look of rotting from the inside out. You could hear it softly choking. I walked south to Oxford Street, found a cab and climbed in. The driver locked his meter and pressed up against the windshield, took the weather on the chin and stayed with the avenues that crossed the city in straight lines. Subway stations on the Central line were barred and locked, the last trains gone. The cabbie counted off the passing station signs—Tottenham Court Road, Holborn, Chancery Lane— just to hear a voice in the night. Unseen city dragged by the cab window. I drew a knuckle across the misted glass and made three vertical marks in a row, like a tally on a slate. One for the Gladstone bag on the seat beside me with most of a million dollars inside. Two for the B-picture actress, handy with a .38, who was waiting to take delivery in my office. And three for Willard, who wanted them both—the money and the woman who'd double-crossed him—and wasn't about to rely on me handing either one of them back. I scrubbed the window clear and told the cabdriver to pull over at the top of Snow Hill.

FIFTY

The Thornburgh's night porter had his door shut tight and dance tunes playing on the short wave of his radio. I put on all the lights in the lobby, took the stair and switched on more on every floor, then cut out at the fifth. At the end of the corridor, in the recess outside my office, a ceiling light threw a beam across a wreath of cigarette smoke, turning slow circles under a green metal shade. From where I stood the row of seats tucked out of sight. All I saw was a slim ankle fitted in a two-tone shoe and a wrist rubbing out the cigarette. The wrist wore a bracelet around the cuff of a tight kid glove, catching the light at every turn. Even at that distance the cut stones looked the kind of class the Thornburgh had always promised. I put a key in my office door and switched on a light of my own, hoisted Charlie's bag on the desk and took a bottle from the drawer to shake off the fog. Then I went back to invite Mrs. Allynson in. I had two stiff measures poured and the stopper back in the bottle before I looked her over. She was standing behind the customer chair taking out a hat pin, coat unbuttoned and a purse hooked under her arm. A strand of hair caught in the corner of her mouth. She flicked at it and raised a private smile. "You look as if you've seen a ghost."

It had been a long day and anybody else would have looked threadbare. Vivien Allynson was dressed for travel in first class. On a winter night in a cold climate she was wearing a dark blue costume fitted to the hemline and enough jewelry to help the bracelet blend. But the jewelry wasn't the surprise. Or the outfit either, when I remembered where I'd seen it before. As for the dark electric in her eyes, it had been there from the first. She set the hat on a corner of the desk, touched at the strand of hair again, and this time pulled it across her cheek where we both could consider it. "You don't think brunette suits me?" Her little finger looped the hair over a dark wave that lifted off her forehead, exactly like her sister's. "We were the same color, Estelle and I. It was Estelle who changed. She always hated being the redhead."

But it wasn't only the brunette that would let her pass for her sister. In build, in looks, in height, they were already close enough. With the new-dyed hair and the nurse's papers she'd stroll through border control anyplace, as near to looking like her passport as anybody ever does. As for Charlie's bag, she'd pull a mouth at a customs officer and he'd carry it over the frontier for her. She loosed the scarf at her throat. "How far did you expect me to get tonight in high-heels and an evening gown? I needed to change, you said not to go home, and Estelle had a wardrobe full of clothes I'd grown tired of." As if her choices were always between being practical and being sentimental. She cast an eye over the Gladstone. I nodded for her to open it. "Go ahead. Look inside. I never had a key."

She hesitated, then took a step and loosed the straps, got the key from her purse, turned it in the lock and yanked the top wide. For thirty seconds of sweet wonder she stirred close to a million dollars in new, hundred-dollar bills, just to breathe their scent; checked they were the way she left them, fastened up the Gladstone and set it on the floor where she could tap it with her two-tone shoe. I slid one of the glasses across the desk, invited her to take a chair and sat looking at her over the liquor.

Mrs. Allynson wasn't the redhead any longer, but that was just to travel with. The rest she wouldn't know how to change. Wouldn't know how to take the glide out of her walk or the night time out of her look or the money out of her calculation; and especially not how to give up her touchiness about the men in her life who disappointed her. You could say disappointment had set in as long ago as Charlie Ross, a schoolgirl regret, but even he still rankled. As for Joe Willard, he'd trampled on the grown woman and there was no chance of her forgetting it. If learning that he meant to marry Drake's daughter had been a jolt, being passed along to his lawyer had been pure humiliation. The way Willard saw it the payoff had been handsome. It just would never balance out the slap in the face. He'd made a lot of missteps, but his biggest by far was crossing a woman who could even the score. I said, "Allynson asked you for a divorce."

She looked up blankly.

"What else would he do? He'd long ago worked out that he was only ever a commercial arrangement you made with his employer. He wanted to be old-fashioned about your sister and knew you wouldn't even stop to wonder who his new flame might be. He was right. All you asked was how he planned to afford it." She gave some thought to that, then held her glass straight out across the desk. And while we sipped at two new drinks she relaxed and filled out the rest, perhaps because she was the only one who could.

Being around a racketeer's personal lawyer had taught her how unrefined a high-earning fraud can be. She saw word come down from the councilor, noticed her husband creating private companies for Willard, then watched as those companies bought up bombed-out lots around the City. Next thing you knew, Drake's committee released the lots for reconstruction, land values went through the roof, and after a decent interval, Drake, Willard & Co. bought out the private companies, leaving Willard richer twice over. Vivien Allynson marveled at the simple felicity of it all. "I told my husband if he wanted a divorce, he'd better find a way to cut in on Joe.

That was two months ago, about the same time the councilor advised buying land around Cripplegate. I believe you worked out the rest."

Cut in on Joe. Add a fraud to a fraud. As a way of paying for an expensive divorce, she made it sound as elegant and unfussy as falling on a sword. You wondered if she'd ever heard of Michael Garfield before the plan went sour. She drained her whisky. I shrugged. "Some. Not all. When I went to the Garden tonight it was to bring you out of there. You'd murdered your husband, but even so, leaving you to Willard's tender mercies didn't answer. Then you walked in his office and showed me what I'd been missing all along. You're a very attractive woman in any light Mrs. Allynson, but a few hours ago in the shadows of a darkened room you were a lot more than that. You were unmistakable." The last part got me the bored and disheartened look. Naturally it would. Since the day she first walked out in a tight dress she'd been hearing it from any man with half an eye for symmetry, and with plenty more to offer. Except for the bag sitting by her toes, I had nothing that interested her even faintly, and its contents were already promised. I said, "Terry Reilly thought you were unmistakable too."

Her air of boredom died.

I waved my glass at her travel costume. "The boy notices detail. I mean somebody's build, the way they move and wear their clothes. He reads the signs. In his line of work, he has to. Get it wrong and he can end in a heap in an alley, or in a police cell if he's in luck. Reilly never did get a real look at Michael Garfield's killer, he just read the signs. Then hours later he read them again when the same figure followed the nurse into Cloth Court. And we both know that wasn't your husband." She drank lazily and listened, but not as if the idea interested her. "Sure your husband cut in on Joe. And when it all went wrong he made the calls you told him to make: first to Guildhall to leave the professor a message, then to Jarrett to set up a trick at the Raglan, last of all to Garfield's pilot to try to get back the film. But it ended there. He didn't have the stomach for murder."

The building ticked soft as clocks in empty parlors. A breeze rattled the glass panel in the door. "Meantime you knew you were both dead if Willard discovered the shakedown. Not even you would convince him you were the innocent bystander. So you put on your husband's coat and hat and shot Garfield at the river yourself. It was either him and Jarrett or you. And right up until you heard Garfield's car drive away it could have been that simple. After, it was nothing but complication. You sent your husband looking in Jarrett's haunts across the City. His address off Cloth Fair, you went to find yourself. Then at four-thirty in the morning, on a bombed-out lot two blocks away, there he was. Trying to start Garfield's convertible in the freeze."

It had been early in her trigger career, and even though she leaned in under the canvas top to take aim, Jarrett had survived. By the time she caught up with him in the church porch, she had Garfield's house keys in her pocket, and the only thing left was to put the gun to Jarrett's head and squeeze. Then the little sister arrived on the scene, fresh from lighting candles at the crib, and her problems went on multiplying. "You followed her home and for a time you coaxed her out of talking, until in the Viaduct you saw she was too scared to rely on anymore and it was back to being either you or her. Who are we kidding? You didn't need me telling you not to go home tonight. You were never planning to. Your clothes, your sister's passport, even her regular hair color were all at the house in Cloth Court. Her identity card you already had. You took it from her bag when you killed her."

A scent of licorice was crawling under the door.

I turned the telephone around and pushed it where she could reach it. "Wake Littomy. Tell him you've got a suitcase full of money that doesn't belong and you'll explain later. Littomy's decisions are made already. They're too big to unmake. He'll put the murders on your husband and leave you accomplice to a fraud. Meaning five years, less if you wear that costume for the jury. Call him. Tell him to get somebody here fast."

She looked thoughtful about the telephone, but when she reached over it was only to slide her glass toward the bottle again. I poured another. I was doing the same for myself when she lifted the purse out of her lap, slipped off its clasp and pulled out a Webley .45 that only made her wrist look slimmer. Her gun hand rested on the arm of the seat and pointed it around the side of the telephone at my stomach. It might not have been the model she was used to, but she wasn't letting the novelty wear her down. "Really, how can I? Besides, I already have my ticket on a slow boat. You approve. Don't you remember?" We sat that way listening to my heartbeat, until she noticed it was the moral support in her right hand that had all my attention. Her fingers flexed around the grip and the muzzle pointed two inches higher at my chest. "This? Charlie gave it to Estelle. In those phony war days when there were invasion scares. Odd isn't it, how one man expects you'll go down fighting and the next expects you'll just go down?"

I still had the bottle poised for pouring, but it felt weightless. I set it very slowly beside the glass and spread my hands flat on the desk where they wouldn't make her hysterical. "Mrs. Allynson, it isn't that you're not free to leave here, it just isn't advised. You stood Willard up tonight, we were both seen at the Garden and we can expect company. Call the operator and talk to Littomy. Do it now."

She sat stiff and flawless as an Egyptian queen. The hand resting on the purse started buttoning her coat, unhurried. In the end, all she said was, "Your concern is touching but I'll take my chance." Shallow wheezing floated on the silence. The room swam on the scent of licorice. Her eyes lifted over my head. A cool draft chilled the sweat under my collar and cold metal jabbed hard at the cotton wad behind my ear. Mrs. Allynson sighed, raised an eyebrow and went ahead with the same level candor. "Detective Inspector McAlester. Such a surprise. Though hardly what we agreed on."

Two guns in one room and neither of them pointed at anybody but me. I had my chin pressed in my shirtfront. The lump under the cotton wad had a high-voltage current running through it. I hissed at her between my teeth. "The detective inspector is here protecting his investments. He was doing the same when he murdered Dillys Valentine. It surprised her too."

McAlester took the weight off the gun and let my head up. His wheeze turned to the dry gasp he used for a voice. He put a shrug in the gasp. "You find Newman, you find a tramp." And made it sound like Wittgenstein's eighth proposition. "With her ticket bought and money to travel and a gun that's making him nervous because she never used it before. His luck is the police are here. Her luck is they're not here to take her back to the Garden. If the tramp heeded advice, Newman would tell her to stop thinking with her hips and put the gun on the desk." Sometimes it can take a beautiful woman to bring out the poetry in a soul. I thought about what McAlester saw in front of him and decided it wouldn't lose him any sleep. What did he have except a gumshoe he always had the drop on when it mattered and a sometime redhead whose future he owned? Added to which, the .45 in the right hand of the sometime redhead was aimed at the gumshoe, not at him. It amounted to more police arithmetic, and the arithmetic was telling him to add another fiction to the file, subtract the two other people in the room, multiply his chances of tranquility and leave there with the money, undivided. It felt like a bad time to be on the wrong side of the calculation. From where I was sitting, Mrs. Allynson's gun hand looked as if it felt that way too.

The next half-second went as well as it ever does. I was already out of the seat when her lips pressed together. Out of her firing line while her shoulder dipped. Heading flat out for the floor before her hand jerked the .45 from the right arm of the chair. And then McAlester moved. A steam shovel hit flush between my shoulders, and where I was aiming to be when the shooting started took on the remote glow of plans you make in winter for a vacation in the spring. He clawed a handful of my coat while I was taking off sideways and twisted it in a ball, dragged my shoulder half around and used my own weight to slam my face down hard on the edge of the desk. My jaw took splinters out of the wood veneer. I heard my cheekbone crack. The room lurched at an angle and my eye clammed shut, and when the claw let go my jacket, I was already gliding chin-up off a cliff into a night of a thousand constellations. In a room far off in another part of the city a fist beat hollow on a closing door: ...*three* ...*four* ...*five*. Too many to count, until in time the fist stopped hammering, the constellations slipped one by one over the rim of night, and a shutter fell like an axe blade burying in a log. Wittgenstein does that to me every time.

FIFTY-ONE

It might have been daylight. There was no telling. In the bright room time moves undivided and there's no clock on the wall. A bug-eyed desk sergeant had taken my wallet and necktie and belt with the brass buckle, my wristwatch, shoelaces and pocket change. Then made out a receipt for it all as if it bought me a ticket to get in. It's the one contract police ever make with you. For the rest, it's understood that they own your present and intend to lean on your past, and your future is theirs to hand back when and if they decide. Aside from that, you're at liberty: at liberty to reflect on what they might have on you, and the man-hours they can put into making something of it; at liberty to become reacquainted with your own sweat and theirs while they make up their minds.

The bright room was on the snug side of intimate. It had no windows. Only two steel-tube chairs across a bolted-down table, so narrow you could feel their breath in your face, as sour as their mood and as permanent as their point of view. I hadn't seen either of them before. Two City detectives, one older and seated opposite, the other younger and leaner and on his feet, with the chiseled look of a Hero of Soviet Agriculture. The Hero had been straining at a leash all night long, leaning against the back wall and baring his teeth as if the whole point of being there was to help him work up an appetite. All night long we'd been running up against the same thing that bothered him. And since it was something that wouldn't stand aside, no matter how we came at it or how often, we kept on going back and starting over again; because police work had taught him that any ending can follow from any beginning, and his method was to stick with the ending he thought of first.

So we went back every time. Back to the architect who bought his liquor on his highland vacations. Back to the councilor's daughter who saw a newsreel in the Charing Cross Road. Back to the nurse who gave up a flight lieutenant's uniform for a charity cause. And always back to the nurse's sister, who bought herself a cop so the cop would buy a suicide. That was the part the Hero had a problem with. He levered himself off the back wall, walked around to my side of the table and jerked my chin sideways on the point of his thumb. "McAlester did this? Not a chance. Why would he stop at a busted nose?"

A hot needle stitched my eyeball in its socket. I swerved out of his reach. "My nose was busted when you were still in short pants. McAlester was trying to fix it for me." And to his boss, "Junior tries that again, we'll both need a doctor."

We hadn't been introduced. Since he entered the room, he hadn't said a word. Even silent I liked him. He was a man in his fifties, short for a cop, wore a soft striped collar and a relaxed brown suit and had the comfortable build and fugitive eyes of somebody's Irish uncle. He also looked as if he slept nights. The Hero wrapped his fist in his hand and mimed to be let alone for five minutes in the room with me. His boss combed his fingers through a hairline he hadn't seen in twenty years. The room waited, breathless. "Detective Tully is a mite overwrought. Understandably so. He took the call for the dreadful murder of Miss Valentine, and learns tonight you were present at the unfortunate woman's demise.

He no doubt thinks, as I do, that you might have mentioned it at the time. As for your story concerning the late detective inspector, now what in the world do you suppose he might do with that?"

Detective Tully. Who listened all night to how McAlester fixed a lawyer's suicide and took it in his stride, yet every time we got to how Dillys Valentine died, acted as if he had stomach cramps. I pulled hard up against the table and leaned across at his boss. "He knows what he can do with it. I was there. As soon as she started in about Jarrett and police protection, Miss Valentine was a dead woman. Detective Tully is overwrought because he wants McAlester left out of her killing and doesn't see how to do it." I squinted past the glare from the hanging light. "It's the thing he's been right about all night. It can't be done. McAlester's under every stone the detective doesn't want to turn. Check the station record. McAlester hauled Jarrett in for hustling once and once only. Chances are he made him known to Joe Willard at the same time, because three years later when the councilor was honey-trapped, they were all on Willard's payroll. Jarrett was the bait, McAlester made the bust, and Willard's lawyer arrived in the bleak hours to spring him. Obviously it was a setup McAlester kept off the record, but Tully would know. There was a second detective on the vice detail with McAlester that night. Why not ask him who?"

Tully's boss laced his hands on his stomach, stretched and stifled a yawn. A tic had started up along my cheekbone. "Always it's McAlester. McAlester who took over the investigation when Jarrett's murder was reported. McAlester who called the councilor to tell him there was a problem. And when Drake hired me to find out what went on, it was because McAlester had set him up pathetically once before." Drake, eight days ago. The one client I ever had who doubled my rate and wouldn't take no for an answer. Even when your head says it can't be Santa Claus, your heart still goes out to the principle. "So I arrived at the Jarrett murder, and later that morning got a call to meet the acting medical examiner at the Great Eastern Hotel. She's smart, but also new to police work and likely left word where to reach her, which is how McAlester found me at the hotel and tailed me from there to Dillys Valentine. Don't take my word. Talk to Louis in the hotel barbershop, then check police prints at the Valentine murder, because they better not include McAlester's. You just said he let Detective Tully take that call, and it makes sense. Why would he go there himself when he already knew who killed her?" Tully stirred, felt in the breast pocket of his jacket for a toothpick, started using the point to scratch last night's dinner off his sleeve. I peered around the bright light at his boss. "Is Junior not naturally inquisitive? Or is he just strict with himself? There were three people in my office last night. If you think I'm off base about McAlester, tell him to park the toothpick and start with the widow."

Tully brushed off his jacket sleeve and burnished his handiwork on a shirt cuff. His boss looked around as if he might have been in the wrong room all night, then sighed and kicked back his chair and led Tully out the door. A bolt slammed behind them. The light burned on with a generator whine. I got to my feet, walked slow circuits around the bolted-down table and started thinking about cops.

Another day, another headline. Lately, McAlester had been collecting them. But last night in my office he'd hit the heights, and for twenty-four hours he was set to be bigger news than Stalin. Plenty enough to put the commissioner in a spot until Littomy cooked a version of his own for the late editions. Meanwhile, Detective Tully was trying to remake himself as the innocent in the park. And for that, if his boss let him be sporting with the evidence, I was a gift. All I had going for me was a gunshot pattern across my office wall, a face I could have collected in a barroom brawl and a story that ended the second the shooting had started. None of it was impressing Tully. He said what he wanted from me was my part in the gunplay at the Thornburgh last night, and up to now I wasn't even close to the way he wanted to hear it.

All I remembered was getting on my knees, alone in the room so far as I could tell, feeling as if the left side of my face had been split off with a hatchet. My office door was wide open to the corridor. The ceiling light still burned. The scent of gunfire so heavy on the air it started me retching and dragged me onto my feet. My wristwatch had cracked apart when I hit the floor. The clock on my wall said it was past one in the morning.

I was partly right about being alone. Vivien Allynson was gone. The bag along with her. The Webley .45 was tossed on my desk and the chair still sprawled where I dragged it over on my way down. Two gunshots had drilled the plaster, one high in the wall, one close by the window. A third had clipped the window blind and splintered the frame, and a fourth had taken off the right-hand corner of my desk. On the whole, it left the room looking roughed-up rather than rugged. Then again, at the other side of my connecting door there was ruggedness to spare.

The door to the adjoining office was folded back at an odd angle, hanging loose on a shot-through hinge and jammed against the heel of McAlester's shoe. The rest of the detective inspector was stretched along the floor on his stomach, his right hand pinned under his chest, his head turned aside, his left arm reaching overhead in a lazy swimmer's crawl across the Styx. I went in through the door and squatted down, grabbed his shoulder two-handed and heaved him onto his back. The Browning semi-automatic that had shot up my office slipped from McAlester's fingers, spun slowly in a blood pool on the linoleum and stopped like a roulette on red. He still had on his homburg.

You didn't need to be Barnes Wallis. For five short seconds Vivien Allynson had aimed and emptied the Webley from ten feet away while McAlester stood framed in the door. She'd missed her aim once only, and from that range whatever she didn't miss with would have stopped a train. The Webley was built to do that. Flight Lieutenant Ross had given it to his girl to keep the Wehrmacht at bay if need be. But then the gun is only ever a part of it. The detective inspector's luck had been to step in the way of the finest shooting of Mrs. Allynson's short career. A flowering red stitched the right side of his coat from his shoulder to his hip.

Her first shot had notched out the top of McAlester's right arm, left him unable to take aim and made him a barn door for target practice. Jerked high and wide under the impact, his gun hand had loosed four harmless shots and then locked solid on the trigger. From left to right, from start to end, the holes in my walls and desk traced the pattern. The rounds McAlester didn't call on were sitting in the palm of my hand. All thirteen of a fully loaded Browning accounted for. Meaning that Vivien Allynson had walked out unhurt from her introduction to a gunfight, temporarily deafened and certainly shaken up. For the first time, somebody had started shooting back at her, and from ten feet away it's a bracing experience.

I reached the telephone closer and thought about what lay ahead. At that hour, Littomy would be sleeping off the Garden's champagne twenty miles south of the river in some stockbroker lane in Camelot. I could wake him and tell him one of his detectives was dead in my office or I could wait and let him hear it secondhand, which wasn't that much of a choice. Harder yet was to see any bright spots. I'd been in the room when the shooting happened, the murder weapon was in my hip pocket and the widow who used it had flown. It had been that kind of a night. The kind even a police chief has to get out of bed for. I took a deep breath, dialed the operator and gave him Littomy's home number.

City Police don't keep the customer waiting. I pulled the doctor's carbon notes on Jarrett out of a drawer, grabbed the photographs Sybil Willard had handed me with Garfield's diary, dropped them in my wastebasket and tossed in a lighted match. While they burned, I got Garfield's wallet out of the safe, put it on the desk with the Browning and Vivien Allynson's .45 and went back to stir over the ashes.

Then I settled in my neighbor's office chair, listened to rain beads jittering in the corners of the window glass and waited. Twenty minutes later, Detective Tully stepped into my office, damp-straw hair plastered back to his scalp and a jaw right off a poster in a Moscow tractor plant. His boss was two steps behind.

Tully had arrived already on edge. As the night wore on and he began to understand what he had, his mood went backward. You could see his point of view. A fellow officer had been gunned down, four murder investigations meant to be closed were unraveling in front of his eyes, and sooner or later Littomy would have to learn that a recently dead lawyer wasn't the City killer after all. The prospect had started crawling over Detective Tully's skin. What his boss thought about it there was no way to tell. But I could wait. Come morning, Littomy would be putting out his certified version to the press. And before he did that, somebody would want to explain it to me.

Police like to explain. Even when you're satisfied that you've got a thing worked out for yourself, they want to straighten out those ideas in which you are entirely mistaken. They have to clarify the things you saw, or thought you saw, or heard or smelled or tasted, and then tell you how you felt about them, what you were doing at the time, what you remember you were thinking or saying or were thinking of saying. It's a humor with them, like flat feet and colic. Soon, somebody would be arriving to help me out with all of those things, to explain to me what I ought to know and what I would never know about how a senior officer had ended shot dead on my office floor; a result of events too complicated for me to understand, or ever to think of go prying in again. The way a cop sees it, he's the one getting paid to know. You're just the itinerant who happened to be there at the time. So I waited and paced the bright room, no way of telling how long, until somebody dropped by to enlighten me.

Littomy arrived in a business suit half-brother to the one that had graced dinner last night at the Garden, breaking the kind of smile a bank teller will use when your credit doesn't stretch. He dropped a large envelope on the table, set his chair side-on, loosed the top button of the suit jacket and stared at the wall over my head. It drew from him a sigh and a contented look, as if the blank wall was his view over a park in springtime where small children chased and ducks sunned around a pond. I sat on my hands. It's hard to enter in the spirit with somebody who took away your shoelaces.

As if it wearied him, Littomy said, "You were fortunate in encountering Detective Inspector Fels this long night. He finds your account engrossing. Some of its substance he has been able to verify. It appears the late detective inspector did, as you say, bring in your client for questioning those many years ago. Detective Tully, when pressed, concedes he was also present, though our station record omits the event. As to the appalling murder of Miss Valentine, Fels finds that police fingerprints at the scene do indeed include McAlester's. Our forensic colleagues it seems, failed entirely to grasp the anomaly." Littomy weighted the *colleagues* part, then grimaced at the glare flooding in through his private window onto the park. "The question remains how far any of this takes us. Can it be, as you suggest, that McAlester colluded with the lawyer's wife to disguise a murder? It is scarcely conceivable. Might she have offered to reward the detective inspector for his complicity? We have only your surmise for it. What evidence do we have that this lone woman contrived to shoot and kill a trained, armed and highly experienced senior officer? None whatever. We have no trace of her prints on the weapon. Nothing but your own account to indicate she was ever in the building, let alone present in your office last night. Yet your tale is not only that she shot and killed the detective inspector there, you say she left behind both McAlester's handgun and her own. This despite your warning that she was in the gravest personal danger." His jaw jutted so far sideways it looked dislocated. "Does that not seem rather careless of her? In conscience, Newman, your version of events beggars belief."

He said it as if I could include the ducks around the pond in that, and let his gaze wander over my shoulder. A superintendent of police does not seek to impress or win an argument. He means only to let you watch yourself losing, no contest, so that next time your appreciation of police work will be more rounded. It was a reminder that what started in his office late Christmas afternoon was ending in the bright room without my tie or shoelaces. I didn't see it making one of my hundred great cases. I felt for my lip to find where it had grown to. "So, you're skeptical. Tully is skeptical. His boss says so. But even police make mistakes. McAlester's was walking into my office with a gun on me, not on the widow, and that mistake got him killed with the Webley she left behind to frame me for his murder. The gun is clean. I wiped it myself. What else would I do? Mrs. Allynson shot her husband with his own .38 and put his prints on it. She was guaranteed to do the same for me. McAlester's Browning she wouldn't even see, because when the shooting ended he was sprawled on top of it. Besides, with McAlester dead she thought she was safe. Carrying either one of the guns would locate her at a police killing. It would have been next best thing to a signed confession."

There are suits made of stuff so fine they only look better the closer you get. They make them in whispers for old maharajahs, behind soft-lit windows on quiet streets, then line them in silk that weighs less than their eyelashes. Littomy's was such a suit, the shadowed green of burned willow wands flecked with soft ash. I sat wondering how many like it a police superintendent affords. Littomy lifted a corner of his mouth. His fingers played with the row of small buttons on his cuff. "One sees why Detective Tully is affronted by your candor. You admit to entering Jarrett's rooms after being at the scene of his murder. Hours later you were at the Valentine killing, but left to report it anonymously. You hand us Professor Garfield's wallet for mercy's sake, and own that when you removed it from his body you were impersonating a City Police officer! Need I continue? Detective Tully would have

341

you behind bars for any one of those infractions, let alone the events of last night. Yet your candor is highly selective, is it not?"

Littomy's hand flattened on the envelope and slid it across the table. It's the police way; they hand back the things they took from you as if they remembered it's your birthday. I pulled the envelope into my lap and shook out my shoelaces, dropped my wristwatch and wallet in a pocket and kicked off my shoes. Littomy interested himself in a thumbnail while I threaded the laces. You can be bruised and sleepless, shaky and not thinking straight, and still recognize the etiquette for a heart-to-heart.

I slipped my shoes back on and double-tied them, rolled down my shirt collar and ran my hands through my hair. I was tipping a handkerchief out of the envelope, feeling a little less rustic, when Littomy said absently, "McAlester was no doubt a flawed officer. Nonetheless, he noted the interest both you and our medical examiner were taking in the Jarrett murder. Having observed you meeting at the Great Eastern Hotel, he charged Detective Tully with monitoring Dr. Swinford's movements. The detective's reports prove absorbing." He set his chin on his knuckles and gave me his consideration. It was the first time I'd had his eye since he walked in and ducked the hanging light. "This past week, Newman, we observe a pattern. We have a killing on our hands, our temporary medical examiner examines, after which she again meets the private investigator she first summoned to the Great Eastern Hotel following the Jarrett murder. This pattern troubled us. Easy to imagine why the private investigator would maintain contact with our acting examiner; he has a political client with reason to keep abreast of police inquiries. Far harder to imagine what in God's name our examiner thought she was doing. That is, until thirty-six hours ago, when our press was good enough to inform us of our mistreatment of the Beaufort boy, with all pertaining medical detail. Good Christ, man, she ministered to the boy's injuries at my request. Then chose to aid him after he absconded from police guard. Whereupon we discover she is not only the Beaufort family doctor, but close friend to the invalid mother. In plain, and with your assistance, the woman has systematically shielded a suspect from our murder investigation. Why deny it?"

But there wasn't any denying it. Tully had done a job on the doctor, and it didn't make me feel any better that I hadn't once set eyes on him before tonight. Littomy's tone honeyed. "You offer an otherwise fulsome account of this past week's events, yet scarce mention the role of our acting medical examiner. Perhaps because you see more clearly than she does herself that she has entirely betrayed her trust. Therefore, understand me. We may lean toward your version of McAlester's murder. We may even see fit to curb Detective Tully in his pursuit of your most recent crimes and misdemeanors. But as things stand, there is not one hope in hell that the good Dr. Swinford will ever again practice medicine, except in some relic of empire where neither her past nor her future will interest anyone but herself."

He crooked a smile across his teeth that promises to follow you in nightmares. "You might be careless of your own imperfect career, but I doubt you'll condemn the lady doctor to a lifetime's travail in some godforsaken wilderness. No more do I wish to see a murdered police officer's record of service kicked about like a football in the gutter press. So let me explain. After the collapse of his attempted fraud on the grand scale, the lawyer Allynson turned in desperation to a series of appalling murders intended to cover his trail. Understanding he was about to be apprehended for those heinous crimes, he killed himself. Barely twenty-four hours later, while acting to detain the lawyer's wife as accessory, Detective Inspector McAlester died tragically at her hands in your office. His errors of judgment along the way, even the rank disloyalty of Dr. Swinford, will be allowed a decent privacy for the greater good of the force. McAlester will therefore be allowed to go quietly. A hero if need be. Do I make myself clear?"

I made a pad out of my pocket handkerchief and held it up against my mouth. So far, we'd had crimes and misdemeanors, heroes and loyalty, trust and betrayal. At the end of a long night with Junior it was a heady mix. In the end, all I did was nod that he made himself clear, and mumbled past the handkerchief, "So you found her."

Littomy stretched back to look me over, gratified his class had been paying attention. His hands spread as if he might applaud. "Indeed, we did. Our colleagues on the flood recovered a body at first light this morning. Though it carried the identity papers of the late Nurse Greer, it is unquestionably the corpse of her sister. The victim died from a single gunshot wound, no doubt one of the rounds fired by McAlester himself, since recovered from your office wall. Of the airman's Gladstone bag you say she was carrying, there was no trace."

I went on dabbing at my mouth. It was one version. And it was fine. Provided you weren't interested in the detective inspector's shakedown, or where the flight lieutenant's bag had disappeared, or how Willard had been bypassed without a mention from beginning to end. Instead, all it asked you to believe was that the lawyer's widow died from a trick shot, loosed off by McAlester with all the angles wrong, and from the kind of gunshot wound that doesn't bleed; not on your office floor, not along your corridor, not in the elevator cage or down four flights of stairs, and not in the entrance lobby either. Then again, you might prefer the simpler version. The one that had two of Willard's bellhops stooging outside the Thornburgh in the fog, waiting to relieve the widow of the bag she was carrying when she exited and to invite her to a waiting car. She wouldn't run. There wouldn't be any point.

According to Littomy, the body had been picked up at dawn. It was fast work. But that was just the prose. A rich widow mortally gunshot in my office, who crossed half the nighttime City to die alone on the river; that was pure poetry. And when the acting examiner found the gunshot was point blank in the head, as she surely would, it would class as a bona fide miracle. As for Charlie Ross's bag with its royal ransom inside, plus the diamond collection the widow was wearing for travel, River Police had a better chance of finding Amelia Earhart. "Don't tell me. Let me guess. They found the body on a gravel heap on a half-sunk lighter in St. Katharine's Dock, not a quarter-mile from the police launch jetty."

Littomy eyed me sidelong, got as close as he allowed to a show of surprise and in the end decided not to ask. He patted his knees instead, as if the commissioner was waiting to jump in his lap, then unfolded from the chair and stood stooping behind it, his fingertips spread along the seatback. "Be satisfied, man. You've avoided an unholy mire: for the esteemed councilor, your client; for the Beaufort family and their lady doctor; and not least for yourself. The burdens of policing this fair City are not your concern. We know our streets. We understand our officers and their lapses. Leave us to deal with our own. We have the practice." He straightened up to move for the door, then paused for effect. "No airman's Gladstone. River Police did however find the victim's own handbag beside her body with a cartridge box half-full inside; six more rounds for her Webley revolver. No doubt that fact helped Inspector Fels credit some small part of your story." The treacled smile broke again. "But we can't have you leaving us with your bruises undoctored. Our medical examiner must take a look." He slipped a dull silver watch out of his pocket. "Dr. Templeton will be along presently when he returns from luncheon."

It's not often you get what you thought you wanted at the end of a long night in the tank. When Doc Templeton walked in, I was still wondering why I didn't feel better about it. The doctor was small and clipped, his wardrobe a little off-key for a police employee, so fastidious you marveled that he left off the spats. He set his bag down on the table, didn't waste an introduction, pushed his spectacles flat against his eyeballs and had a syringe loaded before he looked around to see who else was in the room. The hand with the syringe waved me to open my shirt, then put a shot in my side and snapped the apparatus back in the bag. It was the work of a motorcycle mechanic, and Doc Templeton was out of there in small, quick steps in less time than it takes to grease a cable. He left the cell door wide. Ready to stroll through when I was dressed. As if the last twelve hours passed with City Police was their way to let me get to know myself better. In the corridor outside, there wasn't even anybody to point the way out.

It was chill afternoon on Snow Hill, the fog all but gone. Courtesy of Doc Templeton, I floated up the rise two feet off the ground, went on past the Thornburgh, turned west to Holborn Viaduct, then dropped down the stair to Farringdon without touching the ground. I headed for Fleet Street with the blood singing under my fingernails, planning to sleep through the rest of a year that had started badly before it got a whole lot worse, but in a room with windows and a light that switched off and a lock on the door I had a key to. I pulled the wires out of the buzzer when I walked in the door. Took the telephone off its cradle and closed the drapes at the windows on the street. Say what you want about The Doc, he knew his poisons. I slept in and out of needle fever for two nights and days, laid out on the couch like a corpse.

UNSUBTLE PRIVATE LIVES

I heard the come and go of the City, faint outside. Sweated and froze and got crawled over by a thousand blind white mice on stilts. For countless hours I waited on the gas flame to make one special shadow play across the ceiling and grinned like a lunatic on vacation each time it came around. I liked it a lot. In all the jagged dreams and racing demons the Doc had cooked up and bottled, it was the thing I liked best of all. It gave me a view off the top of a mile-high mountain, out over a thirsty plain that had a river winding through it. I could trace the river's course right across the ceiling, back into the foothills to the spring where it began, purling out of the tip of a hollow needle from behind an open door. It was Doc Templeton's door. It had his name painted on it. And after his name the strings of letters and sometime alma maters that the Doc could list like a stock price ticker. Through two long nights the letters had danced across the ceiling shadows like starlings homing on a roost, until by now the doctor's needle was running thin and they were lining up, hardening out and separating. I got up on an elbow, wiped a hand across my eyes and tried spelling out six words forming on the door glass in heavy black italics, like a citation. The six words said:

A Bedside Manner Can Be Overrated. I got right up off the couch, stumbled to the bathroom and put my head under an ice-cold faucet.

Two hours before sunrise, the street alight with traffic, newspaper offices flaring yellow at every window and the night shift spilling into breakfast bars. Ask anybody down there about a lawyer and a lawyer's wife and a police detective shot dead and they'd wonder what happened to your weekend. It was Monday morning, dry and cold, and except as color on inside pages the story was through, last week's headlines already and a history of the kind that no one ever can put a name or date to. I dropped the curtain back on the street and went looking in the closet for a suit and a shirt, socks and shoes and a necktie. It didn't matter to me what. All I wanted was to get some air, and put on something that didn't smell to me of a killing.

On Hatton Garden, all that lasted of the snow was heaped in gutters, soot-black in a sharp morning sun that lit up the west side of the street. It whitewashed shop windows, dazzled unaccustomed eyes, pepped the talk of early passersby. I stepped in a door that had its blind drawn up behind the glass and a card at a slant that still said *Closed.* The doorbell made its high, crystal jingle. It was a little before nine o'clock.

At Mayhew's Outfitters to Gentlefolk, a week passed by was but the flicker of an eyelid. Gaslight still burned. The wine-colored drape hung across the back wall. Shelves waited on supplies no supplier had for sale. All that had changed was the heartthrob mannequin in the bow tie and plus fours. This morning, he was wearing a rugged homespun sweater, and all things considered I thought it agreed better with his coloring. His look said he thought so too. Then the drape rattled back on its rail and Mrs. Mayhew was giving me her morning smile that wondered if we might have met before. She was looking spry in a pepper-and-salt tweed, cut so she seemed to fill it all by herself. The trick was putting a spark in her eye. I turned the stiffened side of my face away and waved a hand at her mannequin. "I'm the fellow that bought the scarf Mrs. Mayhew, practically a week ago now."

We waited to let her think back. She brightened when she recollected. "Why yes, of course!" Then thought some more and touched a finger to her bottom lip. "Dear me, I do hope there isn't a flaw."

I gave her back the smile. "No flaw. The scarf is fine. It isn't what I came about."

Since the night in the bright room with Tully and Fels, the councilor's check had been weighing on my wallet. Not that my client was complaining. We hadn't started well but somehow Councilor Drake's business interests and his personal reputation had survived a very tough week that might have come out a whole lot worse. He'd kept his name out of a police murder investigation, avoided a scandal that would have blackballed him from the City, and seeing his daughter leave Joe Willard for a different continent might even have salved whatever conscience he had. All it had cost him was a check, still in my pocket, and a handful of blushes, if you granted his skin was that thin. But a client is still a client, and there hadn't been a way to keep the councilor out of the story I gave Detective Tully. Even when you're being fitted for murder, and even though Tully couldn't use what I gave him without burning City Police, himself included, there are rules about that. It was how I came to be on Hatton Garden discussing stylish neckwear with an outfitter to gentlefolk. I began explaining what I was doing there.

I said I did some work for an important City councilor, locating respected enterprises that would help bring on go-ahead young women in the City. As one of its legion of well-satisfied customers, it had occurred to me that Mayhew's of Hatton Garden might be one such enterprise. I said I thought a keen worker could expect to be useful there, learn something about the high-fashion business and generally broaden her outlook. Not only that, I had someone in mind; a personable young woman who exactly fit the bill. If Mrs. Mayhew was willing, I was authorized to sign over a check from the councilor's charitable fund to cover employing her for a trial period. I had one in my pocket to show. And even though I was certain the firm wouldn't regret giving this particular young woman a try, if it didn't work out for either of the two parties there were positively no obligations. The councilor always insisted on that. I took the check out of my wallet, laid it flat on her glass counter and asked Mrs. Mayhew how the idea sounded to her.

FIFTY-THREE

Commercial real estate has its highs and lows. Ask the Thornburgh. One day you've got a desirable address renting at a premium on the west side of the City. Next day a police hero dies there and the address is a headline for all the wrong reasons in every news sheet in the country. It wasn't the kind of advertising the Thornburgh needed. Added to that, its tenants were going to pieces meeting me alone on the stairs. The building's agent wrote, proposing to move me urgently elsewhere, entirely at the owners' expense. But I liked the setup I had, my contract didn't exclude third-party gunfire and I declined their offer. Days later the owners lost their nerve and their agent got the holes in my wall fixed. It was the last I heard. All the same, a week after the murder mayhem I was still getting the cool look on the stairs, and the bookish secretary didn't stroll in any longer for slow drinks at strange hours. Even George was handing me the mail every morning without a whistle.

It was the middle of a dead afternoon. Fat rain dripped off the roof edges. My neighbor was snapping at her typewriter the other side of our connecting door and I was waiting on a call. I had the *Courier* folded to Carl's column on an inside page. Since Doc Templeton blessed me with his needle arts, it was as close as I wanted to get to the Garfield story. Carl had been wrapping up the City killings all week, using Littomy's script released one day at a time and springing no surprises. On Monday it had been the history of a fraud, perpetrated by a ruthless and murderous lawyer. By Friday it was the tragedy of an upstanding senior police detective in his prime, cut down by the lawyer's wife while resisting arrest. The detective inspector had fallen victim to a train of events he'd remorselessly pursued; a trail of deception and cold murder that City Police had now closed for good. In the circumstances, his rough handling of a young man in questioning was a forgivable and forgettable blemish on a fine career. Carl quoted Littomy on that, and printed a pocket version of the superintendent's stock picture in mid-column, to help us all take his word for it.

I pushed the afternoon edition aside and sat on by the telephone. The call I had out was a routine trace that police could have made ten times faster, for a customer who had no pressing desire to try that avenue. Out of such inhibitions my office rental gets paid. A letter on my desk, arrived that morning, was a longer shot. I picked it up and read it through again. It was from a bureau vice-president of the Carne Organization Inc. of Beverly Hills, California, a heavyweight and exclusive investigative agency where the mink and Cadillac crowd could buy discretion. My name had been mentioned by somebody who knew somebody else, and the bureau chief thought I might make a useful addition to his overseas roster. He wrote that he hoped to hear what I could offer. On the one hand, it was a chance to raise some associate business that wouldn't otherwise come my way, at least not before the Americans came begging to be let back in the empire. Against that was crafting a work of fiction to keep Carne interested. I was mulling for and against when the telephone rang. I lifted it. A loose drawl, lately grown familiar, said, "You're as good as your word, Newman. I'll give you that."

It might have been the days of endless rain. Or the cold shoulder I was getting for lowering the tone of the office neighborhood. More likely I was wearied of fast advice, cheap payoffs and cheaper threats, and not in a mood to let Willard pin a medal on my chest. I cut in. "Is there a point or is this our anniversary?"

There was a pause while he sent somebody out of the room. "You were right about McAlester. When we gave Vivien some time alone, she was able to recall the deal they struck. You set both of them up. I don't even want to know why. A talent like yours should be working for me."

So it was settled. Now I had talent. On the confession of a sometime B-movie actress and racketeer lawyer's wife, who knew she was making her last car ride and had nothing left to lose. Willard wouldn't waste sentiment, and you doubted she was given much time to recollect; no more to him now than the new-minted brunette his two guns had picked up outside the Thornburgh, wearing jewels he'd paid for and carrying false papers, a steamer ticket and a bag with his missing million dollars inside. "Neither of them was set up. Vivien Allynson had a way out and didn't take it. McAlester went there for the shakedown and got in her line of fire. They made choices. They could have made different choices and surprised us both. But surprises aren't in your book. When you see your next one you still won't like it. Go make your pitch at somebody else and stay off my line. It gets me a living in ways you won't understand." Willard let the silence hang on the wire, said *Have it your way* and ended the call.

I sat listening to the afternoon drift by, thought about calling the doctor and decided she needed time to herself. Then the snapping typewriter wound down, heels tapped across the room behind me and lights switched off. A quiet Friday ended early for the weekend and a door locked shut. The corridor echoed heels again before the whole floor muted to a string of clicks and empty murmurs. I still had the telephone in my hand. It started ringing the instant I dropped it back on the riser.

The call still wasn't the trace I had out, but for this one I lost the wearied mood and sat up and listened. When it ended I got up from the desk and collected my coat off the rack. It was at the top of Snow Hill I remembered I hadn't turned the key in my door. I should have. In light of recent events, the Thornburgh's agent had circularized all tenants. He said the answer to everybody's peace of mind was for us all to get stricter with security.

FIFTY-FOUR

I paid the taxi, walked the drive to the Beaufort place in a rain shower and dragged on the bell-pull under the porch. The smell of wood smoke was blunting the chill on the air and Ernest seemed satisfied to see me again. He led along the hallway with the log fire and showed me to the same study as before, left with my coat over his arm and came back with a silver tray and two straight whiskies. Mr. Beaufort, he said, would be along to join me shortly, and left the glasses on the cartwheel table by the hearth, one either side of a journal with a marbled hardcover. Ernest would know better than to bring out the Buccleuch tonight, and I hadn't thought about Garfield's diary in a week. I turned my back on both of them and looked around the study.

The French doors had drapes drawn across the view. The workbench was a litter of typesheets, plans and photographs. The rest looked much as it had on one uneasy afternoon before New Year. Wet logs smoked in the chimney. Blanche the debutante glowed in her red dress, in a small, soft light of her own, and the same dark scent of old money clotted the air. A heel scuffed in the doorway and Guy Beaufort stepped into the room, dressed in country worsted with a watchchain and a spotted bow tie. His retriever ambled ahead and sneezed on the rug, and when he saw where the dog flopped Beaufort pointed me at an armchair under his wife's portrait, where he could catch her wideawake look over my shoulder. Ten days ago, getting an audience had meant arm-twisting a friend of the family. Tonight, he'd telephoned my office with a personal invitation. I was interested to hear why.

Beaufort settled his chin on his bow tie, clasped the whisky glass to his stomach, and put on the hardball manner from Christmas night at the Waldorf as if nothing had happened in between. He pointed around his glass at the diary on the table. "What interest do you have in this?"

The diary's cover glowed in the light from Blanche's portrait. I made the mouth that says there are things you can get by without. "Less now than when Henry was in the frame for the City killings. I didn't think your son had murdered anybody and Garfield's journal might have helped his case. Or maybe not. At the time it seemed better to know which. It still might tell where Professor Garfield found his coliseum, and I'm curious about that, but without Henry's help curious is as far as I get." I reached for the glass and waved it at his bow tie. "I don't know yet why I'm invited, only that it wouldn't be to pass the cocktail hour. Let's go on with Professor Garfield and those editions lining his study in Guildhall; the ones with Greek or Latin on the left side and a crib in English on the right. They're handsome, but isn't the crib strictly luxury? The kind of schooling a Beaufort gets, you wouldn't need Greek or Latin translating any more than the professor did."

Beaufort looked up across the table and didn't disagree. I hunched forward over the liquor. "On Christmas Eve you took a call from Drake that put a stop on your work until he got the professor's latest report. Edgar Levin says it made for a lousy Christmas, and probably it did. But you're not the man to let that rest. Garfield was in Guildhall late that afternoon, a telephone message in his wallet says so. You went to see him there in his study with Homer and Horace." A flame wrapped around a log and set shadows chasing along the hearth. "Levin left that part out. He didn't want to give me the idea of you paying Garfield a heated visit just hours before he was murdered." I shrugged. "Still, the possibility crossed my mind."

Beaufort slid his whisky on the table, patted his breast pocket for eyeglasses and shunted the dog aside with his shoe. He was climbing in the high chair at his drawing board before he said, "My son is not here to assist you. He's traveling with a mutual acquaintance. Tomorrow they arrive at Johannesburg, and from there intend to pay a visit to Sir Bernard."

There are some things you wonder if you heard. I sat up, undecided which part sounded craziest: that the Beaufort family doctor had taken his son with her on the lam, or the way he said *Sir Bernard* as if we all rowed in the same eight. Either way, Johannesburg was four days' flying by the clipper route, meaning the doctor had moved while Littomy was still putting a shine on the police story, and before he could change his mind Henry was gone. Africa, meet Kathryn Swinford. May the best man win.

He fitted the eyeglasses on his nose. "On the morning after his detective was killed, Littomy suspended Kathryn from duty and recalled Templeton from leave; first to perform the postmortems on his officer and the Allynson woman, then to review every examination she'd made in his absence." He swung around to the bench and cast about for something. "Naturally, Kathryn was badly shaken. It was a humiliation and a threat. She made plans to leave immediately and brought Professor Garfield's papers to me. Both she and my son tell me we are indebted to you, Newman. I dislike debts. We are not, as you say, here for cocktails." He put on an angle light on the bench, found a pen and taped a sheet of drafting paper to his drawing board. I got out of the chair and went over, stood at his side as he started to draw and watched a landscape emerge that I recognized from the first swift, clean lines. No detail wasted. It was impressive. Beaufort talked as he worked. "Certainly I went to see Professor Garfield that afternoon. As the Corporation's chief adviser, I felt entitled to understand his purpose."

He inked a broad river across the foot of the sheet and a bridge in the bottom right corner, then added the wharf and a garrison fort, and the grid of streets and buildings on the river's north bank. Signed and framed I might have bought it for my office wall. Beaufort stopped there and eased back on the high chair out of the beam from the angle light. "Professor Garfield obliged me. He said he meant to extend his search for an amphitheater *inside* the City wall. It struck me more as a pipe dream than a serious proposal. As archaeology it was wholly perplexing."

The dog yawned. Probably I didn't look wonderstruck either. Beaufort peered at both of us over his eyeglasses and thought about how simple he could keep it. It wasn't the pipe dream that bothered him. It was why Garfield would go looking there at all, when every Roman amphitheater was always found outside, not inside, a city wall. He reached along the bench for a wad of documents hanging off a tag like a mandarin's fan. "Garfield was systematic. He recorded every drawing, measurement, site map and photograph that came his way. I have his catalogue here, completed until the very last. Moreover, in his diary he listed a half-dozen of those catalogue numbers only days before he died. Without, however, explaining the meaning of his list."

Maybe the list in the professor's diary wasn't explained, but Beaufort had pulled the half-dozen records anyway. They were the ones tagged together in the paper fan in his hand. He said in his opinion they told a story, and since his son had a fixed idea that the Beaufort family owed me, if I wanted the story I could have it. The slipper hound lifted an ear, wetted his nose and inched nearer the hearth.

Right up until Christmas Eve, Michael Garfield's year had been on a roll. London's Roman fort had made his name overnight and anybody else might have relaxed in the glow, but according to Beaufort all it did was give the professor one more big idea. The Luftwaffe's area bombing hadn't just led Garfield to a buried Roman fort, it had shown him the fort's foundations were older than the Roman wall itself, and by a century or more. In case I didn't get that straight off the bat, Beaufort said in Garfield's circle that little nugget had made bigger waves than the Cold War.

To begin with, not even the professor realized what it meant. But when the first snowfall stopped his excavations and Henry left town for the holiday, he had time alone to think. When he did, he saw that a thing he'd always taken as given, he could be getting wrong. The nickel dropped that if Roman London had a garrison fort before it had a city wall, then what if it had an amphitheater too? And if it did, what had he been doing all these years looking for it outside a wall that the Romans hadn't even built yet; before there *was* any outside or inside? The idea made him dizzy. It sent him poring over site records he'd always ruled out and listing them at the end of Drake's report. Then, two days before Christmas, he came across a handful that stopped him in his tracks, wrote their catalogue numbers in his diary and dropped his original report in the wastebasket, obsolete. Beaufort's hand swept over his bird's-eye drawing, north across the Thames, of a riverside Roman settlement before it got its wall. The way it had looked to Garfield when he had his epiphany. He went slack on the high chair and raised me an eyebrow. I grunted I was keeping up. So did his dog.

The excavation records that made Garfield sit up were from six of his own trial sites that had looked ordinary at the time, close by each other but otherwise unconnected. All six had hit a band of rough stonework foundation at the same level, four feet wide and set on two strings of Roman red tile. Against that, the foundations were in the wrong place to be interesting, and anyway every one of them lay in an odd alignment nobody could explain, not even the professor. The things you miss seeing are the things that aren't supposed to be there. The sites had been logged and let go. At first I guessed Garfield would be kicking himself, then realized he'd be too cock-a-hoop up to care. So cock-a-hoop he made new drawings of all six sites in hours, measured angles between the alignments, projected the angles into a curve and saw that his fragments of foundation were anything but unconnected. His calculations showed they were one small part of an oval, and no ordinary oval at that. When this one was standing it had been more than three hundred feet long and not a lot less wide. There was no curved structure in the Roman world, Beaufort said, that got even close to that. Not unless the professor was looking at his coliseum.

Beaufort spread out the records Garfield had listed in his diary: plans and sections of six small excavations, an ancient map of a City Ward, the oval geometries of a buried coliseum, a photograph taken from the air. He pulled the map closer and traced the line of one of its streets with the wrong end of his pen. "Professor Garfield compared his projections with a four-hundred-year-old plan of the City, the earliest we have. The western Roman Empire had collapsed more than a thousand years before, yet the curve of this medieval street exactly follows the line he calculated for his coliseum. Our sixteenth-century mapmaker calls it Ketton Street. To later Londoners it was Cat Eaton. Today we know it as Gresham Street, barely a hundred feet south of the Roman garrison fort." It wasn't yet case proven, but when the snowfall eased and Garfield took his last flight over the City, he saw its street pattern with different eyes. Beaufort tapped his pen on the aerial shot and slid his glasses down his nose. "This also is his, I take it. His catalogue lists five photographs taken on his final flight, all five showing the same feature on the ground. We have them here, though none bears any date or catalogue number."

It's the way an expensive schooling teaches you to ask a question. I said, "They're his. Printed off his negatives. The professor's killer took the originals from his body."

Beaufort let that go around. He said in that case, the feature Garfield went to photograph that day from the air had been a church; more exactly, the church on Gresham Street he saw every working day from his office window on Guildhall Yard. He meant St. Lawrence Jewry, named for the quarter's medieval Jewish ghetto and burned in the blitz. Always, Beaufort said, it had been an archaeologist's puzzle, as obvious now as when it was whole. The church had been standing all of eight centuries with its north side built out of square, and as Garfield laid out his geometries, he saw the reason why. It had been more than a medieval off-day. His calculations said that when its builders cleared their site, they'd struck the same line of ancient masonry as his own six trial excavations, then decided they could clip costs by using it for their own foundations. When the snow eased, the professor wanted pictures from the air that would let him show it. Beaufort made a tracing of the curve of Garfield's coliseum and placed it over the aerial shot. The north wall of the ghetto church fitted exactly the line of the Roman arena, older by a thousand years.

I thought along the unraveling line of Beaufort's story, about its ovals and alignments and old Jewish ghettos, forgotten excavations and strings of red tile. It had Garfield written all through it like Brighton rock. Garfield who drove Henry crazy with his everlasting fussing. Garfield who tied City grandees in knots. But it left something we hadn't settled. I leaned over to put a finger on the curve on the old map. "This is Gresham Street?"

"Quite. Even today it follows the contour of the Roman arena."

"So Garfield's coliseum...?"

"Lies approximately thirty feet beneath Guildhall Yard."

And there it was. The reason Garfield hired Gerry Fulton to fly him over the City on a snow-white afternoon. The reason he dumped a report going nowhere to start another that Drake's committee couldn't refuse. The proofs were in a handful of records listed in his diary. The photographs from the airplane were his illustration. And the magic of it was, the professor's coliseum had been sitting outside his office window all along. Legionaries had drilled there, gladiators had fought and died, right under his wheels every time he parked his car.

Beaufort screwed the top back on his pen, thought about squaring the papers on his bench then thought again. He straightened the spotted bow tie and tugged on his shirt cuffs while the last note died. You thought he might mop his brow and milk the applause. I put in a cigarette and said: "Without Garfield's diary nobody else will ever find it."

He was ready to climb down off the high chair and checked himself, pushed aside the angle light and settled back in. It didn't take much adding up. Garfield had been temperamentally reckless, surrounded by bright young men and inclined to mix pleasure with business. Such things make for crowded and unsubtle private lives, and his diary could give away plenty besides the keys to his coliseum. Enough to make him dangerous to have known, and not only for Henry. Willard's nose for blackmail had told him so. Guy Beaufort could do better than that. He could read it in the original.

I looked across at Blanche's portrait. A light had gone out of her eyes and the ingénue air with it, until all she had left was a spare, nervous smile for what she saw coming. I nodded over at her picture. "You'll bury the professor's diary the same way you buried Blanche's friend. That was the gist of the talk I got in the Nile Room. Whatever it takes to protect your son. The thing is, protecting Henry is what Kathryn Swinford thought she was doing all along. She still does. It's why she got him out of the country. She has no idea yet that you cut her loose, does she?"

Beaufort twisted around from the drawing bench. His eyes followed mine to Blanche's stricken look in the portrait on the wall. "Littomy knew his stand-in examiner was never going to bend evidence to make the police story stick. For that he needed Templeton back and a reason to fire his deputy that would guarantee her silence. So he made you an offer: give him enough on his temporary examiner to get her cashiered and in return he'd lose Henry's file. She was trying to keep your son out of a police frame for murder, and you gave Littomy every move she made. You're the only one who could have." Over by the armchair his dog moaned, and didn't like what it heard any more than Blanche did. I half sat on Beaufort's workbench where I could look in his eye. "Betraying a friend of the family was just a necessary step. You didn't think twice about it. One step more and Henry is home free. Go ahead. We can both watch it burn."

Beaufort peeled off his glasses with the look that said he always thought I might catch up in the end. He stepped down from the chair, collected Garfield's diary from the cartwheel table and carried it to the hearth, then leaned in over the beech logs to slot it in the flames. We watched its marbled covers char and curl, then turn bright, liquid gold without catching light. Michael Garfield's diary melted in front of our eyes, his coliseum dreams with it, and when Beaufort looked up I was halfway through the door. I stopped it with my shoe. "That afternoon while you waited for Garfield in his office you took down a copy of Homer from a shelf, then put it back next to Horace. Horace was a Latin. Homer was Greek. The professor never mixed the two. My bloodhound said to mention it." I pulled my toe out of the door and let it swing shut.

Ernest was at the end of the hallway. All evening he'd been looking down in the mouth. I folded my cigarette in an ashtray on a stand and he helped me into my coat. "You're going to miss her, Ernest."

"We shall indeed, Mr. Newman. If I may venture to say, Miss Kathryn performs an improving effect upon all members of the household."

I took my hat and Ernest lifted down a telephone from its oakwood box on the wall. He set it beside the ashtray, then lifted the receiver the regulation six inches from his ear. I answered the back of his head while he steadied himself to dial. "She does at that, Ernest. She does at that." When the cab ground up the drive, he had the cord reeled in, the telephone dusted and locked back in its box on the wall.

ALEKHINE IN THE ENDGAME

The rain had slowed to chill, fitful drizzle. Liverpool Street was jammed with crowds homebound for the weekend. I got out of a taxi at the rail station entrance and walked back along the traffic to the Great Eastern. Its frontage was touching the clouds. I climbed the hotel steps, went in through the main entrance, crossed the foyer and looked in at the barbershop door. Louis was standing at the street window surveying passersby, waiting on trade from the hotel's late arrivals. He glanced over when I walked in and didn't look surprised. I stood while the bell danced on the doorframe, not even sure why I was there. "I came late, not to put a scare in your customers."

The left side of my face still had the look of pie filling. Louis took it in and didn't argue the point. He came over to the door to the hotel lobby and switched the *Open* sign to *Closed*, then went to the street door and did the same. "Day's done, Mr. Newman, I've been expecting you. Take a seat and a hot towel. Can't say you'll look any better, but your face will want to thank you." He set the chair almost flat and loosed my collar, laid on the dry heat of the towel and wound it around my teeth to mingle with the bruises. We didn't talk. Louis collected his copy of the day's *Courier*, stood close by the chair and read whatever caught his eye, in murmurs like stories at bedtime. The hotel hummed softly, and when time came to change the towel, he said in the same lullaby, "It's a curious thing, Mr. Newman. You remember Irene who that young fellow Terry got fired? Well, she visited the hotel yesterday to see a girlfriend here, and the friend says Irene got a new employment in the City. But what I hear, how she came by it makes no sense. You hear anything, Mr. Newman?"

I lay soaking the heat and said what I'd heard. "She'll be fresh air, Louis. The gentlefolk need livening up."

He sounded doubtful. "Well I'm happy for her, Mr. Newman. Her friend is not so sure. She says independent ideas will make the girl trouble at home."

But Voigt wasn't going to make trouble. His daughter's new employment had arrived care of Councilor Drake, and the councilor was too close to Willard to think of fooling with. Besides, in that pepper and salt costume Mrs. Mayhew was irresistible, and her new sales clerk would get the customers hopping. I said through the wrap, "Voigt is taken care of. Irene will be fine. Tell her friend not to worry and give it a chance."

Louis uncoiled the towel and set it aside, took a step back to gauge the result and then clucked the side of his cheek. "I know you're right." I hadn't expected that. He raised the back of the chair upright and caught my eye in the mirror. "I did a thing myself since you were here last. I got a headstone making for Miss Dillys. She never did admit the year she was born, and I don't like to dwell on the day she died, so I said just to put her name on it. One day I'll get it fixed for her under the blossoms. It can't make a difference to the lady, I know, but I didn't see how I could let it go by."

I said Miss Dillys would appreciate that and got out of the chair, left Louis checking his till roll and putting out lights and went out the way I came in, through the hotel foyer to the exit on Liverpool Street. The rail station crowd had thinned. Night was crawling in a deep, wet hole. The City and everything in it felt as appealing as a policemen's ball. I looked along the street to the cab stand, then backed up through the revolving door, re-crossed the foyer to the coat check and climbed the stair.

The dining room was hushed as a lay-reading. A handful of company men were getting slick with gin on ice. A party of retired tea planters dined around a table under the dome, their wives dressed in silk shawls for a cool night at a hill station. I took the same window table as before and ordered something solid, and then a bottle from the list to help it shine. And while the planters mumbled in their starch fronts and their memsahibs forgot the names of servants, I ate a dinner and drank a bottle to the City's sometime temporary medical examiner and wondered where she might be tonight.

Dinner at the Great Eastern is the long haul for the leisured. It gave me time to wonder a lot of things about her. I thought about her notions of Good Form that Louis would approve, and about her clipped style straight out of the girls' dormitory that sent me cross-eyed. I thought about fires that lit her cheeks when she got maddened, her hips in a long white dress, her sweet tooth and high ideals and the smile she kept under wraps in daylight. It was a beginning and I was warming to the theme, sent after another bottle to help fill in the gaps and looked around at the tables already emptying.

In the Dome Room, you eat with enough silver lying about to start another Colorado rush, with linen napkins patterned white on white and crystal glasses set in lines like Russian dolls. Then all evening a waiter takes them away, one item at a time, like Alekhine in the endgame. The new bottle arrived. Another glass disappeared in the blink of an eye. The last one I had left was filled, red as sundown on the Veldt, and as it poured, I knew where—exactly where—she would be tonight.

A flying boat on the Johannesburg run lays up on the Zambezi overnight, riding the current at a wooden jetty upriver from Victoria Falls. No question, the doctor would stay the night at the one first-rate hotel in town. Right now, she would be taking the view from its terrace, hips pressed against the stone balustrade in the moonlight. She'd have on her up-country breeches belted tight in her waist and the shirt she hadn't handed back to me, watching the spray hang high above the falls, lost in the spell of it. Next morning, she'd get back on the clipper for the leg to Jo'burg, then take the slow train winding east. Tonight, she'd be rehearsing a speech for Sir Bernard that she knew could get her disowned, to explain the how and why of things she couldn't let go by.

Louis would understand. But I doubted it would explain to Uncle Bernard. Probably the doctor doubted it too. The truth was, she'd started out with nothing more than an instinct about Blanche's boy, then realized her instincts were more reliable than the police investigation she was a part of. From that point on, she'd decided the boy had to be protected, left the rulebook behind and used whatever and whoever came to hand, including the shamus she ran into along the way. She'd made mistakes. Ridden her luck. And it helped that her intuition hadn't been wrong. Though I didn't see that cutting much ice with the judge over sundowners on his veranda.

It would be tough out there under the jacarandas. She would hear from the judge how the law makes no accommodations with romantics, and that City Police hadn't expected to hire one. Also, that if any part of that came as surprise to her then she wasn't cut out for the work. It would be hard arguing with a Master of the Bench. But you guessed his niece would give it her best shot anyway, because she wouldn't know how not to. I was thinking somebody ought to warn the old boy what was coming his way when the colonials began drifting out, arm in arm. Waiters ghosted. The company men were long gone. My table was cleared except for the glass in my hand. I held it up to the light, turned it around through a hundred shades of red and wished the doctor all the good luck in the world. Then drank and set the empty glass on its side and called Alekhine over for the check.

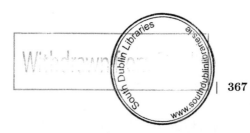